THE RESCUE

Joseph Conrad (originally Józef Teodor Konrad Korzeniowski) was born in the Ukraine in 1857 and grew up under Tsarist autocracy. His parents, ardent Polish patriots, died when he was a child, following their exile for anti-Russian activities, and he came under the protection of his tradition-conscious uncle, Tadeusz Bobrowski, who watched over him for the next twenty-five years. In 1874 Bobrowski conceded to his nephew's passionate desire to go to sea, and Conrad travelled to Marseilles, where he served in French merchant vessels before joining a British ship in 1878. In 1886 he obtained British nationality and his Master's certificate in the British Merchant Service. Eight years later he left the sea to devote himself to writing, publishing his first novel, *Almayer's Folly*, in 1895. The following year he married Jessie George and eventually settled in Kent, where he produced within fifteen years such modern classics as *Youth*, *Heart of Darkness*, *Lord Jim*, *Typhoon*, *Nostromo*, *The Secret Agent* and *Under Western Eyes*. He continued to write until his death in 1924. Today Conrad is generally regarded as one of the greatest writers of fiction in English – his third language. He once described himself as being concerned 'with the ideal value of things, events and people'; in the Preface to *The Nigger of the 'Narcissus'* he defined his task as 'by the power of the written word . . . before all, to make you *see*'.

JOSEPH CONRAD

THE RESCUE

A ROMANCE OF THE SHALLOWS

Alas! quod she, that ever this sholde happe!
For wende I never, by possibilitee,
That swich a monstre or Merveille mighte be!

THE FRANKELEYN'S TALE

PENGUIN BOOKS

PENGUIN BOOKS

Published by the Penguin Group
Penguin Books Ltd, 27 Wrights Lane, London W8 5TZ, England
Penguin Putnam Inc., 375 Hudson Street, New York, New York 10014, USA
Penguin Books Australia Ltd, Ringwood, Victoria, Australia
Penguin Books Canada Ltd, 10 Alcorn Avenue, Toronto, Ontario, Canada M4V 3B2
Penguin Books (NZ) Ltd, 182–190 Wairau Road, Auckland 10, New Zealand

Penguin Books Ltd, Registered Offices: Harmondsworth, Middlesex, England

First published in 1920
Published in Penguin Books 1950
9 10

Printed in England by Clays Ltd, St Ives plc
Set in Linotype Granjon

CONTENTS

Author's Note
page 9

PART ONE
The Man and the Brig
page 13

PART TWO
The Shore of Refuge
page 59

PART THREE
The Capture
page 105

PART FOUR
The Gift of the Shallows
page 173

PART FIVE
*The Point of Honour and the
Point of Passion*
page 217

PART SIX
*The Claim of Life and the
Toll of Death*
page 295

AUTHOR'S NOTE

OF the three long novels of mine which suffered an interruption, *The Rescue* was the one that had to wait the longest for the good pleasure of the Fates. I am betraying no secret when I state here that it had to wait precisely for twenty years. I laid it aside at the end of the summer of 1898 and it was about the end of the summer of 1918 that I took it up again with the firm determination to see the end of it and helped by the sudden feeling that I might be equal to the task.

This does not mean that I turned to it with elation. I was well aware and perhaps even too much aware of the dangers of such an adventure. The amazingly sympathetic kindness which men of various temperaments, diverse views and different literary tastes have been for years displaying toward my word has done much for me, has done all – except giving me that overweening self-confidence which may assist an adventurer sometimes but in the long run ends by leading him to the gallows.

As the characteristic I want most to impress upon these short Author's Notes prepared for my first Collected Edition is that of absolute frankness, I hasten to declare that I founded my hopes not on my supposed merits but on the continued goodwill of my readers. I may say at once that my hopes have been justified out of all proportion to my deserts. I met with the most considerate, most delicately expressed criticism free from all antagonism and in its conclusions showing an insight which in itself could not fail to move me deeply, but was associated also with enough commendation to make me feel rich beyond the dreams of avarice – I mean an artist's avarice which seeks its treasure in the hearts of men and women.

No! Whatever the preliminary anxieties might have been this adventure was not to end in sorrow. Once more Fortune favoured audacity; and yet I have never forgotten the jocular translation of *Audaces fortuna juvat* offered to me by my tutor when I was a small boy: 'The Audacious get bitten.' However he took care to mention that there were various kinds of audacity. Oh, there are, there are! ... There is, for instance, the kind of audacity almost indistinguishable from impudence ... I must believe that in this case I have not been impudent for I am conscious of having been bitten.

The truth is that when *The Rescue* was laid aside it was not laid aside in despair. Several reasons contributed to this abandonment and, no doubt, the first of them was the growing sense of general difficulty in the handling of the subject. The contents and the course of the story I had clearly in my mind. But as to the way of presenting the facts, and perhaps in a certain measure as to the nature of the facts themselves, I had many doubts. I mean the telling, representative facts, helpful to carry on the idea, and, at the same time, of such a nature as not to demand an elaborate creation of the atmosphere to the detriment of the action. I did not see how I could avoid becoming wearisome in the presentation of detail and in the pursuit of clearness. I saw the action plainly enough. What I had lost for the moment was the sense of the proper formula of expression, the only formula that would suit. This, of course, weakened my confidence in the intrinsic worth and in the possible interest of the story – that is, in my invention. But I suspect that all the trouble was, in reality, the doubt of my prose, the doubt of its adequacy, of its power to master both the colours and the shades.

It is difficult to describe, exactly as I remember it, the complex state of my feelings; but those of my readers who take an interest in artistic perplexities will understand me best when I point out that I dropped *The Rescue* not to give myself up to idleness, regrets or dreaming, but to begin *The Nigger of the Narcissus* and to go on with it without hesitation and without a pause. A comparison of any page of *The Rescue* with any page of *The Nigger* will furnish an ocular demonstration of the nature and the inward meaning of this first crisis of my writing life. For it was a crisis undoubtedly. The laying aside of a work so far advanced was a very awful decision to take. It was wrung from me by a sudden conviction that *there* only was the road of salvation, the clear way out for an uneasy conscience. The finishing of *The Nigger* brought to my troubled mind the comforting sense of an accomplished task, and the first consciousness of a certain sort of mastery which could accomplish something with the aid of propitious stars. Why I did not return to *The Rescue* at once, then, was not for the reason that I had grown afraid of it. Being able now to assume a firm attitude I said to myself deliberately: 'That thing can wait.' At the same time I was just as certain in my mind that *Youth*, a story which I had then, so to speak, on the tip of my pen, could *not* wait. Neither could *Heart of Darkness* be put off; for the practical reason that Mr Wm Blackwood having requested me to write something for the No. M. of his magazine I had to stir up at once the subject of that tale which had been long lying quiescent in my mind; because, obviously, the venerable Maga at her patriarchal age of 1000 numbers could not be kept waiting. Then *Lord Jim*, with about seventeen pages already written at odd times, put in his claim which was irresistible. Thus every stroke of the pen was taking me further away from the abandoned *Rescue*, not without some compunction on my part but with a gradually diminishing resistance; till at last I let myself go, as if recognizing a superior influence against which it was useless to contend.

The years passed and the pages grew in number, and the long reveries of which they were the outcome stretched wide between me and the deserted *Rescue* like the smooth hazy spaces of a dreamy sea. Yet I never actually lost sight of that dark speck in the misty distance. It had grown very small but it asserted itself with the appeal of old associations. It seemed to me that it would be a base thing for me to slip out of the world leaving it out there all alone, waiting for its fate – that would never come!

Sentiment, pure sentiment as you see, prompted me in the last instance to face the pains and hazards of that return. As I moved slowly towards the abandoned body of the tale it loomed up big amongst the glittering shallows of the coast, lonely but not forbidding. There was nothing about it of a grim derelict. It had an air of expectant life. One after another I made out the familiar faces watching my approach with faint smiles of amused recognition. They had known well enough that I was bound to come back to them. But their eyes met mine seriously, as was only to be expected since I, myself, felt very serious as I stood amongst them again after years of absence. At once, without wasting words, we went to work together on our renewed life; and every moment I felt more strongly that They Who had Waited bore no grudge to the man who, however widely he may have wandered at times, had played truant only once in his life.

1920   J.C.

PART ONE

THE MAN AND THE BRIG

THE shallow sea that foams and murmurs on the shores of the thousand islands, big and little, which make up the Malay Archipelago has been for centuries the scene of adventurous undertakings. The vices and the virtues of four nations have been displayed in the conquest of that region that even to this day has not been robbed of all the mystery and romance of its past – and the race of men who had fought against the Portuguese, the Spaniards, the Dutch and the English, has not been changed by the unavoidable defeat. They have kept to this day their love of liberty, their fanatical devotion to their chiefs, their blind fidelity in friendship and hate – all their lawful and unlawful instincts. Their country of land and water – for the sea was as much their country as the earth of their islands – has fallen a prey to the western race – the reward of superior strength if not of superior virtue. Tomorrow the advancing civilization will obliterate the marks of a long struggle in the accomplishment of its inevitable victory.

The adventurers who began that struggle have left no descendants. The ideas of the world changed too quickly for that. But even far into the present century they have had successors. Almost in our own day we have seen one of them – a true adventurer in his devotion to his impulse – a man of high mind and of pure heart, lay the foundation of a flourishing state on the ideas of pity and justice. He recognized chivalrously the claims of the conquered; he was a disinterested adventurer, and the reward of his noble instincts is in the veneration with which a strange and faithful race cherish his memory.

Misunderstood and traduced in life, the glory of his achievement has vindicated the purity of his motives. He belongs to history. But there were others – obscure adventurers who had not his advantages of birth, position, and intelligence; who had only his sympathy with the people of forests and sea he understood and loved so well. They cannot be said to be forgotten since they have not been known at all. They were lost in the common crowd of seamen-traders of the Archipelago, and if they emerged from their obscurity it was only to be condemned as law-breakers. Their lives were thrown away for a cause that had no right to exist in the face of an irresistible and orderly progress – their thoughtless lives guided by a simple feeling.

But the wasted lives, for the few who know, have tinged with romance the region of shallow waters and forest-clad islands, that lies far east, and still mysterious between the deep waters of two oceans.

I

OUT of the level blue of a shallow sea Carimata raises a lofty barrenness of grey and yellow tints, the drab eminence of its arid heights. Separated by a narrow strip of water, Suroeton, to the west, shows a curved and ridged outline resembling the backbone of a stooping giant. And to the eastward a troop of insignificant islets stand effaced, indistinct, with vague features that seem to melt into the gathering shadows. The night following from the eastward the retreat of the setting sun advanced slowly, swallowing the land and the sea; the land broken, tormented and abrupt; the sea smooth and inviting with its easy polish of continuous surface to wanderings facile and endless.

There was no wind, and a small brig that had lain all the afternoon a few miles to the northward and westward of Carimata had hardly altered its position half a mile during all these hours. The calm was absolute, a dead, flat calm, the stillness of a dead sea and of a dead atmosphere. As far as the eye could reach there was nothing but an impressive immobility. Nothing moved on earth, on the waters, and above them in the unbroken lustre of the sky. On the unruffled surface of the straits the brig floated tranquil and upright as if bolted solidly, keel to keel, with its own image reflected in the unframed and immense mirror of the sea. To the south and east the double islands watched silently the double ship that seemed fixed amongst them forever, a hopeless captive of the calm, a helpless prisoner of the shallow sea.

Since midday, when the light and capricious airs of these seas had abandoned the little brig to its lingering fate, her head had swung slowly to the westward and the end of her slender and polished jib-boom, projecting boldly beyond the graceful curve of the bow, pointed at the setting sun, like a spear poised high in the hand of an enemy. Right aft by the wheel the Malay quartermaster stood with his bare brown feet firmly planted on the wheel-grating, and holding the spokes at right angles, in a solid grasp, as though the ship had been running before a gale. He stood there perfectly motionless, as if petrified but ready to tend the helm as soon as fate would permit the brig to gather way through the oily sea.

The only other human being then visible on the brig's deck was the person in charge: a white man of low stature, thick-set with shaven cheeks, a grizzled moustache, and a face tinted a scarlet hue by the burning suns and by the sharp salt breezes of the seas. He had thrown off his light jacket, and clad only in white trousers and a thin cotton singlet, with his stout arms crossed on his breast – upon which they showed like two thick lumps of raw flesh – he prowled about from side to side of the half-poop. On his bare feet he wore a pair of straw sandals, and his head was protected by an enormous pith hat – once white but now very dirty – which gave to the whole man the aspect of a phenomenal and animated mushroom. At times he would interrupt his uneasy shuffle athwart the break of the poop, and stand motionless with a vague gaze fixed on the image of the brig in the calm water. He could also see down there his own head and shoulders leaning out over the rail and he would stand long, as if interested by his own features, and mutter vague curses on the calm which lay upon the ship like an immovable burden; immense and burning.

At last, he sighed profoundly, nerved himself for a great effort, and making a start away from the rail managed to drag his slippers as far as the binnacle. There he stopped again, exhausted and bored. From under the lifted glass panes of the cabin skylight near by came the feeble chirp of a canary, which appeared to give him some satisfaction. He listened, smiled faintly, muttered 'Dicky, poor Dick –' and fell back into the immense silence of the world. His eyes closed, his head hung low over the hot brass of the binnacle top. Suddenly he stood up with a jerk and said sharply in a hoarse voice:

'You've been sleeping – you. Shift the helm. She has got stern way on her.'

The Malay, without the least flinch of feature or pose, as if he had been an inanimate object called suddenly into life by some hidden magic of the words, spun the wheel rapidly, letting the spokes pass through his hands; and when the motion had stopped with a grinding noise, caught hold again and held on grimly. After a while, however, he turned his head slowly over his shoulder, glanced at the sea, and said in an obstinate tone:

'No catch wind – no get way.'

'No catch – no catch – that's all you know about it,' growled the red-faced seaman. 'By and by catch Ali –' he went on with sudden condescension. 'By and by catch, and then the helm will be the right way. See?'

The stolid seacannie appeared to see, and for that matter to hear nothing. The white man looked at the impassive Malay with disgust, then glanced around the horizon – then again at the helmsman and ordered curtly:

'Shift the helm back again. Don't you feel the air from aft? You are like a dummy standing there.'

The Malay revolved the spokes again with disdainful obedience, and the red-faced man was moving forward grunting to himself, when through the open skylight the hail 'On deck there!' arrested him short, attentive, and with a sudden change to amiability in the expression of his face.

'Yes, sir,' he said, bending his ear toward the opening.

'What's the matter up there?' asked a deep voice from below.

The red-faced man in a tone of surprise said:

'Sir?'

'I hear that rudder grinding hard up and hard down. What are you up to, Shaw? Any wind?'

'Ye-es,' drawled Shaw, putting his head down the skylight and speaking into the gloom of the cabin. 'I thought there was a light air, and – but it's gone now. Not a breath anywhere under the heavens.'

He withdrew his head and waited a while by the skylight, but heard only the chirping of the indefatigable canary, a feeble twittering that seemed to ooze through the drooping red blossoms of geraniums growing in flower-pots under the glass panes. He strolled away a step or two before the voice from down below called hurriedly:

'Hey, Shaw? Are you there?'

'Yes, Captain Lingard,' he answered, stepping back.

'Have we drifted anything this afternoon?'

'Not an inch, sir, not an inch. We might as well have been at anchor.'

'It's always so,' said the invisible Lingard. His voice changed its tone as he moved in the cabin, and directly afterward burst out with a clear intonation while his head appeared above the slide of the cabin entrance: 'Always so! The currents don't begin till it's dark, when a man can't see against what confounded thing he is being drifted, and then the breeze will come. Dead on end, too, I don't doubt.'

Shaw moved his shoulders slightly. The Malay at the wheel, after making a dive to see the time by the cabin clock through the skylight, rang a double stroke on the small bell aft. Directly forward, on the main deck, a shrill whistle arose, long drawn, modulated, dying away softly. The master of the brig stepped out of the companion upon the deck of his vessel, glanced aloft at the yards laid dead square; then, from the door-step, took a long, lingering look round the horizon.

He was about thirty-five, erect and supple. He moved freely, more like a man accustomed to stride over plains and hills, than like one who from his earliest youth had been used to counteract by sudden swayings of his body the rise and roll of cramped decks of small craft, tossed by the caprice of angry or playful seas.

He wore a grey flannel shirt, and his white trousers were held by a blue silk scarf wound tightly round his narrow waist. He had come up only for a moment, but finding the poop shaded by the main-topsail he remained on deck bareheaded. The light chestnut hair curled close about his well-shaped head, and the clipped beard glinted vividly when he passed across a narrow strip of sunlight, as if every hair in it had been a wavy and attenuated gold wire. His mouth was lost in the heavy moustache; his nose was straight, short, slightly blunted at the end; a broad band of deeper red stretched under the eyes, clung to the cheek bones. The eyes gave the face its remarkable expression. The eyebrows, darker than the hair, pencilled a straight line below the wide and unwrinkled brow much whiter than the sun-burnt face. The eyes, as if glowing with the light of a hidden fire, had a red glint in their greyness that gave a scrutinizing ardour to the steadiness of their gaze.

That man, once so well known, and now so completely for-gotten amongst the charming and heartless shores of the shallow sea, had amongst his fellows the nickname of 'Red-Eyed Tom'. He was proud of his luck but not of his good sense. He was proud of his brig, of the speed of his craft, which was reckoned the swiftest country vessel in those seas, and proud of what she represented.

She represented a run of luck on the Victorian goldfields; his sagacious moderation; long days of planning, of loving care in building; the great joy of his youth, the incomparable freedom of the seas; a perfect because a wandering home; his indepen-dence, his love – and his anxiety. He had often heard men say that Tom Lingard cared for nothing on earth but for his brig – and in his thoughts he would smilingly correct the statement by adding that he cared for nothing *living* but the brig.

To him she was as full of life as the great world. He felt her live in every motion, in every roll, in every sway of her tapering masts, of those masts whose painted trucks move forever, to a seaman's eye, against the clouds or against the stars. To him she was always precious – like old love; always desirable – like a strange woman; always tender – like a mother; always faithful – like the favourite daughter of a man's heart.

For hours he would stand elbow on rail, his head in his hand

and listen – and listen in dreamy stillness to the cajoling and promising whisper of the sea, that slipped past in vanishing bubbles along the smooth black-painted sides of his craft. What passed in such moments of thoughtful solitude through the mind of that child of generations of fishermen from the coast of Devon, who like most of his class was dead to the subtle voices, and blind to the mysterious aspects of the world – the man ready for the obvious, no matter how startling, how terrible or menacing, yet defenceless as a child before the shadowy impulses of his own heart; what could have been the thoughts of such a man, when once surrendered to a dreamy mood, it is difficult to say.

No doubt he, like most of us, would be uplifted at times by the awakened lyricism of his heart into regions charming, empty, and dangerous. But also, like most of us, he was unaware of his barren journeys above the interesting cares of this earth. Yet from these, no doubt absurd and wasted moments, there remained on the man's daily life a tinge as that of a glowing and serene half-light. It softened the outlines of his rugged nature; and these moments kept close the bond between him and his brig.

He was aware that his little vessel could give him something not to be had from anybody or anything in the world; something specially his own. The dependence of that solid man of bone and muscle on that obedient thing of wood and iron, acquired from that feeling the mysterious dignity of love. She – the craft – had all the qualities of a living thing: speed, obedience, trustworthiness, endurance, beauty, capacity to do and to suffer – all but life. He – the man – was the inspirer of that thing that to him seemed the most perfect of its kind. His will was its will, his thought was its impulse, his breath was the breath of its existence. He felt all this confusedly, without ever shaping this feeling into the soundless formulas of thought. To him she was unique and dear, this brig of three hundred and fourteen tons register – a kingdom!

And now, bareheaded and burly, he walked the deck of his kingdom with a regular stride. He stepped out from the hip, swinging his arms with the free motion of a man starting out for a fifteen-mile walk into open country; yet at every twelfth stride he had to turn about sharply and pace back the distance to the taffrail.

Shaw, with his hands stuck in his waistband, had hooked himself with both elbows to the rail, and gazed apparently at the deck between his feet. In reality he was contemplating a little house with a tiny front garden, lost in a maze of riverside streets in the east end of London. The circumstance that he had not, as yet, been able to make the acquaintance of his son – now aged eighteen months – worried him slightly, and was the cause of that flight of his fancy into the murky atmosphere of his home. But it was a placid flight followed by a quick return. In less than two minutes he was back in the brig. 'All there,' as his saying was. He was proud of being always 'all there'.

He was abrupt in manner and grumpy in speech with the seamen. To his successive captains, he was outwardly as deferential as he knew how, and as a rule inwardly hostile – so very few seemed to him of the 'all there' kind. Of Lingard, with whom he had only been a short time – having been picked up in Madras Roads out of a home ship, which he had to leave after a thumping row with the master – he generally approved, although he recognized with regret that this man, like most others, had some absurd fads; he defined them as 'bottom-upwards notions'.

He was a man – as there were many – of no particular value to anybody but himself, and of no account but as chief mate of the brig, and the only white man on board of her besides the captain. He felt himself immeasurably superior to the Malay seamen whom he had to handle, and treated them with lofty toleration, notwithstanding his opinion that at a pinch those chaps would be found emphatically 'not there'.

As soon as his mind came back from his home leave, he detached himself from the rail and, walking forward, stood by the break of the poop, looking along the port side of the main deck. Lingard on his own side stopped in his walk and also gazed absentmindedly before him. In the waist of the brig, in the narrow spars that were lashed on each side of the hatchway, he could see a group of men squatting in a circle around a wooden tray piled up with rice, which stood on the just swept deck. The dark-faced, soft-eyed, silent men, squatting on their hams, fed decorously with an earnestness that did not exclude reserve.

Of the lot, only one or two wore *sarongs*, the others having submitted – at least at sea – to the indignity of European trousers. Only two sat on the spars. One, a man with a child-like, light yellow face, smiling with fatuous imbecility under the wisps of straight coarse hair dyed a mahogany tint, was the *tindal* of the crew – a kind of boatswain's or *serang's* mate. The other, sitting beside him on the booms, was a man nearly black, not much bigger than a large ape, and wearing on his wrinkled face that look of comical truculence which is often characteristic of men from the south-western coast of Sumatra.

This was the *kassab* or store-keeper, the holder of a position of dignity and ease. The *kassab* was the only one of the crew taking their evening meal who noticed the presence on deck of their commander. He muttered something to the *tindal* who directly cocked his old hat on one side, which senseless action invested him with an altogether foolish appearance. The others heard, but went on somnolently feeding with spidery movements of their lean arms.

The sun was no more than a degree or so above the horizon, and from the heated surface of the waters a slight low mist began to rise; a mist thin, invisible to the human eye; yet strong enough to change the sun into a mere glowing red disc, a disc vertical and hot, rolling down to the edge of the horizontal and cold-looking disc of the shining sea. Then the edges touched and the circular expanse of water took on suddenly a tint, sombre, like a frown; deep, like the brooding meditation of evil.

The falling sun seemed to be arrested for a moment in his descent by the sleeping waters, while from it, to the motionless brig, shot out on the polished and dark surface of the sea a track of light, straight and shining, respiendent and direct; a path of gold and crimson and purple, a path that seemed to lead dazzling and terrible from the earth straight into heaven through the portals of a glorious death. It faded slowly. The sea vanquished the light. At last only a vestige of the sun remained, far off, like a red spark floating on the water. It lingered, and all at once – without warning – went out as if extinguished by a treacherous hand.

'Gone,' cried Lingard, who had watched intently yet missed the last moment. 'Gone! Look at the cabin clock, Shaw!'

'Nearly right, I think, sir. Three minutes past six.'

The helmsman struck four bells sharply. Another barefooted seacannie glided on the far side of the poop to relieve the wheel, and the *serang* of the brig came up the ladder to take charge of the deck from Shaw. He came up to the compass, and stood waiting silently.

'The course is south by east when you get the wind, *Serang*,' said Shaw, distinctly.

'Sou' by eas',' repeated the elderly Malay with grave earnestness.

'Let me know when she begins to steer,' added Lingard.

'Ya, Tuan,' answered the man, glancing rapidly at the sky. 'Wind coming,' he muttered.

'I think so, too,' whispered Lingard as if to himself.

The shadows were gathering rapidly round the brig. A mulatto put his head out of the companion and called out:

'Ready, sir.'

'Let's get a mouthful of something to eat, Shaw,' said Lingard. 'I say, just take a look around before coming below. It will be dark when we come up again.'

'Certainly, sir,' said Shaw, taking up a long glass and putting it to his eye. 'Blessed thing,' he went on in snatches while he worked the tubes in and out, 'I can't – never somehow – Ah! I've got it right at last!'

He revolved slowly on his heels, keeping the end of the tube on the sky-line. Then he shut the instrument with a click, and said decisively:

'Nothing in sight, sir.'

He followed his captain down below rubbing his hands cheerfully.

For a good while there was no sound on the poop of the brig. Then the seacannie at the wheel spoke dreamily:

'Did the *malim* say there was no one on the sea?'

'Yes,' grunted the *serang* without looking at the man behind him.

'Between the islands there was a boat,' pronounced the man very softly.

The *serang*, his hands behind his back, his feet slightly apart, stood very straight and stiff by the side of the compass stand. His face, now hardly visible, was as inexpressive as the door of a safe.

'Now, listen to me,' insisted the helmsman in a gentle tone. The man in authority did not budge a hair's breadth. The seacannie bent down a little from the height of the wheel grating.

'I saw a boat,' he murmured with something of the tender obstinacy of a lover begging for a favour. 'I saw a boat, O Haji Wasub ! Ya ! Haji Wasub !'

The *serang* had been twice a pilgrim, and was not insensible to the sound of his rightful title. There was a grim smile on his face.

'You saw a floating tree, O Sali,' he said, ironically.

'I am Sali, and my eyes are better than the bewitched brass thing that pulls out to a great length,' said the pertinacious helmsman. 'There was a boat, just clear of the easternmost island. There was a boat, and they in her could see the ship on the light of the west – unless they are blind men lost on the sea. I have seen her. Have you seen her, too, O Haji Wasub ?'

'Am I a fat white man ?' snapped the *serang*. 'I was a man of the sea before you were born, O Sali ! The order is to keep silence and mind the rudder, lest evil befall the ship.'

After these words he resumed his rigid aloofness. He stood, his legs slightly apart, very stiff and straight, a little on one side of the compass stand. His eyes travelled incessantly from the illuminated card to the shadowy sails of the brig and back again, while his body was motionless as if made of wood and built into the ship's frame. Thus, with a forced and tense watchfulness, Haji Wasub, *serang* of the brig *Lightning*, kept the captain's watch unwearied and wakeful, a slave to duty.

In half an hour after sunset the darkness had taken complete possession of earth and heavens. The islands had melted into the night. And on the smooth water of the Straits, the little brig lying so still, seemed to sleep profoundly, wrapped up in a scented mantle of starlight and silence.

2

It was half-past eight o'clock before Lingard came on deck again. Shaw – now with a coat on – trotted up and down the poop leaving behind him a smell of tobacco smoke. An irregularly glowing spark seemed to run by itself in the darkness before the rounded form of his head. Above the masts of the brig the dome of the clear heaven was full of lights that flickered, as if some mighty breathings high up there had been swaying about the flame of the stars. There was no sound along the brig's decks, and the heavy shadows that lay on it had the aspect, in that silence, of secret places concealing crouching forms that waited in perfect stillness for some decisive event. Lingard struck a match to light his cheroot, and his powerful face with narrowed eyes stood out for a moment in the night and vanished suddenly. Then two shadowy forms and two red sparks moved backward and forward on the poop. A larger, but a paler and oval patch of light from the compass lamps lay on the brasses of the wheel and on the breast of the Malay standing by the helm. Lingard's voice, as if unable altogether to master the enormous silence of the sea, sounded muffled, very calm – without the usual deep ring in it.

'Not much change, Shaw,' he said.

'No, sir, not much. I can just see the island – the big one – still in the same place. It strikes me, sir, that, for calms, this here sea is a devil of loc-ality.'

He cut 'locality' in two with an emphatic pause. It was a good word. He was pleased with himself for thinking of it. He went on again:

'Now – since noon, this big island –'

'Carimata, Shaw,' interrupted Lingard.

'Aye, sir; Carimata – I mean. I must say – being a stranger hereabouts – I haven't got the run of those –'

26

He was going to say 'names' but checked himself and said, 'appellations', instead, sounding every syllable lovingly.

'Having for these last fifteen years,' he continued, 'sailed regularly from London in East-Indiamen, I am more at home over there – in the Bay.'

He pointed into the night toward the northwest and stared as if he could see from where he stood that Bay of Bengal where – as he affirmed – he would be so much more at home.

'You'll soon get used –' muttered Lingard, swinging in his rapid walk past his mate. Then he turned round, came back, and asked sharply:

'You said there was nothing afloat in sight before dark? Hey?'

'Not that I could see, sir. When I took the deck again at eight, I asked that *serang* whether there was anything about; and I understood him to say there was no more as when I went below at six. This is a lonely sea at times – ain't it, sir? Now, one would think at this time of the year the homeward-bounders from China would be pretty thick here.'

'Yes,' said Lingard, 'we have met very few ships since we left Pedra Branca over the stern. Yes; it has been a lonely sea. But for all that, Shaw, this sea, if lonely, is not blind. Every island in it is an eye. And now, since our squadron has left for the China waters –'

He did not finish his sentence. Shaw put his hands in his pockets, and propped his back against the skylight, comfortably.

'They say there is going to be a war with China,' he said in a gossiping tone, 'and the French are going along with us as they did in the Crimea five years ago. It seems to me we're getting mighty good friends with the French. I've not much of an opinion about that. What do you think, Captain Lingard?'

'I have met their men-of-war in the Pacific,' said Lingard, slowly. 'The ships were fine and the fellows in them were civil enough to me – and very curious about my business,' he added with a laugh. 'However, I wasn't there to make war on them. I had a rotten old cutter then, for trade, Shaw,' he went on with animation.

'Had you, sir?' said Shaw without any enthusiasm. 'Now give me a big ship – a ship, I say, that one may –'

'And later on, some years ago,' interrupted Lingard, 'I chummed with a French skipper in Ampanam – being the only two white men in the whole place. He was a good fellow, and free with his red wine. His English was difficult to understand, but he could sing songs in his own language about ah-moor – Ah-moor means love, in French – Shaw.'

'So it does, sir – so it does. When I was second mate of a Sunderland barque, in forty-one, in the Mediterranean, I could pay out their lingo as easy as you would a five-inch warp over a ship's side –'

'Yes, he was a proper man,' pursued Lingard, meditatively, as if for himself only. 'You could not find a better fellow for company ashore. He had an affair with a Bali girl, who one evening threw a red blossom at him from within a doorway, as we were going together to pay our respects to the Rajah's nephew. He was a good-looking Frenchman, he was – but the girl belonged to the Rajah's nephew, and it was a serious matter. The old Rajah got angry and said the girl must die. I don't think the nephew cared particularly to have her krissed; but the old fellow made a great fuss and sent one of his own chief men to see the thing done – and the girl had enemies – her own relations approved! We could do nothing. Mind, Shaw, there was absolutely nothing else between them but that unlucky flower which the Frenchman pinned to his coat – and afterward, when the girl was dead, wore under his shirt, hung round his neck in a small box. I suppose he had nothing else to put it into.'

'Would those savages kill a woman for that?' asked Shaw, incredulously.

'Aye! They are pretty moral there. That was the first time in my life I nearly went to war on my own account, Shaw. We couldn't talk those fellows over. We couldn't bribe them, though the Frenchman offered the best he had, and I was ready to back him to the last dollar, to the last rag of cotton, Shaw! No use – they were that blamed respectable. So, says the Frenchman to me: "My friend, if they won't take our gunpowder for a gift let us burn it to give them lead." I was armed as you see now; six eight-pounders on the main deck and a long eighteen on the forecastle – and I wanted to try 'em. You may believe me ! However, the Frenchman had nothing but a few old muskets; and the beggars got to windward of us by fair words, till one morning a boat's crew from the Frenchman's ship found the girl lying dead on the beach. They put an end to our plans. She was out of her trouble anyhow, and no reasonable man will fight for a dead woman. I was never vengeful, Shaw, and – after all – she didn't throw that flower at me. But it broke the Frenchman up altogether. He began to mope, did no business, and shortly afterward sailed away. I cleared a good many pence out of that trip, I remember.'

With these words he seemed to come to the end of his memories of that trip. Shaw stifled a yawn.

'Women are the cause of a lot of trouble,' he said, dispassionately. 'In the *Morayshire*, I remember, we had once a passenger – an old gentleman – who was telling us a yarn about them old-time Greeks fighting for ten years about some woman. The Turks kidnapped her, or something. Anyway, they fought in Turkey; which I may well believe. Them Greeks and Turks were always fighting. My father was master's mate on board one of the three-deckers at the battle of Navarino – and that was when we went to help those Greeks. But this affair about a woman was long before that time.'

'I should think so,' muttered Lingard, hanging over the rail, and watching the fleeting gleams that passed deep down in the water, along the ship's bottom.

'Yes. Times are changed. They were unenlightened in those old days. My grandfather was a preacher and, though my father served in the navy, I don't hold with war. Sinful the old gentleman called it – and I think so, too. Unless with Chinamen, or niggers, or such people as must be kept in order and won't listen to reason; having not sense enough to know what's good for them, when it's explained to them by their betters – missionaries, and such like au-tho-ri-ties. But to fight ten years. And for a woman !'

'I have read the tale in a book,' said Lingard, speaking down over the side as if setting his words gently afloat upon the sea. 'I have read the tale. She was very beautiful.'

'That only makes it worse, sir – if anything. You may depend on it she was no good. Those pagan times will never come back, thank God. Ten years of murder and unrighteousness! And for a woman! Would anybody do it now? Would you do it, sir? Would you –'

The sound of a bell struck sharply interrupted Shaw's discourse. High aloft, some dry block sent out a screech, short and lamentable, like a cry of pain. It pierced the quietness of the night to the very core, and seemed to destroy the reserve which it had imposed upon the tones of the two men, who spoke now loudly.

'Throw the cover over the binnacle,' said Lingard in his duty voice. 'The thing shines like a full moon. We mustn't show more lights than we can help, when becalmed at night so near the land. No use in being seen if you can't see yourself – is there? Bear that in mind, Mr Shaw. There may be some vagabonds prying about –'

'I thought all this was over and done for,' said Shaw, busying himself with the cover, 'since Sir Thomas Cochrane swept along the Borneo coast with his squadron some years ago. He did a rare lot of fighting – didn't he? We heard about it from the chaps of the sloop *Diana* that was refitting in Calcutta when I was there in the *Warwick Castle*. They took some king's town up a river hereabouts. The chaps were full of it.'

'Sir Thomas did good work,' answered Lingard, 'but it will be a long time before the seas are as safe as the English Channel is in peace time. I spoke about that light more to get you in the way of things to be attended to in these seas than for anything else. Did you notice how few native craft we've sighted for all these days we have been drifting about – one may say – in this sea?'

'I can't say I have attached any significance to the fact, sir.'

'It's a sign that something is up. Once set a rumour afloat in these waters, and it will make its way from island to island, without any breeze to drive it along.'

'Being myself a deep-water man sailing steadily out of home ports nearly all my life,' said Shaw with great deliberation, 'I cannot pretend to see through the peculiarities of them out-of-the-way parts. But I can keep a lookout in an ordinary way, and I have noticed that craft of any kind seemed scarce, for the last few days: considering that we had land aboard of us – one side or another – nearly every day.'

'You will get to know the peculiarities, as you call them, if you remain any time with me,' remarked Lingard, negligently.

'I hope I shall give satisfaction, whether the time be long or short!' said Shaw, accentuating the meaning of his words by the distinctness of his utterance. 'A man who has spent thirty-two years of his life on salt water can say no more. If being an officer of home ships for the last fifteen years I don't understand the heathen ways of them there savages, in matters of seamanship and duty, you will find me all there, Captain Lingard.'

'Except, judging from what you said a little while ago – except in the matter of fighting,' said Lingard, with a short laugh.

'Fighting! I am not aware that anybody wants to fight me. I am a peaceable man, Captain Lingard, but when put to it, I could fight as well as any of them flat-nosed chaps we have to make shift with, instead of a proper crew of decent Christians. Fighting!' he went on with unexpected pugnacity of tone, 'Fighting! If anybody comes to fight me, he will find me all there, I swear!'

'That's all right. That's all right,' said Lingard, stretching his arms above his head and wriggling his shoulders. 'My word! I do wish a breeze would come to let us get away from here. I am rather in a hurry, Shaw.'

'Indeed, sir! Well, I never yet met a thorough seafaring man who was not in a hurry when a con-demned spell of calm had him by the heels. When a breeze comes ... just listen to this, sir!'

'I hear it,' said Lingard. 'Tide-rip, Shaw.'

'So I presume, sir. But what a fuss it makes. Seldom heard such a –'

On the sea, upon the furthest limits of vision, appeared an ad-

vancing streak of seething foam, resembling a narrow white ribbon, drawn rapidly along the level surface of the water by its
two ends, which were lost in the darkness. It reached the brig,
passed under, stretching out on each side; and on each side the
water became noisy, breaking into numerous and tiny wavelets,
a mimicry of an immense agitation. Yet the vessel in the midst of
this sudden and loud disturbance remained as motionless and
steady as if she had been securely moored between the stone walls
of a safe dock. In a few moments the line of foam and ripple
running swiftly north passed at once beyond sight and earshot,
leaving no trace on the unconquerable calm.

'Now this is very curious –' began Shaw.

Lingard made a gesture to command silence. He seemed to
listen yet, as if the wash of the ripple could have had an echo
which he expected to hear. And a man's voice that was heard
forward had something of the impersonal ring of voices thrown
back from hard and lofty cliffs upon the empty distances of the
sea. It spoke in Malay – faintly.

'What?' hailed Shaw. 'What is it?'

Lingard put a restraining hand for a moment on his chief
officer's shoulder, and moved forward smartly. Shaw followed,
puzzled. The rapid exchange of incomprehensible words thrown
backward and forward through the shadows of the brig's main
deck from his captain to the lookout man and back again, made
him feel sadly out of it, somehow.

Lingard had called out sharply – 'What do you see?'

The answer direct and quick was – 'I hear, Tuan. I hear oars.'

'Whereabouts?'

'The night is all around us. I hear them near.'

'Port or starboard?'

There was a short delay in answer this time. On the quarter-
deck, under the poop, bare feet shuffled. Somebody coughed. At
last the voice forward said doubtfully:

'*Kanan.*'

'Call the *serang*, Mr Shaw,' said Lingard, calmly, 'and have
the hands turned up. They are all lying about the decks. Look
sharp now. There's something near us. It's annoying to be
caught like this,' he added in a vexed tone.

He crossed over to the starboard side, and stood listening, one hand grasping the royal back-stay, his ear turned to the sea, but he could hear nothing from there. The quarter-deck was filled with subdued sounds. Suddenly, a long, shrill whistle soared, reverberated loudly amongst the flat surfaces of motionless sails, and gradually grew faint as if the sound had escaped and gone away, running upon the water. Haji Wasub was on deck and ready to carry out the white man's commands. Then silence fell again on the brig, until Shaw spoke quietly.

'I am going forward now, sir, with the *tindal*. We're all at stations.'

'Aye, Mr Shaw. Very good. Mind they don't board you – but I can hear nothing. Not a sound. It can't be much.'

'The fellow has been dreaming, no doubt. I have good ears, too, and –'

He went forward and the end of his sentence was lost in an indistinct growl. Lingard stood attentive. One by one the three seacannies off duty appeared on the poop and busied themselves around a big chest that stood by the side of the cabin companion. A rattle and clink of steel weapons turned out on the deck was heard, but the men did not even whisper. Lingard peered steadily into the night, then shook his head.

'*Serang*!' he called, half aloud.

The spare old man ran up the ladder so smartly that his bony feet did not seem to touch the steps. He stood by his commander, his hands behind his back; a figure indistinct but straight as an arrow.

'Who was looking out?' asked Lingard.

'Badroon, the Bugis,' said Wasub, in his crisp, jerky manner.

'I can hear nothing. Badroon heard the noise in his mind.'

'The night hides the boat.'

'Have you seen it?'

'Yes, Tuan. Small boat. Before sunset. By the land. Now coming here – near. Badroon heard him.'

'Why didn't you report it, then?' asked Lingard, sharply.

'*Malim* spoke. He said: "Nothing there," while I could see. How could I know what was in his mind or yours, Tuan?'

'Do you hear anything now?'

33

'No. They stopped now. Perhaps lost the ship – who knows? Perhaps afraid –'

'Well!' muttered Lingard, moving his feet uneasily. 'I believe you lie. What kind of boat?'

'White men's boat. A four-men boat, I think. Small. Tuan, I hear him now! There!'

He stretched his arm straight out, pointing abeam for a time, then his arm fell slowly.

'Coming this way,' he added with decision.

From forward Shaw called out in a startled tone:

'Something on the water, sir! Broad on this bow!'

'All right!' called back Lingard.

A lump of blacker darkness floated into his view. From it came over the water English words – deliberate, reaching him one by one; as if each had made its own difficult way through the profound stillness of the night.

'What – ship – is – that – pray?'

'English brig,' answered Lingard, after a short moment of hesitation.

'A brig! I thought you were something bigger,' went on the voice from the sea with a tinge of disappointment in its deliberate tone. 'I am coming alongside – if – you – please.'

'No! you don't!' called Lingard back, sharply. The leisurely drawl of the invisible speaker seemed to him offensive, and woke up a hostile feeling. 'No! you don't if you care for your boat. Where do you spring from? Who are you – anyhow? How many of you are there in that boat?'

After these emphatic questions there was an interval of silence. During that time the shape of the boat became a little more distinct. She must have carried some way on her yet, for she loomed up bigger and nearly abreast of where Lingard stood, before the self-possessed voice was heard again:

'I will show you.'

Then, after another short pause, the voice said, less loud but very plain:

'Strike on the gunwale. Strike hard, John!' and suddenly a blue light blazed out, illuminating with a livid flame a round

34

patch in the night. In the smoke and splutter of that ghastly halo appeared a white, four-oared gig with five men sitting in her in a row. Their heads were turned toward the brig with a strong expression of curiosity on their faces, which, in this glare, brilliant and sinister, took on a deathlike aspect and resembled the faces of interested corpses. Then the bowman dropped into the water the light he held above his head and the darkness, rushing back at the boat, swallowed it with a loud and angry hiss.

'Five of us,' said the composed voice out of the night that seemed now darker than before. 'Four hands and myself. We belong to a yacht – a British yacht –'

'Come on board!' shouted Lingard. 'Why didn't you speak at once? I thought you might have been some masquerading Dutchmen from a dodging gunboat.'

'Do I speak like a blamed Dutchman? Pull a stroke, boys – oars! Tend bow, John.'

The boat came alongside with a gentle knock, and a man's shape began to climb at once up the brig's side with a kind of ponderous agility. It poised itself for a moment on the rail to say down into the boat – 'Sheer off a little, boys,' then jumped on deck with a thud, and said to Shaw who was coming aft: 'Good evening ... Captain, sir?'

'No. On the poop!' growled Shaw.

'Come up here. Come up,' called Lingard, impatiently.

The Malays had left their stations and stood clustered by the main mast in a silent group. Not a word was spoken on the brig's decks, while the stranger made his way to the waiting captain. Lingard saw approaching him a short, dapper man, who touched his cap and repeated his greeting in a cool drawl: 'Good evening ... Captain, sir?'

'Yes, I am the master – what's the matter? Adrift from your ship? Or what?'

'Adrift? No! We left her four days ago, and have been pulling that gig in a calm, nearly ever since. My men are done. So is the water. Lucky thing I sighted you.'

'You sighted me!' exclaimed Lingard. 'When? What time?'

'Not in the dark, you may be sure. We've been knocking about

35

amongst some islands to the southward, breaking our hearts tugging at the oars in one channel, then in another – trying to get clear. We got round an islet – a barren thing, in shape like a loaf of sugar – and I caught sight of a vessel a long way off. I took her bearing in a hurry and we buckled to; but another of them currents must have had hold of us, for it was a long time before we managed to clear that islet. I steered by the stars, and, by the Lord Harry, I began to think I had missed you somehow – because it must have been you I saw.'

'Yes, it must have been. We had nothing in sight all day,' assented Lingard. 'Where's your vessel?' he asked, eagerly.

'Hard and fast on middling soft mud – I should think about sixty miles from here. We are the second boat sent off for assistance. We parted company with the other on Tuesday. She must have passed to the northward of you today. The chief officer is in her with orders to make for Singapore. I am second, and was sent off toward the Straits here on the chance of falling in with some ship. I have a letter from the owner. Our gentry are tired of being stuck in the mud and wish for assistance.'

'What assistance did you expect to find down here?'

'The letter will tell you that. May I ask, Captain, for a little water for the chaps in my boat? And I myself would thank you for a drink. We haven't had a mouthful since this afternoon. Our breaker leaked out somehow.'

'See to it, Mr Shaw,' said Lingard. 'Come down the cabin, Mr –'

'Carter is my name.'

'Ah! Mr Carter. Come down, come down,' went on Lingard, leading the way down the cabin stairs.

The steward had lighted the swinging lamp, and had put a decanter and bottles on the table. The cuddy looked cheerful, painted white, with gold mouldings round the panels. Opposite the curtained recess of the stern windows there was a sideboard with a marble top, and, above it, a looking-glass in a gilt frame. The semicircular couch round the stern had cushions of crimson plush. The table was covered with a black Indian tablecloth embroidered in vivid colours. Between the beams of the poop-deck were fitted racks for muskets, the barrels of which glinted in the light. There were twenty-four of them between the four beams. As many sword-bayonets of an old pattern encircled the polished teakwood of the rudder-casing with a double belt of brass and steel. All the doors of the state-rooms had been taken off the hinges and only curtains closed the doorways. They seemed to be made of yellow Chinese silk, and fluttered all together, the four of them, as the two men entered the cuddy.

Carter took in all at a glance, but his eyes were arrested by a circular shield hung slanting above the brass hilts of the bayonets. On its red field, in relief and brightly gilt, was represented a sheaf of conventional thunderbolts darting down the middle between the two capitals T. L. Lingard examined his guest curiously. He saw a young man, but looking still more youthful, with a boyish smooth face much sunburnt, twinkling blue eyes, fair hair and a slight moustache. He noticed his arrested gaze.

'Ah, you're looking at that thing. It's a present from the builder of this brig. The best man that ever launched a craft. It's supposed to be the ship's name between my initials – flash of lightning – d'you see? The brig's name is *Lightning* and mine is Lingard.'

'Very pretty thing that: shows the cabin off well,' murmured Carter, politely.

They drank, nodding at each other, and sat down.

'Now for the letter,' said Lingard.

Carter passed it over the table and looked about, while Lingard took the letter out of an open envelope, addressed to the commander of any British ship in the Java Sea. The paper was thick, had an embossed heading: 'Schooner-yacht *Hermit*' and was dated four days before. The message said that on a hazy night the yacht had gone ashore upon some outlying shoals off the coast of Borneo. The land was low. The opinion of the sailing-master was that the vessel had gone ashore at the top of high water, spring tides. The coast was completely deserted to all appearance. During the four days they had been stranded there they had sighted in the distance two small native vessels, which did not approach. The owner concluded by asking any commander of a homeward-bound ship to report the yacht's position in Anjer on his way through Sunda Straits – or to any British or Dutch man-of-war he might meet. The letter ended by anticipatory thanks, the offer to pay any expenses in connection with the sending of messages from Anjer, and the usual polite expressions.

Folding the paper slowly in the old creases, Lingard said – 'I am not going to Anjer – nor anywhere near.'

'Any place will do, I fancy,' said Carter.

'Not the place where I am bound to,' answered Lingard, opening the letter again and glancing at it uneasily. 'He does not describe very well the coast, and his latitude is very uncertain,' he went on. 'I am not clear in my mind where exactly you are stranded. And yet I know every inch of that land – over there.'

Carter cleared his throat and began to talk in his slow drawl. He seemed to dole out facts, to disclose with sparing words the features of the coast, but every word showed the minuteness of his observation, the clear vision of a seaman able to master quickly the aspect of a strange land and of a strange sea. He presented, with concise lucidity, the picture of the tangle of reefs and sandbanks, through which the yacht had miraculously blundered in the dark before she took the ground.

'The weather seems clear enough at sea,' he observed, finally, and stopped to drink a long draught. Lingard, bending over the table, had been listening with eager attention. Carter went on in his curt and deliberate manner:

'I noticed some high trees on what I take to be the mainland to the south – and whoever has business in that bight was smart enough to whitewash two of them: one on the point, and another farther in. Landmarks, I guess ... What's the matter, Captain?'

Lingard had jumped to his feet, but Carter's exclamation caused him to sit down again.

'Nothing, nothing ... Tell me, how many men have you in that yacht?'

'Twenty-three, besides the gentry, the owner, his wife and a Spanish gentleman – a friend they picked up in Manila.'

'So you were coming from Manila?'

'Aye. Bound for Batavia. The owner wishes to study the Dutch colonial system. Wants to expose it, he says. One can't help hearing a lot when keeping watch aft – you know how it is. Then we are going to Ceylon to meet the mail-boat there. The owner is going home as he came out, overland through Egypt. The yacht would return round the Cape, of course.'

'A lady?' said Lingard. 'You say there is a lady on board. Are you armed?'

'Not much,' replied Carter, negligently. 'There are a few muskets and two sporting guns aft; that's about all – I fancy it's too much, or not enough,' he added with a faint smile.

Lingard looked at him narrowly.

'Did you come out from home in that craft?' he asked.

'Not I! I am not one of them regular yacht hands. I came out of the hospital in Hongkong. I've been two years on the China coast.'

He stopped, then added in an explanatory murmur:

'Opium clippers – you know. Nothing of brass buttons about me. My ship left me behind, and I was in want of work. I took this job but I didn't want to go home particularly. It's slow work after sailing with old Robinson in the *Ly-e-moon*. That was my ship. Heard of her, Captain?'

'Yes, yes,' said Lingard hastily. 'Look here, Mr Carter, which way was your chief officer trying for Singapore? Through the Straits of Rhio?'

'I suppose so,' answered Carter in a slightly surprised tone; 'why do you ask?'

'Just to know ... What is it, Mr Shaw?'

'There's a black cloud rising to the northward, sir, and we shall get a breeze directly,' said Shaw from the doorway.

He lingered there with his eyes fixed on the decanters.

'Will you have a glass?' said Lingard, leaving his seat. 'I will go up and have a look.'

He went on deck. Shaw approached the table and began to help himself, handling the bottles in profound silence and with exaggerated caution, as if he had been measuring out of fragile vessels a dose of some deadly poison. Carter, his hands in his pockets, and leaning back, examined him from head to foot with a cool stare. The mate of the brig raised the glass to his lips, and glaring above the rim at the stranger, drained the contents slowly.

'You have a fine nose for finding ships in the dark, Mister,' he said, distinctly, putting the glass on the table with extreme gentleness.

'Eh? What's that? I sighted you just after sunset.'

'And you knew where to look, too,' said Shaw, staring hard.

'I looked to the westward where there was still some light, as any sensible man would do,' retorted the other a little impatiently. 'What are you trying to get at?'

'And you have a ready tongue to blow about yourself – haven't you?'

'Never saw such a man in my life,' declared Carter, with a return of his nonchalant manner. 'You seem to be troubled about something.'

'I don't like boats to come sneaking up from nowhere in particular, alongside a ship when I am in charge of the deck. I can keep a lookout as well as any man out of home ports, but I hate to be circumvented by muffled oars and such ungentlemanlike tricks. Yacht officer – indeed. These seas must be full of such yachtsmen. I consider you played a mean trick on me. I told my old man there was nothing in sight at sunset – and no more there was. I believe you blundered upon us by chance – for all your boasting about sunsets and bearings. Gammon! I know you came on blindly on top of us, and with muffled oars, too. D'ye call that decent?'

'If I did muffle the oars it was for a good reason. I wanted to slip past a cove where some native craft were moored. That was common prudence in such a small boat, and not armed – as I am. I saw you right enough, but I had no intention to startle anybody. Take my word for it.'

'I wish you had gone somewhere else,' growled Shaw. 'I hate to be put in the wrong through accident and untruthfulness – there! Here's my old man calling me –'

He left the cabin hurriedly and soon afterward Lingard came down, and sat again facing Carter across the table. His face was grave but resolute.

'We shall get the breeze directly,' he said.

'Then, sir,' said Carter, getting up, 'if you will give me back that letter I shall go on cruising about here to speak some other ship. I trust you will report us wherever you are going.'

'I am going to the yacht and I shall keep the letter,' answered Lingard with decision. 'I know exactly where she is, and I must go to the rescue of those people. It's most fortunate you've fallen in with me, Mr Carter. Fortunate for them and fortunate for me,' he added in a lower tone.

'Yes,' drawled Carter reflectively. 'There may be a tidy bit of salvage money if you should get the vessel off, but I don't think you can do much. I had better stay out here and try to speak some gunboat –'

'You must come back to your ship with me,' said Lingard, authoritatively. 'Never mind the gunboats.'

'That wouldn't be carrying out my orders,' argued Carter. 'I've got to speak a homeward-bound ship or a man-of-war – that's plain enough. I am not anxious to knock about for days in an open boat, but – let me fill my fresh-water breaker, Captain, and I will be off.'

'Nonsense,' said Lingard, sharply. 'You've got to come with me to show the place and – and help. I'll take your boat in tow.'

Carter did not seem convinced. Lingard laid a heavy hand on his shoulder.

'Look here, young fellow. I am Tom Lingard and there's not a white man among these islands, and very few natives, that have not heard of me. My luck brought you into my ship – and now I've got you, you must stay. You must!'

The last 'must' burst out loud and sharp like a pistol-shot. Carter stepped back.

'Do you mean you would keep me by force?' he asked, startled.

'Force,' repeated Lingard. 'It rests with you. I cannot let you speak any vessel. Your yacht has gone ashore in a most incon-

41

venient place – for me; and with your boats sent off here and there, you would bring every infernal gunboat buzzing to a spot that was as quiet and retired as the heart of man could wish. You stranding just on that spot of the whole coast was my bad luck. And that I could not help. You coming upon me like this is my good luck. And that I hold!'

He dropped his clenched fist, big and muscular, in the light of the lamp on the black cloth, amongst the glitter of glasses, with the strong fingers closed tight upon the firm flesh of the palm. He left it there for a moment as if showing Carter that luck he was going to hold. And he went on:

'Do you know into what hornet's nest your stupid people have blundered? How much d'ye think their lives are worth, just now? Not a brass farthing if the breeze fails me for another twenty-four hours. You may well open your eyes. It is so! And it may be too late now, while I am arguing with you here.'

He tapped the table with his knuckles, and the glasses, waking up, jingled a thin, plaintive finale to his speech. Carter stood leaning against the sideboard. He was amazed by the unexpected turn of the conversation; his jaw dropped slightly and his eyes never swerved for a moment from Lingard's face. The silence in the cabin lasted only a few seconds, but to Carter, who waited breathlessly, it seemed very long. And all at once he heard in it, for the first time, the cabin clock tick distinctly, in pulsating beats, as though a little heart of metal behind the dial had been started into sudden palpitation.

'A gunboat!' shouted Lingard, suddenly, as if he had seen only in that moment, by the light of some vivid flash of thought, all the difficulties of the situation. 'If you don't go back with me there will be nothing left for you to go back to – very soon. Your gunboat won't find a single ship's rib or a single corpse left for a landmark. That she won't. It isn't a gunboat skipper you want. I am the man you want. You don't know your luck when you see it, but I know mine, I do – and – look here –'

He touched Carter's chest with his forefinger, and said with a sudden gentleness of tone:

'I am a white man inside and out; I won't let inoffensive

people – and a woman, too – come to harm if I can help it. And if I can't help, nobody can. You understand – nobody! There's no time for it. But I am like any other man that is worth his salt: I won't let the end of an undertaking go by the board while there is a chance to hold on – and it's like this –'

His voice was persuasive – almost caressing; he had hold now of a coat button and tugged at it slightly as he went on in a confidential manner:

'As it turns out, Mr Carter, I would – in a manner of speaking – I would as soon shoot you where you stand as let you go to raise an alarm all over this sea about your confounded yacht. I have other lives to consider – and friends – and promises – and – and myself, too. I shall keep you,' he concluded, sharply.

Carter drew a long breath. On the deck above, the two men could hear soft footfalls, short murmurs, indistinct words spoken near the skylight. Shaw's voice rang out loudly in growling tones:

'Furl the royals, you *tindal*!'

'It's the queerest old go,' muttered Carter, looking down on to the floor. 'You are a strange man. I suppose I must believe what you say – unless you and that fat mate of yours are a couple of escaped lunatics that got hold of a brig by some means. Why, that chap up there wanted to pick a quarrel with me for coming aboard, and now you threaten to shoot me rather than let me go. Not that I care much about that; for some time or other you would get hanged for it; and you don't look like a man that will end that way. If what you say is only half true, I ought to get back to the yacht as quick as ever I can. It strikes me that your coming to them will be only a small mercy, anyhow – and I may be of some use – But this is the queerest ... May I go in my boat?'

'As you like,' said Lingard. 'There's a rain squall coming.'

'I am in charge and will get wet along of my chaps. Give us a good long line, Captain.'

'It's done already,' said Lingard. 'You seem a sensible sailor-man and can see that it would be useless to try and give me the slip.'

'For a man so ready to shoot, you seem very trustful,' drawled Carter. 'If I cut adrift in a squall, I stand a pretty fair chance not to see you again.'

'You just try,' said Lingard, drily. 'I have eyes in this brig, young man, that will see your boat when you couldn't see the ship. You are of the kind I like, but if you monkey with me I will find you – and when I find you I will run you down as surely as I stand here.'

Carter slapped his thigh and his eyes twinkled.

'By the Lord Harry!' he cried. 'If it wasn't for the men with me, I would try for sport. You are so cocksure about the lot you can do, Captain. You would aggravate a saint into open mutiny.'

His easy good humour had returned; but after a short burst of laughter, he became serious.

'Never fear,' he said, 'I won't slip away. If there is to be any throat-cutting – as you seem to hint – mine will be there, too, I promise you, and ...'

He stretched his arms out, glanced at them, shook them a little.

'And this pair of arms to take care of it,' he added, in his old, careless drawl.

But the master of the brig sitting with both his elbows on the table, his face in his hands, had fallen unexpectedly into a meditation so concentrated and so profound that he seemed neither to hear, see, nor breathe. The sight of that man's complete absorption in thought was to Carter almost more surprising than any other occurrence of that night. Had his strange host vanished suddenly from before his eyes, it could not have made him feel more uncomfortably alone in that cabin where the pertinacious clock kept ticking off the useless minutes of the calm before it would, with the same steady beat, begin to measure the aimless disturbance of the storm.

3

AFTER waiting a moment, Carter went on deck. The sky, the sea, the brig itself had disappeared in a darkness that had become impenetrable, palpable, and stifling. An immense cloud had come up running over the heavens, as if looking for the little craft, and now hung over it, arrested. To the south there was a livid trembling gleam, faint and sad, like a vanishing memory of destroyed starlight. To the north, as if to prove the impossible, an incredibly blacker patch outlined on the tremendous blackness of the sky the heart of the coming squall. The glimmers in the water had gone out and the invisible sea all around lay mute and still as if it had died suddenly of fright.

Carter could see nothing. He felt about him people moving; he heard them in the darkness whispering faintly as if they had been exchanging secrets important or infamous. The night effaced even words, and its mystery had captured everything and every sound – had left nothing free but the unexpected that seemed to hover about one, ready to stretch out its stealthy hand in a touch sudden, familiar, and appalling. Even the careless disposition of the young ex-officer of an opium-clipper was affected by the ominous aspect of the hour. What was this vessel? What were those people? What would happen tomorrow? To the yacht? To himself? He felt suddenly without any additional reason but the darkness that it was a poor show, anyhow, a dashed poor show for all hands. The irrational conviction made him falter for a second where he stood and he gripped the slide of the companionway hard.

Shaw's voice right close to his ear relieved and cleared his troubled thoughts.

'Oh! it's you, Mister. Come up at last,' said the mate of the brig slowly. 'It appears we've got to give you a tow now. Of all the rum in-cidents, this beats all. A boat sneaks up from nowhere and turns out to be a long-expected friend! For you are one of them friends the skipper was going to meet somewhere here.

45

Ain't you now? Come! I know more than you may think. Are we off to – you may just as well tell – off to – h'm ha … you know?'

'Yes. I know. Don't you?' articulated Carter, innocently.

Shaw remained very quiet for a minute.

'Where's my skipper?' he asked at last.

'I left him down below in a kind of trance. Where's my boat?'

'Your boat is hanging astern. And my opinion is that you are as uncivil as I've proved you to be untruthful. Egzz-actly.'

Carter stumbled toward the taffrail and in the first step he made came full against somebody who glided away. It seemed to him that such a night brings men to a lower level. He thought that he might have been knocked on the head by anybody strong enough to lift a crow-bar. He felt strangely irritated. He said loudly, aiming his words at Shaw whom he supposed somewhere near:

'And my opinion is that you and your skipper will come to a sudden bad end before –'

'I thought you were in your boat. Have you changed your mind?' asked Lingard in his deep voice close to Carter's elbow.

Carter felt his way along the rail, till his hand found a line that seemed, in the calm, to stream out of its own accord into the darkness. He hailed his boat, and directly heard the wash of water against her bows as she was hauled quickly under the counter. Then he loomed up shapeless on the rail, and the next moment disappeared as if he had fallen out of the universe. Lingard heard him say:

'Catch hold of my leg, John.' There were hollow sounds in the boat, a voice growled 'All right.'

'Keep clear of the counter,' said Lingard, speaking in quiet warning tones into the night. 'The brig may get a lot of stern-way on her should this squall not strike her fairly.'

'Aye, aye. I will mind,' was the muttered answer from the water.

Lingard crossed over to the port side, and looked steadily at the sooty mass of approaching vapours. After a moment he said curtly, 'Brace up for the port tack, Mr Shaw,' and remained silent, with his face to the sea. A sound, sorrowful and startling like the sigh of some immense creature, travelling across the starless space, passed above the vertical and lofty spars of the motionless brig.

It grew louder, then suddenly ceased for a moment, and the taut rigging of the brig was heard vibrating its answer in a singing note to this threatening murmur of the winds. A long and slow undulation lifted the level of the waters, as if the sea had drawn a deep breath of anxious suspense. The next minute an immense disturbance leaped out of the darkness upon the sea, kindling upon it a livid clearness of foam, and the first gust of the squall boarded the brig in a stinging flick of rain and spray. As if overwhelmed by the suddenness of the fierce onset, the vessel remained for a second upright where she floated, shaking with tremendous jerks from trucks to keel; while high up in the night the invisible canvas was heard rattling and beating about violently.

Then, with a quick double report, as of heavy guns, both topsails filled at once and the brig fell over swiftly on her side. Shaw was thrown headlong against the skylight, and Lingard, who had encircled the weather rail with his arm, felt the vessel under his feet dart forward smoothly, and the deck become less slanting – the speed of the brig running off a little now, easing the overturning strain of the wind upon the distended surfaces of the sails. It was only the fineness of the little vessel's lines and the perfect shape of her hull that saved the canvas, and perhaps the spars, by enabling the ready craft to get way upon herself with such lightning-like rapidity. Lingard drew a long breath and yelled jubilantly at Shaw who was struggling up against wind and rain to his commander's side.

'She'll do. Hold on everything.'

Shaw tried to speak. He swallowed great mouthfuls of tepid water which the wind drove down his throat. The brig seemed to sail through undulating waves that passed swishing between the masts and swept over the decks with the fierce rush and noise of a cataract. From every spar and every rope a ragged sheet of water streamed flicking to leeward. The overpowering deluge

47

seemed to last for an age; became unbearable – and, all at once, stopped. In a couple of minutes the shower had run its length over the brig and now could be seen like a straight grey wall, going away into the night under the fierce whispering of dissolving clouds. The wind eased. To the northward, low down in the darkness, three stars appeared in a row, leaping in and out between the crests of waves like the distant heads of swimmers in a running surf; and the retreating edge of the cloud, perfectly straight from east to west, slipped along the dome of the sky like an immense hemispheric iron shutter pivoting down smoothly as if operated by some mighty engine. An inspiring and penetrating freshness flowed together with the shimmer of light, through the augmented glory of the heaven, a glory exalted, undimmend, and strangely startling as if a new world had been created during the short flight of the stormy cloud. It was a return to life, a return to space; the earth coming out from under a pall to take its place in the renewed and immense scintillation of the universe.

The brig, her yards slightly checked in, ran with an easy motion under the topsails, jib and driver, pushing contemptuously aside the turbulent crowd of noisy and agitated waves. As the craft went swiftly ahead she unrolled behind her over the uneasy darkness of the sea a broad ribbon of seething foam shot with wispy gleams of dark discs escaping from under the rudder. Far away astern, at the end of a line no thicker than a black thread, which dipped now and then its long curve in the bursting froth, a toy-like object could be made out, elongated and dark, racing after the brig over the snowy whiteness of her wake.

Lingard walked aft, and, with both his hands on the taffrail, looked eagerly for Carter's boat. The first glance satisfied him that the yacht's gig was towing easily at the end of the long scope of line, and he turned away to look ahead and to leeward with a steady gaze. It was then half an hour past midnight and Shaw, relieved by Wasub, had gone below. Before he went, he said to Lingard, 'I will be off, sir, if you're not going to make more sail yet.' 'Not yet for a while,' had answered Lingard in a preoccupied manner; and Shaw departed aggrieved at such a neglect of making the best of a good breeze.

On the main deck dark-skinned men, whose clothing clung to their shivering limbs as if they had been overboard, had finished recoiling the braces, and clearing the gear. The *kassab*, after having hung the fore-topsail halyards in the becket, strutted into the waist toward a row of men who stood idly with their shoulders against the side of the long boat amidships. He passed along looking up close at the stolid faces. Room was made for him, and he took his place at the end.

'It was a great rain and a mighty wind, O men,' he said, dogmatically, 'but no wind can ever hurt this ship. That I knew while I stood minding the sail which is under my care.'

A dull and inexpressive murmur was heard from the men. Over the high weather rail, a topping wave flung into their eyes a handful of heavy drops that stung like hail. There were low groans of indignation. A man sighed. Another emitted a spasmodic laugh through his chattering teeth. No one moved away. The little *kassab* wiped his face and went on in his cracked voice, to the accompaniment of the swishing sounds made by the seas that swept regularly astern along the ship's side.

'Have you heard him shout at the wind – louder than the wind? I have heard, being far forward. And before, too, in the many years I served this white man I have heard him often cry magic words that make all safe. *Ya-wa!* This is truth. Ask Wasub who is a Haji, even as I am.'

'I have seen white men's ships with their masts broken – also wrecked like our own *praus*,' remarked sadly a lean, lank fellow who shivered beside the *kassab*, hanging his head and trying to grasp his shoulder blades.

'True,' admitted the *kassab*. 'They are all the children of Satan but to some more favour is shown. To obey such men on the sea or in a fight is good. I saw him who is master here fight with wild men who eat their enemies – far away to the eastward – and I dealt blows by his side without fear; for the charms he, no doubt, possesses protect his servants also. I am a believer and the Stoned One can not touch my forehead. Yet the reward of victory

comes from the accursed. For six years have I sailed with that
white man; first as one who minds the rudder, for I am a man
of the sea, born in a *prau*, and am skilled in such work. And
now, because of my great knowledge of his desires, I have the
care of all things in this ship.'

Several voices muttered 'True. True.' They remained apathetic
and patient, in the rush of wind, under the repeated short flights
of strays. The slight roll of the ship balanced them stiffly all together where they stood propped against the big boat. The
breeze humming between the inclined masts enveloped their
dark and silent figures in the unceasing resonance of its breath.

The brig's head had been laid so as to pass a little to windward of the small islands of the Carimata group. They had been
till then hidden in the night, but now both men on the lookout
reported land ahead in one long cry. Lingard, standing to leeward abreast of the wheel, watched the islet first seen. When it
was nearly abeam of the brig he gave his orders, and Wasub
hurried off to the main deck. The helm was put down, the yards
on the main came slowly square and the wet canvas of the main-
topsail clung suddenly to the mast after a single heavy flap. The
dazzling streak of the ship's wake vanished. The vessel lost her
way and began to dip her bows into the quick succession of the
running head seas. And at every slow plunge of the craft, the
song of the wind would swell louder amongst the waving spars,
with a wild and mournful note.

Just as the brig's boat had been swung out, ready for lowering,
the yacht's gig hauled up by its line appeared tossing and splashing on the lee quarter. Carter stood up in the stern sheets balancing himself cleverly to the disordered motion of his cockleshell.
He hailed the brig twice to know what was the matter, not being
able from below and in the darkness to make out what that confused group of men on the poop were about. He got no answer,
though he could see the shape of a man standing by himself aft,
and apparently watching him. He was going to repeat his hail
for the third time when he heard the rattling of tackles followed
by a heavy splash, a burst of voices, scrambling hollow sounds –
and a dark mass detaching itself from the brig's side swept past
him on the crest of a passing wave. For less than a second he

could see on the shimmer of the night sky the shape of a boat, the heads of men, the blades of oars pointing upward while being got out hurriedly. Then all this sank out of sight, reappeared once more far off and hardly discernible, before vanishing for good.

'Why, they've lowered a boat!' exclaimed Carter, falling back in his seat. He remembered that he had seen only a few hours ago three native *praus* lurking amongst those very islands. For a moment he had the idea of casting off to go in chase of that boat, so as to find out ... Find out what? He gave up his idea at once. What could he do?

The conviction that the yacht, and everything belonging to her, were in some indefinite but very real danger, took afresh a strong hold of him, and the persuasion that the master of the brig was going there to help did not by any means assuage his alarm. The fact only served to complicate his uneasiness with a sense of mystery.

The white man who spoke as if that sea was all his own, or as if people intruded upon his privacy by taking the liberty of getting wrecked on a coast where he and his friends did some queer business, seemed to him an undesirable helper. That the boat had been lowered to communicate with the *praus* seen and avoided by him in the evening he had no doubt. The thought had flashed on him at once. It had an ugly look. Yet the best thing to do after all was to hang on and get back to the yacht and warn them ... Warn them against whom? The man had been perfectly open with him. Warn them against what? It struck him that he hadn't the slightest conception of what would happen, of what was even likely to happen. That strange rescuer himself was bringing the news of danger. Danger from the natives of course. And yet he was in communication with those natives. That was evident. That boat going off in the night ... Carter swore heartily to himself. His perplexity became positive bodily plain as he sat, wet, uncomfortable, and still, one hand on the tiller, thrown up and down in headlong swings of his boat. And before his eyes, towering high, the black hull of the brig also rose and fell, setting her stern down in the sea, now and again, with a tremendous and foaming splash. Not a sound from her reached Carter's ears. She seemed an abandoned craft but for the outline of a man's head and body still visible in a watchful attitude above the taffrail.

Carter told his bowman to haul up closer and hailed:

'Brig ahoy. Anything wrong?'

He waited, listening. The shadowy man still watched. After some time a curt 'No' came back in answer.

'Are you going to keep hove-to long?' shouted Carter.

'Don't know. Not long. Drop your boat clear of the ship. Drop clear. Do damage if you don't.'

'Slack away, John!' said Carter in a resigned tone to the elderly seaman in the bow. 'Slack away and let us ride easy to the full scope. They don't seem very talkative on board there.'

Even while he was speaking the line ran out and the regular undulations of the passing seas drove the boat away from the brig. Carter turned a little in his seat to look at the land. It loomed up dead to leeward like a lofty and irregular cone only a mile or a mile and a half distant. The noise of the surf beating upon its base was heard against the wind in measured detonations. The fatigue of many days spent in the boat asserted itself above the restlessness of Carter's thoughts and, gradually, he lost the notion of the passing time without altogether losing the consciousness of his situation.

In the intervals of that benumbed stupor – rather than sleep – he was aware that the interrupted noise of the surf had grown into a continuous great rumble, swelling periodically into a loud roar; that the high islet appeared now bigger, and that a white fringe of foam was visible at its feet. Still there was no stir or movement of any kind on board the brig. He noticed that the wind was moderating and the sea going down with it, and then dozed off again for a minute. When next he opened his eyes with a start, it was just in time to see with surprise a new star soar noiselessly straight up from behind the land, take up its position in a brilliant constellation – and go out suddenly. Two more followed, ascending together, and after reaching about the same elevation, expired side by side.

'Them's rockets, sir – ain't they?' said one of the men in a muffled voice.

'Aye, rockets,' grunted Carter. 'And now, what's the next move?' he muttered to himself dismally.

He got his answer in the fierce swishing whirr of a slender ray of fire that, shooting violently upward from the sombre hull of the brig, dissolved at once into a dull red shower of falling sparks. Only one, white and brilliant, remained alone poised high overhead, and after glowing vividly for a second, exploded with a feeble report. Almost at the same time he saw the brig's head fall off the wind, made out the yards swinging round to fill the main topsail, and heard distinctly the thud of the first wave thrown off by the advancing bows. The next minute the tow-line got the strain and his boat started hurriedly after the brig with a sudden jerk.

Leaning forward, wide awake and attentive, Carter steered. His men sat one behind another with shoulders up, and arched backs, dozing, uncomfortable but patient, upon the thwarts. The care requisite to steer the boat properly in the track of the seething and disturbed water left by the brig in her rapid course prevented him from reflecting much upon the incertitude of the future and upon his own unusual situation.

Now he was only exceedingly anxious to see the yacht again, and it was with a feeling of very real satisfaction that he saw all plain sail being made on the brig. Through the remaining hours of the night he sat grasping the tiller and keeping his eyes on the shadowy and high pyramid of canvas gliding steadily ahead of his boat with a slight balancing movement from side to side.

4

It was noon before the brig, piloted by Lingard through the deep channels between the outer coral reefs, rounded within pistol-shot a low hummock of sand which marked the end of a long stretch of stony ledges that, being mostly awash, showed a black head only, here and there amongst the hissing brown froth of the yellow sea. As the brig drew clear of the sandy patch there appeared, dead to windward and beyond a maze of broken water, sandspits, and clusters of rocks, the black hull of the yacht heeling over, high and motionless upon the great expanse of glittering shallows. Her long, naked spars were inclined slightly as if she had been sailing with a good breeze. There was to the lookers-on aboard the brig something sad and disappointing in the yacht's aspect as she lay perfectly still in an attitude that in a seaman's mind is associated with the idea of rapid motion.

'Here she is!' said Shaw, who, clad in a spotless white suit, came just then from forward where he had been busy with the anchors. 'She is well on, sir – isn't she? Looks like a mudflat to me from here.'

'Yes. It is a mudflat,' said Lingard, slowly raising the long glass to his eyes. 'Haul the mainsail up, Mr Shaw,' he went on while he took a steady look at the yacht. 'We will have to work in short tacks here.'

He put the glass down and moved away from the rail. For the next hour he handled his little vessel in the intricate and narrow channel with careless certitude, as if every stone, every grain of sand upon the treacherous bottom had been plainly disclosed to his sight. He handled her in the fitful and unsteady breeze with a matter-of-fact audacity that made Shaw, forward at his station, gasp in sheer alarm. When heading toward the inshore shoals the brig was never put round till the quick, loud cries of the leadsmen announced that there were no more than three feet of water under her keel; and when standing toward the steep inner edge of the long reef, where the lead was of no use, the helm would be put down only when the cutwater touched the faint line of the bordering foam. Lingard's love for his brig was a man's love, and was so great that it could never be appeased unless he called on her to put forth all her qualities and her power, to repay his exacting affection by a faithfulness tried to the very utmost limit of endurance. Every flutter of the sails flew down from aloft along the taut leeches, to enter his heart in a sense of acute delight; and the gentle murmur of water alongside, which, continuous and soft, showed that in all her windings his incomparable craft had never, even for an instant, ceased to carry her way, was to him more precious and inspiring than the soft whisper of tender words would have been to another man. It was in such moments that he lived intensely, in a flush of strong feeling that made him long to press his little vessel to his breast. She was his perfect world full of trustful joy.

The people on board the yacht, who watched eagerly the first sail they had seen since they had been ashore on that deserted part of the coast, soon made her out, with some disappointment, to be a small merchant brig beating up tack for tack along the inner edge of the reef – probably with the intention to communicate and offer assistance. The general opinion among the seafaring portion of her crew was that little effective assistance could be expected from a vessel of that description. Only the sailing-master of the yacht remarked to the boatswain (who had the advantage of being his first cousin): 'This man is well acquainted here; you can see that by the way he handles his brig. I shan't be sorry to have somebody to stand by us. Can't tell when we will get off this mud, George.'

A long board, sailed very close, enabled the brig to fetch the southern limit of discoloured water over the bank on which the yacht had stranded. On the very edge of the muddy patch she was put in stays for the last time. As soon as she had paid off on the other tack, sail was shortened smartly, and the brig commenced the stretch that was to bring her to her anchorage, under her topsails, lower staysails and jib. There was then less than a quarter of a mile of shallow water between her and the yacht; but while that vessel had gone ashore with her head to the eastward the brig was moving slowly in a west-northwest direction, and consequently sailed – so to speak – past the whole length of the yacht. Lingard saw every soul in the schooner on deck, watching his advent in a silence which was as unbroken and perfect as that on board his own vessel.

A little man with a red face framed in white whiskers waved a gold-laced cap above the rail in the waist of the yacht. Lingard raised his arm in return. Further aft, under the white awnings, he could see two men and a woman. One of the men and the lady were in blue. The other man, who seemed very tall and stood with his arm entwined round an awning stanchion above his head, was clad in white. Lingard saw them plainly. They looked at the brig through binoculars, turned their faces to one another, moved their lips, seemed surprised. A large dog put his forepaws on the rail, and, lifting up his big, black head, sent out three loud and plaintive barks, then dropped down out of sight. A sudden stir and an appearance of excitement amongst all hands on board the yacht was caused by their perceiving that the boat towing astern of the stranger was their own second gig.

Arms were outstretched with pointing fingers. Someone shouted out a long sentence of which not a word could be made out; and then the brig, having reached the western limit of the bank, began to move diagonally away, increasing her distance from the yacht but bringing her stern gradually into view. The people aft, Lingard noticed, left their places and walked over to the taffrail so as to keep him longer in sight.

When about a mile off the bank and nearly in line with the stern of the yacht the brig's topsails fluttered and the yards came down slowly on the caps; the fore and aft canvas ran down; and for some time she floated quietly with folded wings upon the transparent sheet of water, under the radiant silence of the sky. Then her anchor went to the bottom with a rumbling noise resembling the roll of distant thunder. In a moment her head tended to the last puffs of the northerly airs and the ensign at the peak stirred, unfurled itself slowly, collapsed, flew out again, and finally hung down straight and still, as if weighted with lead.

'Dead calm, sir,' said Shaw to Lingard. 'Dead calm again. We got into this funny place in the nick of time, sir.'

They stood for a while side by side, looking round upon the coast and the sea. The brig had been brought up in the middle of a broad belt of clear water. To the north rocky ledges showed in black and white lines upon the slight swell setting in from there. A small island stood out from the broken water like the square tower of some submerged building. It was about two miles distant from the brig. To the eastward the coast was low; a coast of green forests fringed with dark mangroves. There was in its sombre dullness a clearly defined opening, as if a small piece had been cut out with a sharp knife. The water in it shone like a patch of polished silver. Lingard pointed it out to Shaw.

'This is the entrance to the place where we are going,' he said. Shaw stared, round-eyed.

'I thought you came here on account of this here yacht,' he stammered, surprised.

'Ah. The yacht,' said Lingard, musingly, keeping his eyes on the break in the coast. 'The yacht –' He stamped his foot suddenly. 'I would give all I am worth and throw in a few days of life into the bargain if I could get her off and away before to-night.'

He calmed down, and again stood gazing at the land. A little within the entrance from behind the wall of forests an invisible fire belched out steadily the black and heavy convolutions of thick smoke, which stood out high, like a twisted and shivering pillar against the clear blue of the sky.

'We must stop that game, Mr Shaw,' said Lingard abruptly.

'Yes, sir. What game?' asked Shaw, looking round in wonder.

'This smoke,' said Lingard, impatiently. 'It's a signal.'

'Certainly, sir – though I don't see how we can do it. It seems far inland. A signal for what, sir?'

'It was not meant for us,' said Lingard in an unexpectedly savage tone. 'Here, Shaw, make them put a blank charge into that forecastle gun. Tell 'em to ram hard the wadding and grease the mouth. We want to make a good noise. If old Jörgenson hears it, that fire will be out before you have time to turn round twice ... In a minute, Mr Carter.'

The yacht's boat had come alongside as soon as the brig had been brought up, and Carter had been waiting to take Lingard on board the yacht. They both walked now to the gangway. Shaw, following his commander, stood by to take his last orders.

'Put all the boats in the water, Mr Shaw,' Lingard was saying, with one foot on the rail, ready to leave his ship, 'and mount the four-pounder swivel in the long-boat's bow. Cast off the sea lashings of the guns, but don't run 'em out yet. Keep the topsails loose and the jib ready for setting, I may want the sails in a hurry. Now, Mr Carter, I am ready for you.'

'Shove off, boys,' said Carter as soon as they were seated in the boat. 'Shove off, and give way for a last pull before you get a long rest.'

The men lay back on their oars, grunting. Their faces were drawn, grey and streaked with the dried salt sprays. They had the worried expression of men who had a long call made upon their endurance. Carter, heavy-eyed and dull, steered for the yacht's gangway. Lingard asked as they were crossing the brig's bows:

'Water enough alongside your craft, I suppose?'

'Yes. Eight to twelve feet,' answered Carter, hoarsely. 'Say, Captain! Where's your show of cut-throats? Why! This sea is as empty as a church on a week-day.'

The booming report, nearly over his head, of the brig's eighteen-pounder interrupted him. A round puff of white vapour, spreading itself lazily, clung in fading shreds about the foreyard. Lingard, turning half round in the stern sheets, looked at the smoke on the shore. Carter remained silent, staring sleepily at the yacht they were approaching. Lingard kept watching the smoke so intensely that he almost forgot where he was, till Carter's voice pronouncing sharply at his ear the words 'way enough', recalled him to himself.

They were in the shadow of the yacht and coming alongside her ladder. The master of the brig looked upward into the face of a gentleman, with long whiskers and a shaved chin, staring down at him over the side through a single eyeglass. As he put his foot on the bottom step he could see the shore smoke still ascending, unceasing and thick; but even as he looked the very base of the black pillar rose above the ragged line of tree-tops. The whole thing floated clear away from the earth, and rolling itself into an irregularly shaped mass, drifted out to seaward, travelling slowly over the blue heavens, like a threatening and lonely cloud.

PART TWO

THE SHORE OF REFUGE

I

The coast off which the little brig, floating upright above her anchor, seemed to guard the high hull of the yacht has no distinctive features. It is land without form. It stretches away without cap or bluff, long and low – indefinitely; and when the heavy gusts of the northeast monsoon drive the thick rain slanting over the sea, it is seen faintly under the grey sky, black and with a blurred outline like the straight edge of a dissolving shore. In the long season of unclouded days, it presents to view only a narrow band of earth that appears crushed flat upon the vast level of waters by the weight of the sky, whose immense dome rests on it in a line as fine and true as that of the sea horizon itself.

Notwithstanding its nearness to the centres of European power, this coast has been known for ages to the armed wanderers of these seas as 'The Shore of Refuge'. It has no specific name on the charts, and geography manuals don't mention it at all; but the wreckage of many defeats unerringly drifts into its creeks. Its approaches are extremely difficult for a stranger. Looked at from seaward, the innumerable islets fringing what, on account of its vast size, may be called the mainland, merge into a background that presents not a single landmark to point the way through the intricate channels. It may be said that in a belt of sea twenty miles broad along that low shore there is much more coral, mud, sand, and stones than actual sea water. It was amongst the outlying shoals of this stretch that the yacht had gone ashore and the events consequent upon her stranding took place.

The diffused light of the short daybreak showed the open water to the westward, sleeping, smooth and grey, under a faded heaven. The straight coast threw a heavy belt of gloom along the shoals, which, in the calm of expiring night, were unmarked by the slightest ripple. In the faint dawn the low clumps of bushes on the sandbanks appeared immense.

Two figures, noiseless like two shadows, moved slowly over the beach of a rocky islet, and stopped side by side on the very edge of the water. Behind them, between the mats from which they had arisen, a small heap of black embers smouldered quietly. They stood upright and perfectly still, but for the slight movement of their heads from right to left and back again as they swept their gaze through the grey emptiness of the waters where, about two miles distant, the hull of the yacht loomed up to seaward, black and shapeless, against the wan sky.

The two figures looked beyond without exchanging as much as a murmur. The taller of the two grounded, at arm's length, the stock of a gun with a long barrel; the hair of the other fell down to its waist; and, near by, the leaves of creepers drooping from the summit of the steep rock stirred no more than the festooned stone. The faint light, disclosing here and there a gleam of white sandbanks and the blurred hummocks of islets scattered within the gloom of the coast, the profound silence, the vast stillness all round, accentuated the loneliness of the two human beings who, urged by a sleepless hope, had risen thus, at break of day, to look afar upon the veiled face of the sea.

'Nothing!' said the man with a sigh, and as if awakening from a long period of musing.

He was clad in a jacket of coarse blue cotton, of the kind a poor fisherman might own, and he wore it wide open on a muscular chest the colour and smoothness of bronze. From the twist of threadbare *sarong* wound tightly on the hips protruded outward to the left the ivory hilt, ringed with six bands of gold, of a weapon that would not have disgraced a ruler. Silver glittered about the flintlock and the hardwood stock of his gun. The red and gold handkerchief folded round his head was of costly stuff, such as is woven by high-born women in the households of chiefs, only the gold threads were tarnished and the silk frayed in the folds. His head was thrown back, the dropped eyelids narrowed the gleam of his eyes. His face was hairless, the nose short with mobile nostrils, and the smile of careless good-humour seemed to have been permanently wrought, as if with a delicate tool, into the slight hollows about the corners of rather full lips.

His upright figure had a negligent elegance. But in the careless face, in the easy gestures of the whole man there was something attentive and restrained.

After giving the offing a last searching glance, he turned and, facing the rising sun, walked bare-footed on the elastic sand. The trailed butt of his gun made a deep furrow. The embers had ceased to smoulder. He looked down at them pensively for awhile, then called over his shoulder to the girl who had remained behind, still scanning the sea:

'The fire is out, Immada.'

At the sound of his voice the girl moved toward the mats. Her black hair hung like a mantle. Her *sarong*, the kilt-like garment which both sexes wear, had the national check of grey and red, but she had not completed her attire by the belt, scarves, the loose upper wrappings, and the head-covering of a woman. A black silk jacket, like that of a man of rank, was buttoned over her bust and fitted closely to her slender waist. The edge of a stand-up collar, stiff with gold embroidery, rubbed her cheek. She had no bracelets, no anklets, and although dressed practically in man's clothes, had about her person no weapon of any sort. Her arms hung down in exceedingly tight sleeves slit a little way up from the wrist, gold-braided and with a row of small gold buttons. She walked, brown and alert, all of a piece, with short steps, the eyes lively in an impassive little face, the arched mouth closed firmly; and her whole person breathed in its rigid grace the fiery gravity of youth at the beginning of the task of life – at the beginning of beliefs and hopes.

This was the day of Lingard's arrival upon the coast, but, as is known, the brig, delayed by the calm, did not appear in sight of the shallows till the morning was far advanced. Disappointed in their hope to see the expected sail shining in the first rays of the rising sun, the man and the woman, without attempting to re-light the fire, lounged on their sleeping mats. At their feet a common canoe, hauled out of the water, was, for more security, moored by a grass rope to the shaft of a long spear planted firmly on the white beach, and the incoming tide lapped monotonously against its stern.

The girl, twisting up her black hair, fastened it with slender wooden pins. The man, reclining at full length, had made room on his mat for the gun – as one would do for a friend – and, supported on his elbow, looked toward the yacht with eyes whose fixed dreaminess like a transparent veil would show the slow passage of every gloomy thought by deepening gradually into a sombre stare.

'We have seen three sunrises on this islet, and no friend came from the sea,' he said without changing his attitude, with his back toward the girl who sat on the other side of the cold embers.

'Yes; and the moon is waning,' she answered in a low voice. 'The moon is waning. Yet he promised to be here when the nights are light and the water covers the sandbanks as far as the bushes.'

'The traveller knows the time of his setting out, but not the time of his return,' observed the man, calmly.

The girl sighed.

'The nights of waiting are long,' she murmured.

'And sometimes they are vain,' said the man with the same composure. 'Perhaps he will never return.'

'Why?' exclaimed the girl.

'The road is long and the heart may grow cold,' was the answer in a quiet voice. 'If he does not return it is because he has forgotten.'

'Oh, Hassim, it is because he is dead,' cried the girl, indignantly.

The man, looking fixedly to seaward, smiled at the ardour of her tone.

They were brother and sister, and though very much alike, the family resemblance was lost in the more general traits common to the whole race.

They were natives of Wajo and it is a common saying amongst the Malay race that to be a successful traveller and trader a man must have some Wajo blood in his veins. And with those people trading, which means also travelling afar, is a romantic and an honourable occupation. The trader must possess an adventurous spirit and a keen understanding; he should have the fearlessness of youth and the sagacity of age; he should be diplomatic and courageous, so as to secure the favour of the great and inspire fear in evil-doers.

These qualities naturally are not expected in a shopkeeper or a Chinaman pedlar; they are considered indispensable only for a man who, of noble birth and perhaps related to the ruler of his own country, wanders over the seas in a craft of his own and with many followers; carries from island to island important news as well as merchandise; who may be trusted with secret messages and valuable goods; a man who, in short, is as ready to intrigue and fight as to buy and sell. Such is the ideal trader of Wajo.

Trading, thus understood, was the occupation of ambitious men who played an occult but important part in all those national risings, religious disturbances, and also in the organized piratical movements on a large scale which, during the first half of the last century, affected the fate of more than one native dynasty and, for a few years at least, seriously endangered the Dutch rule in the East. When, at the cost of much blood and gold, a comparative peace had been imposed on the islands the same occupation, though shorn of its glorious possibilities, remained attractive for the most adventurous of a restless race. The younger sons and relations of many a native ruler traversed the seas of the Archipelago, visited the innumerable and little-known islands, and the then practically unknown shores of New Guinea; every spot where European trade had not penetrated – from Aru to Atjeh, from Sumbawa to Palawan.

2

It was in the most unknown perhaps of such spots, a small bay on the coast of New Guinea, that young Pata Hassim, the nephew of one of the greatest chiefs of Wajo, met Lingard for the first time.

He was a trader after the Wajo manner, and in a stout sea-going *prau* armed with two guns and manned by young men who were related to his family by blood or dependence, had come in there to buy some birds of paradise skins for the old Sultan of Ternate; a risky expedition undertaken not in the way of business but as a matter of courtesy toward the aged Sultan who had entertained him sumptuously in that dismal brick palace at Ternate for a month or more.

While lying off the village, very much on his guard, waiting for the skins and negotiating with the treacherous coast-savages who are the go-betweens in that trade, Hassim saw one morning Lingard's brig come to an anchor in the bay, and shortly afterward observed a white man of great stature with a beard that shone like gold land from a boat and stroll on unarmed, though followed by four Malays of the brig's crew, toward the native village.

Hassim was struck with wonder and amazement at the cool recklessness of such a proceeding; and, after, in true Malay fashion, discussing with his people for an hour or so the urgency of the case, he also landed, but well escorted and armed, with the intention of going to see what would happen.

The affair really was very simple, 'such as' – Lingard would say – 'such as might have happened to anybody.' He went ashore with the intention to look for some stream where he could conveniently replenish his water casks, this being really the motive which had induced him to enter the bay.

While, with his men close by and surrounded by a mop-headed, sooty crowd, he was showing a few cotton handkerchiefs, and trying to explain by signs the object of his landing, a spear, lunged from behind, grazed his neck. Probably the Papuan wanted only to ascertain whether such a creature could be killed or hurt, and most likely firmly believed that it could not; but one of Lingard's seamen at once retaliated by striking at the experimenting savage with his *parang* – three such choppers brought for the purpose of clearing the bush, if necessary, being all the weapons the party from the brig possessed.

A deadly tumult ensued with such suddenness that Lingard,

turning round swiftly, saw his defender, already speared in three places, fall forward at his feet. Wasub, who was there, and afterward told the story once a week on an average, used to hornify his hearers by showing how the man blinked his eyes quickly before he fell. Lingard was unarmed. To the end of his life he remained incorrigibly reckless in that respect, explaining that he was 'much too quick tempered to carry firearms on the chance of a row. And if put to it,' he argued, 'I can make shift to kill a man with my fist anyhow; and then – don't ye see – you know what you're doing and are not so apt to start a trouble from sheer temper or funk – see?'

In this case he did his best to kill a man with a blow from the shoulder and catching up another by the middle flung him at the naked, wild crowd. 'He hurled men about as the wind hurls broken boughs. He made a broad way through our enemies!' related Wasub in his jerky voice. It is more probable that Lingard's quick movements, and the amazing aspect of such a strange being, caused the warriors to fall back before his rush.

Taking instant advantage of their surprise and fear, Lingard, followed by his men, dashed along the kind of ruinous jetty leading to the village which was erected as usual over the water. They darted into one of the miserable huts built of rotten mats and bits of decayed canoes, and in this shelter, showing daylight through all its sides, they had time to draw breath and realize that their position was not much improved.

The women and children screaming had cleared out into the bush, while at the shore end of the jetty the warriors capered and yelled, preparing for a general attack. Lingard noticed with mortification that his boat-keeper apparently had lost his head, for, instead of swimming off to the ship to give the alarm, as he was perfectly able to do, the man actually struck out for a small rock a hundred yards away and was frantically trying to climb up its perpendicular side. The tide being out, to jump into the horrible mud under the houses would have been almost certain death. Nothing remained therefore – since the miserable dwelling would not have withstood a vigorous kick, let alone a siege –

but to rush back on shore and regain possession of the boat. To this Lingard made up his mind quickly and, arming himself with a crooked stick he found under his hand, sallied forth at the head of his three men. As he bounded along, far in advance, he had just time to perceive clearly the desperate nature of the undertaking, when he heard two shots fired to his right. The solid mass of black bodies and frizzly heads in front of him wavered and broke up. They did not run away, however.

Lingard pursued his course, but now with that thrill of exultation which even a faint prospect of success inspires in a sanguine man. He heard a shout of many voices far off, then there was another report of a shot, and a musket ball fired at long range spurted a tiny jet of sand between him and his wild enemies. His next bound would have carried him into their midst had they awaited his onset, but his uplifted arm found nothing to strike. Black backs were leaping high or gliding horizontally through the grass toward the edge of the bush.

He flung his stick at the nearest pair of black shoulders and stopped short. The tall grasses swayed themselves into rest, a chorus of yells and piercing shrieks died out in a dismal howl, and all at once the wooded shores and the blue bay seemed to fall under the spell of a luminous stillness. The change was as startling as the awakening from a dream. The sudden silence struck Lingard as amazing.

He broke it by lifting his voice in a stentorian shout, which arrested the pursuit of his men. They retired reluctantly, glaring back angrily at the wall of a jungle where not a single leaf stirred. The strangers, whose opportune appearance had decided the issue of that adventure, did not attempt to join in the pursuit but halted in a compact body on the ground lately occupied by the savages.

Lingard and the young leader of the Wajo traders met in the splendid light of noonday, and amidst the attentive silence of their followers, on the very spot where the Malay seaman had lost his life. Lingard, striding up from one side, thrust out his open palm; Hassim responded at once to the frank gesture and they exchanged their first hand-clasp over the prostrate body, as if fate had already exacted the price of a death for the most ominous of her gifts – the gift of friendship that sometimes contains the whole good or evil of a life.

'I'll never forget this day,' cried Lingard in a hearty tone; and the other smiled quietly.

Then after a short pause – 'Will you burn the village for vengeance?' asked the Malay with a quick glance down at the dead Lascar who, on his face and with stretched arms, seemed to cling desperately to that earth of which he had known so little.

Lingard hesitated.

'No,' he said, at last. 'It would do good to no one.'

'True,' said Hassim, gently, 'but was this man your debtor – a slave?'

'Slave?' cried Lingard. 'This is an English brig. Slave? No. A free man like myself.'

'*Hai.* He is indeed free now,' muttered the Malay with another glance downward. 'But who will pay the bereaved for his life?'

'If there is anywhere a woman or child belonging to him, I – my *serang* would know – I shall seek them out,' cried Lingard, remorsefully.

'You speak like a chief,' said Hassim, 'only our great men do not go to battle with naked hands. O you white men! O the valour of you white men!'

'It was folly, pure folly,' protested Lingard, 'and this poor fellow has paid for it.'

'He could not avoid his destiny,' murmured the Malay. 'It is in my mind my trading is finished now in this place,' he added, cheerfully.

Lingard expressed his regret.

'It is no matter, it is no matter,' assured the other courteously, and after Lingard had given a pressing invitation for Hassim and his two companions of high rank to visit the brig, the two parties separated.

The evening was calm when the Malay craft left its berth near the shore and was rowed slowly across the bay to Lingard's anchorage. The end of a stout line was thrown on board, and that night the white man's brig and the brown man's *prau* swung together to the same anchor.

The sun setting to seaward shot its last rays between the headlands, when the body of the killed Lascar, wrapped up decently in a white sheet, according to Mohammedan usage, was lowered gently below the still waters of the bay upon which his curious glances, only a few hours before, had rested for the first time. At the moment the dead man, released from slip-ropes, disappeared without a ripple before the eyes of his shipmates, the bright flash and the heavy report of the brig's bow gun were succeeded by the muttering echoes of the encircling shores and by the loud cries of sea birds that, wheeling in clouds, seemed to scream after the departing seaman a wild and eternal good-bye. The master of the brig, making his way aft with hanging head, was followed by low murmurs of pleased surprise from his crew as well as from the strangers who crowded the main deck. In such acts performed simply, from conviction, what may be called the romantic side of the man's nature came out; that responsive sensitiveness to the shadowy appeals made by life and death, which is the groundwork of a chivalrous character.

Lingard entertained his three visitors far into the night. A sheep from the brig's sea stock was given to the men of the *prau*, while in the cabin, Hassim and his two friends, sitting in a row on the stern settee, looked very splendid with costly metals and flawed jewels. The talk, conducted with hearty friendship on Lingard's part, and on the part of the Malays with the well-bred air of discreet courtesy, which is natural to the better class of that people, touched upon many subjects and, in the end, drifted to politics.

'It is in my mind that you are a powerful man in your own country,' said Hassim, with a circular glance at the cuddy.

'My country is upon a far-away sea where the light breezes are as strong as the winds of the rainy weather here,' said Lingard; and there were low exclamations of wonder. 'I left it very young, and I don't know about my power there where great men alone are as numerous as the poor people in all your islands, Tuan

Hassim. But here,' he continued, 'here, which is also my country – being an English craft and worthy of it, too – I am powerful enough. In fact, I am Rajah here. This bit of my country is all my own.'

The visitors were impressed, exchanged meaning glances, nodded at each other.

'Good, good,' said Hassim at last, with a smile. 'You carry your country and your power with you over the sea. A Rajah upon the sea. Good!'

Lingard laughed thunderously while the others looked amused.

'Your country is very powerful – we know,' began again Hassim after a pause, 'but is it stronger than the country of the Dutch who steal our land?'

'Stronger?' cried Lingard. He opened a broad palm. 'Stronger? We could take them in our hand like this –' and he closed his fingers triumphantly.

'And do you make them pay tribute for their land?' inquired Hassim with eagerness.

'No,' answered Lingard in a sobered tone; 'this, Tuan Hassim, you see, is not the custom of white men. We could, of course – but it is not the custom.'

'Is it not?' said the other with a sceptical smile. 'They are stronger than we are and they want tribute from us. And sometimes they get it – even from Wajo where every man is free and wears a *kris*.'

There was a period of dead silence while Lingard looked thoughtful and the Malays gazed stonily at nothing.

'But we burn our powder amongst ourselves,' went on Hassim, gently, 'and blunt our weapons upon one another.'

He sighed, paused, and then changing to an easy tone began to urge Lingard to visit Wajo 'for trade and to see friends,' he said, laying his hand on his breast and inclining his body slightly.

'Aye. To trade with friends,' cried Lingard with a laugh, 'for such a ship' – he waved his arm – 'for such a vessel as this is like a household where there are many behind the curtain. It is as costly as a wife and children.'

The guests rose and took their leave.

'You fired three shots for me, Panglima Hassim,' said Lingard, seriously, 'and I have had three barrels of powder put on board your *prau*; one for each shot. But we are not quits.'

The Malay's eyes glittered with pleasure.

'This is indeed a friend's gift. Come to see me in my country !'

'I promise,' said Lingard, 'to see you – some day.'

The calm surface of the bay reflected the glorious night sky, and the brig with the *prau* riding astern seemed to be suspended amongst the stars in a peace that was almost unearthly in the perfection of its unstirring silence. The last hand-shakes were exchanged on deck, and the Malays went aboard their own craft. Next morning, when a breeze sprang up soon after sunrise, the brig and the *prau* left the bay together. When clear of the land Lingard made all sail and sheered alongside to say good-bye before parting company – the brig, of course, sailing three feet to the *prau*'s one. Hassim stood on the high deck aft.

'Prosperous road,' hailed Lingard.

'Remember the promise !' shouted the other. 'And come soon !' he went on, raising his voice as the brig forged past. 'Come soon – lest what perhaps is written should come to pass !'

The brig shot ahead.

'What?' yelled Lingard in a puzzled tone, 'what's written?'

He listened. And floating over the water came faintly the words:

'No one knows !'

3

'My word! I couldn't help liking the chap,' would shout Lingard when telling the story; and looking around at the eyes that glittered at him through the smoke of cheroots, this Brixham trawler-boy, afterward a youth in colliers, deep-water man, gold-digger, owner and commander of 'the finest brig afloat', knew that by his listeners – seamen, traders, adventurers like himself –

this was accepted not as the expression of a feeling, but as the highest commendation he could give his Malay friend.

'By heavens! I shall go to Wajo!' he cried, and a semicircle of heads nodded grave approbation while a slightly ironical voice said deliberately – 'You are a made man, Tom, if you get on the right side of that Rajah of yours.'

'Go in – and look out for yourself,' cried another with a laugh.

A little professional jealousy was unavoidable, Wajo, on account of its chronic state of disturbance, being closed to the white traders; but there was no real ill-will in the banter of these men, who, rising with handshakes, dropped off one by one. Lingard went straight aboard his vessel and, till morning, walked the poop of the brig with measured steps. The riding lights of ships twinkled all round him; the lights ashore twinkled in rows, the stars twinkled above his head in a black sky; and reflected in the black water of the roadstead twinkled far below his feet. And all these innumerable and shining points were utterly lost in the immense darkness. Once he heard faintly the rumbling chain of some vessel coming to anchor far away somewhere outside the official limits of the harbour. A stranger to the port – thought Lingard – one of us would have stood right in. Perhaps a ship from home? And he felt strangely touched at the thought of that ship, weary with months of wandering, and daring not to approach the place of rest. At sunrise, while the big ship from the West, her sides streaked with rust and grey with the salt of the sea, was moving slowly in to take up a berth near the shore, Lingard left the roadstead on his way to the eastward.

A heavy gulf thunderstorm was raging, when after a long passage and at the end of a sultry calm day, wasted in drifting helplessly in sight of his destination, Lingard, taking advantage of fitful gusts of wind, approached the shores of Wajo. With characteristic audacity, he held on his way, closing in with a coast to which he was a stranger, and on a night that would have appalled any other man; while at every dazzling flash, Hassim's native land seemed to leap nearer at the brig – and

73

disappear instantly as though it had crouched low for the next spring out of an impenetrable darkness. During the long day of the calm, he had obtained from the deck and from aloft, such good views of the coast, and had noted the lay of the land and the position of the dangers so carefully that, though at the precise moment when he gave the order to let go the anchor, he had been for some time able to see no further than if his head had been wrapped in a woollen blanket, yet the next flickering bluish flash showed him the brig, anchored almost exactly where he had judged her to be, off a narrow white beach near the mouth of a river.

He could see on the shore a high cluster of bamboo huts perched upon piles, a small grove of tall palms all bowed together before the blast like stalks of grass, something that might have been a palisade of pointed stakes near the water, and far off, a sombre background resembling an immense wall – the forest-clad hills. Next moment, all this vanished utterly from his sight, as if annihilated, and, before he had time to turn away, came back to view with a sudden crash, appearing unscathed and motionless under hooked darts of flame, like some legendary country of immortals, withstanding the wrath and fire of Heaven.

Made uneasy by the nature of his holding ground, and fearing that in one of the terrific off-shore gusts the brig would start her anchor, Lingard remained on deck to watch over the safety of his vessel. With one hand upon the lead-line which would give him instant warning of the brig beginning to drag, he stood by the rail, most of the time deafened and blinded, but also fascinated by the repeated swift visions of an unknown shore, a sight always so inspiring, as much perhaps by its vague suggestion of danger as by the hopes of success it never fails to awaken in the heart of a true adventurer. And its immutable aspect of profound and still repose, seen thus under streams of fire and in the midst of a violent uproar, made it appear inconceivably mysterious and amazing.

Between the squalls there were short moments of calm, while now and then even the thunder would cease as if to draw breath.

74

During one of those intervals, Lingard, tired and sleepy, was beginning to doze where he stood, when suddenly it occurred to him that, somewhere below, the sea had spoken in a human voice. It had said, 'Praise be to God –' and the voice sounded small, clear, and confident, like the voice of a child speaking in a cathedral. Lingard gave a start and thought – I've dreamed this – and directly the sea said very close to him, 'Give a rope.'

The thunder growled wickedly, and Lingard, after shouting to the men on deck, peered down at the water, until at last he made out floating close alongside the upturned face of a man with staring eyes that gleamed at him and then blinked quickly to a flash of lightning. By that time all hands in the brig were wildly active and many ropes-ends had been thrown over. Then together with a gust of wind, and as if blown on board, a man tumbled over the rail and fell all in a heap upon the deck. Before any one had the time to pick him up, he leaped to his feet, causing the people around him to step back hurriedly. A sinister blue glare showed the bewildered faces and the petrified attitudes of men completely deafened by the accompanying peal of thunder. After a time, as if to beings plunged in the abyss of eternal silence, there came to their ears an unfamiliar thin, far-away voice saying:

'I seek the white man.'

'Here,' cried Lingard. Then, when he had the stranger, dripping and naked but for a soaked waist-cloth, under the lamp of the cabin, he said, 'I don't know you.'

'My name is Jaffir, and I come from Pata Hassim, who is my chief and your friend. Do you know this?'

He held up a thick gold ring, set with a fairly good emerald.

'I have seen it before on the Rajah's finger,' said Lingard, looking very grave.

'It is the witness of the truth I speak – the message from Hassim is – "Depart and forget!"'

'I don't forget,' said Lingard, slowly. 'I am not that kind of man. What folly is this?'

It is unnecessary to give at full length the story told by Jaffir. It appears that on his return home, after the meeting with

Lingard, Hassim found his relative dying and a strong party formed to oppose his rightful successor. The old Rajah Tulla died late at night and – as Jaffir put it – before the sun rose there were already blows exchanged in the courtyard of the ruler's *dalam*. This was the preliminary fight of a civil war, fostered by foreign intrigues; a war of jungle and river, of assaulted stockades and forest ambushes. In this contest, both parties – according to Jaffir – displayed great courage, and one of them an unswerving devotion to what, almost from the first, was a lost cause. Before a month elapsed Hassim, though still chief of an armed band, was already a fugitive. He kept up the struggle, however, with some vague notion that Lingard's arrival would turn the tide.

'For weeks we lived on wild rice; for days we fought with nothing but water in our bellies,' declaimed Jaffir in the tone of a true fire-eater.

And then he went on to relate how, driven steadily down to the sea, Hassim, with a small band of followers, had been for days holding the stockade by the waterside.

'But every night some men disappeared,' confessed Jaffir. 'They were weary and hungry and they went to eat with their enemies. We are only ten now – ten men and a woman with the heart of a man, who are tonight starving, and tomorrow shall die swiftly. We saw your ship afar all day; but you have come too late. And for fear of treachery and lest harm should befall you – his friend – the Rajah gave me the ring and I crept on my stomach over the sand, and I swam in the night – and I, Jaffir, the best swimmer in Wajo, and the slave of Hassim, tell you – his message to you is "Depart and forget" – and this is his gift – take !'

He caught hold suddenly of Lingard's hand, thrust roughly into it the ring, and then for the first time looked round the cabin with wondering but fearless eyes. They lingered over the semicircle of bayonets and rested fondly on the musket-racks. He grunted in admiration.

'*Ya-wa*, this is strength !' he murmured as if to himself. 'But it has come too late.'

'Perhaps not,' cried Lingard.

'Too late,' said Jaffir, 'we are ten only, and at sunrise we go out to die.' He went to the cabin door and hesitated there with a puzzled air, being unused to locks and door handles.

'What are you going to do?' asked Lingard.

'I shall swim back,' replied Jaffir. 'The message is spoken and the night can not last for ever.'

'You can stop with me,' said Lingard, looking at the man searchingly.

'Hassim waits,' was the curt answer.

'Did he tell you to return?' asked Lingard.

'No! What need!' said the other in a surprised tone.

Lingard seized his hand impulsively.

'If I had ten men like you!' he cried.

'We are ten, but they are twenty to one,' said Jaffir, simply.

Lingard opened the door.

'Do you want anything that a man can give?' he asked.

The Malay had a moment of hesitation, and Lingard noticed the sunken eyes, the prominent ribs, and the worn-out look of the man.

'Speak out,' he urged with a smile; 'the bearer of a gift must have a reward.'

'A drink of water and a handful of rice for strength to reach the shore,' said Jaffir, sturdily. 'For over there' – he tossed his head – 'we had nothing to eat today.'

'You shall have it – give it to you with my own hands,' muttered Lingard.

He did so, and thus lowered himself in Jaffir's estimation for a time. While the messenger, squatting on the floor, ate without haste but with considerable earnestness, Lingard thought out a plan of action. In his ignorance as to the true state of affairs in the country, to save Hassim from the immediate danger of his position was all that he could reasonably attempt. To that end Lingard proposed to swing out his long-boat and send her close inshore to take off Hassim and his men. He knew enough of Malays to feel sure that on such a night the besiegers, now certain of success, and being, Jaffir said, in possession of everything that could float, would not be very vigilant, especially on the sea front of the stockade. The very fact of Jaffir having managed to swim off undetected proved that much. The brig's boat could – when the frequency of lightning abated – approach unseen close to the beach, and the defeated party, either stealing out one by one or making a rush in a body, would embark and be received in the brig.

This plan was explained to Jaffir, who heard it without the slightest mark of interest, being apparently too busy eating. When the last grain of rice was gone, he stood up, took a long pull at the water bottle, muttered: 'I hear. Good. I will tell Hassim,' and tightening the rag round his loins, prepared to go. 'Give me time to swim ashore,' he said, 'and when the boat starts, put another light beside the one that burns now like a star above your vessel. We shall see and understand. And don't send the boat till there is less lightning: a boat is bigger than a man in the water. Tell the rowers to pull for the palm-grove and cease when an oar, thrust down with a strong arm, touches the bottom. Very soon they will hear our hail; but if no one comes they must go away before daylight. A chief may prefer death to life, and we who are left are all of true heart. Do you understand, O big man?'

'The chap has plenty of sense,' muttered Lingard to himself, and when they stood side by side on the deck, he said: 'But there may be enemies on the beach, O Jaffir, and they also may shout to deceive my men. So let your hail be *Lightning*! Will you remember?'

For a time Jaffir seemed to be choking.

'Lit-ing! Is that right? I say – is that right, O strong man?' Next moment he appeared upright and shadowy on the rail.

'Yes. That's right. Go now,' said Lingard, and Jaffir leaped off, becoming invisible long before he struck the water. Then there was a splash; after a while a spluttering voice cried faintly, 'Lit-ing! Ah, ha!' and suddenly the next thunder-squall burst upon the coast. In the crashing flares of light Lingard had again and again the quick vision of a white beach, the inclined palm-trees of the grove, the stockade by the sea, the forest far away: a vast landscape mysterious and still – Hassim's native country sleeping unmoved under the wrath and fire of Heaven.

4

A TRAVELLER visiting Wajo today may, if he deserves the confidence of the common people, hear the traditional account of the last civil war, together with the legend of a chief and his sister, whose mother had been a great princess suspected of sorcery and on her death-bed had communicated to these two the secrets of the art of magic. The chief's sister especially, 'with the aspect of a child and the fearlessness of a great fighter', became skilled in casting spells. They were defeated by the son of their uncle, because – will explain the narrator simply – 'The courage of us Wajo people is so great that magic can do nothing against it. I fought in that war. We had them with their backs to the sea.' And then he will go on to relate in an awed tone how on a certain night 'when there was such a thunderstorm as has been never heard of before or since' a ship, resembling the ships of white men, appeared off the coast, 'as though she had sailed down from the clouds. She moved,' he will affirm, 'with her sails bellying against the wind; in size she was like an island; the lightning played between her masts which were as high as the summits of mountains; a star burned low through the clouds above her. We knew it for a star at once because no flame of man's kindling could have endured the wind and rain of that night. It was such a night that we on the watch hardly dared look upon the sea. The heavy rain was beating down our eyelids. And when day came, the ship was nowhere to be seen, and in the stockade where the day before there were a hundred or more at our mercy, there was no one. The chief, Hassim, was gone, and the lady who was a princess in the country – and nobody knows what became of them from that day to this. Sometimes traders from our parts talk of having heard of them here, and heard of them there, but these are the lies of men who go afar for gain. We who live in the country believe that the ship sailed back into the clouds whence the Lady's magic made her come. Did we not see the ship with our own eyes? And as to Rajah Hassim and his sister, Mas Immada, some men say one thing and some another, but God alone knows the truth.'

Such is the traditional account of Lingard's visit to the shores of Boni. And the truth is he came and went the same night; for, when the dawn broke on a cloudy sky the brig, under reefed canvas and smothered in sprays, was storming along to the southward on her way out of the Gulf. Lingard, watching over the rapid course of his vessel, looked ahead with anxious eyes and more than once asked himself with wonder, why, after all, was he thus pressing her under all the sail she could carry. His hair was blown about by the wind, his mind was full of care and the indistinct shapes of many new thoughts, and under his feet, the obedient brig dashed headlong from wave to wave.

Her owner and commander did not know where he was going. That adventurer had only a confused notion of being on the threshold of a big adventure. There was something to be done, and he felt he would have to do it. It was expected of him. The seas expected it; the land expected it. Men also. The story of war and of suffering; Jaffir's display of fidelity, the sight of Hassim and his sister, the night, the tempest, the coast under streams of fire – all this made one inspiring manifestation of a life calling to him distinctly for interference. But what appealed to him most was the silent, the complete, unquestioning, and apparently uncurious, trust of these people. They came away from death straight into his arms as it were, and remained in them passive as though there had been no such thing as doubt or hope or desire. This amazing unconcern seemed to put him under a heavy load of obligation.

He argued to himself that had not these defeated men expected everything from him they could not have been so indifferent to his action. Their dumb quietude stirred him more than the most ardent pleading. Not a word, not a whisper, not a questioning look even! They did not ask! It flattered him.

He was also rather glad of it, because if the unconscious part of him was perfectly certain of its action, he, himself, did not know what to do with those bruised and battered beings a playful fate had delivered suddenly into his hands.

He had received the fugitives personally, had helped some over the rail; in the darkness, slashed about by lightning, he had guessed that not one of them was unwounded, and in the midst of tottering shapes he wondered how on earth they had managed to reach the long-boat that had brought them off. He caught unceremoniously in his arms the smallest of these shapes and carried it into the cabin, then without looking at his light burden ran up again on deck to get the brig under way. While shouting out orders he was dimly aware of someone hovering near his elbow. It was Hassim.

'I am not ready for war,' he explained, rapidly, over his shoulder, 'and tomorrow there may be no wind.'

Afterward for a time he forgot everybody and everything while he conned the brig through the few outlying dangers. But in half an hour, and running off with the wind on the quarter, he was quite clear of the coast and breathed freely. It was only then that he approached two others on that poop where he was accustomed in moments of difficulty to commune alone with his craft. Hassim had called his sister out of the cabin; now and then Lingard could see them with fierce distinctness, side by side, and with twined arms, looking toward the mysterious country that seemed at every flash to leap away farther from the brig – unscathed and fading.

The thought uppermost in Lingard's mind was: 'What on earth am I going to do with them?' And no one seemed to care what he would do. Jaffir, with eight others quartered on the main hatch, looked to each other's wounds and conversed interminably in low tones, cheerful and quiet, like well-behaved children. Each of them had saved his *kris*, but Lingard had to make a distribution of cotton cloth out of his trade-goods. Whenever he passed by them, they all looked after him gravely. Hassim and Immada lived in the cuddy. The chief's sister took the air only in the evening and those two could be heard every night, invisible

81

and murmuring in the shadows of the quarter-deck. Every Malay on board kept respectfully away from them.

Lingard, on the poop, listened to the soft voices, rising and falling, in a melancholy cadence; sometimes the woman cried out as if in anger or in pain. He would stop short. The sound of a deep sigh would float up to him on the stillness of the night. Attentive stars surrounded the wandering brig and on all sides their light fell through a vast silence upon a noiseless sea. Lingard would begin again to pace the deck, muttering to himself.

'Belarab's the man for this job. His is the only place where I can look for help, but I don't think I know enough to find it. I wish I had old Jörgenson here – just for ten minutes.'

This Jörgenson knew things that had happened a long time ago, and lived amongst men efficient in meeting the accidents of the day, but who did not care what would happen tomorrow and who had no time to remember yesterday. Strictly speaking, he did not live amongst them. He only appeared there from time to time. He lived in the native quarter, with a native woman, in a native house standing in the middle of a plot of fenced ground where grew plantains, and furnished only with mats, cooking pots, a queer fishing net on two sticks, and a small mahogany case with a lock and a silver plate engraved with the words 'Captain H. C. Jörgenson. Barque *Wild Rose.*'

It was like an inscription on a tomb. The *Wild Rose* was dead, and so was Captain H. C. Jörgenson, and the sextant case was all that was left of them. Old Jörgenson, gaunt and mute, would turn up at meal times on board any trading vessel in the Roads, and the stewards – Chinamen or mulattos – would sulkily put on an extra plate without waiting for orders. When the seamen traders forgathered noisily round a glittering cluster of bottles and glasses on a lighted verandah, old Jörgenson would emerge up the stairs as if from a dark sea, and, stepping up with a kind of tottering jauntiness, would help himself in the first tumbler to hand.

'I drink to you all. No – no chair.'

He would stand silent over the talking group. His taciturnity was as eloquent as the repeated warning of the slave of the feast.

His flesh had gone the way of all flesh, his spirit had sunk in the turmoil of his past, but his immense and bony frame survived as if made of iron. His hands trembled but his eyes were steady. He was supposed to know details about the end of mysterious men and of mysterious enterprises. He was an evident failure himself, but he was believed to know secrets that would make the fortune of any man; yet there was also a general impression that his knowledge was not of that nature which would make it profitable for a moderately prudent person.

This powerful skeleton, dressed in faded blue serge and without any kind of linen, existed anyhow. Sometimes, if offered the job, he piloted a home ship through the Straits of Rhio, after, however, assuring the captain:

'You don't want a pilot; a man could go through with his eyes shut. But if you want me, I'll come. Ten dollars.'

Then, after seeing his charge clear of the last island of the group he would go back thirty miles in a canoe, with two old Malays who seemed to be in some way his followers. To travel thirty miles at sea under the equatorial sun and in a cranky dugout where once down you must not move, is an achievement that requires the endurance of a fakir and the virtue of a salamander. Ten dollars was cheap and generally he was in demand. When times were hard he would borrow five dollars from any of the adventurers with the remark:

'I can't pay you back very soon, but the girl must eat, and if you want to know anything, I can tell you.'

It was remarkable that nobody ever smiled at that 'anything'. The usual thing was to say:

'Thank you, old man; when I am pushed for a bit of information I'll come to you.'

Jörgenson nodded then and would say: 'Remember that unless you young chaps are like we men who ranged about here years ago, what I could tell you would be worse than poison.'

It was from Jörgenson, who had his favourites with whom he was less silent, that Lingard had heard of Darat-es-Salam, the 'Shore of Refuge'. Jörgenson had, as he expressed it, 'known the inside of that country just after the high old times when the

white-clad Padris preached and fought all over Sumatra till the
Dutch shook in their shoes.' Only he did not say 'shook' and
'shoes' but the above paraphrase conveys well enough his contemptuous meaning. Lingard tried now to remember and piece
together the practical bits of old Jörgenson's amazing tales; but
all that had remained with him was an approximate idea of the
locality and a very strong but confused notion of the dangerous
nature of its approaches. He hesitated, and the brig, answering in
her movements to the state of the man's mind, lingered on the
road, seemed to hesitate also, swinging this way and that on the
days of calm.

It was just because of that hesitation that a big New York
ship, loaded with oil in cases for Japan, and passing through the
Billiton passage, sighted one morning a very smart brig being
hove-to right in the fair-way and a little to the east of Carimata.
The lank skipper, in a frock-coat, and the big mate with heavy
moustaches, judged her almost too pretty for a Britisher, and
wondered at the man on board laying his topsail to the mast for
no reason that they could see. The big ship's sails fanned her
along, flapping in the light air, and when the brig was last seen
far astern she had still her mainyard aback as if waiting for someone. But when, next day, a London tea-clipper passed on the
same track, she saw no pretty brig hesitating, all white and still
at the parting of the ways. All that night Lingard had talked
with Hassim while the stars streamed from east to west like an
immense river of sparks above their heads. Immada listened,
sometimes exclaiming low, sometimes holding her breath. She
clapped her hands once. A faint dawn appeared.

'You shall be treated like my father in the country,' Hassim
was saying. A heavy dew dripped off the rigging and the
darkened sails were black on the pale azure of the sky. 'You
shall be the father who advises for good –'

'I shall be a steady friend, and as a friend I want to be treated
– no more,' said Lingard. 'Take back your ring.'

'Why do you scorn my gift?' asked Hassim, with a sad and
ironic smile.

'Take it,' said Lingard. 'It is still mine. How can I forget that, when facing death, you thought of my safety? There are many dangers before us. We shall be often separated – to work better for the same end. If ever you and Immada need help at once and I am within reach, send me a message with this ring and if I am alive I will not fail you.' He looked around at the pale daybreak. 'I shall talk to Belarab straight – like we whites do. I have never seen him, but I am a strong man. Belarab must help us to re-conquer your country and when our end is attained I won't let him eat you up.'

Hassim took the ring and inclined his head.

'It's time for us to be moving,' said Lingard. He felt a slight tug at his sleeve. He looked back and caught Immada in the act of pressing her forehead to the grey flannel. 'Don't, child!' he said, softly.

The sun rose above the faint blue line of the Shore of Refuge.

The hesitation was over. The man and the vessel, working in accord, had found their way to the faint blue shore. Before the sun had descended half-way to its rest the brig was anchored within a gunshot of the slimy mangroves, in a place where for a hundred years or more no white man's vessel had been entrusted to the hold of the bottom. The adventurers of two centuries ago had no doubt known of that anchorage for they were very ig-norant and incomparably audacious. If it is true, as some say, that the spirits of the dead haunt the places where the living have sinned and toiled, then they might have seen a white long-boat, pulled by eight oars and steered by a man sunburnt and bearded, a cabbage-leaf hat on head, and pistols in his belt, skirt-ing the black mud, full of twisted roots, in search of a likely opening.

Creek after creek was passed and the boat crept on slowly like a monstrous water-spider with a big body and eight slender legs ... Did you follow with your ghostly eyes the quest of this obscure adventurer of yesterday, you shades of forgotten ad-venturers who, in leather jerkins and sweating under steel helmets, attacked with long rapiers the palisades of the strange heathen, or, musket on shoulder and match in cock, guarded timber blockhouses built upon the banks of rivers that command good trade? You, who, wearied with the toil of fighting, slept wrapped in frieze mantles on the sand of quiet beaches, dreaming of fabulous diamonds and a far-off home.

'Here's an opening,' said Lingard to Hassim, who sat at his side, just as the sun was setting away to his left. 'Here's an opening big enough for a ship. It's the entrance we are looking for, I believe. We shall pull all night up this creek if necessary and it's the very devil if we don't come upon Belarab's lair before daylight.'

He shoved the tiller hard over and the boat, swerving sharply, vanished from the coast.

And perhaps the ghosts of old adventurers nodded wisely their ghostly heads and exchanged the ghost of a wistful smile.

5

'WHAT's the matter with King Tom of late?' would ask someone when, all the cards in a heap on the table, the traders lying back in their chairs took a spell from a hard gamble.

'Tom has learned to hold his tongue, he must be up to some dam' good thing,' opined another; while a man with hooked features and of German extraction who was supposed to be agent for a Dutch crockery house – the famous 'Sphinx' mark – broke in resentfully:

'Nefer mind him, shentlemens, he's matt, matt as a Marsh Hare. Dree monats ago I call on board his prig to talk pizness. And he says like dis – "Glear oudt." "Vat for?" I say. "Glear oudt before I shuck you oferboard." Gott-for-dam! Iss dat the vay to talk pizness? I vant sell him ein liddle case first chop grockery for trade and –'

'Ha, ha, ha! I don't blame Tom,' interrupted the owner of a pearling schooner, who had come into the Roads for stores. 'Why, Mosey, there isn't a mangy cannibal left in the whole of New Guinea that hasn't got a cup and saucer of your providing. You've flooded the market, *savee*?'

Jörgenson stood by, a skeleton at the gaming table.

'Because you are a Dutch spy,' he said, suddenly, in an awful tone.

The agent of the Sphinx mark jumped up in a sudden fury.

'Vat? Vat? Shentlemens, you all know me!' Not a muscle moved in the faces around. 'Know me,' he stammered with wet lips. 'Vat, fünf year – berfegtly acquaint – grockery – Verfluchte sponsher. Ich? Spy. Vat for spy? Vordammte English pedlars!'

The door slammed. 'Is that so?' asked a New England voice. 'Why don't you let daylight into him?'

'Oh, we can't do that here,' murmured one of the players. 'Your deal, Trench, let us get on.'

'Can't you?' drawled the New England voice. 'You law-abiding, get-a-summons, act-of-parliament lot of sons of Belial – can't you? Now, look a-here, these Colt pistols I am selling –' He took the pearler aside and could be heard talking earnestly in the corner. 'See – you load – and – see?' There were rapid clicks. 'Simple, isn't it? And if any trouble – say with your divers' – *click, click, click* – 'Through and through – like a sieve – warranted to cure the worst kind of cussedness in any nigger. Yes, siree! A case of twenty-four or single specimens – as you like. No? Shot-guns – rifles? No! Waal, I guess you're of no use to me, but I could do a deal with that Tom – what d'ye call him? Where d'ye catch him? Everywhere – eh? Waal – that's nowhere. But I shall find him some day – yes, siree.'

Jörgenson, utterly disregarded, looked down dreamily at the falling cards. 'Spy – I tell you,' he muttered to himself. 'If you want to know anything, ask me.'

When Lingard returned from Wajo – after an uncommonly long absence – everyone remarked a great change. He was less talkative and not so noisy, he was still hospitable but his hospitality was less expansive, and the man who was never so happy as when discussing impossibly wild projects with half a dozen congenial spirits often showed a disinclination to meet his best friends. In a word, he returned much less of a good fellow than he went away. His visits to the Settlements were not less frequent, but much shorter; and when there he was always in a hurry to be gone.

During two years the brig had, in her way, as hard a life of it as the man. Swift and trim she flitted amongst the islands of little known groups. She could be descried afar from lonely headlands, a white speck travelling fast over the blue sea; the apathetic keepers of rare lighthouses dotting the great highway to the east came to know the cut of her topsails. They saw her passing east, passing west. They had faint glimpses of her flying with masts aslant in the mist of a rain-squall, or could observe her at leisure, upright and with shivering sails, forging ahead through a long day of unsteady airs. Men saw her battling with a heavy monsoon in the Bay of Bengal, lying becalmed in the Java Sea, or gliding out suddenly from behind a point of land, graceful and silent in the clear moonlight. Her activity was the subject of excited but low-toned conversations, which would be interrupted when her master appeared.

'Here he is. Came in last night,' whispered the gossiping group.

Lingard did not see the covert glances of respect tempered by irony; he nodded and passed on.

'Hey, Tom! No time for a drink?' would shout someone.

He would shake his head without looking back – far away already.

Florid and burly he could be seen, for a day or two, getting out of dusty *gharries*, striding in sunshine from the Occidental Bank to the Harbour Office, crossing the Esplanade, disappearing down a street of Chinese shops, while at his elbow and as tall as himself, old Jörgenson paced along, lean and faded, obstinate and disregarded, like a haunting spirit from the past eager to step back into the life of men.

Lingard ignored this wreck of an adventurer, sticking to him closer than his shadow, and the other did not try to attract attention. He waited patiently at the doors of offices, would vanish at tiffin time, would invariably turn up again in the evening and then he kept his place till Lingard went aboard for the night. The police-*peons* on duty looked disdainfully at the phantom of

Captain H. C. Jörgenson, Barque *Wild Rose*, wandering on the silent quay or standing still for hours at the edge of the sombre roadstead speckled by the anchor lights of ships – an adventurous soul longing to recross the water of oblivion.

The *sampan*-men, sculling lazily homeward past the black hull of the brig at anchor, could hear far into the night the drawl of the New England voice escaping through the lifted panes of the cabin skylight. Snatches of nasal sentences floated in the stillness around the still craft.

'Yes, siree! Mexican war rifles – good as new – six in a case – my people in Baltimore – that's so. Hundred and twenty rounds thrown in for each specimen – marked to suit your re-quirements. Suppose – musical instruments, this side up with care – how's that for your taste? No, no! Cash down – my people in Balt – Shooting sea-gulls you say? Waal! It's a risky business – see here – ten per cent discount – it's out of my own pocket –'

As time wore on, and nothing happened, at least nothing that one could hear of, the excitement died out. Lingard's new attitude was accepted as only 'his way'. There was nothing in it, maintained some. Others dissented. A good deal of curiosity, however, remained and the faint rumour of something big being in preparation followed him into every harbour he went to, from Rangoon to Hongkong.

He felt nowhere so much at home as when his brig was anchored on the inner side of the great stretch of shoals. The centre of his life had shifted about four hundred miles – from the Straits of Malacca to the Shore of Refuge – and when there he felt himself within the circle of another existence, governed by his impulse, nearer his desire. Hassim and Immada would come down to the coast and wait for him on the islet. He always left them with regret.

At the end of the first stage in each trip, Jörgenson waited for him at the top of the boat-stairs and without a word fell into step at his elbow. They seldom exchanged three words in a day; but one evening about six months before Lingard's last trip, as they were crossing the short bridge over the canal where native craft lie moored in clusters, Jörgenson lengthened his stride and came

abreast. It was a moonlight night and nothing stirred on earth
but the shadows of high clouds. Lingard took off his hat and
drew in a long sigh in the tepid breeze. Jörgenson spoke suddenly in a cautious tone: 'The new Rajah Tulla smokes opium
and is sometimes dangerous to speak to. There is a lot of dis-
content in Wajo amongst the big people.'

'Good! Good!' whispered Lingard, excitedly, off his guard
for once. Then – 'How the devil do you know anything about
it?' he asked.

Jörgenson pointed at the mass of *praus*, coasting boats and
sampans that, jammed up together in the canal, lay covered with
mats and flooded by the cold moonlight with here and there a
dim lantern burning amongst the confusion of high sterns, spars,
masts, and lowered sails.

'There!' he said, as they moved on, and their hatted and
clothed shadows fell heavily on the queer-shaped vessels that
carry the fortunes of brown men upon a shallow sea. 'There! I
can sit with them, I can talk to them, I can come and go as I
like. They know me now – it's time – thirty-five years. Some of
them give a plate of rice and a bit of fish to the white man.
That's all I get – after thirty-five years – given up to them.'

He was silent for a time.

'I was like you once,' he added, and then laying his hand on
Lingard's sleeve, murmured – 'Are you very deep in this thing?'

'To the very last cent,' said Lingard, quietly, and looking
straight before him.

The glitter of the roadstead went out, and the masts of
anchored ships vanished in the invading shadow of a cloud.

'Drop it,' whispered Jörgenson.

'I am in debt,' said Lingard, slowly, and stood still.

'Drop it!'

'Never dropped anything in my life.'

'Drop it!'

'By God, I won't!' cried Lingard, stamping his foot.

There was a pause.

'I was like you – once,' repeated Jörgenson. 'Five and thirty
years – never dropped anything. And what you can do is only
child's play to some jobs I have had on my hands – understand

that – great man as you are, Captain Lingard of the *Lightning* . . . You should have seen the *Wild Rose*,' he added with a sudden break in his voice.

Lingard leaned over the guard-rail of the pier. Jörgenson came closer.

'I set fire to her with my own hands!' he said in a vibrating tone and very low, as if making a monstrous confession.

'Poor devil,' muttered Lingard, profoundly moved by the tragic enormity of the act. 'I suppose there was no way out?'

'I wasn't going to let her rot to pieces in some Dutch port,' said Jörgenson, gloomily. 'Did you ever hear of Dawson?'

'Something – I don't remember now –' muttered Lingard, who felt a chill down his back at the idea of his own vessel decaying slowly in some Dutch port. 'He died – didn't he?' he asked, absently, while he wondered whether he would have the pluck to set fire to the brig – in an emergency.

'Cut his throat on the beach below Fort Rotterdam,' said Jörgenson. His gaunt figure wavered in the unsteady moonshine as though made of mist. 'Yes. He broke some trade regulation or other and talked big about law-courts and legal trials to the lieutenant of the *Komet*. "Certainly," says the hound. "Jurisdiction of Macassar, I will take your schooner there." Then coming into the roads he tows her full tilt on a ledge of rocks on the north side – smash! When she was half full of water he takes his hat off to Dawson. "There's the shore," says he – "go and get your legal trial, you – Englishman –"' He lifted a long arm and shook his fist at the moon which dodged suddenly behind a cloud. 'All was lost. Poor Dawson walked the streets for months barefooted and in rags. Then one day he begged a knife from some charitable soul, went down to take a last look at the wreck, and –'

'I don't interfere with the Dutch,' interrupted Lingard, impatiently. 'I want Hassim to get back his own –'

'And suppose the Dutch want the things just so,' returned Jörgenson. 'Anyway there is a devil in such work – drop it!'

'Look here,' said Lingard, 'I took these people off when they were in their last ditch. That means something. I ought not to have meddled and it would have been all over in a few hours. I must have meant something when I interfered, whether I knew it or not. I meant it then – and did not know it. Very well. I mean it now – and do know it. When you save people from death you take a share in their life. That's how I look at it.'

Jörgenson shook his head.

'Foolishness!' he cried, then asked softly in a voice that trembled with curiosity – 'Where did you leave them?'

'With Belarab,' breathed out Lingard. 'You knew him in the old days.'

'I knew him, I knew his father,' burst out the other in an excited whisper. 'Whom did I not know? I knew Sentot when he was King of the South Shore of Java and the Dutch offered a price for his head – enough to make any man's fortune. He slept twice on board the *Wild Rose* when things had begun to go wrong with him. I knew him, I knew all his chiefs, the priests, the fighting men, the old regent who lost heart and went over to the Dutch, I knew –' he stammered as if the words could not come out, gave it up and sighed – 'Belarab's father escaped with me,' he began again, quietly, 'and joined the Padris in Sumatra. He rose to be a great leader. Belarab was a youth then. Those were the times. I ranged the coast – and laughed at the cruisers; I saw every battle fought in the Battak country – and I saw the Dutch run; I was at the taking of Singal and escaped. I was the white man who advised the chiefs of Manangkabo. There was a lot about me in the Dutch papers at the time. They said I was a Frenchman turned Mohammedan –' he swore a great oath, and, reeling against the guard-rail, panted, muttering curses on newspapers.

'Well, Belarab has the job in hand,' said Lingard, composedly. 'He is the chief man on the Shore of Refuge. There are others, of course. He has sent messages north and south. We must have men.'

'All the devils unchained,' said Jörgenson. 'You have done it and now – look out – look out ...'

'Nothing can go wrong as far as I can see,' argued Lingard. 'They all know what's to be done. I've got them in hand. You don't think Belarab unsafe? Do you?'

'Haven't seen him for fifteen years – but the whole thing's unsafe,' growled Jörgenson.

'I tell you I've fixed it so that nothing can go wrong. It would be better if I had a white man over there to look after things generally. There is a good lot of stores and arms – and Belarab would bear watching – no doubt. Are you in any want?' he added, putting his hand in his pocket.

'No, there's plenty to eat in the house,' answered Jörgenson, curtly. 'Drop it,' he burst out. 'It would be better for you to jump overboard at once. Look at me. I came out a boy of eighteen. I can speak English, I can speak Dutch, I can speak every cursed lingo of these islands – I remember things that would make your hair stand on end – but I have forgotten the language of my own country. I've traded, I've fought, I never broke my word to white or native. And, look at me. If it hadn't been for the girl I would have died in a ditch ten years ago. Everything left me – youth, money, strength, hope – the very sleep. But she stuck by the wreck.'

'That says a lot for her and something for you,' said Lingard, cheerily.

Jörgenson shook his head.

'That's the worst of all,' he said with slow emphasis. 'That's the end. I came to them from the other side of the earth and they took me and – see what they made of me.'

'What place do you belong to?' asked Lingard.

'Tromsö,' groaned out Jörgenson; 'I will never see snow again,' he sobbed out, his face in his hands.

Lingard looked at him in silence.

'Would you come with me?' he said. 'As I told you, I am in want of a –'

'I would see you damned first!' broke out the other, savagely. 'I am an old white loafer, but you don't get me to meddle in their infernal affairs. They have a devil of their own –'

'The thing simply can't fail. I've calculated every move. I've guarded against everything. I am no fool.'

'Yes – you are. Good night.'

'Well, good-bye,' said Lingard, calmly.

93

He stepped into his boat, and Jörgenson walked up the jetty. Lingard, clearing the yoke lines, heard him call out from a distance:

'Drop it!'

'I sail before sunrise,' he shouted in answer, and went on board.

When he came up from his cabin after an uneasy night, it was dark yet. A lank figure strolled across the deck.

'Here I am,' said Jörgenson, huskily. 'Die there or here – all one. But, if I die there, remember the girl must eat.'

Lingard was one of the few who had seen Jörgenson's girl. She had a wrinkled brown face, a lot of tangled grey hair, a few black stumps of teeth, and had been married to him lately by an enterprising young missionary from Bukit Timah. What her appearance might have been once when Jörgenson gave for her three hundred dollars and several brass guns, it was impossible to say. All that was left of her youth was a pair of eyes, undimmed and mournful, which, when she was alone, seemed to look stonily into the past of two lives. When Jörgenson was near they followed his movements with anxious pertinacity. And now within the *sarong* thrown over the grey head they were dropping unseen tears while Jörgenson's girl rocked herself to and fro, squatting alone in a corner of the dark hut.

'Don't you worry about that,' said Lingard, grasping Jörgenson's hand. 'She shall want for nothing. All I expect you to do is to look a little after Belarab's morals when I am away. One more trip I must make, and then we shall be ready to go ahead. I've foreseen every single thing. Trust me!'

In this way did the restless shade of Captain H. C. Jörgenson recross the water of oblivion to step back into the life of men.

6

FOR two years, Lingard, who had thrown himself body and soul into the great enterprise, had lived in the long intoxication of slowly preparing success. No thought of failure had crossed his mind, and no price appeared too heavy to pay for such a magnificent achievement. It was nothing less than bringing Hassim triumphantly back to that country seen once at night under the low clouds and in the incessant tumult of thunder. When at the conclusion of some long talk with Hassim, who for the twentieth time perhaps had related the story of his wrongs and his struggle, he lifted his big arm and shaking his fist above his head, shouted: 'We will stir them up. We will wake up the country!' he was, without knowing it in the least, making a complete confession of the idealism hidden under the simplicity of his strength. He would wake up the country! That was the fundamental and unconscious emotion on which were engrafted his need of action, the primitive sense of what was due to justice, to gratitude, to friendship, the sentimental pity for the hard lot of Immada – poor child – the proud conviction that of all the men in the world, in his world, he alone had the means and the pluck 'to lift up the big end' of such an adventure.

Money was wanted and men were wanted, and he had obtained enough of both in two years from that day when, pistols in his belt and a cabbage-leaf hat on head, he had unexpectedly, and at early dawn, confronted in perfect silence that mysterious Belarab, who himself was for a moment too astounded for speech at the sight of a white face.

The sun had not yet cleared the forests of the interior, but a sky already full of light arched over a dark oval lagoon, over wide fields as yet full of shadows, that seemed slowly changing into the whiteness of the morning mist. There were huts, fences, palisades, big houses that, erected on lofty piles, were seen above the tops of clustered fruit trees, as if suspended in the air.

Such was the aspect of Belarab's settlement when Lingard set his eyes on it for the first time. There were all these things, a great number of faces at the back of the spare and muffled-up figure confronting him, and in the swiftly increasing light a complete stillness that made the murmur of the word '*Marhaba*' (welcome), pronounced at last by the chief, perfectly audible to every one of his followers. The bodyguards who stood about him in black skull-caps and with long-shafted lances preserved an impassive aspect. Across open spaces men could be seen running to the waterside. A group of women standing on a low knoll gazed intently, and nothing of them but the heads showed above the unstirring stalks of a maize field. Suddenly within a cluster of empty huts near by the voice of an invisible hag was heard scolding with shrill fury an invisible young girl:

'Strangers! You want to see the strangers? O devoid of all decency! Must I so lame and old husk the rice alone? May evil befall thee and the strangers! May they never find favour! May they be pursued with swords! I am old. I am old. There is no good in strangers! O girl! May they burn.'

'Welcome,' repeated Belarab, gravely, and looking straight into Lingard's eyes.

Lingard spent six days that time in Belarab's settlement. Of these, three were passed in observing each other without a question being asked or a hint given as to the object in view. Lingard lounged on the fine mats with which the chief had furnished a small bamboo house outside a fortified enclosure, where a white flag with a green border fluttered on a high and slender pole but still below the walls of long, high-roofed buildings, raised forty feet or more on hardwood posts.

Far away the inland forests were tinted a shimmering blue, like the forests of a dream. On the seaward side the belt of great trunks and matted undergrowth came to the western shore of the oval lagoon; and in the pure freshness of the air the groups of brown houses reflected in the water or seen above the waving green of the fields, the clumps of palm trees, the fenced-in plantations, the groves of fruit trees, made up a picture of sumptuous prosperity.

Above the buildings, the men, the women, the still sheet of water and the great plain of crops glistening with dew, stretched the exalted, the miraculous peace of a cloudless sky. And no road seemed to lead into this country of splendour and stillness. One could not believe the unquiet sea was so near, with its gifts and its unending menace. Even during the months of storms, the great clamour rising from the whitened expanse of the Shallows dwelt high in the air in a vast murmur, now feeble now stronger, that seemed to swing back and forth on the wind above the earth without any one being able to tell whence it came. It was like the solemn chant of a waterfall swelling and dying away above the woods, the fields, above the roofs of houses and the heads of men, above the secret peace of that hidden and flourishing settlement of vanquished fanatics, fugitives, and outcasts.

Every afternoon Belarab, followed by an escort that stopped outside the door, entered alone the house of his guest. He gave the salutation, inquired after his health, conversed about insignificant things with an inscrutable mien. But all the time the steadfast gaze of his thoughtful eyes seemed to seek the truth within that white face. In the cool of the evening, before the sun had set, they talked together, passing and repassing between the rugged pillars of the grove near the gate of the stockade. The escort, away in the oblique sunlight, followed with their eyes the strolling figures appearing and vanishing behind the trees. Many words were pronounced, but nothing was said that would disclose the thoughts of the two men. They clasped hands demonstratively before separating, and the heavy slam of the gate was followed by the triple thud of the wooden bars dropped into iron clamps.

On the third night, Lingard was awakened from a light sleep by the sound of whispering outside. A black shadow obscured the stars in the doorway, and a man, entering suddenly, stood above his couch while another could be seen squatting – a dark lump on the threshold of the hut.

'Fear not. I am Belarab,' said a cautious voice.

'I was not afraid,' whispered Lingard. 'It is the man coming in the dark and without warning who is in danger.'

'And did you not come to me without warning? I said "welcome" – it was as easy for me to say "kill him".'

'You were within reach of my arm. We would have died together,' retorted Lingard, quietly.

The other clicked his tongue twice, and his indistinct shape seemed to sink half-way through the floor.

'It was not written thus before we were born,' he said, sitting cross-legged near the mats, and in a deadened voice. 'Therefore you are my guest. Let the talk between us be straight like the shaft of a spear and shorter than the remainder of this night. What do you want?'

'First, your long life,' answered Lingard, leaning forward toward the gleam of a pair of eyes, 'and then – your help.'

7

THE faint murmur of the words spoken on that night lingered for a long time in Lingard's ears, more persistent than the memory of an uproar; he looked with a fixed gaze at the stars burning peacefully in the square of the doorway, while after listening in silence to all he had to say, Belarab, as if seduced by the strength and audacity of the white man, opened his heart without reserve. He talked of his youth surrounded by the fury of fanaticism and war, of battles on the hills, of advances through the forests, of men's unswerving piety, of their unextinguishable hate. Not a single wandering cloud obscured the gentle splendour of the rectangular patch of sunlight framed in the opaque blackness of the hut. Belarab murmured on of a succession of reverses, of the ring of disasters narrowing round men's fading hopes and undiminished courage. He whispered of defeat and flight, of the days of despair, of the nights without sleep, of unending pursuit, of the bewildered horror and sombre fury, of their women and children killed in the stockade before the besieged sallied forth to die.

'I have seen all this before I was in years a man,' he cried, low.

His voice vibrated. In the pause that succeeded they heard a light sigh of the sleeping follower who, clasping his legs above his ankles, rested his forehead on his knees.

'And there was amongst us,' began Belarab again, 'one white

man who remained to the end, who was faithful with his strength, with his courage, with his wisdom. A great man. He had great riches but a greater heart.'

The memory of Jörgenson, emaciated and grey-haired, and trying to borrow five dollars to get something to eat for the girl, passed before Lingard suddenly upon the pacific glitter of the stars.

'He resembled you,' pursued Belarab, abruptly. 'We escaped with him, and in his ship came here. It was a solitude. The forest came near to the sheet of water, the rank grass waved upon the heads of tall men. Telal, my father, died of weariness; we were only a few, and we all nearly died of trouble and sadness – here. On this spot! And no enemies could tell where we had gone. It was the Shore of Refuge – and starvation.'

He droned on in the night, with rising and falling inflections. He told how his desperate companions wanted to go out and die fighting on the sea against ships from the west, the ships with high sides and white sails; and how, unflinching and alone, he kept them battling with the thorny bush, with the rank grass, with the soaring and enormous trees. Lingard, leaning on his elbow and staring through the door, recalled the image of the wide fields outside, sleeping now, in an immensity of serenity and starlight. This quiet and almost invisible talker had done it all; in him was the origin, the creation, the fate; and in the wonder of that thought the shadowy murmuring figure acquired a gigantic greatness of significance, as if it had been the embodiment of some natural force, of a force forever masterful and undying.

'And even now my life is unsafe as if I were their enemy,' said Belarab, mournfully. 'Eyes do not kill, nor angry words; and curses have no power, else the Dutch would not grow fat living on our land, and I would not be alive tonight. Do you understand? Have you seen the men who fought in the old days? They have not forgotten the times of war. I have given them homes and quiet hearts and full bellies. I alone. And they curse my name in the dark, in each other's ears – because they can never forget.'

This man, whose talk had been of war and violence, discovered unexpectedly a passionate craving for security and peace. No one would understand him. Some of those who would not understand had died. His white teeth gleamed cruelly in the dark. But there were others he could not kill. The fools. He wanted the land and the people in it to be forgotten as if they had been swallowed by the sea. But they had neither wisdom nor patience. Could they not wait? They chanted prayers five times every day, but they had not the faith.

'Death comes to all – and to the believers the end of trouble. But you white men who are too strong for us, you also die. You die. And there is a Paradise as great as all earth and all Heaven together, but not for you – not for you !'

Lingard, amazed, listened without a sound. The sleeper snored faintly. Belarab continued very calm after this almost involuntary outburst of a consoling belief. He explained that he wanted somebody at his back, somebody strong and whom he could trust, some outside force that would awe the unruly, that would inspire their ignorance with fear, and make his rule secure. He groped in the dark and seizing Lingard's arm above the elbow pressed it with force – then let go. And Lingard understood why his temerity had been so successful.

Then and there, in return for Lingard's open support, a few guns and a little money, Belarab promised his help for the conquest of Wajo. There was no doubt he could find men who would fight. He could send messages to friends at a distance and there were also many unquiet spirits in his own district ready for any adventure. He spoke of these men with fierce contempt and an angry tenderness, in mingled accents of envy and disdain. He was wearied by their folly, by their recklessness, by their impatience – and he seemed to resent these as if they had been gifts of which he himself had been deprived by the fatality of his wisdom. They would fight. When the time came Lingard had only to speak, and a sign from him would send them to a vain death – those men who could not wait for an opportunity on this earth or for the eternal revenge of Heaven.

He ceased, and towered upright in the gloom.

'Awake!' he exclaimed, low, bending over the sleeping man.

Their black shapes, passing in turn, eclipsed for two successive moments the glitter of the stars, and Lingard, who had not stirred, remained alone. He lay back full length with an arm thrown across his eyes.

When three days afterward he left Belarab's settlement, it was on a calm morning of unclouded peace. All the boats of the brig came up into the lagoon armed and manned to make more impressive the solemn fact of a concluded alliance. A staring crowd watched his imposing departure in profound silence and with an increased sense of wonder at the mystery of his apparition. The progress of the boats was smooth and slow while they crossed the wide lagoon. Lingard looked back once. A great stillness had laid its hand over the earth, the sky, and the men; upon the immobility of landscape and people. Hassim and Immada, standing out clearly by the side of the chief, raised their arms in a last salutation; and the distant gesture appeared sad, futile, lost in space, like a sign of distress made by castaways in the vain hope of an impossible help.

He departed, he returned, he went away again, and each time those two figures, lonely on some sandbank of the Shallows, made at him the same futile sign of greeting or good-bye. Their arms at each movement seemed to draw closer around his heart the bond of a protecting affection. He worked prosaically, earning money to pay the cost of the romantic necessity that had invaded his life. And the money ran like water out of his hands. The owner of the New England voice remitted not a little of it to his people in Baltimore. But import houses in the ports of the Far East had their share. It paid for a fast *prau* which, commanded by Jaffir, sailed into unfrequented bays and up unexplored rivers, carrying secret messages, important news, generous bribes. A good part of it went to the purchase of the *Emma*.

The *Emma* was a battered and decrepit old schooner that, in the decline of her existence, had been much ill-used by a paunchy white trader of cunning and gluttonous aspect. This man boasted outrageously afterward of the good price he had got 'for that rotten old hooker of mine – you know'. The *Emma* left port mysteriously in company with the brig and henceforth vanished from the seas forever. Lingard had her towed up the creek and ran her aground upon that shore of the lagoon farthest from Belarab's settlement. There had been at that time a great rise of waters, which retiring soon after left the old craft cradled in the mud, with her bows grounded high between the trunks of two big trees, and leaning over a little as though after a hard life she had settled wearily to an everlasting rest. There, a few months later, Jörgenson found her when, called back into the life of men, he reappeared, together with Lingard, in the Land of Refuge.

'She is better than a fort on shore,' said Lingard, as side by side they leant over the taffrail, looking across the lagoon on the houses and palm groves of the settlement. 'All the guns and powder I have got together so far are stored in her. Good idea, wasn't it? There will be, perhaps, no other such flood for years, and now they can't come alongside unless right under the counter, and only one boat at a time. I think you are perfectly safe here; you could keep off a whole fleet of boats; she isn't easy to set fire to; the forest in front is better than a wall. Well?'

Jörgenson assented in grunts. He looked at the desolate emptiness of the decks, at the stripped spars, at the dead body of the dismantled little vessel that would know the life of the seas no more. The gloom of the forest fell on her, mournful like a winding sheet. The bushes of the bank tapped their twigs on the bluff of her bows, and a pendent spike of tiny brown blossoms swung to and fro over the ruins of her windlass.

Hassim's companions garrisoned the old hulk, and Jörgenson, left in charge, prowled about from stem to stern, taciturn and anxiously faithful to his trust. He had been received with astonishment, respect – and awe. Belarab visited him often. Sometimes those whom he had known in their prime years ago, during a struggle for faith and life, would come to talk with the white man. Their voices were like the echoes of stirring events, in the pale glamour of a youth gone by. They nodded their old heads. Do you remember? – they said. He remembered only too well! He was like a man raised from the dead, for whom the fascinating trust in the power of life is tainted by the black scepticism of the grave.

Only at times the invincible belief in the reality of existence would come back, insidious and inspiring. He squared his shoulders, held himself straight, and walked with a firmer step. He felt a glow within him and the quickened beat of his heart. Then he calculated in silent excitement Lingard's chances of success, and he lived for a time with the life of that other man who knew nothing of the black scepticism of the grave. The chances were good, very good.

'I should like to see it through,' Jörgenson muttered to himself ardently; and his lustreless eyes would flash for a moment.

PART THREE

THE CAPTURE

'SOME people,' said Lingard, 'go about the world with their eyes
shut. You are right. The sea is free to all of us. Some work on it,
and some play the fool on it – and I don't care. Only you may
take it from me that I will let no man's play interfere with
my work. You want me to understand you are a very great
man –'

Mr Travers smiled, coldly.

'Oh, yes,' continued Lingard, 'I understand that well enough.
But remember you are very far from home, while I, here, I am
where I belong. And I belong where I am. I am just Tom Lingard, no more, no less, wherever I happen to be, and – you may
ask –' A sweep of his hand along the western horizon entrusted with perfect confidence the remainder of his speech to the
dumb testimony of the sea.

He had been on board the yacht for more than an hour, and
nothing, for him, had come of it but the birth of an unreasoning
hate. To the unconscious demand of these people's presence, of
their ignorance, of their faces, of their voices, of their eyes, he
had nothing to give but a resentment that had in it a germ of
reckless violence. He could tell them nothing because he had
not the means. Their coming at this moment, when he had wandered beyond that circle which race, memories, early associations, all the essential conditions of one's origin, trace round
every man's life, deprived him in a manner of the power of
speech. He was confounded. It was like meeting exacting
spectres in a desert.

He stared at the open sea, his arms crossed, with a reflective
fierceness. His very appearance made him utterly different from
everyone on board that vessel. The grey shirt, the blue sash, one
rolled-up sleeve baring a sculptural forearm, the negligent
masterfulness of his tone and pose were very distasteful to Mr
Travers, who, having made up his mind to wait for some kind
of official assistance, regarded the intrusion of that inexplicable

man with suspicion. From the moment Lingard came on board
the yacht, every eye in that vessel had been fixed upon him.
Only Carter, within earshot and leaning with his elbow upon
the rail, stared down at the deck as if overcome with drowsiness
or lost in thought.

Of the three other persons aft, Mr Travers kept his hands in
the side pockets of his jacket and did not conceal his growing
disgust.

On the other side of the deck, a lady, in a long chair, had a
passive attitude that to Mr d'Alcacer, standing near her, seemed
characteristic of the manner in which she accepted the necessities of existence. Years before, as an attaché of his Embassy in
London, he had found her an interesting hostess. She was even
more interesting now, since a chance meeting and Mr Travers'
offer of a passage to Batavia had given him an opportunity of
studying the various shades of scorn which he suspected to be
the secret of her acquiescence in the shallowness of events and
the monotony of a worldly existence.

There were things that from the first he had not been able to
understand; for instance, why she should have married Mr
Travers. It must have been from ambition. He could not help
feeling that such a successful mistake would explain completely
her scorn and also her acquiescence. The meeting in Manila had
been utterly unexpected to him, and he accounted for it to his
uncle, the Governor-General of the colony, by pointing out that
Englishmen, when worsted in the struggle of love or politics,
travel extensively as if by encompassing a large portion of earth's
surface they hoped to gather fresh strength for a renewed contest. As to himself, he judged – but did not say – that his contest with fate was ended, though he also travelled, leaving behind him in the capitals of Europe a story in which there was
nothing scandalous but the publicity of an excessive feeling, and
nothing more tragic than the early death of a woman whose brilliant perfections were no better known to the great world than
the discreet and passionate devotion she had innocently inspired.

The invitation to join the yacht was the culminating point of
many exchanged civilities, and was mainly prompted by Mr

Travers' desire to have somebody to talk to. D'Alcacer had accepted with the reckless indifference of a man to whom one method of flight from a relentless enemy is as good as another. Certainly the prospect of listening to long monologues on commerce, administration, and politics did not promise much alleviation to his sorrow; and he could not expect much else from Mr Travers, whose life and thought, ignorant of human passion, were devoted to extracting the greatest possible amount of personal advantage from human institutions. D'Alcacer found, however, that he could attain a measure of forgetfulness – the most precious thing for him now – in the society of Edith Travers.

She had awakened his curiosity, which he thought nothing and nobody on earth could do any more.

These two talked of things indifferent and interesting, certainly not connected with human institutions, and only very slightly with human passions; but d'Alcacer could not help being made aware of her latent capacity for sympathy developed in those who are disenchanted with life or death. How far she was disenchanted he did not know, and did not attempt to find out. This restraint was imposed upon him by the chivalrous respect he had for the secrets of women and by a conviction that deep feeling is often impenetrably obscure, even to those it masters for their inspiration or their ruin. He believed that even she herself would never know; but his grave curiosity was satisfied by the observation of her mental state, and he was not sorry that the stranding of the yacht prolonged his opportunity.

Time passed on that mudbank as well as anywhere else, and it was not from a multiplicity of events, but from the lapse of time alone, that he expected relief. Yet in the sameness of days upon the Shallows, time, flowing ceaselessly, flowed imperceptibly; and, since every man clings to his own, be it joy, be it grief, he was pleased after the unrest of his wanderings to be able to fancy the whole universe and even time itself apparently come to a standstill; as if unwilling to take him away further from his sorrow, which was fading indeed but undiminished, as things fade, not in the distance but in the mist.

2

'D'ALCACER was a man of nearly forty, lean and sallow, with hollow eyes and a drooping brown moustache. His gaze was penetrating and direct, his smile frequent and fleeting. He observed Lingard with great interest. He was attracted by that elusive something – a line, a fold, perhaps the form of the eye, the droop of an eyelid, the curve of a cheek, that trifling trait which on no two faces on earth is alike, that in each face is the very foundation of expression, as if, all the rest being heredity, mystery, or accident, it alone had been shaped consciously by the soul within.

Now and then he bent slightly over the slow beat of a red fan in the curve of the deck chair to say a few words to Mrs Travers, who answered him without looking up, without a modulation of tone or a play of feature, as if she had spoken from behind the veil of an immense indifference stretched between her and all men, between her heart and the meaning of events, between her eyes and the shallow sea which, like her gaze, appeared profound, forever stilled, and seemed, far off in the distance of a faint horizon, beyond the reach of eye, beyond the power of hand or voice, to lose itself in the sky.

Mr Travers stepped aside, and speaking to Carter, overwhelmed him with reproaches.

'You misunderstood your instructions,' murmured rapidly Mr Travers. 'Why did you bring this man here? I am surprised –'

'Not half so much as I was last night,' growled the young seaman, without any reverence in his tone, very provoking to Mr Travers.

'I perceive now you were totally unfit for the mission I entrusted you with,' went on the owner of the yacht.

'It's he who got hold of me,' said Carter. 'Haven't you heard him yourself, sir?'

'Nonsense,' whispered Mr Travers, angrily. 'Have you any idea what his intentions may be?'

'I half believe,' answered Carter, 'that his intention was to shoot me in his cabin last night if I –'

'That's not the point,' interrupted Mr Travers. 'Have you any opinion as to his motives in coming here?'

Carter raised his weary, bloodshot eyes in a face scarlet and peeling as though it had been licked by a flame. 'I know no more than you do, sir. Last night when he had me in that cabin of his, he said he would just as soon shoot me as let me go to look for any other help. It looks as if he were desperately bent upon getting a lot of salvage money out of a stranded yacht.'

Mr Travers turned away, and, for a moment, appeared immersed in deep thought. This accident of stranding upon a deserted coast was annoying as a loss of time. He tried to minimize it by putting in order the notes collected during the year's travel in the East. He had sent off for assistance; his sailing-master, very crestfallen, made bold to say that the yacht would most likely float at the next spring tides; d'Alcacer, a person of undoubted nobility though of inferior principles, was better than no company, in so far at least that he could play picquet.

Mr Travers had made up his mind to wait. Then suddenly this rough man, looking as if he had stepped out from an engraving in a book about buccaneers, broke in upon his resignation with mysterious allusions to danger, which sounded absurd yet were disturbing; with dark and warning sentences that sounded like disguised menaces.

Mr Travers had a heavy and rather long chin which he shaved. His eyes were blue, a chill, naïve blue. He faced Lingard untouched by travel, without a mark of weariness or exposure, with the air of having been born invulnerable. He had a full, pale face; and his complexion was perfectly colourless, yet amazingly fresh, as if he had been reared in the shade.

He thought:

'I must put an end to this preposterous hectoring. I won't be intimidated into paying for services I don't need.'

Mr Travers felt a strong disgust for the impudence of the attempt; and all at once, incredibly, strangely, as though the thing, like a contest with a rival or a friend, had been of profound importance to his career, he felt inexplicably elated at the thought of defeating the secret purposes of that man.

Lingard, unconscious of everything and everybody, contemplated the sea. He had grown on it, he had lived with it; it had enticed him away from home; on it his thoughts had expanded and his hand had found work to do. It had suggested endeavour, it had made him owner and commander of the finest brig afloat; it had lulled him into a belief in himself, in his strength, in his luck – and suddenly, by its complicity in a fatal accident, it had brought him face to face with a difficulty that looked like the beginning of disaster.

He had said all he dared to say – and he perceived that he was not believed. This had not happened to him for years. It had never happened. It bewildered him as if he had suddenly discovered that he was no longer himself. He had come to them and had said: 'I mean well by you. I am Tom Lingard –' and they did not believe! Before such scepticism he was helpless, because he had never imagined it possible. He had said: 'You are in the way of my work. You are in the way of what I can not give up for any one; but I will see you through all safe if you will only trust me – me, Tom Lingard.' And they would not believe him! It was intolerable. He imagined himself sweeping their disbelief out of his way. And why not? He did not know them, he did not care for them, he did not even need to lift his hand against them! All he had to do was to shut his eyes now for a day or two, and afterward he could forget that he had ever seen them. It would be easy. Let their disbelief vanish, their folly disappear, their bodies perish ... It was that – or ruin!

3

LINGARD's gaze, detaching itself from the silent sea, travelled slowly over the silent figures clustering forward, over the faces of the seamen attentive and surprised, over the faces never seen before yet suggesting old days – his youth – other seas – the distant shores of early memories. Mr Travers gave a start also, and the hand which had been busy with his left whisker went into the pocket of his jacket, as though he had plucked out something worth keeping. He made a quick step toward Lingard.

'I don't see my way to utilize your services,' he said, with cold finality.

Lingard, grasping his beard, looked down at him thoughtfully for a short time.

'Perhaps it's just as well,' he said, very slowly, 'because I did not offer my services. I've offered to take you on board my brig for a few days, as your only chance of safety. And you asked me what were my motives. My motives! If you don't see them they are not for you to know.'

And these men who, two hours before, had never seen each other, stood for a moment close together, antagonistic, as if they had been life-long enemies, one short, dapper and glaring upward, the other towering heavily, and looking down in contempt and anger.

Mr d'Alcacer, without taking his eyes off them, bent low over the deck chair.

'Have you ever seen a man dashing himself at a stone wall?' he asked, confidentially.

'No,' said Mrs Travers, gazing straight before her above the slow flutter of the fan. 'No, I did not know it was ever done; men burrow under or slip round quietly while they look the other way.'

'Ah! you define diplomacy,' murmured d'Alcacer. 'A little of it here would do no harm. But our picturesque visitor has none of it. I've a great liking for him.'

'Already!' breathed out Mrs Travers, with a smile that touched her lips with its bright wing and was flown almost before it could be seen.

'There is liking at first sight,' affirmed d'Alcacer, 'as well as love at first sight — the *coup de foudre* — you know.'

She looked up for a moment, and he went on, gravely:

'I think it is the truest, the most profound of sentiments. You do not love because of what is in the other. You love because of something that is in you – something alive – in yourself.' He struck his breast lightly with the tip of one finger. 'A capacity in you. And not everyone may have it – not everyone deserves to be touched by fire from heaven.'

'And die,' she said.

He made a slight movement.

'Who can tell? That is as it may be. But it is always a privilege, even if one must live a little after being burnt.'

Through the silence between them, Mr Travers' voice came plainly, saying with irritation :

'I've told you already that I do not want you. I've sent a messenger to the governor of the Straits. Don't be importunate.'

Then Lingard, standing with his back to them, growled out something which must have exasperated Mr Travers, because his voice was pitched higher :

'You are playing a dangerous game, I warn you. Sir John, as it happens, is a personal friend of mine. He will send a cruiser –' and Lingard interrupted recklessly loud :

'As long as she does not get here for the next ten days, I don't care. Cruisers are scarce just now in the Straits; and to turn my back on you is no hanging matter anyhow. I would risk that, and more ! Do you hear? And more !'

He stamped his foot heavily, Mr Travers stepped back.

'You will gain nothing by trying to frighten me,' he said. 'I don't know who you are.'

Every eye in the yacht was wide open. The men, crowded upon each other, stared stupidly like a flock of sheep. Mr Travers pulled out a handkerchief and passed it over his forehead. The face of the sailing-master who leaned against the main mast – as near as he dared to approach the gentry – was shining and crimson between white whiskers, like a glowing coal between two patches of snow.

D'Alcacer whispered :

'It is a quarrel, and the picturesque man is angry. He is hurt.'

Mrs Travers' fan rested on her knees, and she sat still as if waiting to hear more.

'Do you think I ought to make an effort for peace?' asked d'Alcacer.

She did not answer, and after waiting a little, he insisted:

'What is your opinion? Shall I try to mediate – as a neutral, as a benevolent neutral? I like that man with the beard.'

The interchange of angry phrases went on aloud, amidst general consternation.

'I would turn my back on you only I am thinking of these poor devils here,' growled Lingard, furiously. 'Did you ask them how they feel about it?'

'I ask no one,' spluttered Mr Travers. 'Everybody here depends on my judgement.'

'I am sorry for them then,' pronounced Lingard with sudden deliberation, and leaning forward with his arms crossed on his breast.

At this Mr Travers positively jumped, and forgot himself so far as to shout:

'You are an impudent fellow. I have nothing more to say to you.'

D'Alcacer, after muttering to himself, 'This is getting serious,' made a movement, and could not believe his ears when he heard Mrs Travers say rapidly with a kind of fervour:

'Don't go, pray; don't stop them. Oh! This is truth – this is anger – something real at last.'

D'Alcacer leaned back at once against the rail.

Then Mr Travers, with one arm extended, repeated very loudly:

'Nothing more to say. Leave my ship at once!'

And directly the black dog, stretched at his wife's feet, muzzle on paws and blinking yellow eyes, growled discontentedly at the noise. Mrs Travers laughed a faint, bright laugh, that seemed to escape, to glide, to dart between her white teeth. D'Alcacer, concealing his amazement, was looking down at her gravely: and after a slight gasp, she said with little bursts of merriment between every few words:

'No, but this is – such – such a fresh experience for me to hear – to see something – genuine and human. Ah! ah! one would think they had waited all their lives for this opportunity – ah! ah! ah! All their lives – for this! ah! ah! ah!'

These strange words struck d'Alcacer as perfectly just, as throwing an unexpected light. But after a smile, he said, seriously:

'This reality may go too far. A man who looks so picturesque is capable of anything. Allow me –' And he left her side, moving toward Lingard, loose-limbed and gaunt, yet having in his whole bearing, in his walk, in every leisurely movement, an air of distinction and ceremony.

Lingard spun round with aggressive mien to the light touch on his shoulder, but as soon as he took his eyes off Mr Travers, his anger fell, seemed to sink without a sound at his feet like a rejected garment.

'Pardon me,' said d'Alcacer, composedly. The slight wave of his hand was hardly more than an indication, the beginning of a conciliating gesture. 'Pardon me; but this is a matter requiring perfect confidence on both sides. Don Martin, here, who is a person of importance ...'

'I've spoken my mind plainly. I have said as much as I dare. On my word I have,' declared Lingard with an air of good temper.

'Ah!' said d'Alcacer, reflectively, 'then your reserve is a matter of pledged faith – of – of honour?'

Lingard also appeared thoughtful for a moment.

'You may put it that way. And I owe nothing to a man who couldn't see my hand when I put it out to him as I came aboard.'

'You have so much the advantage of us here,' replied d'Alcacer, 'that you may well be generous and forget that oversight; and then just a little more confidence ...'

'My dear d'Alcacer, you are absurd,' broke in Mr Travers, in a calm voice but with white lips. 'I did not come out all this way to shake hands promiscuously and receive confidences from the first adventurer that comes along.'

D'Alcacer stepped back with an almost imperceptible inclination of the head at Lingard, who stood for a moment with twitching face.

'I *am* an adventurer,' he burst out, 'and if I hadn't been an adventurer, I would have had to starve or work at home for such people as you. If I weren't an adventurer, you would be most likely lying dead on this deck with your cut throat gaping at the sky.'

Mr Travers waved this speech away. But others also had heard. Carter listened watchfully and something, some alarming notion seemed to dawn all at once upon the thick little sailing-master, who rushed on his short legs, and tugging at Carter's sleeve, stammered desperately:

'What's he saying? Who's he? What's up? Are the natives unfriendly? My book says: "Natives friendly all along this coast!" My book says –'

Carter, who had glanced over the side, jerked his arm free.

'You go down into the pantry, where you belong, Skipper, and read that bit about the natives over again,' he said to his superior officer, with savage contempt. 'I'll be hanged if some of them ain't coming aboard now to eat you – book and all. Get out of the way, and let the gentlemen have the first chance of a row.'

Then addressing Lingard, he drawled in his old way:

'That crazy mate of yours has sent your boat back, with a couple of visitors in her, too.'

Before he apprehended plainly the meaning of these words, Lingard caught sight of two heads rising above the rail, the head of Hassim and the head of Immada. Then their bodies ascended into view as though these two beings had gradually emerged from the Shallows. They stood for a moment on the platform looking down on the deck as if about to step into the unknown, then descended and walking aft entered the half-light under the awning shading the luxurious surroundings, the complicated emotions of the, to them, inconceivable existences.

Lingard without waiting a moment cried:

'What news, O Rajah?'

Hassim's eyes made the round of the schooner's decks. He had left his gun in the boat and advanced empty handed, with a tranquil assurance as if bearing a welcome offering in the faint smile of his lips. Immada, half hidden behind his shoulder, followed lightly, her elbows pressed close to her side. The thick fringe of her eyelashes was dropped like a veil; she looked youthful and brooding; she had an aspect of shy resolution.

They stopped within arm's length of the whites, and for some time nobody said a word. Then Hassim gave Lingard a significant glance, and uttered rapidly with a slight toss of the head that indicated in a manner the whole of the yacht:

'I see no guns!'

'N – no!' said Lingard, looking suddenly confused. It had occurred to him that for the first time in two years or more he had forgotten, utterly forgotten, these people's existence.

Immada stood slight and rigid with downcast eyes. Hassim, at his ease, scrutinized the faces, as if searching for elusive points of similitude or for subtle shades of difference.

'What is this new intrusion?' asked Mr Travers, angrily.

'These are the fisher-folk, sir,' broke in the sailing-master, 'we've observed these three days past flitting about in a canoe; but they never had the sense to answer our hail; and yet a bit of fish for your breakfast –?' He smiled obsequiously, and all at once, without provocation, began to bellow:

'Hey! Johnnie! Hab got fish? Fish! One peecee fish! Eh? *Savee*? Fish! Fish –' He gave it up suddenly to say in a deferential tone – 'Can't make them savages understand anything, sir,' and withdrew as if after a clever feat.

Hassim looked at Lingard.

'Why did the little white man make that outcry?' he asked, anxiously.

'Their desire is to eat fish,' said Lingard in an enraged tone.

Then before the air of extreme surprise which incontinently appeared on the other's face, he could not restrain a short and hopeless laugh.

'Eat fish,' repeated Hassim, staring. 'O you white people! O you white people! Eat fish! Good! But why make that noise? And why did you send them here without guns?' After a significant glance down upon the slope of the deck caused by the vessel being on the ground, he added with a slight nod at Lingard – 'And without knowledge?'

'You should not have come here, O Hassim,' said Lingard,
testily. 'Here no one understands. They take a rajah for a fisherman –'

'*Ya-wa* ! A great mistake, for, truly, the chief of ten fugitives
without a country is much less than the headman of a fishing
village,' observed Hassim, composedly. Immada sighed. 'But
you, Tuan, at least know the truth,' he went on with quiet irony;
then after a pause – 'We came here because you had forgotten to
look toward us, who had waited, sleeping little at night, and, in
the day, watching with hot eyes the empty water at the foot of
the sky for you.'

Immada murmured, without lifting her head:

'You never looked for us. Never, never once.'

'There was too much trouble in my eyes,' explained Lingard
with that patient gentleness of tone and face which, every time
he spoke to the young girl, seemed to disengage itself from his
whole person, enveloping his fierceness, softening his aspect,
such as the dreamy mist that in the early radiance of the morning weaves a veil of tender charm about a rugged rock in mid-
ocean. 'I must look now to the right and to the left as in a
time of sudden danger,' he added after a moment and she whispered an appalled 'Why?' so low that its pain floated away in
the silence of attentive men, without response, unheard, ignored,
like the pain of an impalpable thought.

4

D'ALCACER, standing back, surveyed them all with a profound
and alert attention. Lingard seemed unable to tear himself away
from the yacht, and remained, checked, as it were in the act of
going, like a man who has stopped to think out the last thing to
say; and that stillness of a body, forgotten by the labouring mind,
reminded Carter of that moment in the cabin, when alone he
had seen this man thus wrestling with his thought, motionless
and locked in the grip of his conscience.

Mr Travers muttered audibly through his teeth:

'How long is this performance going to last? I have desired you to go.'

'Think of these poor devils,' whispered Lingard, with a quick glance at the crew huddled up near by.

'You are the kind of man I would be least disposed to trust – in any case,' said Mr Travers, incisively, very low, and with an inexplicable but very apparent satisfaction. 'You are only wasting your time here.'

'You – You –' He stammered and stared. He chewed with growls some insulting word and at last swallowed it with an effort. 'My time pays for your life,' he said.

He became aware of a sudden stir, and saw that Mrs Travers had risen from her chair.

She walked impulsively toward the group on the quarter-deck, making straight for Immada. Hassim had stepped aside and his detached gaze of a Malay gentleman passed by her as if she had been invisible.

She was tall, supple, moving freely. Her complexion was so dazzling in the shade that it seemed to throw out a halo round her head. Upon a smooth and wide brow an abundance of pale fair hair, fine as silk, undulating like the sea, heavy like a helmet, descended low without a trace of gloss, without a gleam in its coils, as though it had never been touched by a ray of light; and a throat white, smooth, palpitating with life, a round neck modelled with strength and delicacy, supported gloriously that radiant face and that pale mass of hair unkissed by sunshine.

She said with animation:

'Why, it's a girl!'

Mrs Travers extorted from d'Alcacer a fresh tribute of curiosity. A strong puff of wind fluttered the awnings and one of the screens blowing out wide let in upon the quarter-deck the rippling glitter of the Shallows, showing to d'Alcacer the luminous vastness of the sea, with the line of the distant horizon, dark like the edge of the encompassing night, drawn at the height of Mrs Travers' shoulder ... Where was it he had seen her last – a long time before, on the other side of the world?

There was also the glitter of splendour around her then, and an impression of luminous vastness. The encompassing night, too, was there, the night that waits for its time to move forward upon the glitter, the splendour, the men, the women.

He could not remember for the moment, but he became convinced that of all the women he knew, she alone seemed to be made for action. Every one of her movements had firmness, ease, the meaning of a vital fact, the moral beauty of a fearless expression. Her supple figure was not dishonoured by any faltering of outlines under the plain dress of dark blue stuff moulding her form with bold simplicity.

She had only very few steps to make, but before she had stopped, confronting Immada, d'Alcacer remembered her suddenly as he had seen her last, out West, far away, impossibly different, as if in another universe, as if presented by the fantasy of a fevered memory. He saw her in a luminous perspective of palatial drawing rooms, in the restless eddy and flow of a human sea, at the foot of walls high as cliffs, under lofty ceilings that like a tropical sky flung light and heat upon the shallow glitter of uniforms, of stars, of diamonds, of eyes sparkling in the weary or impassive faces of the throng at an official reception. Outside he had found the unavoidable darkness with its aspect of patient waiting, a cloudy sky holding back the dawn of a London morning. It was difficult to believe.

Lingard, who had been looking dangerously fierce, slapped his thigh and showed signs of agitation.

'By heavens, I had forgotten all about you!' he pronounced in dismay.

Mrs Travers fixed her eyes on Immada. Fair-haired and white she asserted herself before the girl of olive face and raven locks with the maturity of perfection, with the superiority of the flower over the leaf, of the phrase that contains a thought over the cry that can only express an emotion. Immense spaces and countless centuries stretched between them: and she looked at her as when one looks into one's own heart with absorbed curiosity, with still wonder, with an immense compassion. Lingard murmured, warningly:

'Don't touch her.'

Mrs Travers looked at him.

'Do you think I could hurt her?' she asked, softly, and was so startled to hear him mutter a gloomy 'Perhaps,' that she hesitated before she smiled.

'Almost a child! And so pretty! What a delicate face,' she said, while another deep sigh of the sea-breeze lifted and let fall the screens, so that the sound, the wind, and the glitter seemed to rush in together and bear her words away into space. 'I had no idea of anything so charmingly gentle,' she went on in a voice that without effort glowed, caressed, and had a magic power of delight to the soul. 'So young! And she lives here – does she? On the sea – or where? Lives –' Then faintly, as if she had been in the act of speaking, removed instantly to a great distance, she was heard again: 'How does she live?'

Lingard had hardly seen Edith Travers till then. He had seen no one really but Mr Travers. He looked and listened with something of the stupor of a new sensation.

Then he made a distinct effort to collect his thoughts and said with a remnant of anger:

'What have you got to do with her? She knows war. Do you know anything about it? And hunger, too, and thirst, and unhappiness; things you have only heard about. She has been as near death as I am to you – and what is all that to any of you here?'

'That child!' she said in slow wonder.

Immada turned upon Mrs Travers her eyes black as coal, sparkling and soft like a tropical night; and the glances of the two women, their dissimilar and inquiring glances met, seemed to touch, clasp, hold each other with the grip of an intimate contact. They separated.

'What are they come for? Why did you show them the way to this place?' asked Immada, faintly.

Lingard shook his head in denial.

'Poor girl,' said Mrs Travers. 'Are they all so pretty?'

'Who – all?' mumbled Lingard. 'There isn't another one like her if you were to ransack the islands all round the compass.'

'Edith!' ejaculated Mr Travers in a remonstrating, acrimonious voice, and everyone gave him a look of vague surprise.

Then Mrs Travers asked:

'Who is she?'

Lingard very red and grave declared curtly:

'A princess.'

Immediately he looked round with suspicion. No one smiled. D'Alcacer, courteous and nonchalant, lounged up close to Mrs Travers' elbow.

'If she is a princess, then this man is a knight,' he murmured with conviction. 'A knight as I live! A descendant of the immortal hidalgo errant upon the sea. It would be good for us to have him for a friend. Seriously I think that you ought –'

The two stepped aside and spoke low and hurriedly.

'Yes, you ought –'

'How can I?' she interrupted, catching the meaning like a ball.

'By saying something.'

'Is it really necessary?' she asked, doubtfully.

'It would do no harm,' said d'Alcacer with sudden carelessness; 'a friend is always better than an enemy.'

'Always?' she repeated, meaningly. 'But what could I say?'

'Some words,' he answered; 'I should think any words in your voice –'

'Mr d'Alcacer!'

'Or you could perhaps look at him once or twice as though he were not exactly a robber,' he continued.

'Mr d'Alcacer, are you afraid?'

'Extremely,' he said, stooping to pick up the fan at her feet. 'That is the reason I am so anxious to conciliate. And you must not forget that one of your queens once stepped on the cloak of perhaps such a man.'

Her eyes sparkled and she dropped them suddenly.

'I am not a queen,' she said, coldly.

'Unfortunately not,' he admitted; 'but then the other was a woman with no charm but her crown.'

At that moment Lingard, to whom Hassim had been talking earnestly, protested aloud:

'I never saw these people before.'

Immada caught hold of her brother's arm. Mr Travers said harshly:

'Oblige me by taking these natives away.'

'Never before,' murmured Immada as if lost in ecstasy. D'Alcacer glanced at Mrs Travers and made a step forward.

'Could not the difficulty, whatever it is, be arranged, Captain?' he said with careful politeness. 'Observe that we are not only men here –'

'Let them die!' cried Immada, triumphantly.

Though Lingard alone understood the meaning of these words, all on board felt oppressed by the uneasy silence which followed her cry.

'Ah! He is going. Now, Mrs Travers,' whispered d'Alcacer.

'I hope!' said Mrs Travers, impulsively, and stopped as if alarmed at the sound.

Lingard stood still.

'I hope,' she began again, 'that this poor girl will know happier days –' she hesitated.

Lingard waited, attentive and serious.

'Under your care,' she finished. 'And I believe you meant to be friendly to us.'

'Thank you,' said Lingard with dignity.

'You and d'Alcacer,' observed Mr Travers, austerely, 'are unnecessarily detaining this – ah – person, and – ah – friends – ah!'

'I had forgotten you – and now – what? One must – it is hard – hard –' went on Lingard, disconnectedly, while he looked into Mrs Travers' violet eyes, and felt his mind overpowered and troubled as if by the contemplation of vast distances. 'I – you don't know – I – you – cannot . . . Ha! It's all that man's doing,' he burst out.

For a time, as if beside himself, he glared at Mrs Travers, then flung up one arm and strode off toward the gangway, where Hassim and Immada waited for him, interested and patient. With a single word 'Come,' he preceded them down into the boat. Not a sound was heard on the yacht's deck, while these three disappeared one after another below the rail as if they had descended into the sea.

5

THE afternoon dragged itself out in silence. Mrs Travers sat pensive and idle with her fan on her knees. D'Alcacer, who thought the incident should have been treated in a conciliatory spirit, attempted to communicate his view to his host, but that gentleman, purposely misunderstanding his motive, overwhelmed him with so many apologies and expressions of regret at the irksome and perhaps inconvenient delay 'which you suffer from through your good-natured acceptance of our invitation' that the other was obliged to refrain from pursuing the subject further.

'Even my regard for you, my dear d'Alcacer, could not induce me to submit to such a bare-faced attempt at extortion,' affirmed Mr Travers with uncompromising virtue. 'The man wanted to force his services upon me, and then put in a heavy claim for salvage. That is the whole secret – you may depend on it. I detected him at once, of course.' The eye-glass glittered perspicuously. 'He underrated my intelligence; and what a violent scoundrel! The existence of such a man in the time we live in is a scandal.'

D'Alcacer retired, and, full of vague forebodings, tried in vain for hours to interest himself in a book. Mr Travers walked up and down restlessly, trying to persuade himself that his indignation was based on purely moral grounds. The glaring day, like a mass of white-hot iron withdrawn from the fire, was losing gradually its heat and its glare in a richer deepening of tone. At the usual time two seamen, walking noiselessly aft in their yachting shoes, rolled up in silence the quarter-deck screens; and the coast, the shallows, the dark islets and the snowy sandbanks uncovered thus day after day were seen once more in their aspect of dumb watchfulness. The brig, swung end on in the foreground, her squared yards crossing heavily the soaring symmetry of the rigging, resembled a creature instinct with life, with the power of springing into action lurking in the light grace of its repose.

A pair of stewards in white jackets with brass buttons appeared on deck and began to flit about without a sound, laying the table for dinner on the flat top of the cabin skylight. The sun, drifting away toward other lands, toward other seas, toward other men; the sun, all red in a cloudless sky raked the yacht with a parting salvo of crimson rays that shattered themselves into sparks of fire upon the crystal and silver of the dinner-service, put a short flame into the blades of knives, and spread a rosy tint over the white of plates. A trail of purple, like a smear of blood on a blue shield, lay over the sea.

On sitting down Mr Travers alluded in a vexed tone to the necessity of living on preserves, all the stock of fresh provisions for the passage to Batavia having been already consumed. It was distinctly unpleasant.

'I don't travel for my pleasure, however,' he added; 'and the belief that the sacrifice of my time and comfort will be productive of some good to the world at large would make up for any amount of privations.'

Mrs Travers and d'Alcacer seemed unable to shake off a strong aversion to talk, and the conversation, like an expiring breeze, kept on dying out repeatedly after each languid gust. The large silence of the horizon, the profound repose of all things visible, enveloping the bodies and penetrating the souls with their quieting influence, stilled thought as well as voice. For a long time no one spoke. Behind the taciturnity of the masters the servants hovered without noise.

Suddenly, Mr Travers, as if concluding a train of thought, muttered aloud:

'I own with regret I did in a measure lose my temper; but then you will admit that the existence of such a man is a disgrace to civilization.'

This remark was not taken up and he returned for a time to

the nursing of his indignation, at the bottom of which, like a monster in a fog, crept a bizarre feeling of rancour. He waved away an offered dish.

'This coast,' he began again, 'has been placed under the sole protection of Holland by the Treaty of 1820. The Treaty of 1820 creates special rights and obligations . . .'

Both his hearers felt vividly the urgent necessity to hear no more. D'Alcacer, uncomfortable on a camp-stool, sat stiff and stared at the glass stopper of a carafe. Mrs Travers turned a little sideways and leaning on her elbow rested her head on the palm of her hand like one thinking about matters of profound import. Mr Travers talked; he talked inflexibly, in a harsh blank voice, as if reading a proclamation. The other two, as if in a state of incomplete trance, had their ears assailed by fragments of official verbiage.

'An international understanding – the duty to civilize – failed to carry out – compact – Canning –' D'Alcacer became attentive for a moment '– not that this attempt, almost amusing in its impudence, influences my opinion. I won't admit the possibility of any violence being offered to people of our position. It is the social aspect of such an incident I am desirous of criticizing.'

Here d'Alcacer lost himself again in the recollection of Mrs Travers and Immada looking at each other – the beginning and the end, the flower and the leaf, the phrase and the cry. Mr Travers' voice went on dogmatic and obstinate for a long time. The end came with a certain vehemence.

'And if the inferior race must perish, it is a gain, a step toward the perfecting of society which is the aim of progress.'

He ceased. The sparks of sunset in crystal and silver had gone out, and around the yacht the expanse of coast and Shallows seemed to await, unmoved, the coming of utter darkness. The dinner was over a long time ago and the patient stewards had been waiting, stoical in the downpour of words like sentries under a shower.

Mrs Travers rose nervously and going aft began to gaze at the coast. Behind her the sun, sunk already, seemed to force through the mass of waters the glow of an unextinguishable fire, and below her feet, on each side of the yacht, the lustrous sea, as if reflecting the colour of her eyes, was tinged a sombre violet hue.

D'Alcacer came up to her with quiet footsteps and for some time they leaned side by side over the rail in silence. Then he said – 'How quiet it is!' and she seemed to perceive that the quietness of that evening was more profound and more significant than ever before. Almost without knowing it she murmured – 'It's like a dream.' Another long silence ensued; the tranquillity of the universe had such an august ampleness that the sounds remained on the lips as if checked by the fear of profanation. The sky was limpid like a diamond, and under the last gleams of sunset the night was spreading its veil over the earth. There was something precious and soothing in the beautifully serene end of that expiring day, of the day vibrating, glittering and ardent, and dying now in infinite peace, without a stir, without a tremor, without a sigh – in the certitude of resurrection.

Then all at once the shadow deepened swiftly, the stars came out in a crowd, scattering a rain of pale sparks upon the blackness of the water, while the coast stretched low down, a dark belt without a gleam. Above it the top-hamper of the brig loomed indistinct and high.

Mrs Travers spoke first.

'How unnaturally quiet! It is like a desert of land and water without a living soul.'

'One man at least dwells in it,' said d'Alcacer, lightly, 'and if he is to be believed there are other men, full of evil intentions.'

'Do you think it is true?' Mrs Travers asked.

Before answering d'Alcacer tried to see the expression of her face but the obscurity was too profound already.

'How can one see a dark truth on such a dark night?' he said, evasively. 'But it is easy to believe in evil, here or anywhere else.'

She seemed to be lost in thought for a while.

'And that man himself?' she asked.

After some time d'Alcacer began to speak slowly.

'Rough, uncommon, decidedly uncommon of his kind. Not at

all what Don Martin thinks him to be. For the rest – mysterious
to me. He is *your* countryman after all –'

She seemed quite surprised by that view.

'Yes,' she said, slowly. 'But you know, I can not – what shall
I say? – imagine him at all. He has nothing in common with
the mankind I know. There is nothing to begin upon. How does
such a man live? What are his thoughts? His actions? His
affections? His –'

'His conventions,' suggested d'Alcacer. 'That would include
everything.'

Mr Travers appeared suddenly behind them with a glowing
cigar in his teeth. He took it between his fingers to declare with
persistent acrimony that no amount of 'scoundrelly intimidation'
would prevent him from having his usual walk. There was
about three hundred yards to the southward of the yacht a sandbank nearly a mile long, gleaming a silvery white in the darkness, plumetted in the centre with a thicket of dry bushes that
rustled very loud in the slightest stir of the heavy night air. The
day after the stranding they had landed on it 'to stretch their
legs a bit', as the sailing-master defined it, and every evening
since, as if exercising a privilege or performing a duty, the
three paced there for an hour backward and forward lost in
dusky immensity, threading at the edge of water the belt of
damp sand, smooth, level, elastic to the touch like living flesh
and sweating a little under the pressure of their feet.

This time d'Alcacer alone followed Mr Travers. Mrs Travers
heard them get into the yacht's smallest boat, and the night-
watchman, tugging at a pair of sculls, pulled them off to the
nearest point. Then the man returned. He came up the ladder
and she heard him say to someone on deck:

'Orders to go back in an hour.'

His footsteps died out forward, and a somnolent, unbreathing
repose took possession of the stranded yacht.

6

AFTER a time this absolute silence which she almost could feel pressing upon her on all sides induced in Mrs Travers a state of hallucination. She saw herself standing alone, at the end of time, on the brink of days. All was unmoving as if the dawn would never come, the stars would never fade, the sun would never rise any more; all was mute, still, dead – as if the shadow of the outer darkness, the shadow of the uninterrupted, of the ever-lasting night that fills the universe, the shadow of the night so profound and so vast that the blazing suns lost in it are only like sparks, like pin-pricks of fire, the restless shadow that like a sus-picion of an evil truth darkens everything upon the earth on its passage, had enveloped her, had stood arrested as if to remain with her forever.

And there was such a finality in that illusion, such an accord with the trend of her thought that when she murmured into the darkness a faint 'so be it' she seemed to have spoken one of those sentences that resume and close a life.

As a young girl, often reproved for her romantic ideas, she had dreams where the sincerity of a great passion appeared like the ideal fulfilment and the only truth of life. Entering the world she discovered that ideal to be unattainable because the world is too prudent to be sincere. Then she hoped that she could find the truth of life in ambition which she understood as a lifelong devotion to some unselfish ideal. Mr Travers' name was on men's lips; he seemed capable of enthusiasm and of de-votion; he impressed her imagination by his impenetrability. She married him, found him enthusiastically devoted to the nursing of his own career, and had nothing to hope for now.

That her husband should be bewildered by the curious mis-understanding which had taken place and also permanently grieved by her disloyalty to his respectable ideals was only natural. He was, however, perfectly satisfied with her beauty, her brilliance, and her useful connections. She was admired; she was envied; she was surrounded by splendour and adulation; the days went on rapid, brilliant, uniform, without a glimpse of sincerity or true passion, without a single true emotion – not even that of a great sorrow. And swiftly and stealthily they had led her on and on, to this evening, to this coast, to this sea, to this moment of time and to this spot on the earth's surface where she felt unerringly that the moving shadow of the unbroken night had stood still to remain with her forever.

'So be it!' she murmured, resigned and defiant, at the mute and smooth obscurity that hung before her eyes in a black curtain without a fold; and as if in answer to that whisper a lantern was run up to the foreyard-arm of the brig. She saw it ascend swinging for a short space, and suddenly remain motionless in the air, piercing the dense night between the two vessels by its glance of flame that strong and steady seemed, from afar, to fall upon her alone.

Her thoughts, like a fascinated moth, went fluttering toward that light – that man – that girl, who had known war, danger, seen death near, had obtained evidently the devotion of that man. The occurrences of the afternoon had been strange in themselves, but what struck her artistic sense was the vigour of their presentation. They outlined themselves before her memory with the clear simplicity of some immortal legend. They were mysterious, but she felt certain they were absolutely true. They embodied artless and masterful feelings; such, no doubt, as had swayed mankind in the simplicity of its youth. She envied, for a moment, the lot of that humble and obscure sister. Nothing stood between that girl and the truth of her sensations. She could be sincerely courageous, and tender and passionate and – well – ferocious. Why not ferocious? She could know the truth of terror – and of affection, absolutely, without artificial trammels, without the pain of restraint.

Thinking of what such life could be Mrs Travers felt invaded by that inexplicable exaltation which the consciousness of their physical capacities so often gives to intellectual beings. She glowed with a sudden persuasion that she also could be equal to such an existence; and her heart was dilated with a momentary longing to know the naked truth of things; the naked truth of life and passion buried under the growth of centuries.

She glowed and, suddenly, she quivered with the shock of coming to herself as if she had fallen down from a star. There was a sound of rippling water and a shapeless mass glided out of the dark void she confronted. A voice below her feet said:

'I made out your shape – on the sky.'

A cry of surprise expired on her lips and she could only peer downward. Lingard, alone in the brig's dinghy, with another stroke sent the light boat nearly under the yacht's counter, laid his sculls in, and rose from the thwart. His head and shoulders loomed up alongside and he had the appearance of standing upon the sea. Involuntarily Mrs Travers made a movement of retreat.

'Stop,' he said, anxiously, 'don't speak loud. No one must know. Where do your people think themselves, I wonder? In a dock at home? And you –'

'My husband is not on board,' she interrupted, hurriedly.

'I know.'

She bent a little more over the rail.

'Then you are having us watched. Why?'

'Somebody must watch. Your people keep such a good look-out – don't they? Yes. Ever since dark one of my boats has been dodging astern here, in the deep water. I swore to myself I would never see one of you, never speak to one of you here, that I would be dumb, blind, deaf. And – here I am!'

Mrs Travers' alarm and mistrust were replaced by an immense curiosity, burning, yet quiet, too, as if before the inevitable work of destiny. She looked downward at Lingard. His head was bared, and, with one hand upon the ship's side, he seemed to be thinking deeply.

'Because you had something more to tell us,' Mrs Travers suggested, gently.

'Yes,' he said in a low tone and without moving in the least.

'Will you come on board and wait?' she asked.

'Who? I! I!' He lifted his head so quickly as to startle her. 'I have nothing to say to him; and I'll never put my foot on board this craft. I've been told to go. That's enough.'

'He is accustomed to be addressed deferentially,' she said after a pause, 'and you –'

'Who is he?' asked Lingard, simply.

These three words seemed to her to scatter her past in the air – like smoke. They robbed all the multitude of mankind of every vestige of importance. She was amazed to find that on this night, in this place, there could be no adequate answer to the searching naïveness of that question.

'I didn't ask for much,' Lingard began again. 'Did I? Only that you all should come on board my brig for five days. That's all ... Do I look like a liar? There are things I could not tell him. I couldn't explain – I couldn't – not to him – to no man – to no man in the world –'

His voice dropped.

'Not to myself,' he ended as if in a dream.

'We have remained unmolested so long here,' began Mrs Travers, a little unsteadily, 'that it makes it very difficult to believe in danger now. We saw no one all these days except those two people who came for you. If you may not explain –'

'Of course, you can't be expected to see through a wall,' broke in Lingard. 'This coast's like a wall, but I know what's on the other side ... A yacht here of all things that float! When I set eyes on her I could fancy she hadn't been more than an hour from home. Nothing but the look of her spars made me think of old times. And then the faces of the chaps on board. I seemed to know them all. It was like homecoming to me when I wasn't thinking of it. And I hated the sight of you all.'

'If we are exposed to any peril,' she said after a pause during which she tried to penetrate the secret of passion hidden behind that man's words, 'it need not affect you. Our other boat is gone to the Straits and effective help is sure to come very soon.'

'Affect me! Is that precious watchman of yours coming aft? I don't want anybody to know I came here again begging, even of you. Is he coming aft? ... Listen! I've stopped your other boat.'

His head and shoulders disappeared as though he had dived into a denser layer of obscurity floating on the water. The watchman, who had the intention to stretch himself in one of the deck chairs, catching sight of the owner's wife, walked straight to the lamp that hung under the ridge pole of the awning, and after fumbling with it for a time went away forward with an indolent gait.

'You dared!' Mrs Travers whispered down in an intense tone; and, directly, Lingard's head emerged again below her with an upturned face.

'It was dare – or give up. The help from the Straits would have been too late anyhow if I hadn't the power to keep you safe; and if I had the power I could see you through it – alone. I expected to find a reasonable man to talk to. I ought to have known better. You come from too far to understand these things. Well, I dared; I've sent after your other boat a fellow who, with me at his back, would try to stop the governor of the Straits himself. He will do it. Perhaps it's done already. You have nothing to hope for. But I am here. You said you believed I meant well –'

'Yes,' she murmured.

'That's why I thought I would tell you everything. I had to begin with this business about the boat. And what do you think of me now? I've cut you off from the rest of the earth. You people would disappear like a stone in the water. You left one foreign port for another. Who's there to trouble about what became of you? Who would know? Who could guess? It would be months before they began to stir.'

'I understand,' she said, steadily, 'we are helpless.'

'And alone,' he added.

After a pause she said in a deliberate, restrained voice:

'What does this mean? Plunder, captivity?'

'It would have meant death if I hadn't been here,' he answered.

'But you have the power to –'

'Why, do you think, you are alive yet?' he cried. 'Jörgenson has been arguing with them on shore,' he went on, more calmly, with a swing of his arm toward where the night seemed darkest. 'Do you think he would have kept them back if they hadn't expected me every day? His words would have been nothing without my fist.'

She heard a dull blow struck on the side of the yacht and concealed in the same darkness that wrapped the unconcern of the earth and sea, the fury and the pain of hearts; she smiled above his head, fascinated by the simplicity of images and expressions.

Lingard made a brusque movement, the lively little boat being unsteady under his feet, and she spoke slowly, absently, as if her thought had been lost in the vagueness of her sensations.

'And this – this – Jörgenson, you said? Who is he?'

'A man,' he answered, 'a man like myself.'

'Like yourself?'

'Just like myself,' he said with strange reluctance, as if admitting a painful truth. 'More sense, perhaps, but less luck. Though, since your yacht has turned up here, I begin to think that my luck is nothing much to boast of either.'

'Is our presence here so fatal?'

'It may be death to some. It may be worse than death to me. And it rests with you in a way. Think of that! I can never find such another chance again. But that's nothing! A man who has saved my life once and that I passed my word to would think I had thrown him over. But that's nothing! Listen! As true as I stand here in my boat talking to you, I believe the girl would die of grief.'

'You love her,' she said, softly.

'Like my own daughter,' he cried, low.

Mrs Travers said, 'Oh !' faintly, and for a moment there was a silence, then he began again :

'Look here. When I was a boy in a trawler, and looked at you yacht people, in the Channel ports, you were as strange to me as the Malays here are strange to you. I left home sixteen years ago and fought my way all round the earth. I had the time to forget where I began. What are you to me against these two? If I was to die here on the spot would you care? No one would care at home. No one in the whole world – but these two.'

'What can I do?' she asked, and waited, leaning over.

He seemed to reflect, then, lifting his head, spoke gently :

'Do you understand the danger you are in? Are you afraid?'

135

'I understand the expression you used, of course. Understand the danger?' she went on. 'No – decidedly no. And – honestly – I am not afraid.'

'Aren't you?' he said in a disappointed voice. 'Perhaps you don't believe me? I believed you, though, when you said you were sure I meant well. I trusted you enough to come here asking for your help – telling you what no one knows.'

'You mistake me,' she said with impulsive earnestness. 'This is so extraordinarily unusual – sudden – outside my experience.'

'Aye!' he murmured, 'what would you know of danger and trouble? You! But perhaps by thinking it over –'

'You want me to think myself into a fright!' Mrs Travers laughed lightly, and in the gloom of his thought this flash of joyous sound was incongruous and almost terrible. Next moment the night appeared brilliant as day, warm as sunshine; but when she ceased the returning darkness gave him pain as if it had struck heavily against his breast. 'I don't think I could do that,' she finished in a serious tone.

'Couldn't you?' He hesitated, perplexed. 'Things are bad enough to make it no shame. I tell you,' he said, rapidly, 'and I am not a timid man, I may not be able to do much if you people don't help me.'

'You want me to pretend I am alarmed?' she asked, quickly.

'Aye, to pretend – as well you may. It's a lot to ask of you – who perhaps never had to make-believe a thing in your life – isn't it?'

'It is,' she said after a time.

The unexpected bitterness of her tone struck Lingard with dismay.

'Don't be offended,' he entreated. 'I've got to plan a way out of this mess. It's no play either. Could you pretend?'

'Perhaps, if I tried very hard. But to what end?'

'You must all shift aboard the brig,' he began, speaking quickly, 'and then we may get over this trouble without coming to blows. Now, if you were to say that you wish it; that you feel unsafe in the yacht – don't you see?'

'I see,' she pronounced, thoughtfully.

'The brig is small but the cuddy is fit for a lady,' went on Lingard with animation.

'Has it not already sheltered a princess?' she commented, coolly.

'And I shall not intrude.'

'This is an inducement.'

'Nobody will dare to intrude. You needn't even see me.'

'This is almost decisive, only –'

'I know my place.'

'Only, I might not have the influence,' she finished.

'That I can not believe,' he said, roughly. 'The long and the short of it is you don't trust me because you think that only people of your own condition speak the truth always.'

'Evidently,' she murmured.

'You say to yourself – here's a fellow deep in with pirates, thieves, niggers –'

'To be sure –'

'A man I never saw the like before,' went on Lingard, head-long, 'a – ruffian.'

He checked himself, full of confusion. After a time he heard her saying, calmly:

'You are like other men in this, that you get angry when you can not have your way at once.'

'I angry!' he exclaimed in deadened voice. 'You do not understand. I am thinking of you also – it is hard on me –'

'I mistrust not you, but my own power. You have produced an unfortunate impression on Mr Travers.'

'Unfortunate impression! He treated me as if I had been a long-shore loafer. Never mind that. He is your husband. Fear in those you care for is hard to bear for any man. And so, he –'

'What Machiavellism!'

'Eh, what did you say?'

'I only wondered where you had observed that. On the sea?'

'Observed what?' he said, absently. Then pursuing his idea – 'One word from you ought to be enough.'

'You think so?'

'I am sure of it. Why, even I, myself –'

'Of course,' she interrupted. 'But don't you think that after parting with you on such – such – inimical terms, there would be a difficulty in resuming relations?'

'A man like me would do anything for money – don't you see?'

After a pause she asked:

'And would you care for that argument to be used?'

'As long as you know better!'

His voice vibrated – she drew back disturbed, as if unexpectedly he had touched her.

'What can there be at stake?' she began, wonderingly.

'A kingdom,' said Lingard.

Mrs Travers leaned far over the rail, staring, and their faces, one above the other, came very close together.

'Not for yourself?' she whispered.

He felt the touch of her breath on his forehead and remained still for a moment, perfectly still as if he did not intend to move or speak any more.

'Those things,' he began, suddenly, 'come in your way, when you don't think, and they get all round you before you know what you mean to do. When I went into that bay in New Guinea I never guessed where that course would take me to. I could tell you a story. You would understand! You! You!'

He stammered, hesitated, and suddenly spoke, liberating the visions of two years into the night where Mrs Travers could follow them as if outlined in words of fire.

7

His tale was as startling as the discovery of a new world. She was being taken along the boundary of an exciting existence, and she looked into it through the guileless enthusiasm of the narrator. The heroic quality of the feelings concealed what was disproportionate and absurd in that gratitude, in that friendship, in that inexplicable devotion. The headlong fierceness of purpose invested his obscure design of conquest with the proportions of a great enterprise. It was clear that no vision of a subjugated world could have been more inspiring to the most famous adventurer of history.

From time to time he interrupted himself to ask, confidently, as if he had been speaking to an old friend, 'What would you have done?' and hurried on without pausing for approval.

It struck her that there was a great passion in all this, the beauty of an implanted faculty of affection that had found itself, its immediate need of an object and the way of expansion; a tenderness expressed violently; a tenderness that could only be satisfied by backing human beings against their own destiny. Perhaps her hatred of convention, trammelling the frankness of her own impulses, had rendered her more alert to perceive what is intrinsically great and profound within the forms of human folly, so simple and so infinitely varied according to the region of the earth and to the moment of time.

What of it that the narrator was only a roving seaman; the kingdom of the jungle, the men of the forest, the lives obscure! That simple soul was possessed by the greatness of the idea; there was nothing sordid in its flaming impulses. When she once understood that, the story appealed to the audacity of her thoughts, and she became so charmed with what she heard that she forgot where she was. She forgot that she was personally close to that tale which she saw detached, far away from her, truth of fiction, presented in picturesque speech, real only by the response of her emotion.

Lingard paused. In the cessation of the impassioned murmur she began to reflect. And at first it was only an oppressive notion of there being some significance that really mattered in this man's story. That mattered to her. For the first time the shadow of danger and death crossed her mind. Was that the significance? Suddenly, in a flash of acute discernment, she saw herself involved helplessly in that story, as one is involved in a natural cataclysm.

He was speaking again. He had not been silent more than a minute. It seemed to Mrs Travers that years had elapsed, so different now was the effect of his words. Her mind was agitated as if his coming to speak and confide in her had been a tremendous occurrence. It was a fact of her own existence; it was part of the story also. This was the disturbing thought. She heard him pronounce several names: Belarab, Daman, Tengga, Ningrat. These belonged now to her life and she was appalled to find she was unable to connect these names with any human appearance. They stood out alone, as if written on the night; they took on a symbolic shape; they imposed themselves upon her senses. She whispered as if pondering: 'Belarab, Daman, Ningrat,' and these barbarous sounds seemed to possess an exceptional energy, a fatal aspect, the savour of madness.

'Not one of them but has a heavy score to settle with the whites. What's that to me! I had somehow to get men who would fight. I risked my life to get that lot. I made them promises which I shall keep – or –! Can you see now why I dared to stop your boat? I am in so deep that I care for no Sir John in the world. When I look at the work ahead I care for nothing. I gave you one chance – one good chance. That I had to do. No! I suppose I didn't look enough of a gentleman. Yes! Yes! That's it. Yet I know what a gentleman is. I lived with them for years. I chummed with them – yes – on gold-fields and in other places where a man has got to show the stuff that's in him. Some of them write from home to me here – such as you see me, because I – never mind! And I know what a gentleman would do. Come! Wouldn't he treat a stranger fairly? Wouldn't he remember that no man is a liar till you prove him so? Wouldn't he keep his word wherever given? Well, I am going to do that. Not a hair of your head shall be touched as long as I live!'

She had regained much of her composure but at these words she felt that staggering sense of utter insecurity which is given one by the first tremor of an earthquake. It was followed by an expectant stillness of sensations. She remained silent. He thought she did not believe him.

'Come! What on earth do you think brought me here – to – to – talk like this to you? There was Hassim – Rajah Tulla, I should say – who was asking me this afternoon: "What will you do now with these, your people?" I believe he thinks yet I fetched you here for some reason. You can't tell what crooked notion they will get into their thick heads. It's enough to make one swear.' He swore. 'My people! are you? How much? Say – how much? You're no more mine than I am yours. Would any of you fine folks at home face black ruin to save a fishing smack's crew from getting drowned?'

Notwithstanding that sense of insecurity which lingered faintly in her mind she had no image of death before her. She felt intensely alive. She felt alive in a flush of strength, with an impression of novelty as though life had been the gift of this very moment. The danger hidden in the night gave no sign to awaken her terror, but the workings of a human soul, simple and violent, were laid bare before her and had the disturbing charm of an unheard-of experience. She was listening to a man who concealed nothing. She said, interrogatively:

'And yet you have come?'

'Yes,' he answered, 'to you – and for you only.'

The flood tide running strong over the banks made a placid trickling sound about the yacht's rudder.

'I would not be saved alone.'

'Then you must bring them over yourself,' he said in a sombre tone. 'There's the brig. You have me – my men – my guns. You know what to do.'

'I will try,' she said.

'Very well. I am sorry for the poor devils forward there if you fail. But of course you won't. Watch that light on the brig. I had it hoisted on purpose. The trouble may be nearer than we think. Two of my boats are gone scouting and if the news they bring me is bad the light will be lowered. Think what that means. And I've told you what I have told nobody. Think of my feelings also. I told you because I – because I had to.'

He gave a shove against the yacht's side and glided away from under her eyes. A rippling sound died out.

She walked away from the rail. The lamp and the skylights shone faintly along the dark stretch of the decks. This evening was like the last – like all the evenings before.

'Is all this I have heard possible?' she asked herself. 'No – but it is true.'

She sat down in a deck chair to think and found she could only remember. She jumped up. She was sure somebody was hailing the yacht faintly. Was that man hailing? She listened, and hearing nothing was annoyed with herself for being haunted by a voice.

'He said he could trust me. Now, what is this danger? What is danger?' she meditated.

Footsteps were coming from forward. The figure of the watchman flitted vaguely over the gangway. He was whistling softly and vanished. Hollow sounds in the boat were succeeded by a splash of oars. The night swallowed these slight noises. Mrs Travers sat down again and found herself much calmer.

She had the faculty of being able to think her own thoughts – and the courage. She could take no action of any kind till her husband's return. Lingard's warnings were not what had impressed her most. This man had presented his innermost self unclothed by any subterfuge. There were in plain sight his desires, his perplexities, affections, doubts, his violence, his folly; and the existence they made up was lawless but not vile. She had too much elevation of mind to look upon him from any other but a strictly human standpoint. If he trusted her (how strange; why should he? Was he wrong?) she accepted the trust with scrupulous fairness. And when it dawned upon her that of all the men in the world this unquestionably was the one she knew best, she had a moment of wonder followed by an impression of profound sadness. It seemed an unfortunate matter that concerned her alone.

Her thought was suspended while she listened attentively for the return of the yacht's boat. She was dismayed at the task before her. Not a sound broke the stillness and she felt as if she were lost in empty space. Then suddenly someone amidships yawned immensely and said: 'Oh, dear! Oh, dear!' A voice asked: 'Ain't they back yet?' A negative grunt answered.

Mrs Travers found that Lingard was touching, because he could be understood. How simple was life, she reflected. She was

frank with herself. She considered him apart from social or-
ganization. She discovered he had no place in it. How delight-
ful! Here was a human being and the naked truth of things
was not so very far from her notwithstanding the growth of
centuries. Then it occurred to her that this man by his action
stripped her at once of her position, of her wealth, of her rank,
of her past. 'I am helpless. What remains?' she asked herself. Nothing! Anybody there might have suggested: 'Your
presence.' She was too artificial yet to think of her beauty;
and yet the power of personality is part of the naked truth of
things.

She looked over her shoulder, and saw the light at the brig's
foreyard-arm burning with a strong, calm flame in the dust of
starlight suspended above the coast. She heard the heavy bump
as of a boat run headlong against the ladder. They were back!
She rose in sudden and extreme agitation. What should she say?
How much? How to begin? Why say anything? It would be
absurd, like talking seriously about a dream. She would not
dare! In a moment she was driven into a state of mind bordering on distraction. She heard somebody run up the gangway
steps. With the idea of gaining time she walked rapidly aft to
the taffrail. The light of the brig faced her without a flicker,
enormous amongst the suns scattered in the immensity of the
night.

She fixed her eyes on it. She thought: 'I shan't tell him anything. Impossible. No! I shall tell everything.' She expected
every moment to hear her husband's voice and the suspense was
intolerable because she felt that then she must decide. Somebody on deck was babbling excitedly. She devoutly hoped
d'Alcacer would speak first and thus put off the fatal moment.
A voice said roughly: 'What's that?' and in the midst of her
distress she recognized Carter's voice, having noticed that young
man who was of a different stamp from the rest of the crew.
She came to the conclusion that the matter could be related
jocularly, or – why not pretend fear? At that moment the brig's
yard-arm light she was looking at trembled distinctly, and she
was dumbfounded as if she had seen a commotion in the fir-

mament. With her lips open for a cry she saw it fall straight down several feet, flicker, and go out. All perplexity passed from her mind. This first fact of the danger gave her a thrill of quite a new emotion. Something had to be done at once. For some remote reason she felt ashamed of her hesitations.

She moved swiftly forward and under the lamp came face to face with Carter who was coming aft. Both stopped, staring, the light fell on their faces, and both were struck by each other's expression. The four eyes shone wide.

'You have seen?' she asked, beginning to tremble.

'How do you know?' he said, at the same time, evidently surprised.

Suddenly she saw that everybody was on deck.

'The light is down,' she stammered.

'The gentlemen are lost,' said Carter. Then he perceived she did not seem to understand. 'Kidnapped off the sandbank,' he continued, looking at her fixedly to see how she would take it. She seemed calm. 'Kidnapped like a pair of lambs! Not a squeak,' he burst out with indignation. 'But the sandbank is long and they might have been at the other end. You were on deck, ma'am?' he asked.

'Yes,' she muttered. 'In the chair here.'

'We were all down below. I had to rest a little. When I came up the watchman was asleep. He swears he wasn't, but I know better. Nobody heard any noise, unless you did. But perhaps you were asleep?' he asked, deferentially.

'Yes – no – I must have been,' she said, faintly.

8

LINGARD's soul was exalted by his talk with Mrs Travers, by the strain of incertitude and by extreme fatigue. On returning on board he asked after Hassim and was told that the Rajah and his sister had gone off in their canoe promising to return before midnight. The boats sent to scout between the islets north and south of the anchorage had not come back yet. He went into his cabin and throwing himself on the couch closed his eyes thinking: 'I must sleep or I shall go mad.'

At times he felt an unshaken confidence in Mrs Travers – then he remembered her face. Next moment the face would fade, he would make an effort to hold on to the image, fail – and then become convinced without the shadow of a doubt that he was utterly lost, unless he let all these people be wiped off the face of the earth.

'They all heard that man order me out of his ship,' he thought, and thereupon for a second or so he contemplated without flinching the lurid image of a massacre. 'And yet I had to tell her that not a hair of her head shall be touched. Not a hair.'

And irrationally at the recollection of these words there seemed to be no trouble of any kind left in the world. Now and then, however, there were black instants when from sheer weariness he thought of nothing at all; and during one of these he fell asleep, losing the consciousness of external things as suddenly as if he had been felled by a blow on the head.

When he sat up, almost before he was properly awake, his first alarmed conviction was that he had slept the night through. There was a light in the cuddy and through the open door of his cabin he saw distinctly Mrs Travers pass out of view across the lighted space.

'They did come on board after all,' he thought – 'how is it I haven't been called!'

He darted into the cuddy. Nobody! Looking up at the clock in the skylight he was vexed to see it had stopped till his ear caught the faint beat of the mechanism. It was going then! He could not have been asleep more than ten minutes. He had not been on board more than twenty!

So it was only a deception; he had seen no one. And yet he remembered the turn of the head, the line of the neck, the colour of the hair, the movement of the passing figure. He returned spiritlessly to his state-room muttering, 'No more sleep for me tonight,' and came out directly, holding a few sheets of paper covered with a high, angular handwriting.

This was Jörgenson's letter written three days before and
entrusted to Hassim. Lingard had read it already twice, but he
turned up the lamp a little higher and sat down to read it again.
On the red shield above his head the gilt sheaf of thunderbolts
darting between the initials of his name seemed to be aimed
straight at the nape of his neck as he sat with bared elbows
spread on the table, poring over the crumpled sheets.

The letter began:

Hassim and Immada are going out tonight to look for you. You
are behind your time and every passing day makes things worse.

Ten days ago three of Belarab's men, who had been collecting
turtles' eggs on the islets, came flying back with a story of a ship
stranded on the outer mudflats. Belarab at once forbade any boats
from leaving the lagoon. So far good. There was a great excitement
in the village. I judge it must be a schooner – probably some fool of
a trader. However, you will know all about her when you read this.
You may say I might have pulled out to sea to have a look for myself. But besides Belarab's orders to the contrary, which I would
attend to for the sake of example, all you are worth in this world,
Tom, is here in the *Emma*, under my feet, and I would not leave
my charge even for half a day. Hassim attended the council held
every evening in the shed outside Belarab's stockade. That holy man
Ningrat was for looting that vessel. Hassim reproved him saying
that the vessel probably was sent by you because no white men were
known to come inside the shoals. Belarab backed up Hassim. Ningrat
was very angry and reproached Belarab for keeping him, Ningrat,
short of opium to smoke. He began by calling him 'O! son,' and
ended by shouting 'O! you worse than an unbeliever!' There was a
hullabaloo. The followers of Tengga were ready to interfere and
you know how it is between Tengga and Belarab. Tengga always
wanted to oust Belarab, and his chances were getting pretty good before you turned up and armed Belarab's bodyguard with muskets.
However, Hassim stopped that row, and no one was hurt that time.
Next day, which was Friday, Ningrat, after reading the prayers in the
mosque, talked to the people outside. He bleated and capered like an
old goat, prophesying misfortune, ruin, and extermination if these
whites were allowed to get away. He is mad but then they think him
a saint, and he had been fighting the Dutch for years in his young
days. Six of Belarab's guard marched down the village street carrying

muskets at full cock and the crowd cleared out. Ningrat was spirited away by Tengga's men into their master's stockade. If it was not for the fear of you turning up any moment there would have been a party-fight that evening. I think it is a pity Tengga is not chief of the land instead of Belarab. A brave and foresighted man, however treacherous at heart, can always be trusted to a certain extent. One can never get anything clear from Belarab. Peace! Peace! You know his fad. And this fad makes him act silly. The peace racket will get him into a row. It may cost him his life in the end. However, Tengga does not feel himself strong enough yet to act with his own followers only and Belarab has, on my advice, disarmed all villagers. His men went into the houses and took away by force all the firearms and as many spears as they could lay hands on. The women screamed abuse of course, but there was no resistance. A few men were seen clearing out into the forest with their arms. Note this for it means there is another power beside Belarab's in the village. The growing power of Tengga.

One morning – four days ago – I went to see Tengga. I found him by the shore trimming a plank with a small hatchet while a slave held an umbrella over his head. He is amusing himself in building a boat just now. He threw his hatchet down to meet me and led me by the hand to a shady spot. He told me frankly he had sent out two good swimmers to observe the stranded vessel. These men stole down the creek in a canoe and when on the sea coast swam from sandbank to sandbank until they approached unobserved – I think – to about fifty yards from that schooner. What can that craft be? I can't make it out. The men reported there were three chiefs on board. One with a glittering eye, one a lean man in white, and another without any hair on the face and dressed in a different style. Could it be a woman? I don't know what to think. I wish you were here. After a lot of chatter Tengga said: 'Six years ago I was ruler of a country and the Dutch drove me out. The country was small but nothing is too small for them to take. They pretended to give it back to my nephew – may he burn! I ran away or they would have killed me. I am nothing here – but I remember. These white people out there cannot run away and they are very few. There is perhaps a little to loot. I would give it to my men who followed me in my calamity because I am their chief and my father was the chief of their fathers.' I pointed out the imprudence of this. He said: 'The dead do not show the way.' To this I remarked that the ignorant do not give information. Tengga kept quiet for a while, then said: 'We must not touch them because their skin is like yours and to kill them would be wrong, but at the bidding of you whites we may go and fight with people of our own skin and our own faith – and that is good. I have promised to Tuan Lingard twenty men and a *prau* to make war in Wajo. The men are good and look at the *prau*; it is swift and strong.' I must say, Tom, the *prau* is the best craft of the kind I have ever seen. I said you paid him well for the help. 'And I also would pay,' says he, 'if you let me have a few guns and a little powder for my men. You and I shall share the loot of that ship outside, and Tuan Lingard will not know. It is only a little game. You have plenty of guns and powder under your care.' He meant in the *Emma*. On that I spoke out pretty straight and we got rather warm until at last he gave me to understand that as he had about forty followers of his own and I had only nine of Hassim's chaps to defend the *Emma* with, he could very well go for me and get the lot. 'And then,' says he, 'I would be so strong that everybody would be on my side.' I discovered in the course of further talk that there is a notion amongst many people that you have come to grief in some way and won't show up here any more. After this I saw the position was serious and I was in a hurry to get back to the *Emma*, but pretending I did not care I smiled and thanked Tengga for giving me warning of his intentions about me and the *Emma*. At this he nearly choked himself with his betel quid and fixing me with his little eyes, muttered: 'Even a lizard will give a fly the time to say its prayers.' I turned my back on him and was very thankful to get beyond the throw of a spear. I haven't been out of the *Emma* since.

9

THE letter went on to enlarge on the intrigues of Tengga, the wavering conduct of Belarab, and the state of the public mind. It noted every gust of opinion and every event, with an earnestness of belief in their importance befitting the chronicle of a crisis in the history of an empire. The shade of Jörgenson had, indeed, stepped back into the life of men. The old adventurer looked on with a perfect understanding of the value of trifles, using his eyes for that other man whose conscience would have the task to unravel the tangle. Lingard lived through those days in the Settlement and was thankful to Jörgenson; only as he lived not from day to day but from sentence to sentence of the writing, there was an effect of bewildering rapidity in the succession of events that made him grunt with surprise sometimes or growl – 'What?' to himself angrily and turn back several lines or a whole page more than once. Toward the end he had a heavy frown of perplexity and fidgeted as he read:

– and I began to think I could keep things quiet till you came or those wretched white people got their schooner off, when Sheriff Daman arrived from the north on the very day he was expected, with two Illanun *praus*. He looks like an Arab. It was very evident to me he can wind the two Illanun *pangerans* round his little finger. The two *praus* are large and armed. They came up the creek, flags and streamers flying, beating drums and gongs, and entered the lagoon with their decks full of armed men brandishing two-handed swords and sounding the war cry. It is a fine force for you, only Belarab who is a perverse devil would not receive Sheriff Daman at once. So Daman went to see Tengga who detained him a very long time. Leaving Tengga he came on board the *Emma*, and I could see directly there was something up.

He began by asking me for the ammunition and weapons they are to get from you, saying he was anxious to sail at once toward Wajo, since it was agreed he was to precede you by a few days. I replied that that was true enough but that I could not think of giving him the powder and muskets till you came. He began to talk about you and hinted that perhaps you will never come. 'And no matter,' says he, 'here is Rajah Hassim and the Lady Immada and we would fight for them if no white man was left in the world. Only we must have something to fight with.' He pretended then to forget me altogether and talked with Hassim while I sat listening. He began to boast how well he got along the Bruni coast. No Illanun *prau* had passed down that coast for years.

Immada wanted me to give the arms he was asking for. The girl is beside herself with fear of something happening that would put a stopper on the Wajo expedition. She has set her mind on getting her country back. Hassim is very reserved but he is very anxious, too. Daman got nothing from me, and that very evening the *praus* were ordered by Belarab to leave the lagoon. He does not trust the Illanuns – and small blame to him. Sheriff Daman went like a lamb. He has no powder for his guns. As the *prau* passed by the *Emma* he shouted to me he was going to wait for you outside the creek. Tengga has given him a man who would show him the place. All this looks very queer to me.

Look out outside then. The *praus* are dodging amongst the islets. Daman visits Tengga. Tengga called on me as a good friend to try and persuade me to give Daman the arms and gunpowder he is so anxious to get. Somehow or other they tried to get around Belarab, who came to see me last night and hinted I had better do so. He is anxious for these Illanuns to leave the neighbourhood. He thinks that if they loot the schooner they will be off at once. That's all he wants now. Immada has been to see Belarab's women and stopped two nights in the stockade. Belarab's youngest wife – he got married six weeks ago – is on the side of Tengga's party because she thinks Belarab would get a share of the loot and she got into her silly head there are jewels and silks in that schooner. What between Tengga worrying him outside and the women worrying him at home, Belarab had such a lively time of it that he concluded he would go to pray at his father's tomb. So for the last two days he has been away camping in that unhealthy place. When he comes back he will be down with fever as sure as fate and then he will be no good for anything. Tengga lights up smoky fires often. Some signal to Daman. I go ashore with Hassim's men and put them out. This is risking a fight every time – for Tengga's men look very black at us. I don't know what the next move may be. Hassim's as true as steel. Immada is very unhappy. They will tell you many details I have no time to write.

The last page fluttered on the table out of Lingard's fingers. He sat very still for a moment looking straight before him, then went on deck.

'Our boats back yet?' he asked Shaw, whom he saw prowling on the quarter-deck.

'No, sir, I wish they were. I am waiting for them to go and turn in,' answered the mate in an aggrieved manner.

'Lower that lantern forward there,' cried Lingard, suddenly, in Malay.

'This trade isn't fit for a decent man,' muttered Shaw to himself, and he moved away to lean on the rail, looking moodily to seaward. After a while: 'There seems to be commotion on board that yacht,' he said. 'I see a lot of lights moving about her decks. Anything wrong, do you think, sir?'

'No, I know what it is,' said Lingard in a tone of elation. She has done it! he thought.

He returned to the cabin, put away Jörgenson's letter and pulled out the drawer of the table. It was full of cartridges. He took a musket down, loaded it, then took another and another. He hammered at the waddings with fierce joyousness. The ramrods rang and jumped. It seemed to him he was doing his share of some work in which that woman was playing her part faithfully. 'She has done it,' he repeated, mentally. 'She will sit in the cuddy. She will sleep in my berth. Well, I'm not ashamed of the brig. By heavens – no! I shall keep away; never come near them as I've promised. Now there's nothing more to say. I've told her everything at once. There's nothing more.'

He felt a heaviness in his burning breast, in all his limbs, as if the blood in his veins had become molten lead.

'I shall get the yacht off. Three, four days – no, a week.'

He found he couldn't do it under a week. It occurred to him he would see her every day till the yacht was afloat. No, he wouldn't intrude, but he was master and owner of the brig after all. He didn't mean to skulk like a whipped cur about his own decks.

'It'll be ten days before the schooner is ready. I'll take every scrap of ballast out of her. I'll strip her – I'll take her lower masts out of her, by heavens! I'll make sure. Then another week to fit out – and – good-bye. Wish I had never seen them. Good-bye – forever. Home's the place for them. Not for me. On another coast she would not have listened. Ah, but she is a woman – every inch of her. I shall shake hands. Yes. I shall take her hand – just before she goes. Why the devil not? I am master here after all – in this brig – as good as any one – by heavens, better than any one – better than any one on earth.'

He heard Shaw walk smartly forward above his head hailing:

'What's that – a boat?'

A voice answered indistinctly.

'One of my boats is back,' thought Lingard. 'News about Daman perhaps. I don't care if he kicks. I wish he would. I would soon show her I can fight as well as I can handle the brig. Two *praus*. Only two *praus*. I wouldn't mind if there were twenty. I would sweep 'em off the sea – I would blow 'em out of the water – I would make the brig walk over them. "Now," I'd say to her, "you who are not afraid, look how it's done!" '

He felt light. He had the sensation of being whirled high in the midst of an uproar and as powerless as a feather in a hurricane. He shuddered profoundly. His arms hung down, and he stood before the table staring like a man overcome by some fatal intelligence.

Shaw, going into the wait to receive what he thought was one of the brig's boats, came against Carter making his way aft hurriedly.

'Hullo! Is it you again?' he said, swiftly, barring the way.

'I come from the yacht,' began Carter with some impatience.

'Where else could you come from?' said Shaw. 'And what might you want now?'

'I want to see your skipper.'

'Well, you can't,' declared Shaw, viciously. 'He's turned in for the night.'

'He expects me,' said Carter, stamping his foot. 'I've got to tell him what happened.'

'Don't you fret yourself, young man,' said Shaw in a superior manner; 'he knows all about it.'

They stood suddenly silent in the dark. Carter seemed at a loss what to do. Shaw, though surprised by it, enjoyed the effect he had produced.

'Damn me, if I did not think so,' murmured Carter to himself; then drawling coolly asked – 'And perhaps you know, too?'

'What do you think? Think I am a dummy here? I ain't mate of this brig for nothing.'

'No, you are not,' said Carter with a certain bitterness of tone. 'People do all kinds of queer things for a living, and I am not particular myself, but I would think twice before taking your billet.'

'What? What do you in-si-nu-ate? My billet? You ain't fit for it, you yacht-swabbing, brass-buttoned impostor.'

'What's this? Any of our boats back?' asked Lingard from the poop. 'Let the seacannie in charge come to me at once.'

'There's only a message from the yacht,' began Shaw, deliberately.

'Yacht! Get the deck lamps along here in the waist! See the ladder lowered. Bear a hand, *Serang*! Mr Shaw! Burn the flare up aft. Two of them! Give light to the yacht's boats that will be coming alongside. Steward! Where's that steward? Turn him out then.'

Bare feet began to patter all around Carter. Shadows glided swiftly.

'Are these flares coming? Where's the quartermaster on duty?' shouted Lingard in English and Malay. 'This way, come here! Put it on a rocket stick – can't you? Hold over the side – thus! Stand by with the lines for the boats forward there. Mr Shaw – we want more light!'

'Aye, aye, sir,' called out Shaw, but he did not move, as if dazed by the vehemence of his commander.

'That's what we want,' muttered Carter under his breath. 'Impostor! What do you call yourself?' he said half aloud to Shaw.

The ruddy glare of the flares disclosed Lingard from head to foot, standing at the break of the poop. His head was bare, his face, crudely lighted, had a fierce and changing expression in the sway of flames.

'What can be his game,' thought Carter, impressed by the powerful and wild aspect of that figure. 'He's changed somehow since I saw him first,' he reflected.

It struck him the change was serious, not exactly for the worse, perhaps – and yet ... Lingard smiled at him from the poop.

Carter went up the steps and without pausing informed him of what had happened.

'Mrs Travers told me to go to you at once. She's very upset as you may guess,' he drawled, looking Lingard hard in the face. Lingard knitted his eyebrows. 'The hands, too, are scared,' Carter went on. 'They fancy the savages, or whatever they may be who stole the owner, are going to board the yacht every minute. I don't think so myself but –'

'Quite right – most unlikely,' muttered Lingard.

'Aye, I daresay you know all about it,' continued Carter, coolly, 'the men are startled and no mistake, but I can't blame them very much. There isn't enough even of carving knives aboard to go round. One old signal gun! A poor show for better men than they.'

'There's no mistake I suppose about this affair?' asked Lingard.

'Well, unless the gentlemen are having a lark with us at hide and seek. The man says he waited ten minutes at the point, then pulled slowly along the bank looking out, expecting to see them walking back. He made the trunk of a tree apparently stranded on the sand and as he was sculling past he says a man jumped up from behind that log, flung a stick at him and went off running. He backed water at once and began to shout "Are you there, sir?" No one answered. He could hear the bushes rustle and some strange noises like whisperings. It was very dark. After calling out several times, and waiting on his oars, he got frightened and pulled back to the yacht. That is clear enough. The only doubt in my mind is if they are alive or not. I didn't let on to Mrs Travers. That's a kind of thing you keep to yourself, of course.'

'I don't think they are dead,' said Lingard, slowly, and as if thinking of something else.

'Oh! If you say so it's all right,' said Carter with deliberation.

'What?' asked Lingard, absently; 'fling a stick, did they? Fling a spear!'

'That's it!' assented Carter, 'but I didn't say anything. I only wondered if the same kind of stick hadn't been flung at the owner, that's all. But I suppose you know your business best, Captain.'

Lingard, grasping his whole beard, reflected profoundly, erect and with bowed head in the glare of the flares.

'I suppose you think it's my doing?' he asked, sharply, without looking up.

Carter surveyed him with a candidly curious gaze.

'Well, Captain, Mrs Travers did let on a bit to me about our chief-officer's boat. You've stopped it, haven't you? How she got to know God only knows. She was sorry she spoke, too, but it wasn't so much of news to me as she thought. I can put two and two together, sometimes. Those rockets, last night, eh? I wished I had bitten my tongue out before I told you about our first gig. But I was taken unawares. Wasn't I? I put it to you: wasn't I? And so I told her when she asked me what passed between you and me on board this brig, not twenty-four hours ago. Things look different now, all of a sudden. Enough to scare a woman, but she is the best man of them all on board. The others are fairly off the chump because it's a bit dark and something has happened they ain't used to. But she has something on her mind. I can't make her out!' He paused, wriggled his shoulders slightly – 'No more than I can make you out,' he added.

'That's your trouble, is it?' said Lingard, slowly.

'Aye, Captain. Is it all clear to you? Stopping boats, kidnapping gentlemen. That's fun in a way, only – I am a youngster to you – but is it clear to you? Old Robinson wasn't particular, you know, and he –'

'Clearer than daylight,' cried Lingard, hotly. 'I can't give up –'

He checked himself. Carter waited. The flare bearers stood rigid, turning their faces away from the flame, and in the play of gleams at its foot the mast near by, like a lofty column, ascended in the great darkness. A lot of ropes ran up slanting into a dark void and were lost to sight, but high aloft a brace block gleamed white, the end of a yard-arm could be seen suspended in the air and as if glowing with its own light. The sky had clouded over the brig without a breath of wind.

'Give up,' repeated Carter, with an uneasy shuffle of feet.

'Nobody,' finished Lingard. 'I can't. It's as clear as daylight. I can't! No! Nothing!'

He stared straight out afar, and after looking at him Carter felt moved by a bit of youthful intuition to murmur, 'That's bad,' in a tone that almost in spite of himself hinted at the dawning of a befogged compassion.

He had a sense of confusion within him, the sense of mystery without. He had never experienced anything like it all the time when serving with old Robinson in the *Ly-e-moon*. And yet he had seen and taken part in some queer doings that were not clear to him at the time. They were secret but they suggested something comprehensible. This affair did not. It had somehow a subtlety that affected him. He was uneasy as if there had been a breath of magic on events and men giving to this complication of a yachting voyage a significance impossible to perceive, but felt in the words, in the gestures, in the events, which made them all strangely, obscurely startling.

He was not one who could keep track of his sensations, and besides he had not the leisure. He had to answer Lingard's questions about the people of the yacht. No, he couldn't say Mrs Travers was what you may call frightened. She seemed to have something in her mind. Oh, yes! The chaps were in a funk. Would they fight? Anybody would fight when driven to it, funk or no funk. That was his experience. Naturally one liked to have something better than a handspike to do it with. Still –

In the pause Carter seemed to weigh with composure the chances of men with handspikes.

'What do you want to fight us for?' he asked, suddenly.

Lingard started.

'I don't,' he said; 'I wouldn't be asking you.'

'There's no saying what you would do, Captain,' replied Carter; 'it isn't twenty-four hours since you wanted to shoot me.'

'I only said I would, rather than let you go raising trouble for me,' explained Lingard.

'One night isn't like another,' mumbled Carter, 'but how am I to know? It seems to me you are making trouble for yourself as fast as you can.'

'Well, supposing I am,' said Lingard with sudden gloominess. 'Would your men fight if I armed them properly?'

'What – for you or for themselves?' asked Carter.

'For the woman,' burst out Lingard. 'You forget there's a woman on board. I don't care *that* for their carcases.'

Carter pondered conscientiously.

'Not tonight,' he said at last. 'There's one or two good men amongst them, but the rest are struck all of a heap. Not tonight. Give them time to get steady a bit if you want them to fight.'

He gave facts and opinions with a mixture of loyalty and mistrust. His own state puzzled him exceedingly. He couldn't make out anything, he did not know what to believe and yet he had an impulsive desire, an inspired desire to help the man. At times it appeared a necessity – at others policy; between whiles a great folly, which perhaps did not matter because he suspected himself of being helpless anyway. Then he had moments of anger. In those moments he would feel in his pocket the butt of a loaded pistol. He had provided himself with the weapon, when directed by Mrs Travers to go on board the brig.

'If he wants to interfere with me, I'll let drive at him and take my chance of getting away,' he had explained, hurriedly.

He remembered how startled Mrs Travers looked. Of course, a woman like that – not used to hear such talk. Therefore it was no use listening to her, except for good manners' sake. Once bit, twice shy. He had no mind to be kidnapped, not he, nor bullied either.

'I can't let him nab me, too. You will want me now, Mrs Travers,' he had said; 'and I promise you not to fire off the old thing unless he jolly well forces me to.'

He was youthfully wise in his resolution not to give way to her entreaties, though her extraordinary agitation did stagger him for a moment. When the boat was already on its way to the brig, he remembered her calling out after him:

'You must not! You don't understand.'

Her voice coming faintly in the darkness moved him, it resembled so much a cry of distress.

'Give way, boys, give way,' he urged his men.

He was wise, resolute, and he was also youthful enough to almost wish it should 'come to it'. And with foresight he even instructed the boat's crew to keep the gig just abaft the main rigging of the brig.

'When you see me drop into her all of a sudden, shove off and pull for dear life.'

Somehow just then he was not so anxious for a shot, but he held on with a determined mental grasp to his fine resolution, lest it should slip away from him and perish in a sea of doubts.

'Hadn't I better get back to the yacht?' he asked, gently.

Getting no answer he went on with deliberation:

'Mrs Travers ordered me to say that no matter how this came about she is ready to trust you. She is waiting for some kind of answer, I suppose.'

'Ready to trust me,' repeated Lingard. His eyes lit up fiercely.

Every sway of flares tossed slightly to and fro the massy shadows of the main deck, where here and there the figure of a man could be seen standing very still with a dusky face and glittering eyeballs.

Carter stole his hand warily into his breast pocket:

'Well, Captain,' he said. He was not going to be bullied, let the owner's wife trust whom she liked.

'Have you got anything in writing for me there?' asked Lingard, advancing a pace, exultingly.

Carter, alert, stepped back to keep his distance. Shaw stared from the side; his rubicund cheeks quivered, his round eyes seemed starting out of his head, and his mouth was open as though he had been ready to choke with pent-up curiosity, amazement, and indignation.

'No! Not in writing,' said Carter, steadily and low.

Lingard had the air of being awakened by a shout. A heavy and darkening frown seemed to fall out of the night upon his forehead and swiftly passed into the night again, and when it departed it left him so calm, his glance so lucid, his mien so composed that it was difficult to believe the man's heart had undergone within the last second the trial of humiliation and of danger. He smiled sadly:

'Well, young man,' he asked with a kind of good-humoured resignation, 'what is it you have there? A knife or a pistol?'

'A pistol,' said Carter. 'Are you surprised, Captain?' He spoke with heat because a sense of regret was stealing slowly within him, as stealthily, as irresistibly as the flowing tide. 'Who began these tricks?' He withdrew his hand, empty, and raised his voice.

'You are up to something I can't make out. You – you are not straight.'

The flares held on high streamed right up without swaying, and in that instant of profound calm the shadows on the brig's deck became as still as the men.

'You think not?' said Lingard, thoughtfully.

Carter nodded. He resented the turn of the incident and the growing impulse to surrender to that man.

'Mrs Travers trusts me though,' went on Lingard with gentle triumph as if advancing an unanswerable argument.

'So she says,' grunted Carter; 'I warned her. She's a baby. They're all as innocent as babies there. And you know it. And I know it. I've heard of your kind. You would dump the lot of us overboard if it served your turn. That's what I think.'

'And that's all.'

Carter nodded slightly and looked away. There was a silence. Lingard's eyes travelled over the brig. The lighted part of the vessel appeared in bright and wavering detail walled and canopied by the night. He felt a light breath on his face. The air was stirring, but the Shallows, silent and lost in the darkness, gave no sound of life.

This stillness oppressed Lingard. The world of his endeavours and his hopes seemed dead, seemed gone. His desire existed homeless in the obscurity that had devoured his corner of the sea, this stretch of the coast, his certitude of success. And here in the midst of what was the domain of his adventurous soul there was a lost youngster ready to shoot him on suspicion of some extravagant treachery. Came ready to shoot! That's good, too! He was too weary to laugh – and, perhaps, too sad. Also the danger of the pistol-shot, which he believed real – the young are rash – irritated him. The night and the spot were full of contradictions. It was impossible to say who in this shadowy warfare was to be an enemy, and who were the allies. So close were the contacts issuing from this complication of a yachting voyage that he seemed to have them all within his breast.

'Shoot me! He is quite up to that trick – damn him. Yet I would trust him sooner than any man in that yacht.'

Such were his thoughts while he looked at Carter, who was biting his lips, in the vexation of the long silence. When they spoke again to each other they talked soberly, with a sense of relief, as if they had come into cool air from an overheated room and when Carter, dismissed, went into his boat, he had practically agreed to the line of action traced by Lingard for the crew of the yacht. He had agreed as if in implicit confidence. It was one of the absurdities of the situation which had to be accepted and could never be understood.

'Do I talk straight now?' had asked Lingard.

'It seems straight enough,' assented Carter with an air of reserve; 'I will work with you so far anyhow.'

'Mrs Travers trusts me,' remarked Lingard again.

'By the Lord Harry!' cried Carter, giving way suddenly to some latent conviction. 'I was warning her against you. Say, Captain, you are a devil of a man. How did you manage it?'

'I trusted her,' said Lingard.

'Did you?' cried the amazed Carter. 'When? How? Where –'

'You know too much already,' retorted Lingard, quietly. 'Waste no time. I will be after you.'

Carter whistled low.

'There's a pair of you I can't make out,' he called back, hurrying over the side.

Shaw took this opportunity to approach. Beginning with hesitation: 'A word with you, sir,' the mate went on to say he was a respectable man. He delivered himself in a ringing, unsteady voice. He was married, he had children, he abhorred illegality. The light played about his obese figure, he had flung his mushroom hat on the deck, he was not afraid to speak the truth. The grey moustache stood out aggressively, his glances were uneasy; he pressed his hands to his stomach convulsively, opened his thick, short arms wide, wished it to be understood he had been chief-officer of home ships, with a spotless character and he hoped 'quite up to his work'. He was a peaceable man, none more; disposed to stretch a point when it 'came to a difference with niggers of some kind – they had to be taught manners and reason' and he was not averse at a pinch to – but here were white people – gentlemen, ladies, not to speak of the crew. He had never spoken to a superior like this before, and this was prudence, his conviction, a point of view, a point of principle, a conscious superiority and a burst of resentment hoarded through years against all the successive and unsatisfactory captains of his existence. There never had been such an opportunity to show he could not be put upon. He had one of them on a string and he was going to lead him a dance. There was courage, too, in it, since he believed himself fallen unawares into the clutches of a particularly desperate man and beyond the reach of law.

A certain small amount of calculation entered the audacity of his remonstrance. Perhaps – it flashed upon him – the yacht's gentry will hear I stood up for them. This could conceivably be of advantage to a man who wanted a lift in the world. 'Owner of a yacht – badly scared – a gentleman – money nothing to him.' Thereupon Shaw declared with heat that he couldn't be an accessory either after or before the fact. Those that never went home – who had nothing to go to perhaps – he interjected, hurriedly, could do as they liked. He couldn't. He had a wife, a family, a little house – paid for – with difficulty. He followed the sea respectably out and home, all regular, not vagabonding here and there, chumming with the first nigger that came along and laying traps for his betters.

One of the two flare bearers sighed at his elbow, and shifted his weight to the other foot.

These two had been keeping so perfectly still that the movement was as startling as if a statue had changed its pose. After looking at the offender with cold malevolence, Shaw went on to speak of law courts, of trials, and of the liberty of the subject; then he pointed out the certitude and the inconvenience of being found out, affecting for the moment the dispassionateness of wisdom.

'There will be fifteen years in gaol at the end of this job for everybody,' said Shaw, 'and I have a boy that don't know his father yet. Fine things for him to learn when he grows up. The innocent are dead certain to catch it along with you. The missus will break her heart unless she starves first. Home sold up.'

He saw a mysterious iniquity in a dangerous relation to himself and began to lose his head. What he really wanted was to have his existence left intact, for his own cherishing and pride. It was a moral aspiration, but in his alarm the native grossness of his nature came clattering out like a devil out of a trap. He would blow the gaff, split, give away the whole show, he would back up honest people, kiss the book, say what he thought, let all the world know ... and when he paused to draw breath, all around him was silent and still. Before the impetus of that respectable passion his words were scattered like chaff driven by a gale and rushed headlong into the night of the Shallows. And in the great obscurity, imperturbable, it heard him say he 'washed his hands of everything'.

'And the brig?' asked Lingard, suddenly.

Shaw was checked. For a second the seaman in him instinctively admitted the claim of the ship.

'The brig. The brig. She's right enough,' he mumbled. He had nothing to say against the brig – not he. She wasn't like the big ships he was used to, but of her kind the best craft he ever ... And with a brusque return upon himself, he protested that he had been decoyed on board under false pretences. It was as bad as being shanghaied when in liquor. It was – upon his soul. And into a craft next thing to a pirate! That was the name for it or his own name was not Shaw. He said this glaring owlishly. Lingard, perfectly still and mute, bore the blows without a sign.

The silly fuss of that man seared his very soul. There was no end to this plague of fools coming to him from the forgotten ends of the earth. A fellow like that could not be told. No one could be told. Blind they came and blind they would go out. He admitted reluctantly, but without doubt, that as if pushed by a force from outside he would have to try and save two of them. To this end he foresaw the probable need of leaving his brig for a time. He would have to leave her with that man. The mate. He had engaged him himself – to make his insurance valid – to be able sometimes to speak – to have near him. Who would have believed such a fool-man could exist on the face of the sea! Who? Leave the brig with him. The brig!

Ever since sunset, the breeze kept off by the heat of the day had been trying to re-establish in the darkness its sway over the Shoals. Its approaches had been heard in the night, its patient murmurs, its foiled sighs; but now a surprisingly heavy puff came in a free rush such as if, far away there to the northward, the last defence of the calm had been victoriously carried. The flames borne down streamed bluishly, horizontal and noisy at the end of tall sticks, like fluttering pennants; and behold, the shadows on the deck went mad and jostled each other as if trying to escape from a doomed craft, the darkness, held up dome-like by the brilliant glare, seemed to tumble headlong upon the brig in an overwhelming downfall, the men stood swaying as if ready to fall under the ruins of a black and noiseless disaster. The blurred outlines of the brig, the masts, the rigging, seemed to shudder in the terror of coming extinction – and then the darkness leaped upward again, the shadows returned to their places, the men were seen distinct, swarthy, with calm faces, with glittering eyeballs. The destruction in the breath had passed, was gone.

A discord of three voices raised together in a drawling wail trailed on the sudden immobility of the air.

'Brig ahoy! Give us a rope!'

The first boat-load from the yacht emerged floating slowly into the pool of purple light wavering round the brig on the black water. Two men squeezed in the bows pulled uncomfortably; in the middle, on a heap of seamen's canvas bags, another sat, insecure, propped with both arms, stiff-legged, angularly helpless. The light from the poop brought everything out in lurid detail, and the boat floating slowly toward the brig had a suspicious and pitiful aspect. The shabby load lumbering her looked somehow as if it had been stolen by those men who resembled castaways. In the stern-sheets, Carter, standing up, steered with his leg. He had a smile of youthful sarcasm.

'Here they are!' he cried to Lingard. 'You've got your own way, Captain. I thought I had better come myself with the first precious lot –'

'Pull around the stern. The brig's on the swing,' interrupted Lingard.

'Aye, aye. We'll try not to smash the brig. We would be lost indeed if – fend off there, John; fend off, old reliable, if you care a pin for your salty hide. I like the old chap,' he said, when he stood by Lingard's side looking down at the boat which was being rapidly cleared by whites and Malays working shoulder to shoulder in silence. 'I like him. He don't belong to that yachting lot either. They picked him up on the road somewhere. Look at the old dog – carved out of a ship's timber – as talkative as a fish – grim as a gutted wreck. That's the man for me. All the others there are married, or going to be, or ought to be, or sorry they ain't. Every man jack of them has a petticoat in tow – dash me! Never heard in all my travels such a jabber about wives and kids. Hurry up with your dunnage – below there! Aye! I had no difficulty in getting them to clear out from the yacht. They never saw a pair of gents stolen before – you understand. It upset all their little notions of what a stranding means, hereabouts. Not that mine aren't mixed a bit, too – and yet I've seen a thing or two.'

His excitement was revealed in this boyish impulse to talk.

'Look,' he said, pointing at the growing pile of bags and bedding on the brig's quarter-deck. 'Look. Don't they mean to sleep soft – and dream of home – maybe. Home. Think of that, Captain. These chaps can't get clear away from it. It isn't like you and me –'

Lingard made a movement.

'I ran away myself when so high. My old man's a Trinity pilot. That's a job worth staying at home for. Mother writes sometimes, but they can't miss me much. There's fourteen of us altogether – eight at home yet. No fear of the old country ever getting undermanned – let die who must. Only let it be a fair game, Captain. Let's have a fair show.'

Lingard assured him briefly he should have it. That was the very reason he wanted the yacht's crew in the brig, he added. Then quiet and grave he inquired whether that pistol was still in Carter's pocket.

'Never mind that,' said the young man, hurriedly. 'Remember who began. To be shot at wouldn't rile me so much – it's being threatened, don't you see, that was heavy on my chest. Last night is very far off though – and I will be hanged if I know what I meant exactly when I took the old thing from its nail. There. More I can't say till all's settled one way or another. Will that do?'

Flushing brick red, he suspended his judgement and stayed his hand with the generosity of youth.

*

Apparently it suited Lingard to be reprieved in that form. He bowed his head slowly. It would do. To leave his life to that youngster's ignorance seemed to redress the balance of his mind against a lot of secret intentions. It was distasteful and bitter as an expiation should be. He also held a life in his hand; a life, and many deaths besides, but these were like one single feather in the scales of his conscience. That he should feel so was unavoidable because his strength would at no price permit itself to be wasted. It would not be – and there was an end to it. All he could do was to throw in another risk into the sea of risks. Thus was he enabled to recognize that a drop of water in the ocean makes a great difference. His very desire, unconquered, but exiled, had left the place where he could constantly hear its voice. He saw it, he saw himself, the past, the future, he saw it all, shifting and indistinct like those shapes the strained eye of a wanderer outlines in darker strokes upon the face of the night.

10

WHEN Lingard went to his boat to follow Carter, who had gone back to the yacht, Wasub, mast and sail on shoulder, preceded him down the ladder. The old man leaped in smartly and busied himself in getting the dinghy ready for his commander.

In that little boat Lingard was accustomed to traverse the Shallows alone. She had a short mast and a lug-sail, carried two easily, floated in a few inches of water. In her he was independent of a crew, and, if the wind failed, could make his way with a pair of sculls taking short cuts over shoal places. There were so many islets and sandbanks that in case of sudden bad weather there was always a lee to be found, and when he wished to land he could pull her up a beach, striding ahead, painter in hand, like a giant child dragging a toy boat. When the brig was anchored within the Shallows it was in her that he visited the lagoon. Once, when caught by a sudden freshening of the sea-breeze, he had waded up a shelving bank carrying her on his head and for two days they had rested together on the sand, while around them the shallow waters raged lividly, and across three miles of foam the brig would time after time dissolve in the mist and re-appear distinct, nodding her tall spars that seemed to touch a weeping sky of lamentable greyness.

Whenever he came into the lagoon tugging with bare arms, Jörgenson, who would be watching the entrance of the creek ever since a muffled detonation of a gun to seaward had warned him of the brig's arrival on the Shore of Refuge, would mutter to himself – 'Here's Tom coming in his nutshell.' And indeed she was in shape somewhat like half a nutshell and also in the colour of her dark varnished planks. The man's shoulders and head rose high above her gunwales; loaded with Lingard's heavy frame she would climb sturdily the steep ridges, slide squatting into the hollows of the sea, or, now and then, take a sedate leap over a short wave. Her behaviour had a stout trustworthiness about it, and she reminded one of a sure-footed mountain-pony carrying over difficult ground a rider much bigger than himself.

Wasub wiped the thwarts, ranged the mast and sail along the side, shipped the rowlocks. Lingard looked down at his old servant's spare shoulders upon which the light from above fell unsteady but vivid. Wasub worked for the comfort of his commander and his single-minded absorption in that task flashed upon Lingard the consolation of an act of friendliness. The elderly Malay at last lifted his head with a deferential murmur; his wrinkled old face with half a dozen wiry hairs pendulous at each corner of the dark lips expressed a kind of weary satisfaction, and the slightly oblique worn eyes stole a discreet upward glance containing a hint of some remote meaning. Lingard found himself compelled by the justice of that obscure claim to murmur as he stepped into the boat:

'These are times of danger.'

He sat down and took up the sculls. Wasub held on to the gunwale as to a last hope of a further confidence. He had served in the brig five years. Lingard remembered that very well. This aged figure had been intimately associated with the brig's life and with his own, appearing silently ready for every incident and emergency in an unquestioning expectation of orders; symbolic of blind trust in his strength, of an unlimited obedience to his will. Was it unlimited?

'We shall require courage and fidelity,' added Lingard, in a tentative tone.

'There are those who know me,' snapped the old man, readily, as if the words had been waiting for a long time. 'Observe, Tuan. I have filled with fresh water the little breaker in the bows.'

'I know you, too,' said Lingard.

'And the wind – and the sea,' ejaculated the *serang*, jerkily. 'These also are faithful to the strong. By Allah ! I who am a pilgrim and have listed to words of wisdom in many places, I tell you, Tuan, there is strength in the knowledge of what is hidden in things without life, as well as in the living men. Will Tuan be gone long?'

'I come back in a short time – together with the rest of the whites from over there. This is the beginning of many stratagems. Wasub ! Daman, the son of a dog, has suddenly made prisoners two of my own people. My face is made black.'

'*Tse* ! *Tse* ! What ferocity is that ! One should not offer shame to a friend or to a friend's brother lest revenge come sweeping like a flood. Yet can an Illanun chief be other than tyrannical? My old eyes have seen much but they never saw a tiger change its stripes. *Ya-wa* ! The tiger can not. This is the wisdom of us ignorant Malay men. The wisdom of white Tuans is great. They think that by the power of many speeches the tiger may –' He broke off and in a crisp, busy tone said: 'The rudder dwells safely under the aftermost seat should Tuan be pleased to sail the

boat. This breeze will not die away before sunrise.' Again his
voice changed as if two different souls had been flitting in and
out of his body. 'No, no, kill the tiger and then the stripes may
be counted without fear – one by one, thus.'

He pointed a frail brown finger and, abruptly, made a mirthless dry sound as if a rattle had been sprung in his throat.

'The wretches are many,' said Lingard.

'Nay, Tuan. They follow their great men even as we in the
brig follow you. That is right.'

Lingard reflected for a moment.

'My men will follow me then,' he said.

'They are poor *calashes* without sense,' commented Wasub
with pitying superiority. 'Some with no more comprehension
than men of the bush freshly caught. There is Sali, the foolish
son of my sister and by your great favour appointed to mind
the tiller of this ship. His stupidity is extreme, but his eyes are
good – nearly as good as mine that by praying and much exercise
can see far into the night.'

Lingard laughed low and then looked earnestly at the *serang*.
Above their heads a man shook a flare over the side and a thin
shower of sparks floated downward and expired before touching
the water.

'So you can see in the night, *O Serang*! Well, then, look and
speak. Speak! Fight – or no fight? Weapons or words? Which
folly? Well, what do you see?'

'A darkness, a darkness,' whispered Wasub at last in a frightened tone. 'There are nights –' He shook his head and muttered.
'Look. The tide has turned. *Ya*, Tuan. The tide has turned.'

Lingard looked downward where the water could be seen,
gliding past the ship's side, moving smoothly, streaked with lines
of froth, across the illuminated circle thrown round the brig by
the lights on her poop. Air bubbles sparkled, lines of darkness,
ripples of glitter, appeared, glided, went astern without a splash,
without a trickle, without a plaint, without a break. The unchecked gentleness of the flow captured the eye by a subtle spell,
fastened insidiously upon the mind a disturbing sense of the ir-
retrievable. The ebbing of the sea athwart the lonely sheen of
flames resembled the eternal ebb-tide of time; and when at last

Lingard looked up, the knowledge of that noiseless passage of the waters produced on his mind a bewildering effect. For a moment the speck of light lost in vast obscurity the brig, the boat, the hidden coast, the Shallows, the very walls and roof of darkness – the seen and the unseen alike seemed to be gliding smoothly onward through the enormous gloom of space. Then, with a great mental effort, he brought everything to a sudden standstill; and only the froth and bubbles went on streaming past ceaselessly, unchecked by the power of his will.

'The tide has turned – you say, *Serang*? Has it –? Well, perhaps it has, perhaps it has,' he finished, muttering to himself.

'Truly it has. Can not Tuan see it run under his own eyes?' said Wasub with an alarmed earnestness. 'Look. Now it is in my mind that a *prau* coming from amongst the southern islands, if steered cunningly in the free set of the current, would approach the bows of this, our brig, drifting silently as a shape without a substance.'

'And board suddenly – is that it?' said Lingard.

'Daman is crafty and the Illanuns are very blood-thirsty. Night is nothing to them. They are certainly valorous. Are they not born in the midst of fighting and are they not inspired by the evil of their hearts even before they can speak? And their chiefs would be leading them while you, Tuan, are going from us even now –'

'You don't want me to go?' asked Lingard.

For a time Wasub listened attentively to the profound silence.

'Can we fight without a leader?' he began again. 'It is the belief in victory that gives courage. And what would poor *calashes* do, sons of peasants and fishermen, freshly caught – without knowledge? They believe in your strength – and in your power – or else – Will those whites that came so suddenly avenge you? They are here like fish within the stakes. *Ya-wa*! Who will bring the news and who will come to find the truth and perchance to carry off your body? You go alone, Tuan!'

'There must be no fighting. It would be a calamity,' insisted Lingard. 'There is blood that must not be spilt.'

'Hear, Tuan!' exclaimed Wasub with heat. 'The waters are running out now.' He punctuated his speech by slight jerks at

the dinghy. 'The waters go and at the appointed time they shall
return. And if between their going and coming the blood of all
the men in the world were poured into it, the sea would not rise
higher at the full by the breadth of my finger nail.'

'But the world would not be the same. You do not see that,
Serang. Give the boat a good shove.'

'Directly,' said the old Malay and his face became impassive.
'Tuan knows when it is best to go, and death sometimes re-
treats before a firm tread like a startled snake. Tuan should take
a follower with him, not a silly youth, but one who has lived –
who has a steady heart – who would walk close behind watchfully – and quietly. Yes. Quietly and with quick eyes – like mine
– perhaps with a weapon – I know how to strike.'

Lingard looked at the wrinkled visage very near his own and
into the peering old eyes. They shone strangely. A tense eagerness was expressed in the squatting figure leaning out toward
him. On the other side, within reach of his arm, the night stood
like a wall – discouraging – opaque – impenetrable. No help
would avail. The darkness he had to combat was too impalpable
to be cleft by a blow – too dense to be pierced by the eye; yet as if
by some enchantment in the words that made this vain offer of
fidelity, it became less overpowering to his sight, less crushing
to his thought. He had a moment of pride which soothed his
heart for the space of two beats. His unreasonable and misjudged
heart, shrinking before the menace of failure, expanded freely
with a sense of generous gratitude. In the threatening dimness
of his emotions this man's offer made a point of clearness, the
glimmer of a torch held aloft in the night. It was priceless, no
doubt, but ineffectual; too small, too far, too solitary. It did not
dispel the mysterious obscurity that had descended upon his
fortunes so that his eyes could no longer see the work of his
hands. The sadness of defeat pervaded the world.

'And what could you do, O Wasub?' he said.

'I could always call out – "Take care, Tuan".'

'And then for these charm-words of mine. Hey? Turn danger
aside? What? But perchance you would die all the same.
Treachery is a strong magic, too – as you said.'

'Yes, indeed! The order might come to your servant. But I –
Wasub – the son of a free man, a follower of Rajahs, a fugitive,
a slave, a pilgrim – diver for pearls, *serang* of white men's ships,
I have had too many masters. Too many. You are the last.' After
a silence he said in an almost indifferent voice: 'If you go, Tuan,
let us go together.'

For a time Lingard made no sound.

'No use,' he said at last. 'No use, *Serang*. One life is enough
to pay for a man's folly – and you have a household.'

'I have two – Tuan; but it is a long time since I sat on the
ladder of a house to talk at ease with neighbours. Yes. Two
households; one in –' Lingard smiled faintly. 'Tuan, let me
follow you.'

'No. You have said it, *Serang* – I am alone. That is true, and
alone I shall go on this very night. But first I must bring all the
white people here. Push.'

'Ready, Tuan? Look out!'

Wasub's body swung over the sea with extended arms. Lingard
caught up the sculls, and as the dinghy darted away from the
brig's side he had a complete view of the lighted poop – Shaw
leaning massively over the taffrail in sulky dejection, the flare
bearers erect and rigid, the heads along the rail, the eyes staring
after him above the bulwarks. The fore-end of the brig was
wrapped in a lurid and sombre mistiness; the sullen mingling of
darkness and of light; her masts pointing straight up could be
tracked by torn gleams and vanished above as if the trucks had
been tall enough to pierce the heavy mass of vapours motionless
overhead. She was beautifully precious. His loving eyes saw her
floating at rest in a wavering halo, between an invisible sky and
an invisible sea, like a miraculous craft suspended in the air. He
turned his head away as if the sight had been too much for him
at the moment of separation, and, as soon as his little boat had
passed beyond the limit of the light thrown upon the water, he
perceived very low in the black void of the west the stern lantern
of the yacht shining feebly like a star about to set, unattainable,
infinitely remote – belonging to another universe.

PART FOUR

THE GIFT OF THE SHALLOWS

I

Lingard brought Mrs Travers away from the yacht, going alone with her in the little boat. During the bustle of the embarkment, and till the last of the crew had left the schooner, he had remained towering and silent by her side. It was only when the murmuring and uneasy voices of the sailors going away in the boats had been completely lost in the distance that his voice was heard, grave in the silence, pronouncing the words – 'Follow me.' She followed him; their footsteps rang hollow and loud on the empty deck. At the bottom of the steps he turned round and said very low:

'Take care.'

He got into the boat and held on. It seemed to him that she was intimidated by the darkness. She felt her arm gripped firmly – 'I've got you,' he said. She stepped in, headlong, trusting herself blindly to his grip, and sank on the stern seat catching her breath a little. She heard a slight splash, and the indistinct side of the deserted yacht melted suddenly into the body of the night.

Rowing, he faced her, a hooded and cloaked shape, and above her head he had before his eyes the gleam of the stern lantern expiring slowly on the abandoned vessel. When it went out without a warning flicker he could see nothing of the stranded yacht's outline. She had vanished utterly like dream; and the occurrences of the last twenty-four hours seemed also to be a part of a vanished dream. The hooded and cloaked figure was part of it, too. It spoke not; it moved not; it would vanish presently. Lingard tried to remember Mrs Travers' features, even as she sat within two feet of him in the boat. He seemed to have taken from that vanished schooner not a woman but a memory – the tormenting recollection of a human being he would see no more.

At every stroke of the short sculls Mrs Travers felt the boat leap forward with her. Lingard, to keep his direction, had to look

175

over his shoulder frequently – 'You will be safe in the brig,' he said. She was silent. A dream! A dream! He lay back vigorously; the water slapped loudly against the blunt bows. The ruddy glow thrown afar by the flares was reflected deep within the hood. The dream had a pale visage, the memory had living eyes.

'I had to come for you myself,' he said.

'I expected it of you.' These were the first words he had heard her say since they had met for the third time.

'And I swore – before you, too – that I would never put my foot on board your craft.'

'It was good of you to –' she began.

'I forgot somehow,' he said, simply.

'I expected it of you,' she repeated. He gave three quick strokes before he asked very gently:

'What more do you expect?'

'Everything,' she said. He was rounding then the stern of the brig and had to look away. Then he turned to her.

'And you trust me to –' he exclaimed.

'I would like to trust you,' she interrupted, 'because –'

Above them a startled voice cried in Malay, 'Captain coming.' The strange sound silenced her. Lingard laid in his sculls and she saw herself gliding under the high side of the brig. A dark, staring face appeared very near her eyes, black fingers caught the gunwale of the boat. She stood up swaying. 'Take care,' said Lingard again, but this time, in the light, did not offer to help her. She went up alone and he followed her over the rail.

The quarter-deck was thronged by men of two races. Lingard and Mrs Travers crossed it rapidly between the groups that moved out of the way on their passage. Lingard threw open the cabin door for her, but remained on deck to inquire about his boats. They had returned while he was on board the yacht, and the two men in charge of them came aft to make their reports. The boat sent north had seen nothing. The boat which had been directed to explore the banks and islets to the south had actually been in sight of Daman's *praus*. The man in charge reported that several fires were burning on the shore, the crews of the two *praus* being encamped on a sandbank. Cooking was going on. They had been near enough to hear the voices. There was a man keeping watch on the ridge; they knew this because they heard him shouting to the people below, by the fires. Lingard wanted to know how they had managed to remain unseen. 'The night was our hiding place,' answered the man in his deep growling voice. He knew nothing of any white men being in Daman's camp. Why should there be? Rajah Hassim and the Lady, his sister, appeared unexpectedly near his boat in their canoe. Rajah Hassim had ordered him then in whispers to go back to the brig at once, and tell Tuan what he had observed. Rajah Hassim said also that he would return to the brig with more news very soon. He obeyed because the Rajah was to him a person of authority, 'having the perfect knowledge of Tuan's mind as we all know.' – 'Enough,' cried Lingard, suddenly.

The man looked up heavily for a moment, and retreated forward without another word. Lingard followed him with irritated eyes. A new power had come into the world, had possessed itself of human speech, had imparted to it a sinister irony of allusion. To be told that someone had 'a perfect knowledge of his mind' startled him and made him wince. It made him aware that now he did not know his mind himself – that it seemed impossible for him ever to regain that knowledge. And the new power not only had cast its spell upon the words he had to hear, but also upon the facts that assailed him, upon the people he saw, upon the thoughts he had to guide, upon the feelings he had to bear. They remained what they had ever been – the visible surface of life open in the sun to the conquering tread of an unfettered will. Yesterday they could have been discerned clearly, mastered and despised; but now another power had come into the world, and had cast over them all the wavering gloom of a dark and inscrutable purpose.

2

RECOVERING himself with a slight start Lingard gave the order to extinguish all the lights in the brig. Now the transfer of the crew from the yacht had been effected there was every advantage in the darkness. He gave the order from instinct, it being the right thing to do in the circumstances. His thoughts were in the cabin of his brig, where there was a woman waiting. He put his hand over his eyes, collecting himself as if before a great mental effort. He could hear about him the excited murmurs of the white men whom in the morning he had so ardently desired to have safe in his keeping. He had them there now; but accident, ill-luck, a cursed folly, had tricked him out of the success of his plan. He would have to go in and talk to Mrs Travers. The idea dismayed him. Of necessity he was not one of those men who have the mastery of expression. To liberate his soul was for him a gigantic undertaking, a matter of desperate effort, of doubtful success. 'I must have it out with her,' he murmured to himself as though at the prospect of a struggle. He was uncertain of everything and everybody; but he was very certain he wanted to look at her.

At the moment he turned to the door of the cabin both flares went out together and the black vault of the night upheld above the brig by the fierce flames fell behind him and buried the deck in sudden darkness. The buzz of strange voices instantly hummed louder with a startled note. 'Hallo!' – 'Can't see a mortal thing' – 'Well, what next?' – insisted a voice – 'I want to know what next?'

Lingard checked himself ready to open the door and waited absurdly for the answer as though in the hope of some suggestion. 'What's up with you? Think yourself lucky,' said somebody. – 'It's all very well – for tonight,' began the voice. – 'What are you fashing yourself for?' remonstrated the other, reasonably, 'we'll get home right enough.' – 'I am not so sure; the second mate he says –' 'Never mind what he says; that 'ere man who has got this brig will see us through. The owner's wife will talk to him – she will. Money can do a lot.' The two voices came nearer, and spoke more distinctly, close behind Lingard. 'Suppose them blooming savages set fire to the yacht. What's to prevent them?' – 'And suppose they do. This 'ere brig's good enough to get away in. Ain't she? Guns and all. We'll get home yet all right. What do you say, John?'

'I say nothing and care less,' said a third voice, peaceful and faint.

'D'you mean to say, John, you would go to the bottom as soon as you would go home? Come now!' – 'To the bottom,' repeated the wan voice, composedly. 'Aye! That's where we all are going to, in one way or another. The way don't matter.'

'Ough! You would give the blues to the funny man of a blooming circus. What would my missus say if I wasn't to turn up never at all?' – 'She would get another man; there's always plenty of fools about.' A quiet and mirthless chuckle was heard in the pause of shocked silence. Lingard, with his hand on the door, remained still. Further off a growl burst out: 'I do hate to be chucked in the dark aboard a strange ship. I wonder where they keep their fresh water. Can't get any sense out of them silly niggers. We don't seem to be more account here than a lot of cattle. Likely as not we'll have to berth on this blooming quarter-deck for God knows how long.' Then again very near Lingard the first voice said, deadened discreetly – 'There's something curious about this here brig turning up sudden-like, ain't there? And that skipper of her – now? What kind of a man is he – anyhow?'

'Oh, he's one of them skippers going about loose. The brig's his own, I am thinking. He just goes about in her looking for what he may pick up honest or dishonest. My brother-in-law has served two commissions in these seas, and was telling me awful yarns about what's going on in them God-forsaken parts. Likely he lied, though. Them man-of-war's men are a holy terror for yarns. Bless you, what do I care who this skipper is? Let him do his best and don't trouble your head. You won't see him again in your life once we get clear.'

'And can he do anything for the owner?' asked the first voice again. – 'Can he! *We* can do nothing – that's one thing certain. The owner may be lying clubbed to death this very minute for all we know. By all accounts these savages here are a crool murdering lot. Mind you, I am sorry for him as much as anybody.' 'Aye, aye,' muttered the other, approvingly. – 'He may not have been ready, poor man,' began again the reasonable voice. Lingard heard a deep sigh. – 'If there's anything as can be done for him, the owner's wife she's got to fix it up with this 'ere skipper. Under Providence he may serve her turn.'

Lingard flung open the cabin door, entered, and, with a slam, shut the darkness out.

'I am, under Providence, to serve your turn,' he said after standing very still for a while, with his eyes upon Mrs Travers. The brig's swing-lamp lighted the cabin with an extraordinary brilliance. Mrs Travers had thrown back her hood. The radiant brightness of the little place enfolded her so close, clung to her with such force that it might have been part of her very essence. There were no shadows on her face; it was fiercely lighted, hermetically closed, of impenetrable fairness.

Lingard looked in unconscious ecstasy at this vision, so amazing that it seemed to have strayed into his existence from beyond the limits of the conceivable. It was impossible to guess her thoughts, to know her feelings, to understand her grief or her joy. But she knew all that was at the bottom of his heart. He had told her himself, impelled by a sudden thought, going to her in darkness, in desperation, in absurd hope, in incredible trust. He had told her what he had told no one on earth, except perhaps, at times, himself, but without words – less clearly. He had told her and she had listened in silence. She had listened leaning over the rail till at last her breath was on his forehead. He remembered this and had a moment of soaring pride and of unutterable dismay. He spoke, with an effort.

'You've heard what I said just now? Here I am.'

'Do you expect me to say something?' she asked. 'Is it necessary? Is it possible?'

'No,' he answered. 'It is said already. I know what you expect from me. Everything.'

'Everything,' she repeated, paused, and added much lower, 'It is the very least.' He seemed to lose himself in thought.

'It is extraordinary,' he reflected half aloud, 'how I dislike that man.' She leaned forward a little.

'Remember those two men are innocent,' she began.

'So am I – innocent. So is everybody in the world. Have you

ever met a man or a woman that was not? They've got to take their chances all the same.'

'I expect you to be generous,' she said.

'To you?'

'Well – to me. Yes – if you like to me alone.'

'To you alone! And you know everything!' His voice dropped. 'You want your happiness.'

She made an impatient movement and he saw her clench the hand that was lying on the table.

'I want my husband back,' she said, sharply.

'Yes. Yes. It's what I was saying. Same thing,' he muttered with strange placidity. She looked at him searchingly. He had a large simplicity that filled one's vision. She found herself slowly invaded by this masterful figure. He was not mediocre. Whatever he might have been he was not mediocre. The glamour of a lawless life stretched over him like the sky over the sea down on all sides to an unbroken horizon. Within, he moved very lonely, dangerous and romantic. There was in him crime, sacrifice, tenderness, devotion, and the madness of a fixed idea. She thought with wonder that of all the men in the world he was indeed the one she knew best and yet she could not foresee the speech or the act of the next minute. She said distinctly:

'You've given me your confidence. Now I want you to give me the life of these two men. The life of two men whom you do not know, whom tomorrow you will forget. It can be done. It must be done. You cannot refuse them to me.' She waited.

'Why can't I refuse?' he whispered, gloomily, without looking up.

'You ask!' she exclaimed. He made no sign. He seemed at a loss for words.

'You ask ... Ah!' she cried. 'Don't you see that I have no kingdoms to conquer?'

3

A SLIGHT change of expression which passed away almost directly showed that Lingard heard the passionate cry wrung from her by the distress of her mind. He made no sign. She perceived clearly the extreme difficulty of her position. The situation was dangerous; not so much the facts of it as the feeling of it. At times it appeared no more actual than a tradition; and she thought of herself as of some woman in a ballad, who has to beg for the lives of innocent captives. To save the lives of Mr Travers and Mr d'Alcacer was more than a duty. It was a necessity, it was an imperative need, it was an irresistible mission. Yet she had to reflect upon the horrors of a cruel and obscure death before she could feel for them the pity they deserved. It was when she looked at Lingard that her heart was wrung by an extremity of compassion. The others were pitiful, but he, the victim of his own extravagant impulses, appeared tragic, fascinating, and culpable. Lingard lifted his head. Whispers were heard at the door and Hassim followed by Immada entered the cabin.

Mrs Travers looked at Lingard, because of all the faces in the cabin his was the only one that was intelligible to her. Hassim began to speak at once, and when he ceased Immada's deep sigh was heard in the sudden silence. Then Lingard looked at Mrs Travers and said:

'The gentlemen are alive. Rajah Hassim here has seen them less than two hours ago, and so has the girl. They are alive and unharmed, so far. And now . . .'

He paused. Mrs Travers, leaning on her elbow, shaded her eyes under the glint of suspended thunderbolts.

'You must hate us,' she muttered.

'Hate you,' he repeated with, as she fancied, a tinge of disdain in his tone. 'No. I hate myself.'

'Why yourself?' she asked, very low.

'For not knowing my mind,' he answered. 'For not knowing

my mind. For not knowing what it is that's got hold of me since – since this morning. I was angry then ... Nothing but very angry ...'

'And now?' she murmured.

'I am ... unhappy,' he said. After a moment of silence which gave to Mrs Travers the time to wonder how it was that this man had succeeded in penetrating into the very depths of her compassion, he hit the table such a blow that all the heavy muskets seemed to jump a little.

Mrs Travers heard Hassim pronounce a few words earnestly and a moan of distress from Immada.

'I believed in you before you ... before you gave me your confidence,' she began. 'You could see that. Could you not?'

He looked at her fixedly. 'You are not the first that believed in me,' he said.

Hassim, lounging with his back against the closed door, kept his eyes on him watchfully and Immada's dark and sorrowful eyes rested on the face of the white woman. Mrs Travers felt as though she were engaged in a contest with them; in a struggle for the possession of that man's strength and of that man's devotion. When she looked up at Lingard she saw on his face – which should have been impassive or exalted, the face of a stern leader or the face of a pitiless dreamer – an expression of utter forgetfulness. He seemed to be tasting the delight of some profound and amazing sensation. And suddenly in the midst of her appeal to his generosity, in the middle of a phrase, Mrs Travers faltered, becoming aware that she was the object of his contemplation.

'Do not! Do not look at that woman!' cried Immada. 'O! Master – look away ...' Hassim threw one arm round the girl's neck. Her voice sank. 'Oh! Master – look at us.' Hassim, drawing her to himself, covered her lips with his hand. She struggled a little like a snared bird and submitted, hiding her face on his shoulder, very quiet, sobbing without noise.

'What do they say to you?' asked Mrs Travers with a faint and pained smile. 'What can they say? It is intolerable to think that their words which have no meaning for me may go straight to your heart ...'

'Look away,' whispered Lingard without making the slightest movement.

Mrs Travers sighed.

'Yes, it is very hard to think that I who want to touch you cannot make myself understood as well as they. And yet I speak the language of your childhood, the language of the man for whom there is no hope but in your generosity.'

He shook his head. She gazed at him anxiously for a moment. 'In your memories then,' she said, and was surprised by the expression of profound sadness that over-spread his attentive face.

'Do you know what I remember?' he said. 'Do you want to know?' She listened with slightly parted lips. 'I will tell you. Poverty, hard work – and death,' he went on, very quietly. 'And now I've told you, and you don't know. That's how it is between us. You talk to me – I talk to you – and we don't know.'

Her eyelids dropped.

'What can I find to say?' she went on. 'What can I do? I mustn't give in. Think! Amongst your memories there must be some face – some voice – some name, if nothing more. I can not believe that there is nothing but bitterness.'

'There's no bitterness,' he murmured.

'O! Brother, my heart is faint with fear,' whispered Immada. Lingard turned swiftly to that whisper.

'Then, they are to be saved,' exclaimed Mrs Travers. 'Ah, I knew ...'

'Bear thy fear in patience,' said Hassim, rapidly, to his sister.

'They are to be saved. You have said it,' Lingard pronounced aloud, suddenly. He felt like a swimmer who, in the midst of superhuman efforts to reach the shore, perceives that the undertow is taking him to sea. He would go with the mysterious current; he would go swiftly – and see the end, the fulfilment both blissful and terrible.

With this state of exaltation in which he saw himself in some incomprehensible way always victorious, whatever might befall, there was mingled a tenacity of purpose. He could not sacrifice his intention, the intention of years, the intention of his life; he could no more part with it and exist than he could cut out his heart and live. The adventurer held fast to his adventure which made him in his own sight exactly what he was.

He considered the problem with cool audacity, backed by a belief in his own power. It was not these two men he had to save; he had to save himself. And looked upon in this way the situation appeared familiar.

Hassim had told him the two white men had been taken by their captors to Daman's camp. The young Rajah, leaving his sister in the canoe, had landed on the sand and had crept to the very edge of light thrown by the fires by which the Illanuns were cooking. Daman was sitting apart by a larger blaze. Two *praus* rode in shallow water near the sandbank; on the ridge, a sentry walked watching the lights of the brig; the camp was full of quiet whispers. Hassim returned to his canoe, then he and his sister, paddling cautiously round the anchored *praus*, in which women's voices could be heard, approached the other end of the camp. The light of the big blaze there fell on the water and the canoe skirted it without a splash, keeping in the night. Hassim, landing for the second time, crept again close to the fires. Each *prau* had, according to the customs of the Illanun rovers when on a raiding expedition, a smaller war-boat and these being light and manageable were hauled up on the sand not far from the big blaze; they sat high on the shelving shore throwing heavy shadows. Hassim crept up toward the largest of them and then standing on tiptoe could look at the camp across the gunwales. The confused talking of the men was like the buzz of insects in a forest. A child wailed on board one of the *praus* and a woman hailed the shore shrilly. Hassim unsheathed his *kris* and held it in his hand.

Very soon – he said – he saw the two white men walking amongst the fires. They waved their arms and talked together, stopping from time to time; they approached Daman; and the short man with the hair on his face addressed him earnestly and at great length. Daman sat crosslegged upon a little carpet with an open Koran on his knees and chanted the versets swaying to and fro with his eyes shut.

The Illanun Chiefs reclining wrapped in cloaks on the ground raised themselves on their elbows to look at the whites. When the short white man finished speaking he gazed down at them for a while, then stamped his foot. He looked angry because no one understood him. Then suddenly he looked very sad; he covered his face with his hands; the tall man put his hand on the short man's shoulder and whispered into his ear. The dry wood of the fires crackled, the Illanuns slept, cooked, talked, but with their weapons at hand. An armed man or two came up to stare at the prisoners and then returned to their fire. The two whites sank down in the sand in front of Daman. Their clothes were soiled, there was sand in their hair. The tall man had lost his hat; the glass in the eye of the short man glittered very much; his back was muddy and one sleeve of his coat torn up to the elbow.

All this Hassim saw and then retreated undetected to that part of the shore where Immada waited for him, keeping the canoe afloat. The Illanuns, trusting to the sea, kept very bad watch of their prisoners, and had he been able to speak with them Hassim thought an escape could have been effected. But they could not have understood his signs and still less his words. He consulted with his sister. Immada murmured sadly; at their feet the ripple broke with a mournful sound no louder than their voices.

Hassim's loyalty was unshaken, but now it led him on not in the bright light of hopes but in the deepened shadow of doubt. He wanted to obtain information for his friend who was so powerful and who perhaps would know how to be constant. When followed by Immada he approached the camp again – this time openly – their appearance did not excite much surprise. It was well known to the Chiefs of the Illanuns that the Rajah for whom they were to fight – if God so willed – was upon the shoals looking out for the coming of the white man who had much wealth and a store of weapons and who was his servant. Daman, who alone understood the exact relation, welcomed them with impenetrable gravity. Hassim took his seat on the carpet at his right hand. A consultation was being held half aloud in short and apparently careless sentences, with long intervals of silence between. Immada, nestling close to her brother, leaned one arm on his shoulder and listened with serious attention and with outward calm as became a princess of Wajo accustomed to consort with warriors and statesmen in moments of danger and in the hours of deliberation. Her heart was beating rapidly, and facing her the silent white men stared at these two known faces, as if across a gulf. Four Illanun Chiefs sat in a row. Their ample cloaks fell from their shoulders, and lay behind them on the sand in which their four long lances were planted upright, each supporting a small oblong shield of wood, carved on the edges and stained a dull purple. Daman stretched out his arm and pointed at the prisoners. The faces of the white men were very quiet. Daman looked at them mutely and ardently, as if consumed by an unspeakable longing.

The Koran, in a silk cover, hung on his breast by a crimson cord. It rested over his heart and, just below the plain buffalo-horn handle of a *kris*, stuck into the twist of his *sarong*, protruded ready to his hand. The clouds thickening over the camp made the darkness press heavily on the glow of scattered fires. 'There is blood between me and the whites,' he pronounced, violently. The Illanun Chiefs remained impassive. There was blood between them and all mankind. Hassim remarked dispassionately that there was one white man with whom it would be wise to remain friendly; and besides, was not Daman his friend already? Daman smiled with half-closed eyes. He was that white man's friend, not his slave. The Illanuns playing with their sword-handles grunted assent. Why, asked Daman, did these strange whites travel so far from their country? The great white man whom they all knew did not want them. No one wanted them. Evil would follow in their footsteps. They were such men as are sent by rulers to examine the aspects of far-off countries and talk of peace and make treaties. Such is the beginning of great sorrows. The Illanuns were far from their country, where no white man dared to come, and therefore they were free to seek their enemies upon the open waters. They had found these two who had come to see. He asked what they had come to see? Was there nothing to look at in their own country?

He talked in an ironic and subdued tone. The scattered heaps of embers glowed a deeper red; the big blaze of the chief's fire sank low and grew dim before he ceased. Straight-limbèd figures rose, sank, moved, whispered on the beach. Here and there a spear-blade caught a red gleam above the black shape of a head.

'The Illanuns seek booty on the sea,' cried Daman. 'Their fathers and the fathers of their fathers have done the same, being fearless like those who embrace death closely.'

A low laugh was heard. 'We strike and go,' said an exulting voice. 'We live and die with our weapons in our hands.' The Illanuns leaped to their feet. They stamped on the sand, flourishing naked blades over the heads of their prisoners. A tumult arose.

When it subsided Daman stood up in a cloak that wrapped him to his feet and spoke again giving advice. The white men sat on the sand and turned their eyes from face to face as if trying to understand. It was agreed to send the prisoners into the lagoon where their fate would be decided by the ruler of the land. The Illanuns only wanted to plunder the ship. They did not care what became of the men. 'But Daman cares,' remarked Hassim to Lingard, when relating what took place. 'He cares, O Tuan !'

Hassim had learned also that the Settlement was in a state of unrest as if on the eve of war. Belarab with his followers was encamped by his father's tomb in the hollow beyond the cultivated fields. His stockade was shut up and no one appeared on the verandahs of the houses within. You could tell there were people inside only by the smoke of the cooking fires. Tengga's followers meantime swaggered about the Settlement behaving tyrannically to those who were peaceable. A great madness had descended upon the people, a madness strong as the madness of love, the madness of battle, the desire to spill blood. A strange fear also had made them wild. The big smoke seen that morning above the forests of the coast was some agreed signal from Tengga to Daman but what it meant Hassim had been unable to find out. He feared for Jörgenson's safety. He said that while one of the war-boats was being made ready to take the captives into the lagoon, he and his sister left the camp quietly and got away in their canoe. The flares of the brig, reflected in a faint loom upon the clouds, enabled them to make straight for the vessel across the banks. Before they had gone half way these flames went out and the darkness seemed denser than any he had known before. But it was no greater than the darkness of his mind – he added. He had looked upon the white men sitting unmoved and silent under the edge of swords; he had looked at Daman, he had heard bitter words spoken; he was looking now at his white friend – and the issue of events he could not see. One can see men's faces but their fate, which is written on their foreheads, one cannot see. He had no more to say, and what he had spoken was true in every word.

4

LINGARD repeated it all to Mrs Travers. Her courage, her intelligence, the quickness of her apprehension, the colour of her eyes and the intrepidity of her glance evoked in him an admiring enthusiasm. She stood by his side. Every moment that fatal illusion clung closer to his soul – like a garment of light – like an armour of fire.

He was unwilling to face the facts. All his life – till that day – had been a wrestle with events in the daylight of this world, but now he could not bring his mind to the consideration of his position. It was Mrs Travers who, after waiting awhile, forced on him the pain of thought by wanting to know what bearing Hassim's news had upon the situation.

Lingard had not the slightest doubt Daman wanted him to know what had been done with the prisoners. That is why Daman had welcomed Hassim, and let him hear the decision and had allowed him to leave the camp on the sandbank. There could be only one object in this; to let him, Lingard, know that the prisoners had been put out of his reach as long as he remained in his brig. Now this brig was his strength. To make him leave his brig was like removing his hand from his sword.

'Do you understand what I mean, Mrs Travers?' he asked.

'They are afraid of me because I know how to fight this brig. They fear the brig because when I am on board her, the brig and I are one. An armed man – don't you see? Without the brig I am disarmed, without me she can't strike. So Daman thinks. He does not know everything but he is not far off the truth. He says to himself that if I man the boats to go after these whites into the lagoon then his Illanuns will get the yacht for sure – and perhaps the brig as well. If I stop here with my brig he holds the two white men and can talk as big as he pleases. Belarab believes in me no doubt, but Daman trusts no man on earth. He simply does not know how to trust any one, because he is always plotting himself. He came to help me and as soon as he found I was not there he began to plot with Tengga. Now he has made a move – a clever move; a cleverer move than he thinks. Why? I'll tell you why. Because I, Tom Lingard, haven't a single white man aboard this brig I can trust. Not one. I only just discovered my mate's got the notion I am some kind of pirate. And all your yacht people think the same. It is as though you had brought a curse on me in your yacht. Nobody believes me. Good God! What have I come to! Even those two – look at them – I say look at them! By all the stars they doubt me! Me!...'

He pointed at Hassim and Immada. The girl seemed frightened. Hassim looked on calm and intelligent with inexhaustible patience. Lingard's voice fell suddenly.

'And by heavens they may be right. Who knows? You? Do you know? They have waited for years. Look. They are waiting with heavy hearts. Do you think that I don't care? Ought I to have kept it all in – told no one – no one – not even you? Are they waiting for what will never come now?'

Mrs Travers rose and moved quickly round the table. 'Can we give anything to this – this Daman or these other men? We could give them more than they could think of asking. I – my husband . . .'

'Don't talk to me of your husband,' he said, roughly. 'You don't know what you are doing.' She confronted the sombre anger of his eyes – 'But I must,' she asserted with heat. – 'Must,' he mused, noticing that she was only half a head less tall than

himself. 'Must! Oh, yes. Of course, you must. Must! Yes. But I
don't want to hear. Give! What can you give? You may have
all the treasures of the world for all I know. No! You can't give
anything...'

'I was thinking of your difficulty when I spoke,' she interrupted. His eyes wandered downward following the line of her
shoulder. – 'Of me – of me!' he repeated.

All this was said almost in whispers. The sound of slow footsteps was heard on deck above their heads. Lingard turned his
face to the open skylight.

'On deck there! Any wind?'

All was still for a moment. Somebody above answered in a
leisurely tone:

'A steady little draught from the northward.'

Then after a pause added in a mutter:

'Pitch dark.'

'Aye, dark enough,' murmured Lingard. He must do something. Now. At once. The world was waiting. The world full of
hopes and fear. What should he do? Instead of answering that
question he traced the ungleaming coils of her twisted hair and
became fascinated by a stray lock at her neck. What should he
do? No one to leave his brig to. The voice that had answered his
question was Carter's voice. 'He is hanging about keeping his
eye on me,' he said to Mrs Travers. She shook her head and tried
to smile. The man above coughed discreetly. 'No,' said Lingard,
'you must understand that you have nothing to give.' The man
on deck who seemed to have lingered by the skylight was heard
saying quietly, 'I am at hand if you want me, Mrs Travers.'
Hassim and Immada looked up. 'You see,' exclaimed Lingard.
'What did I tell you? He's keeping his eye on me! On board my
own ship. Am I dreaming? Am I in a fever? Tell him to come
down,' he said, after a pause. Mrs Travers did so and Lingard
thought her voice very commanding and very sweet. 'There's
nothing in the world I love so much as this brig,' he went on.
'Nothing in the world. If I lost her I would have no standing
room on the earth for my feet. You don't understand this. You
can't.'

Carter came in and shut the cabin door carefully. He looked with serenity at everyone in turn.

'All quiet?' asked Lingard.

'Quiet enough if you like to call it so,' he answered. 'But if you only put your head outside the door you'll hear them all on the quarter-deck snoring against each other, as if there were no wives at home and no pirates at sea.'

'Look here,' said Lingard. 'I found out that I can't trust my mate.'

'Can't you?' drawled Carter. 'I am not exactly surprised. I must say *he* does not snore but I believe it is because he is too crazy to sleep. He waylaid me on the poop just now and said something about evil communications corrupting good manners. Seems to me I've heard that before. Queer thing to say. He tried to make it out somehow that if he wasn't corrupt it wasn't your fault. As if this was any concern of mine. He's as mad as he's fat – or else he puts it on.' Carter laughed a little and leaned his shoulders against a bulkhead.

Lingard gazed at the woman who expected so much from him and in the light she seemed to shed he saw himself leading a column of armed boats to the attack of the Settlement. He could burn the whole place to the ground and drive every soul of them into the bush. He could! And there was a surprise, a shock, a vague horror at the thought of the destructive power of his will. He could give her ever so many lives. He had seen her yesterday, and it seemed to him he had been all his life waiting for her to make a sign. She was very still. He pondered a plan of attack. He saw smoke and flame – and next moment he saw himself alone amongst shapeless ruins with the whispers, with the sigh and moan of the Shallows in his ears. He shuddered, and shaking his head :

'No! I cannot give you all those lives!' he cried.

Then, before Mrs Travers could guess the meaning of this outburst, he declared that as the two captives must be saved he would go alone into the lagoon. He could not think of using force. 'You understand why,' he said to Mrs Travers and she whispered a faint 'Yes.' He would run the risk alone. His hope was in Belarab being able to see where his true interest lay. 'If I can only get at him I would soon make him see,' he mused aloud. 'Haven't I kept his power up for these two years past? And he knows it, too. He feels it.' Whether he would be allowed to reach Belarab was another matter. Lingard lost himself in deep thought. 'He would not dare,' he burst out. Mrs Travers listened with parted lips. Carter did not move a muscle of his youthful and self-possessed face; only when Lingard, turning suddenly, came up close to him and asked with a red flash of eyes and in a lowered voice, 'Could you fight this brig?' something like a smile made a stir amongst the hairs of his little fair moustache.

'Could I?' he said. 'I could try, anyhow.' He paused, and added hardly above his breath, 'For the lady – of course.'

Lingard seemed staggered as though he had been hit in the chest. 'I was thinking of the brig,' he said, gently.

'Mrs Travers would be on board,' retorted Carter.

'What! on board. Ah yes; on board. Where else?' stammered Lingard.

Carter looked at him in amazement. 'Fight! You ask!' he said, slowly. 'You just try me.'

'I shall,' ejaculated Lingard. He left the cabin calling out 'Serang!' A thin cracked voice was heard immediately answering 'Tuan!' and the door slammed to.

'You trust him, Mrs Travers?' asked Carter, rapidly.

'You do not – why?' she answered.

'I can't make him out. If he was another kind of man I would say he was drunk,' said Carter. 'Why is he here at all – he, and this brig of his? Excuse my boldness – but have you promised him anything?'

' I – I promised!' exclaimed Mrs Travers in a bitter tone which silenced Carter for a moment.

'So much the better,' he said at last. 'Let him show what he can do first and ...'

'Here! Take this,' said Lingard, who re-entered the cabin fumbling about his neck. Carter mechanically extended his hand.

'What's this for?' he asked, looking at a small brass key attached to a thin chain.

'Powder magazine. Trap door under the table. The man who has this key commands the brig while I am away. The *serang* understands. You have her very life in your hand there.'

Carter looked at the small key lying in his half-open palm.

'I was just telling Mrs Travers I didn't trust you – not altogether ...'

'I know all about it,' interrupted Lingard, contemptuously. 'You carry a blamed pistol in your pocket to blow my brains out – don't you? What's that to me? I am thinking of the brig. I think I know your sort. You will do.'

'Well, perhaps I might,' mumbled Carter, modestly.

'Don't be rash,' said Lingard, anxiously. 'If you've got to fight use your head as well as your hands. If there's a breeze fight under way. If they should try to board in a calm, trust to the small arms to hold them off. Keep your head and –' He looked intensely into Carter's eyes; his lips worked without a sound as though he had been suddenly struck dumb. 'Don't think about me. What's that to you who I am? Think of the ship,' he burst out. 'Don't let her go! – Don't let her go!' The passion in his voice impressed his hearers who for a time preserved a profound silence.

'All right,' said Carter at last. 'I will stick to your brig as though she were my own; but I would like to see clear through all this. Look here – you are going off somewhere? Alone, you said?'

'Yes. Alone.'

'Very well. Mind, then, that you don't come back with a crowd of those brown friends of yours – or by the Heavens above us I won't let you come within hail of your own ship. Am I to keep this key?'

'Captain Lingard,' said Mrs Travers suddenly. 'Would it not be better to tell him everything?'

'Tell him everything?' repeated Lingard. 'Everything! Yesterday it might have been done. Only yesterday! Yesterday, did I say? Only six hours ago – only six hours ago I had something to tell. You heard it. And now it's gone. Tell him! There's nothing to tell any more.' He remained for a time with bowed head, while before him Mrs Travers, who had begun a gesture of protest, dropped her arms suddenly. In a moment he looked up again.

'Keep the key,' he said, calmly, 'and when the time comes step forward and take charge. I am satisfied.'

'I would like to see clear through all this though,' muttered Carter again. 'And for how long are you leaving us, Captain?' Lingard made no answer. Carter waited awhile. 'Come, sir,' he urged. 'I ought to have some notion. What is it? Two, three days?' Lingard started.

'Days,' he repeated. 'Ah, days. What is it you want to know? Two ... three – what did the old fellow say – perhaps for life.' This was spoken so low that no one but Carter heard the last words. – 'Do you mean it?' he murmured. Lingard nodded. – 'Wait as long as you can – then go,' he said in the same hardly audible voice. 'Go where?' – 'Where you like, nearest port, any port.' – 'Very good. That's something plain at any rate,' commented the young man with imperturbable good humour.

'I go, O Hassim!' began Lingard and the Malay made a slow inclination of the head which he did not raise again till Lingard had ceased speaking. He betrayed neither surprise nor any other emotion while Lingard in a few concise and sharp sentences made him acquainted with his purpose to bring about single-handed the release of the prisoners. When Lingard had ended with the words: 'And you must find a way to help me in the time of trouble, O Rajah Hassim,' he looked up and said:

'Good. You never asked me for anything before.' He smiled at his white friend. There was something subtle in the smile and afterward an added firmness in the repose of the lips. Immada moved a step forward. She looked at Lingard with terror in her black and dilated eyes. She exclaimed in a voice whose vibration startled the hearts of all the hearers with an indefinable sense of alarm, 'He will perish, Hassim! He will perish alone!'

'No,' said Hassim. 'Thy fear is as vain tonight as it was at sunrise. He shall not perish alone.'

Her eyelids dropped slowly. From her veiled eyes the tears fell, vanishing in the silence. Lingard's forehead became furrowed by folds that seemed to contain an infinity of sombre thoughts. 'Remember, O Hassim, that when I promised you to take you back to your country you promised me to be a friend to all white men. A friend to all whites who are of my people, forever.'

'My memory is good, O Tuan,' said Hassim; 'I am not yet back in my country, but is not everyone the ruler of his own heart? Promises made by a man of noble birth live as long as the speaker endures.'

'Good-bye,' said Lingard to Mrs Travers. 'You will be safe here.' He looked all around the cabin. 'I leave you,' he began again and stopped short. Mrs Travers' hand, resting lightly on the edge of the table, began to tremble. 'It's for you . . . Yes. For you alone . . . and it seems it can't be . . .'

It seemed to him that he was saying good-bye to all the world, that he was taking a last leave of his own self. Mrs Travers did not say a word, but Immada threw herself between them and cried:

'You are a cruel woman! You are driving him away from where his strength is. You put madness into his heart, O! Blind – without pity – without shame! . . .'

'Immada,' said Hassim's calm voice. Nobody moved.

'What did she say to me?' faltered Mrs Travers and again repeated in a voice that sounded hard, 'What did she say?'

'Forgive her,' said Lingard. 'Her fears are for me . . .' – 'It's about your going?' Mrs Travers interrupted, swiftly.

'Yes, it is – and you must forgive her.' He had turned away his eyes with something that resembled embarrassment but suddenly he was assailed by an irresistible longing to look again at that woman. At the moment of parting he clung to her with his glance as a man holds with his hands a priceless and disputed possession. The faint blush that overspread gradually Mrs Travers' features gave her face an air of extraordinary and startling animation.

'The danger you run?' she asked, eagerly. He repelled the suggestion by a slighting gesture of the hand. – 'Nothing worth looking at twice. Don't give it a thought,' he said. 'I've been in tighter places.' He clapped his hands and waited till he heard the cabin door open behind his back. 'Steward, my pistols.' The mulatto in slippers, aproned to the chin, glided through the cabin with unseeing eyes as though for him no one there had existed ... – 'Is it my heart that aches so?' Mrs Travers asked herself, contemplating Lingard's motionless figure. 'How long will this sensation of dull pain last? Will it last forever ...' – 'How many changes of clothes shall I put up, sir?' asked the steward, while Lingard took the pistols from him and eased the hammers after putting on fresh caps. – 'I will take nothing this time, steward.' He received in return from the mulatto's hands a red silk hankerchief, a pocket book, a cigar-case. He knotted the handkerchief loosely round his throat; it was evident he was going through the routine of every departure for the shore; he even opened the cigar-case to see whether it had been filled. – 'Hat, sir,' murmured the half-caste. Lingard flung it on his head. – 'Take your orders from this lady, steward – till I come back. The cabin is hers – do you hear?' He sighed, ready to go and seemed unable to lift a foot. – 'I am coming with you,' declared Mrs Travers suddenly in a tone of unalterable decision. He did not look at her; he did not even look up; he said nothing, till after Carter had cried: 'You can't, Mrs Travers!' – when without budging he whispered to himself: – 'Of course.' Mrs Travers had pulled already the hood of her cloak over her head and her face within the dark cloth had turned an intense and unearthly white, in which the violet of her eyes appeared unfathomably mysterious. Carter started forward. – 'You don't know this man,' he almost shouted.

'I do know him,' she said, and before the reproachfully unbelieving attitude of the other she added, speaking slowly and with emphasis: 'There is not, I verily believe, a single thought or act of his life that I don't know.' – 'It's true – it's true,' muttered Lingard to himself. Carter threw up his arms with a groan. 'Stand back,' said a voice that sounded to him like a growl of thunder, and he felt a grip on his hand which seemed to crush every bone. He jerked it away. – 'Mrs Travers! stay,' he cried. They had vanished through the open door and the sound of their footsteps had already died away. Carter turned about bewildered as if looking for help. – 'Who is he, steward? Who in the name of all the mad devils is he?' he asked, wildly. He was confounded by the cold and philosophical tone of the answer: – ' 'Tain't my place to trouble about that, sir – nor yours I guess.' – 'Isn't it!' shouted Carter. 'Why, he has carried the lady off.' The steward was looking critically at the lamp and after a while screwed the light down. – 'That's better,' he mumbled. – 'Good God! What is a fellow to do?' continued Carter, looking at Hassim and Immada who were whispering together and gave him only an absent glance. He rushed on deck and was struck blind instantly by the night that seemed to have been lying in wait for him; he stumbled over something soft, kicked something hard, flung himself on the rail. 'Come back,' he cried. 'Come back, Captain! Mrs Travers! – or let me come, too.'

He listened. The breeze blew cool against his cheek. A black bandage seemed to lie over his eyes. 'Gone,' he groaned, utterly crushed. And suddenly he heard Mrs Travers' voice remote in the depths of the night. – 'Defend the brig,' it said, and these words, pronouncing themselves in the immensity of a lightless universe, thrilled every fibre of his body by the commanding sadness of their tone. 'Defend, defend the brig.' . . . 'I am damned if I do,' shouted Carter in despair. 'Unless you come back! . . . Mrs Travers!'

'. . . as though – I were – on board – myself,' went on the rising cadence of the voice, more distant now, a marvel of faint and imperious clearness.

Carter shouted no more; he tried to make out the boat for a time, and when, giving it up, he leaped down from the rail, the heavy obscurity of the brig's main deck was agitated like a sombre pool by his jump, swayed, eddied, seemed to break up. Blotches of darkness recoiled, drifted away, bare feet shuffled hastily, confused murmurs died out. 'Lascars,' he muttered. 'The crew is all agog.' Afterward he listened for a moment to the faintly tumultuous snores of the white men sleeping in rows, with their heads under the break of the poop. Somewhere about his feet, the yacht's black dog, invisible, and chained to a deck-ringbolt, whined, rattled the thin links, pattered with his claws in his distress at the unfamiliar surroundings, begging for the charity of human notice. Carter stooped impulsively, and was met by a startling lick in the face. – 'Hallo, boy!' He thumped the thick curly sides, stroked the smooth head – 'Good boy, Rover. Down. Lie down, dog. You don't know what to make of it – do you, boy?' The dog became still as death. 'Well, neither do I,' muttered Carter. But such natures are helped by a cheerful contempt for the intricate and endless suggestions of thought. He told himself that he would soon see what was to come of it, and dismissed all speculation. Had he been a little older he would have felt that the situation was beyond his grasp; but he was too young to see it whole and in a manner detached from himself. All these inexplicable events filled him with deep concern – but then on the other hand he had the key of the magazine and he could not find it in his heart to dislike Lingard. He was positive about this at last, and to know that much after the discomfort of an inward conflict went a long way toward a solution. When he followed Shaw into the cabin he could not repress a sense of enjoyment or hide a faint and malicious smile.

'Gone away – did you say? And carried off the lady with him?' discoursed Shaw very loud in the doorway. 'Did he? Well, I am not surprised. What can you expect from a man like that, who leaves his ship in an open roadstead without – I won't say orders – but without as much as a single word to his next in command? And at night at that! That just shows you the kind of man. Is this the way to treat a chief mate? I apprehend he was riled at the little al-ter-cation we had just before you came on board. I told him a truth or two – but – never mind. There's the law and that's enough for me. I am captain as long as he is out of the ship, and if his address before very long is not in one of Her Majesty's jails or other I au-tho-rize you to call me a Dutchman. You mark my words.'

He walked in masterfully, sat down and surveyed the cabin in a leisurely and autocratic manner; but suddenly his eyes became stony with amazement and indignation; he pointed a fat and trembling forefinger.

'Niggers,' he said, huskily. 'In the cuddy! In the cuddy!' He appeared bereft of speech for a time.

Since he entered the cabin Hassim had been watching him in

thoughtful and expectant silence. 'I can't have it,' he continued with genuine feeling in his voice. 'Damme! I've too much respect for myself.' He rose with heavy deliberation; his eyes bulged out in a severe and dignified stare. 'Out you go!' he bellowed, suddenly, making a step forward. – 'Great Scott! What are you up to, mister?' asked in a tone of dispassionate surprise the steward whose head appeared in the doorway. 'These are the Captain's friends.' 'Show me a man's friends and ...' began Shaw, dogmatically, but abruptly passed into the tone of admonition. 'You take your mug out of the way, bottlewasher. They ain't friends of mine. I ain't a vagabond. I know what's due to myself. Quit!' he hissed, fiercely. Hassim, with an alert movement, grasped the handle of his *kris*. Shaw puffed out his cheeks and frowned. – 'Look out! He will stick you like a prize pig,' murmured Carter without moving a muscle. Shaw looked around helplessly – 'And you would enjoy the fun – wouldn't you?' he said with slow bitterness. Carter's distant non-committal smile quite overwhelmed him by its horrid frigidity. Extreme despondency replaced the proper feeling of racial pride in the primitive soul of the mate. 'My God! What luck! What have I done to fall amongst that lot?' he groaned, sat down, and took his big grey head in his hands. Carter drew aside to make room for Immada, who, in obedience to a whisper from her brother, sought to leave the cabin. She passed out after an instant of hesitation, during which she looked up at Carter once. Her brother, motionless in a defensive attitude, protected her retreat. She disappeared; Hassim's grip on his weapon relaxed; he looked in turn at every object in the cabin as if to fix its position in his mind forever, and following his sister, walked out with noiseless footfalls.

They entered the same darkness which had received, enveloped, and hidden the troubled souls of Lingard and Edith, but to these two the light from which they had felt themselves driven away was now like the light of forbidden hopes; it had the awful and tranquil brightness that a light burning on the shore has for an exhausted swimmer about to give himself up to the fateful sea. They looked back; it had disappeared; Carter had shut the cabin door behind them to have it out with Shaw. He wanted to arrive at some kind of working compromise with the nominal commander, but the mate was so demoralized by the novelty of the assaults made upon his respectability that the young defender of the brig could get nothing from him except lamentations mingled with mild blasphemies. The brig slept, and along her quiet deck the voices raised in her cabin – Shaw's appeals and reproaches directed vociferously to heaven, together with Carter's inflexible drawl, mingled into one deadened, modulated, and continuous murmur. The lookouts in the waist, motionless and peering into obscurity, one ear turned to the sea, were aware of that strange resonance like the ghost of a quarrel that seemed to hover at their backs. Wasub, after seeing Hassim and Immada into their canoe, prowled to and fro the whole length of the vessel vigilantly. There was not a star in the sky and no gleam on the water; there was no horizon, no outline, no shape for the eye to rest upon, nothing for the hand to grasp. An obscurity that seemed without limit in space and time had submerged the universe like a destroying flood.

A lull of the breeze kept for a time the small boat in the neighbourhood of the brig. The hoisted sail, invisible, fluttered faintly, mysteriously, and the boat rising and falling bodily to the passage of each invisible undulation of the waters seemed to repose upon a living breast. Lingard, his hand on the tiller, sat up erect, expectant and silent. Mrs Travers had drawn her cloak close around her body. Their glances plunged infinitely deep into a lightless void, and yet they were still so near the brig that the piteous whine of the dog, mingled with the angry rattling of the chain, reached their ears, evoking obscure images of distress and fury. A sharp bark ending in a plaintive howl that seemed raised by the passage of phantoms invisible to men rent the black stillness, as though the instinct of the brute inspired by the soul of night had voiced in a lamentable plaint the fear of shadows. Not far from the brig's boat Hassim and Immada in their canoe, letting their paddles trail in the water, sat in a silent and invincible torpor as if the fitful puffs of wind had carried to their hearts the breath of a subtle poison that, very soon, would make them die.
– 'Have you seen the white woman's eyes?' cried the girl. She

struck her palms together loudly and remained with her arms extended, with her hands clasped. 'O Hassim ! Have you seen her
eyes shining under her eyebrows like rays of light darting under
the arched boughs in a forest? They pierced me. I shuddered at
the sound of her voice ! I saw her walk behind him – and it seems
to me that she does not live on earth – that all this is witchcraft.'

She lamented in the night. Hassim kept silent. He had no illusions and in any other man but Lingard he would have thought
the proceeding no better than suicidal folly. For him Travers and
d'Alcacer were two powerful Rajahs – probably relatives of the
Ruler of the land of the English whom he knew to be a woman;
but why they should come and interfere with the recovery of his
own kingdom was an obscure problem. He was concerned for
Lingard's safety. That the risk was incurred mostly for his sake –
so that the prospects of the great enterprise should not be ruined
by a quarrel over the lives of these whites – did not strike him so
much as may be imagined. There was that in him which made
such an action on Lingard's part appear all but unavoidable. Was
he not Rajah Hassim and was not the other a man of strong
heart, of strong arm, of proud courage, a man great enough to
protect highborn princes – a friend? Immada's words called out a
smile which, like the words, was lost in the darkness. 'Forget
your weariness,' he said gently, 'lest, O Sister, we should arrive
too late.' The coming day would throw its light on some decisive
event. Hassim thought of his own men who guarded the *Emma*
and he wished to be where they could hear his voice. He regretted Jaffir was not there. Hassim was saddened by the absence
from his side of that man who once had carried what he
thought would be his last message to his friend. It had not been
the last. He had lived to cherish new hopes and to face new
troubles and, perchance, to frame another message yet, while
death knocked with the hands of armed enemies at the gate. The
breeze steadied; the succeeding swells swung the canoe smoothly
up the unbroken ridges of water travelling apace along the land.
They progressed slowly; but Immada's heart was more weary
than her arms, and Hassim, dipping the blade of his paddle without a splash, peered right and left, trying to make out the

shadowy forms of islets. A long way ahead of the canoe and holding the same course, the brig's dinghy ran with broad lug extended, making for that narrow and winding passage between the coast and the southern shoals, which led to the mouth of the creek connecting the lagoon with the sea.

Thus on that starless night the Shallows were peopled by uneasy souls. The thick veil of clouds stretched over them, cut them off from the rest of the universe. At times Mrs Travers had in the darkness the impression of dizzy speed, and again it seemed to her that the boat was standing still, that everything in the world was standing still and only her fancy roamed free from all trammels. Lingard, perfectly motionless by her side, steered, shaping his course by the feel of the wind. Presently he perceived ahead a ghostly flicker of faint, livid light which the earth seemed to throw up against the uniform blackness of the sky. The dinghy was approaching the expanse of the Shallows. The confused clamour of broken water deepened its note.

'How long are we going to sail like this?' asked Mrs Travers, gently. She did not recognize the voice that pronounced the word 'Always' in answer to her question. It had the impersonal ring of a voice without a master. Her heart beat fast.

'Captain Lingard!' she cried.

'Yes. What?' he said, nervously, as if startled out of a dream.

'I asked you how long we were going to sail like this,' she repeated, distinctly.

'If the breeze holds we shall be in the lagoon soon after daybreak. That will be the right time, too. I shall leave you on board the hulk with Jörgenson.'

'And you? What will you do?' she asked. She had to wait for a while.

'I will do what I can,' she heard him say at last. There was another pause. 'All I can,' he added.

The breeze dropped, the sail fluttered.

'I have perfect confidence in you,' she said. 'But are you certain of success?'

'No.'

The futility of her question came home to Mrs Travers. In a

few hours of life she had been torn away from all her certitudes, flung into a world of improbabilities. This thought instead of augmenting her distress seemed to soothe her. What she experienced was not doubt and it was not fear. It was something else. It might have been only a great fatigue.

She heard a dull detonation as if in the depth of the sea. It was hardly more than a shock and a vibration. A roller had broken amongst the shoals; the livid clearness Lingard had seen ahead flashed and flickered in expanded white sheets much nearer to the boat now. And all this -- the wan burst of light, the faint shock as of something remote and immense falling into ruins, was taking place outside the limits of her life which remained encircled by an impenetrable darkness and by an impenetrable silence. Puffs of wind blew about her head and expired; the sail collapsed, shivered audibly, stood full and still in turn; and again the sensation of vertiginous speed and of absolute immobility succeeding each other with increasing swiftness merged at last into a bizarre state of headlong motion and profound peace. The darkness enfolded her like the enervating caress of a sombre universe. It was gentle and destructive. Its languor seduced her soul into surrender. Nothing existed and even all her memories vanished into space. She was content that nothing should exist.

Lingard, aware all the time of their contact in the narrow stern sheets of the boat, was startled by the pressure of the woman's head drooping on his shoulder. He stiffened himself still more as though he had tried on the approach of a danger to conceal his life in the breathless rigidity of his body. The boat soared and descended slowly; a region of foam and reefs stretched across her course hissing like a gigantic cauldron; a strong gust of wind drove her straight at it for a moment, then passed on and abandoned her to the regular balancing of the swell. The struggle of the rocks forever overwhelmed and emerging, with the sea forever victorious and repulsed, fascinated the man. He watched it as he would have watched something going on within himself while Mrs Travers slept sustained by his arm, pressed to his side, abandoned to his support. The shoals guarding the Shore of

Refuge had given him his first glimpse of success – the solid support he needed for his action. The Shallows were the shelter of his dreams; their voice had the power to soothe and exalt his thoughts with the promise of freedom for his hopes. Never had there been such a generous friendship ... A mass of white foam whirling about a centre of intense blackness spun silently past the side of the boat ... That woman he held like a captive on his arm had also been given to him by the Shallows.

Suddenly his eyes caught on a distant sandbank the red gleam of Daman's camp fire instantly eclipsed like the wink of a signalling lantern along the level of the waters. It brought to his mind the existence of the two men – those other captives. If the war canoe transporting them into the lagoon had left the sands shortly after Hassim's retreat from Daman's camp, Travers and d'Alcacer were by this time far away up the creek. Every thought of action had become odious to Lingard since all he could do in the world now was to hasten the moment of his separation from that woman to whom he had confessed the whole secret of his life.

And she slept. She could sleep. He looked down at her as he would have looked at the slumbering ignorance of a child, but the life within him had the fierce beat of supreme moments. Near by, the eddies sighed along the reefs, the water soughed amongst the stones, clung round the rocks with tragic murmurs that resembled promises, good-byes, or prayers. From the unfathomable distances of the night came the booming of the swell assaulting the seaward face of the Shallows. He felt the woman's nearness with such intensity that he heard nothing ... Then suddenly he thought of death.

'Wake up!' he shouted in her ear, swinging round in his seat. Mrs Travers gasped; a splash of water flicked her over the eyes and she felt the separate drops run down her cheeks, she tasted them on her lips, tepid and bitter like tears. A swishing undulation tossed the boat on high followed by another and still another; and then the boat with the breeze abeam glided through still water, laying over at a steady angle.

'Clear of the reef now,' remarked Lingard in a tone of relief.

'Were we in any danger?' asked Mrs Travers in a whisper.

'Well, the breeze dropped and we drifted in very close to the rocks,' he answered. 'I had to rouse you. It wouldn't have done for you to wake up suddenly struggling in the water.'

So she had slept! It seemed to her incredible that she should have closed her eyes in this small boat, with the knowledge of their desperate errand, on so disturbed a sea. The man by her side leaned forward, extended his arm, and the boat going off before the wind went on faster on an even keel. A motionless black bank resting on the sea stretched infinitely right in their way in ominous stillness. She called Lingard's attention to it. 'Look at this awful cloud.'

'This cloud is the coast and in a moment we shall be entering the creek,' he said, quietly. Mrs Travers stared at it. Was it land – land! It seemed to her even less palpable than a cloud, a mere sinister immobility above the unrest of the sea, nursing in its depth the unrest of men who, to her mind, were no more real than fantastic shadows.

5

WHAT struck Mrs Travers most, directly she set eyes on him, was the other-world aspect of Jörgenson. He had been buried out of sight so long that his tall, gaunt body, his unhurried, mechanical movements, his set face and his eyes with an empty gaze suggested an invincible indifference to all the possible surprises of the earth. That appearance of a resuscitated man who seemed to be commanded by a conjuring spell strolled along the decks of what was, even to Mrs Travers' eyes, the mere corpse of a ship and turned on her a pair of deep-sunk, expressionless eyes with an almost unearthly detachment. Mrs Travers had never been looked at before with that strange and pregnant abstraction. Yet she didn't dislike Jörgenson. In the early morning light, white from head to foot in a perfectly clean suit of clothes which seemed hardly to contain any limbs, freshly shaven (Jörgenson's sunken cheeks with their withered colouring always had a sort of gloss as though he had the habit of shaving every two hours or so), he looked as immaculate as though he had been indeed a pure spirit superior to the soiling contacts of the material earth. He was disturbing but he was not repulsive. He gave no sign of greeting.

Lingard addressed him at once.

'You have had a regular staircase built up the side of the hulk, Jörgenson,' he said. 'It was very convenient for us to come aboard now, but in case of an attack don't you think . . .'

'I did think.' There was nothing so dispassionate in the world as the voice of Captain H. C. Jörgenson, ex Barque *Wild Rose*, since he had recrossed the Waters of Oblivion to step back into the life of men. 'I did think, but since I don't want to make trouble . . .'

'Oh, you don't want to make trouble,' interrupted Lingard.

'No. Don't believe in it. Do you, King Tom?'

'I may have to make trouble.'

'So you came up here in this small dinghy of yours like this to start making trouble, did you?'

'What's the matter with you? Don't you know me yet, Jörgenson?'

'I thought I knew you. How could I tell that a man like you would come along for a fight bringing a woman with him?'

'This lady is Mrs Travers,' said Lingard. 'The wife of one of the luckless gentlemen Daman got hold of last evening . . . This is Jörgenson, the friend of whom I have been telling you, Mrs Travers.'

Mrs Travers smiled faintly. Her eyes roamed far and near and the strangeness of her surroundings, the overpowering curiosity, the conflict of interest and doubt gave her the aspect of one still new to life, presenting an innocent and naïve attitude before the surprises of experience. She looked very guileless and youthful between those two men. Lingard gazed at her with that unconscious tenderness mingled with wonder, which some men manifest toward girlhood. There was nothing of a conqueror of kingdoms in his bearing. Jörgenson preserved his amazing abstraction which seemed neither to hear nor see anything. But, evidently, he kept a mysterious grip on events in the world of living men because he asked very naturally:

'How did she get away?'

'The lady wasn't on the sandbank,' explained Lingard, curtly.

'What sandbank?' muttered Jörgenson, perfunctorily ... 'Is the yacht looted, Tom?'

'Nothing of the kind,' said Lingard.

'Ah, many dead?' inquired Jörgenson.

'I tell you there was nothing of the kind,' said Lingard impatiently.

'What? No fight!' inquired Jörgenson again without the slightest sign of animation.

'No.'

'And you a fighting man.'

'Listen to me, Jörgenson. Things turned out so that before the time came for a fight it was already too late.' He turned to Mrs Travers still looking about with anxious eyes and a faint smile on her lips. 'While I was talking to you that evening from the boat it was already too late. No. There was never any time for it. I have told you all about myself, Mrs Travers, and you know that I speak the truth when I say too late. If you had only been alone in that yacht going about the seas!'

'Yes,' she struck in, 'but I was not alone.'

Lingard dropped his chin on his breast. Already a foretaste of noonday heat staled the sparkling freshness of the morning. The smile had vanished from Edith Travers' lips and her eyes rested on Lingard's bowed head with an expression no longer curious but which might have appeared enigmatic to Jörgenson if he had looked at her. But Jörgenson looked at nothing. He asked from the remoteness of his dead past, 'What have you left outside, Tom? What is there now?'

'There's the yacht on the shoals, my brig at anchor, and about a hundred of the worst kind of Illanun vagabonds under three chiefs and with two war-*praus* moored to the edge of the bank. Maybe Daman is with them, too, out there.'

'No,' said Jörgenson, positively.

'He has come in,' cried Lingard. 'He brought his prisoners in himself then.'

'Landed by torchlight,' uttered precisely the shade of Captain Jörgenson, late of the Barque *Wild Rose*. He swung his arm pointing across the lagoon and Mrs Travers turned about in that direction.

All the scene was but a great light and a great solitude. Her gaze travelled over the lustrous, dark sheet of empty water to a shore bordered by a white beach empty, too, and showing no sign of human life. The human habitations were lost in the shade of the fruit trees, masked by the cultivated patches of Indian corn and the banana plantations. Near the shore the rigid lines of two stockaded forts could be distinguished flanking the beach, and between them, with a great open space before it, the brown roof slope of an enormous long building that seemed suspended in the air had a great square flag fluttering above it. Something like a small white flame in the sky was the carved white coral finial on the gable of the mosque which had caught full the rays of the sun. A multitude of gay streamers, white and red, flew over the half-concealed roofs, over the brilliant fields and amongst the sombre palm groves. But it might have been a deserted settlement decorated and abandoned by its departed population. Lingard pointed to the stockade on the right.

'That's where your husband is,' he said to Mrs Travers.

'Who is the other?' uttered Jörgenson's voice at their backs. He also was turned that way with his strange sightless gaze fixed beyond them into the void.

'A Spanish gentleman I believe you said, Mrs Travers,' observed Lingard.

'It is extremely difficult to believe that there is anybody there,' murmured Mrs Travers.

'Did you see them both, Jörgenson?' asked Lingard.

'Made out nobody. Too far. Too dark.'

As a matter of fact Jörgenson had seen nothing, about an hour before daybreak, but the distant glare of torches, while the loud shouts of an excited multitude had reached him across the water only like a faint and tempestuous murmur. Presently the lights went away processionally through the groves of trees into the armed stockades. The distant glare vanished in the fading darkness and the murmurs of the invisible crowd ceased suddenly as if carried off by the retreating shadow of the night. Daylight followed swiftly, disclosing to the sleepless Jörgenson the solitude of the shore and the ghostly outlines of the familiar forms of grouped trees and scattered human habitations. He had watched the varied colours come out in the dawn, the wide cultivated Settlement of many shades of green, framed far away by the fine black lines of the forest-edge that was its limit and its protection.

Mrs Travers stood against the rail as motionless as a statue. Her face had lost all its mobility and her cheeks were dead white as if all the blood in her body had flowed back into her heart and had remained there. Her very lips had lost their colour. Lingard caught hold of her arm roughly.

'Don't, Mrs Travers. Why are you terrifying yourself like this? If you don't believe what I say listen to me asking Jörgenson . . .'

'Yes, ask me,' mumbled Jörgenson in his white moustache.

'Speak straight, Jörgenson. What do you think? Are the gentlemen alive?'

'Certainly,' said Jörgenson in a sort of disappointed tone as though he had expected a much more difficult question.

'Is their life in immediate danger?'

'Of course not,' said Jörgenson.

Lingard turned away from the oracle. 'You have heard him, Mrs Travers. You may believe every word he says. There isn't a thought or a purpose in that Settlement,' he continued, pointing at the dumb solitude of the lagoon, 'that this man doesn't know as if they were his own.'

'I know. Ask me,' muttered Jörgenson, mechanically.

Mrs Travers said nothing but made a slight movement and her whole rigid figure swayed dangerously. Lingard put his arm firmly round her waist and she did not seem aware of it till she had turned her head and found Lingard's face very near her own. But his eyes full of concern looked so close into hers that she was obliged to shut them like a woman about to faint.

The effect this produced upon Lingard was such that she felt the tightening of his arm and as she opened her eyes again some of the colour returned to her face. She met the deepened expression of his solitude with a look so steady, with a gaze that in spite of herself was so profoundly vivid that its clearness seemed to Lingard to throw all his past life into shade. – 'I don't feel faint. It isn't that at all,' she declared in a perfectly calm voice. It seemed to Lingard as cold as ice.

'Very well,' he agreed with a resigned smile. 'But you just catch hold of that rail, please, before I let you go.' She, too, forced a smile on her lips.

'What incredulity,' she remarked, and for a time made not the slightest movement. At last, as if making a concession, she rested the tips of her fingers on the rail. Lingard gradually removed his arm. 'And pray don't look upon me as a conventional "weak woman" person, the delicate lady of your own conception,' she said, facing Lingard, with her arm extended to the rail. 'Make that effort please against your own conception of what a woman like me should be. I am perhaps as strong as you are, Captain Lingard. I mean it literally. In my body.' – 'Don't you think I have seen that long ago?' she heard his deep voice protesting – 'And as to my courage,' Mrs Travers continued, her expression charmingly undecided between frowns and smiles; 'didn't I tell you only a few hours ago, only last evening, that I was not capable of thinking myself into a fright; you remember, when you were begging me to try something of the kind. Don't imagine that I would have been ashamed to try. But I couldn't have done it. No. Not even for the sake of somebody else's kingdom. Do you understand me?'

'God knows,' said the attentive Lingard after a time, with an unexpected sigh. 'You people seem to be made of another stuff.'

'What has put that absurd notion into your head?'

'I didn't mean better or worse. And I wouldn't say it isn't good stuff either. What I mean to say is that it's different. One feels it. And here we are.'

'Yes, here we are,' repeated Mrs Travers. 'And as to this moment of emotion, what provoked it is not a concern for anybody or anything outside myself. I felt no terror. I cannot even fix my fears upon any distinct image. You think I am shamelessly heartless in telling you this.'

Lingard made no sign. It didn't occur to him to make a sign. He simply hung on Mrs Travers' words as it were only for the sake of the sound – 'I am simply frank with you,' she continued. 'What do I know of savagery, violence, murder? I have never seen a dead body in my life. The light, the silence, the mysterious emptiness of this place have suddenly affected my imagination, I suppose. What is the meaning of this wonderful peace in which we stand – you and I alone?'

Lingard shook his head. He saw the narrow gleam of the woman's teeth between the parted lips of her smile, as if all the ardour of her conviction had been dissolved at the end of her speech into wistful recognition of their partnership before things outside their knowledge. And he was warmed by something a little helpless in that smile. Within three feet of them the shade of Jörgenson, very gaunt and neat, stared into space.

'Yes. You are strong,' said Lingard. 'But a whole long night sitting in a small boat! I wonder you are not too stiff to stand.'

'I am not stiff in the least,' she interrupted, still smiling. 'I am really a very strong woman,' she added, earnestly. 'Whatever happens you may reckon on that fact.'

Lingard gave her an admiring glance. But the shade of Jörgenson, perhaps catching in its remoteness the sound of the word woman, was sudd nly moved to begin scolding with all the liberty of a ghost, i. a flow of passionless indignation.

'Woman! That's vhat I say. That's just about the last touch – that you, Tom Ling rd, red-eyed Tom, King Tom, and all those fine names, that you should leave your weapons twenty miles behind you, your men, your guns, your brig that is your strength, and come along here with your mouth full of fight, bare-handed and with a woman in tow. – Well – Well!'

'Don't forget, Jörgenson, that the lady hears you,' remonstrated Lingard in a vexed tone . . . 'He doesn't mean to be rude,' he remarked to Mrs Travers quite loud, as if indeed Jörgenson were but an immaterial and feelingless illusion. 'He has forgotten.'

'The woman is not in the least offended. I ask for nothing better than to be taken on that footing.'

'Forgot nothing!' mumbled Jörgenson with a sort of ghostly assertiveness and as it were for his own satisfaction. 'What's the world coming to?'

'It was I who insisted on coming with Captain Lingard,' said Mrs Travers, treating Jörgenson to a fascinating sweetness of tone.

'That's what I say! What is the world coming to? Hasn't King Tom a mind of his own? What has come over him? He's mad! Leaving his brig with a hundred and twenty born and bred pirates of the worst kind in two *praus* on the other side of the sandbank. Did you insist on that, too? Has he put himself in the hands of a strange woman?'

Jörgenson seemed to be asking those questions of himself. Mrs Travers observed the empty stare, the self-communing voice, his unearthly lack of animation. Somehow it made it very easy to speak the whole truth about him.

'No,' she said, 'it is I who am altogether in his hands.'

Nobody would have guessed that Jörgenson had heard a single word of that emphatic declaration if he had not addressed himself to Lingard with the question neither more nor less abstracted than all his other speeches.

'Why then did you bring her along?'

'You don't understand. It was only right and proper. One of the gentlemen is the lady's husband.'

'Oh, yes,' muttered Jörgenson. 'Who's the other?'

'You have been told. A friend.'

'Poor Mr d'Alcacer,' said Mrs Travers. 'What bad luck for him to have accepted our invitation. But he is really a mere acquaintance.'

'I hardly noticed him,' observed Lingard, gloomily. 'He was talking to you over the back of your chair when I came aboard the yacht as if he had been a very good friend.'

'We always understood each other very well,' said Mrs Travers, picking up from the rail the long glass that was lying there. 'I always liked him, the frankness of his mind, and his great loyalty.'

'What did he do?' asked Lingard.

'He loved,' said Mrs Travers, lightly. 'But that's an old story.' She raised the glass to her eyes, one arm extended fully to sustain the long tube, and Lingard forgot d'Alcacer in admiring the firmness of her pose and the absolute steadiness of the heavy glass. She was as firm as a rock after all those emotions and all that fatigue.

Mrs Travers directed the glass instinctively toward the entrance of the lagoon. The smooth water there shone like a piece of silver in the dark frame of the forest. A black speck swept across the field of her vision. It was some time before she could find it again and then she saw, apparently so near as to be within reach of the voice, a small canoe with two people in it. She saw the wet paddles rising and dipping with a flash in the sunlight. She made out plainly the face of Immada, who seemed to be looking straight into the big end of the telescope. The chief and his sister, after resting under the bank for a couple of hours in the middle of the night, had entered the lagoon and were making straight for the hulk. They were already near enough to be perfectly distinguishable to the naked eye if there had been anybody on board to glance that way. But nobody was even thinking of them. They might not have existed except perhaps in the memory of old Jörgenson. But that was mostly busy with all the mysterious secrets of his late tomb.

Mrs Travers lowered the glass suddenly. Lingard came out from a sort of trance and said:

'Mr d'Alcacer. Loved! Why shouldn't he?'

Mrs Travers looked frankly into Lingard's gloomy eyes. 'It isn't that alone, of course,' she said. 'First of all he knew how to love and then ... You don't know how artificial and barren certain kinds of life can be. But Mr d'Alcacer's life was not that. His devotion was worth having.'

'You seem to know a lot about him,' said Lingard, enviously. 'Why do you smile?' She continued to smile at him for a little while. The long brass tube over her shoulder shone like gold against the pale fairness of her bare head. – 'At a thought,' she answered, preserving the low tone of the conversation into which they had fallen as if their words could have disturbed the self-absorption of Captain H. C. Jörgenson. 'At the thought that for all my long acquaintance with Mr d'Alcacer I don't know half as much about him as I know about you.'

'Ah, that's impossible,' contradicted Lingard. 'Spaniard or no Spaniard, he is one of your kind.'

'Tarred with the same brush,' murmured Mrs Travers, with only a half-amused irony. But Lingard continued:

'He was trying to make it up between me and your husband, wasn't he? I was too angry to pay much attention, but I liked him well enough. What pleased me most was the way in which he gave it up. That was done like a gentleman. Do you understand what I mean, Mrs Travers?'

'I quite understand.'

'Yes, you would,' he commented, simply. 'But just then I was too angry to talk to anybody. And so I cleared out on board my own ship and stayed there, not knowing what to do and wishing you all at the bottom of the sea. Don't mistake me, Mrs Travers; it's you, the people aft, that I wished at the bottom of the sea. I had nothing against the poor devils on board. They would have trusted me quick enough. So I fumed there till – till . . .'

'Till nine o'clock or a little after,' suggested Mrs Travers, impenetrably.

'No. Till I remembered you,' said Lingard with the utmost innocence.

'Do you mean to say that you forgot my existence so completely till then? You had spoken to me on board the yacht, you know.'

'Did I? I thought I did. What did I say?'

'You told me not to touch a dusky princess,' answered Mrs Travers with a short laugh. Then with a visible change of mood as if she had suddenly out of a light heart been recalled to the sense of the true situation: 'But indeed I meant no harm to this figure of your dream. And, look over there. She is pursuing you.' Lingard glanced toward the north shore and suppressed an exclamation of remorse. For the second time he discovered that he had forgotten the existence of Hassim and Immada. The canoe was now near enough for its occupants to distinguish plainly the heads of three people above the low bulwark of the *Emma*. Immada let her paddle trail suddenly in the water, with the exclamation, 'I see the white woman there.' Her brother looked over his shoulder and the canoe floated, arrested as if by the sudden power of a spell. – 'They are no dream to me,' muttered Lingard, sturdily. Mrs Travers turned abruptly away to look at the further shore. It was still and empty to the naked eye and seemed to quiver in the sunshine like an immense painted curtain lowered upon the unknown.

'Here's Rajah Hassim coming, Jörgenson. I had an idea he would perhaps stay outside.' Mrs Travers heard Lingard's voice at her back and the answering grunt of Jörgenson. She raised deliberately the long glass to her eye, pointing it at the shore.

She distinguished plainly now the colours in the flutter of the streamers above the brown roofs of the large Settlement, the stir of palm groves, the black shadows inland and the dazzling white beach of coral sand all ablaze in its formidable mystery. She swept the whole range of the view and was going to lower the glass when from behind the massive angle of the stockade there stepped out into the brilliant immobility of the landscape a man in a long white gown and with an enormous black turban surmounting a dark face. Slow and grave he paced the beach ominously in the sunshine, an enigmatical figure in an Oriental tale with something weird and menacing in its sudden emergence and lonely progress.

With an involuntary gasp Mrs Travers lowered the glass. All at once behind her back she heard a low musical voice beginning to pour out incomprehensible words in a tone of passionate pleading. Hassim and Immada had come on board and had approached Lingard. Yes! It was intolerable to feel that this flow of soft speech which had no meaning for her could make its way straight into that man's heart.

PART FIVE

THE POINT OF HONOUR AND
THE POINT OF PASSION

I

'MAY I come in?'

'Yes,' said a voice within. 'The door is open.'

It had a wooden latch. Mr Travers lifted it while the voice of his wife continued as he entered. 'Did you imagine I had locked myself in? Did you ever know me to lock myself in?'

Mr Travers closed the door behind him. 'No, it has never come to that,' he said in a tone that was not conciliatory. In that place which was a room in a wooden hut and had a square opening without glass but with a half-closed shutter he could not distinguish his wife very well at once. She was sitting in an armchair and what he could see best was her fair hair all loose over the back of the chair. There was a moment of silence. The measured footsteps of two men pacing athwart the quarter-deck of the dead ship *Emma* commanded by the derelict shade of Jörgenson could be heard outside.

Jörgenson, on taking up his dead command, had a house of thin boards built on the after deck for his own accommodation and that of Lingard during his flying visits to the Shore of Refuge. A narrow passage divided it in two and Lingard's side was furnished with a camp bedstead, a rough desk, and a rattan armchair. On one of his visits Lingard had brought with him a black seaman's chest and left it there. Apart from these objects and a small looking-glass worth about half a crown and nailed to the wall there was nothing else in there whatever. What was on Jörgenson's side of the deckhouse no one had seen, but from external evidence one could infer the existence of a set of razors.

The erection of that primitive deckhouse was a matter of propriety rather than of necessity. It was proper that the white men should have a place to themselves on board, but Lingard was perfectly accurate when he told Mrs Travers that he had never slept there once. His practice was to sleep on deck. As to Jörgenson, if he did sleep at all he slept very little. It might have been said that he haunted rather than commanded the *Emma*. His white form flitted here and there in the night or stood for hours, silent, contemplating the sombre glimmer of the lagoon. Mr Travers' eyes accustomed gradually to the dusk of the place could now distinguish more of his wife's person than the great mass of honey-coloured hair. He saw her face, the dark eyebrows and her eyes that seemed profoundly black in the half light. He said:

'You couldn't have done so here. There is neither lock nor bolt.'

'Isn't there? I didn't notice. I would know how to protect myself without locks and bolts.'

'I am glad to hear it,' said Mr Travers in a sullen tone and fell silent again surveying the woman in the chair. 'Indulging your taste for fancy dress,' he went on with faint irony.

Mrs Travers clasped her hands behind her head. The wide sleeves slipping back bared her arms to her shoulders. She was wearing a Malay thin cotton jacket, cut low in the neck without a collar and fastened with wrought silver clasps from the throat downward. She had replaced her yachting skirt by a blue check *sarong* embroidered with threads of gold. Mr Travers' eyes travelling slowly down attached themselves to the gleaming instep of an agitated foot from which hung a light leather sandal.

'I had no clothes with me but what I stood in,' said Mrs Travers. 'I found my yachting costume too heavy. It was intolerable. I was soaked in dew when I arrived. So when these things were produced for my inspection . . .'

'By enchantment,' muttered Mr Travers in a tone too heavy for sarcasm.

'No. Out of that chest. There are very fine stuffs there.'

'No doubt,' said Mr Travers. 'The man wouldn't be above plundering the natives . . .' He sat down heavily on the chest. 'A most appropriate costume for this farce,' he continued. 'But do you mean to wear it in open daylight about the decks?'

'Indeed I do,' said Mrs Travers. 'D'Alcacer has seen me already and he didn't seem shocked.'

'You should,' said Mr Travers, 'try to get yourself presented with some bangles for your ankles so that you may jingle as you walk.'

'Bangles are not necessities,' said Mrs Travers in a weary tone and with the fixed upward look of a person unwilling to relinquish her dream. Mr Travers dropped the subject to ask:

'And how long is this farce going to last?'

Mrs Travers unclasped her hands, lowered her glance, and changed her whole pose in a moment.

'What do you mean by farce? What farce?'

'The one which is being played at my expense.'

'You believe that?'

'Not only believe. I feel deeply that it is so. At my expense. It's a most sinister thing,' Mr Travers pursued, still with downcast eyes and in an unforgiving tone. 'I must tell you that when I saw you in that courtyard in a crowd of natives and leaning on that man's arm, it gave me quite a shock.'

'Did I, too, look sinister?' said Mrs Travers, turning her head slightly toward her husband. 'And yet I assure you that I was glad, profoundly glad, to see you safe from danger for a time at least. To gain time is everything . . .'

'I ask myself,' Mr Travers meditated aloud, 'was I ever in danger? Am I safe now? I don't know. I can't tell. No! All this seems an abominable farce.'

There was that in his tone which made his wife continue to look at him with awakened interest. It was obvious that he suffered from a distress which was not the effect of fear; and Mrs Travers' face expressed real concern till he added in a freezing manner: 'The question, however, is as to your discretion.'

She leaned back again in the chair and let her hands rest quietly on her lap. 'Would you have preferred me to remain outside, in the yacht, in the near neighbourhood of these wild men who captured you? Or do you think that they, too, were got up to carry on a farce?'

'Most decidedly.' Mr Travers raised his head, though of course not his voice. 'You ought to have remained in the yacht amongst white men, your servants, the sailing-master, the crew whose duty it was to . . . who would have been ready to die for you.'

'I wonder why they should have – and why I should have asked them for that sacrifice. However, I have no doubt they

would have died. Or would you have preferred me to take up
my quarters on board that man's brig? We were all fairly safe
there. The real reason why I insisted on coming in here was to be
nearer to you – to see for myself what could be or was being done
... But really if you want me to explain my motives then I may
just as well say nothing. I couldn't remain outside for days without news, in a state of horrible doubt. We couldn't even tell
whether you and d'Alcacer were still alive till we arrived here.
You might have been actually murdered on the sandbank, after
Rajah Hassim and the girl had gone away; or killed while going
up the river. And I wanted to know at once, as soon as possible.
It was a matter of impulse. I went off in what I stood without
delaying a moment.'

'Yes,' said Mr Travers. 'And without even thinking of having
a few things put up for me in a bag. No doubt you were in
a state of excitement. Unless you took such a tragic view
that it seemed to you hardly worth while to bother about my
clothes.'

'It was absolutely the impulse of the moment. I could have
done nothing else. Won't you give me credit for it?'

Mr Travers raised his eyes again to his wife's face. He saw it
calm, her attitude reposeful. Till then his tone had been resentful,
dully, without sarcasm. But now he became slightly pompous.

'No. As a matter of fact, as a matter of experience, I can't
credit you with the possession of feelings appropriate to your
origin, social position, and the ideas of the class to which you
belong. It was the heaviest disappointment of my life. I had made
up my mind not to mention it as long as I lived. This, however,
seems an occasion which you have provoked yourself. It isn't at
all a solemn occasion. I don't look upon it as solemn at all. It's
very disagreeable and humiliating. But it has presented itself.
You have never taken a serious interest in the activities of my
life which of course are its distinction and its value. And why
you should be carried away suddenly, by a feeling toward the
mere man I don't understand.'

'Therefore you don't approve,' Mrs Travers commented in an
even tone. 'But I assure you, you may safely. My feeling was

of the most conventional nature, exactly as if the whole world were looking on. After all, we are husband and wife. It's eminently fitting that I should be concerned about your fate. Even the man you distrust and dislike so much (the warmest feeling let me tell you that I ever saw you display) even that man found my conduct perfectly proper. His own word. Proper. So eminently proper that it altogether silenced his objections.'

Mr Travers shifted uneasily on his seat.

'It's my belief, Edith, that if you had been a man you would have led a most irregular life. You would have been a frank adventurer. I mean morally. It has been a great grief to me. You have a scorn in you for the serious side of life, for the ideas and the ambitions of the social sphere to which you belong.'

He stopped because his wife had clasped again her hands behind her head and was no longer looking at him.

'It's perfectly obvious,' he began again. 'We have been living amongst the most distinguished men and women and your attitude to them has been always so – so negative! You would never recognize the importance of achievements, of acquired positions. I don't remember you ever admiring frankly any political or social success. I ask myself what after all you could possibly have expected from life.'

'I could never have expected to hear such a speech from you. As to what I did expect! . . . I must have been very stupid.'

'No, you are anything but that,' declared Mr Travers, conscientiously. 'It isn't stupidity.' He hesitated for a moment. 'It's a kind of wilfulness, I think. I preferred not to think about this grievous difference in our points of view, which, you will admit, I could not have possibly foreseen before we . . .'

A sort of solemn embarrassment had come over Mr Travers. Mrs Travers, leaning her chin on the palm of her hand, stared at the bare matchboard side of the hut.

'Do you charge me with profound girlish duplicity?' she asked, very softly.

The inside of the deckhouse was full of stagnant heat perfumed by a slight scent which seemed to emanate from the loose mass of Mrs Travers' hair. Mr Travers evaded the direct question which struck him as lacking fineness even to the point of impropriety.

'I must suppose that I was not in the calm possession of my insight and judgement in those days,' he said. 'I – I was not in a critical state of mind at the time,' he admitted further; but even after going so far he did not look up at his wife and therefore missed something like the ghost of a smile on Mrs Travers' lips. That smile was tinged with scepticism which was too deep-seated for anything but the faintest expression. Therefore she said nothing, and Mr Travers went on as if thinking aloud:

'Your conduct was, of course, above reproach; but you made for yourself a detestable reputation of mental superiority, expressed ironically. You inspired mistrust in the best people. You were never popular.'

'I was bored,' murmured Mrs Travers in a reminiscent tone and with her chin resting in the hollow of her hand.

Mr Travers got up from the seaman's chest as unexpectedly as if he had been stung by a wasp, but, of course, with a much slower and more solemn motion.

'The matter with you, Edith, is that at heart you are perfectly primitive.' Mrs Travers stood up, too, with a supple, leisurely movement, and raising her hands to her hair turned half away with a pensive remark:

'Imperfectly civilized.'

'Imperfectly disciplined,' corrected Mr Travers after a moment of dreary meditation.

She let her arms fall and turned her head.

'No, don't say that,' she protested with strange earnestness. 'I am the most severely disciplined person in the world. I am tempted to say that my discipline has stopped at nothing short of killing myself. I suppose you can hardly understand what I mean.'

Mr Travers made a slight grimace at the floor.

'I shall not try,' he said. 'It sounds like something that a barbarian, hating the delicate complexities and the restraints of a nobler life, might have said. From you it strikes me as wilful bad taste ... I have often wondered at your tastes. You have always liked extreme opinions, exotic costumes, lawless characters, romantic personalities – like d'Alcacer . . .'

'Poor Mr d'Alcacer,' murmured Mrs Travers.

'A man without any ideas of duty or usefulness,' said Mr Travers, acidly. 'What are you pitying him for?'

'Why! For finding himself in this position out of mere good-nature. He had nothing to expect from joining our voyage, no advantage for his political ambition or anything of the kind. I suppose you asked him on board to break our *tête-à-tête* which must have grown wearisome to you.'

'I am never bored,' declared Mr Travers. 'D'Alcacer seemed glad to come. And, being a Spaniard, the horrible waste of time cannot matter to him in the least.'

'Waste of time!' repeated Mrs Travers, indignantly. 'He may yet have to pay for his good nature with his life.'

Mr Travers could not conceal a movement of anger.

'Ah! I forgot those assumptions,' he said between his clenched teeth. 'He is a mere Spaniard. He takes this farcical conspiracy with perfect nonchalance. Decayed races have their own philosophy.'

'He takes it with a dignity of his own.'

'I don't know what you call his dignity. I should call it lack of self-respect.'

'Why? Because he is quiet and courteous, and reserves his judgement. And allow me to tell you, Martin, that you are not taking our troubles very well.'

'You can't expect from me all those foreign affectations. I am not in the habit of compromising with my feelings.'

Mrs Travers turned completely round and faced her husband. 'You sulk,' she said . . . Mr Travers jerked his head back a little as if to let the word go past. – 'I am outraged,' he declared. Mrs Travers recognized there something like real suffering. – 'I assure you,' she said, seriously (for she was accessible to pity), 'I assure you that this strange Lingard has no idea of your importance. He doesn't know anything of your social and political position and still less of your great ambitions.' Mr Travers listened with some attention. – 'Couldn't you have enlightened him?' he asked.

– 'It would have been no use; his mind is fixed upon his own position and upon his own sense of power. He is a man of the lower classes . . .' – 'He is a brute,' said Mr Travers, obstinately, and for a moment those two looked straight into each other's eyes. – 'Oh,' said Mrs Travers, slowly, 'you are determined not to compromise with your feelings!' An undertone of scorn crept into her voice. 'But shall I tell you what I think? I think,' and she advanced her head slightly toward the pale, unshaven face that confronted her dark eyes; 'I think that for all your blind scorn you judge the man well enough to feel that you can indulge your indignation with perfect safety. Do you hear? With perfect safety!' Directly she had spoken she regretted these words. Really it was unreasonable to take Mr Travers' tricks of character more passionately on this spot of the Eastern Archipelago full of obscure plots and warring motives than in the more artificial atmosphere of the town. After all what she wanted was simply to save his life, not to make him understand anything. Mr Travers opened his mouth and without uttering a word shut it again. His wife turned toward the looking-glass nailed to the wall. She heard his voice behind her.

'Edith, where's the truth in all this?'

She detected the anguish of a slow mind with an instinctive dread of obscure places wherein new discoveries can be made. She looked over her shoulder to say :

'It's on the surface, I assure you. Altogether on the surface.'

She turned again to the looking-glass where her own face met her with dark eyes and a fair mist of hair above the smooth forehead; but her words had produced no soothing effect.

'But what does it mean?' cried Mr Travers. 'Why doesn't the fellow apologize? Why are we kept here? Are we being kept here? Why don't we get away? Why doesn't he take me back on board my yacht? What does he want from me? How did he procure our release from these people on shore who he says intended to cut our throats? Why did they give us up to him instead?'

Mrs Travers began to twist her hair on her head.

'Matters of high policy and of local politics. Conflict of personal interests, mistrust between the parties, intrigues of individuals – you ought to know how that sort of thing works. His diplomacy made use of all that. The first thing to do was not to liberate you but to get you into his keeping. He is a very great man here and let me tell you that your safety depends on his dexterity in the use of his prestige rather than on his power which he cannot use. If you would let him talk to you I am sure he would tell you as much as it is possible for him to disclose.'

'I don't want to be told about any of his rascalities. But haven't you been taken into his confidence?'

'Completely,' admitted Mrs Travers, peering into the small looking-glass.

'What is the influence you brought to bear upon this man? It looks to me as if our fate were in your hands.'

'Your fate is not in my hands. It is not even in his hands. There is a moral situation here which must be solved.'

'Ethics of blackmail,' commented Mr Travers with unexpected sarcasm. It flashed through his wife's mind that perhaps she didn't know him so well as she had supposed. It was as if the polished and solemn crust of hard proprieties had cracked slightly, here and there, under the strain, disclosing the mere wrong-headedness of a common mortal. But it was only manner that had cracked a little; the marvellous stupidity of his conceit remained the same. She thought that this discussion was perfectly useless, and as she finished putting up her hair she said: 'I think we had better go on deck now.'

'You propose to go out on deck like this?' muttered Mr Travers with downcast eyes.

'Like this? Certainly. It's no longer a novelty. Who is going to be shocked?'

Mr Travers made no reply. What she had said of his attitude was very true. He sulked at the enormous offensiveness of men, things, and events; of words and even of glances which he seemed to feel physically resting on his skin like a pain, like a degrading contact. He managed not to wince. But he sulked. His wife continued, 'And let me tell you that those clothes are fit for a princess – I mean they are of the quality, material, and style custom prescribes for the highest in the land, a far-distant

227

land where I am informed women rule as much as the men. In fact they were meant to be presented to an actual princess in due course. They were selected with the greatest care for that child Immada. Captain Lingard . . .'

Mr Travers made an inarticulate noise partaking of a groan and a grunt.

'Well, I must call him by some name and this I thought would be the least offensive for you to hear. After all, the man exists. But he is known also on a certain portion of the earth's surface as King Tom. D'Alcacer is greatly taken by that name. It seems to him wonderfully well adapted to the man, in its familiarity and deference. And if you prefer . . .'

'I would prefer to hear nothing,' said Mr Travers, distinctly. 'Not a single word. Not even from you, till I am a free agent again. But words don't touch me. Nothing can touch me; neither your sinister warnings nor the moods of levity which you think proper to display before a man whose life, according to you, hangs on a thread.'

'I never forget it for a moment,' said Mrs Travers. 'And I not only know that it does but I also know the strength of the thread. It is a wonderful thread. You may say if you like it has been spun by the same fate which made you what you are.'

Mr Travers felt awfully offended. He had never heard anybody, let alone his own self, addressed in such terms. The tone seemed to question his very quality. He reflected with shocked amazement that he had lived with that woman for eight years! And he said to her gloomily:

'You talk like a pagan.'

It was a very strong condemnation which apparently Mrs Travers had failed to hear for she pursued with animation:

'But really, you can't expect me to meditate on it all the time or shut myself up here and mourn the circumstances from morning to night. It would be morbid. Let us go on deck.'

'And you look simply heathenish in this costume,' Mr Travers went on as though he had not been interrupted, and with an accent of deliberate disgust.

Her heart was heavy but everything he said seemed to force

the tone of levity on to her lips. 'As long as I don't look like a guy,' she remarked, negligently, and then caught the direction of his lurid stare which as a matter of fact was fastened on her bare feet. She checked herself, 'Oh, yes, if you prefer I will put on my stockings. But you know I must be very careful of them. It's the only pair I have here. I have washed them this morning in that bathroom which is built over the stern. They are now drying over the rail just outside. Perhaps you will be good enough to pass them to me when you go on deck.'

Mr Travers spun round and went on deck without a word. As soon as she was alone Mrs Travers pressed her hands to her temples, a gesture of distress which relieved her by its sincerity. The measured footsteps of two men came to her plainly from the deck, rhythmic and double with a suggestion of tranquil and friendly intercourse. She distinguished particularly the footfalls of the man whose life's orbit was most remote from her own. And yet the orbits had cut! A few days ago she could not have even conceived of his existence, and now he was the man whose footsteps, it seemed to her, her ears could single unerringly in the tramp of a crowd. It was, indeed, a fabulous thing. In the half light of her over-heated shelter she let an irresolute, frightened smile pass off her lips before she, too, went on deck.

2

AN ingeniously constructed framework of light posts and thin laths occupied the greater part of the deck amidships of the *Emma*. The four walls of that airy structure were made of muslin. It was comparatively lofty. A door-like arrangement of light battens filled with calico was further protected by a system of curtains calculated to baffle the pursuit of mosquitoes that haunted the shores of the lagoon in great singing clouds from sunset till sunrise. A lot of fine mats covered the deck space within the transparent shelter devised by Lingard and Jörgenson to make Mrs Travers' existence possible during the time when the fate of the two men, and indeed probably of everybody else on board the *Emma*, had to hang in the balance. Very soon Lingard's unbidden and fatal guests had learned the trick of stepping in and out of the place quickly. Mr d'Alcacer performed the feat without apparent haste, almost nonchalantly, yet as well as anybody. It was generally conceded that he had never let a mosquito in together with himself. Mr Travers dodged in and out without grace and was obviously much irritated at the necessity. Mrs Travers did it in a manner all her own, with marked cleverness and an unconscious air. There was an improvised table in there and some wicker armchairs which Jörgenson had produced from somewhere in the depths of the ship. It was hard to say what the inside of the *Emma* did not contain. It was crammed with all sorts of goods like a general store. That old hulk was the arsenal and the war-chest of Lingard's political action; she was stocked with muskets and gunpowder, with bales of longcloth, of cotton prints, of silks; with bags of rice and currency brass guns. She contained everything necessary for dealing death and distributing bribes, to act on the cupidity and upon the fears of men, to march and to organize, to feed the friends and to combat the enemies of the cause. She held wealth and power in her flanks, that grounded ship that would swim no more, without masts and with the best part of her deck cumbered by the two structures of thin boards and of transparent muslin.

Within the latter lived the Europeans, visible in the daytime to the few Malays on board as if through a white haze. In the evening the lighting of the hurricane lamps inside turned them into dark phantoms surrounded by a shining mist, against which the insect world rushing in its millions out of the forest on the bank was baffled mysteriously in its assault. Rigidly enclosed by transparent walls, like captives of an enchanted cobweb, they moved about, sat, gesticulated, conversed publicly during the day; and at night when all the lanterns but one were extinguished, their slumbering shapes covered all over by white cotton sheets on the camp bedsteads, which were brought in every evening, conveyed the gruesome suggestion of dead bodies reposing on stretchers. The food, such as it was, was served within that glorified mosquito net which everybody called the 'Cage' without any humorous intention. At meal times the party from the yacht had the company of Lingard who attached to this ordeal a sense of duty performed at the altar of civility and conciliation. He could have no conception how much his presence added to the exasperation of Mr Travers because Mr Travers' manner was too intensely consistent to present any shades. It was determined by an ineradicable conviction that he was a victim held to ransom on some incomprehensible terms by an extraordinary and outrageous bandit. This conviction, strung to the highest pitch, never left him for a moment, being the object of indignant meditation to his mind, and even clinging, as it were, to his very body. It lurked in his eyes, in his gestures, in his ungracious mutters, and in his sinister silences. The shock to his moral being had ended by affecting Mr Travers' physical machine. He was aware of hepatic pains, suffered from excesses of somnolence and suppressed gusts of fury which frightened him secretly. His complexion had acquired a yellow tinge, while his heavy eyes had become bloodshot because of the smoke of the open wood fires during his three days' detention inside Belarab's stockade. His eyes had been always very sensitive to outward conditions. D'Alcacer's fine black eyes were more enduring and his appearance did not differ very much from his ordinary appearance on board the yacht. He had accepted with smiling thanks the offer of a thin blue flannel tunic from Jörgenson. Those two men were much of the same build, though of course d'Alcacer, quietly alive and spiritually watchful, did not resemble Jörgenson, who, without being exactly *macabre*, behaved more like an indifferent but restless corpse. Those two could not be said to have ever conversed together. Conversation with Jörgenson was an impossible thing. Even Lingard never attempted the feat. He propounded questions to Jörgenson much as a magician would interrogate an evoked shade, or gave him curt directions as one would make use of some marvellous automaton. And that was apparently the way in which Jörgenson preferred to be treated. Lingard's real company on board the

Emma was d'Alcacer. D'Alcacer had met Lingard on the easy
terms of a man accustomed all his life to good society in which
the very affectations must be carried on without effort. Whether
affectation, or nature, or inspired discretion, d'Alcacer never let
the slightest curiosity pierce the smoothness of his level, grave
courtesy, lightened frequently by slight smiles which often had
not much connection with the words he uttered, except that
somehow they made them sound kindly and as it were tactful. In
their character, however, those words were strictly neutral.

The only time when Lingard had detected something of a
deeper comprehension in d'Alcacer was the day after the long
negotiations inside Belarab's stockade for the temporary surrender of the prisoners. That move had been suggested to him,
exactly as Mrs Travers had told her husband, by the rivalries of
the parties and the state of public opinion in the Settlement deprived of the presence of the man who, theoretically at least, was
the greatest power and the visible ruler of the Shore of Refuge.
Belarab still lingered at his father's tomb. Whether that man of
the embittered and pacific heart had withdrawn there to meditate upon the unruliness of mankind and the thankless nature of
his task; or whether he had gone there simply to bathe in a particularly clear pool which was a feature of the place, give himself up to the enjoyment of a certain fruit which grew in
profusion there and indulge for a time in a scrupulous performance of religious exercises, his absence from the Settlement was a
fact of the utmost gravity. It is true that the prestige of a long-
unquestioned rulership and the long-settled mental habits of the
people had caused the captives to be taken straight to Belarab's
stockade as a matter of course. Belarab, at a distance, could still
outweigh the power on the spot of Tengga, whose secret purposes were no better known, who was jovial, talkative, outspoken, and pugnacious; but who was not a professed servant of
God famed for many charities and a scrupulous performance of
pious practices, and who also had no father who had achieved a
local saintship. But Belarab, with his glamour of asceticism and
melancholy together with a reputation for severity (for a man so
pious would be naturally ruthless), was not on the spot. The only

favourable point in his absence was the fact that he had taken with him his latest wife, the same lady whom Jörgenson had mentioned in his letter to Lingard as anxious to bring about battle, murder, and the looting of the yacht, not because of in-born wickedness of heart but from a simple desire for silks, jewels and other objects of personal adornment, quite natural in a girl so young and elevated to such a high position. Belarab had selected her to be the companion of his retirement and Lingard was glad of it. He was not afraid of her influence over Belarab. He knew his man. No words, no blandishments, no sulks, scold-ings, or whisperings of a favourite could affect either the resolves or the irresolutions of that Arab whose action ever seemed to hang in mystic suspense between the contradictory speculations and judgements disputing the possession of his will. It was not what Belarab would either suddenly do or leisurely determine upon that Lingard was afraid of. The danger was that in his taci-turn hesitation, which had something hopelessly godlike in its remote calmness, the man would do nothing and leave his white friend face to face with unruly impulses against which Lingard had no means of action but force which he dared not use since it would mean the destruction of his plans and the downfall of his hopes; and worse still would wear an aspect of treachery to Hassim and Immada, those fugitives whom he had snatched away from the jaws of death on a night of storm and had pro-mised to lead back in triumph to their own country he had seen but once, sleeping unmoved under the wrath and fire of heaven.

On the afternoon of the very day he had arrived with her on board the *Emma* – to the infinite disgust of Jörgenson – Lingard held with Mrs Travers (after she had had a couple of hours' rest) a long, fiery, and perplexed conversation. From the nature of the problem it could not be exhaustive; but toward the end of it they were both feeling thoroughly exhausted. Mrs Travers had no longer to be instructed as to facts and possibilities. She was aware of them only too well and it was not her part to advise or argue. She was not called upon to decide or to plead. The situa-tion was far beyond that. But she was worn out with watching the passionate conflict within the man who was both so desperately reckless and so rigidly restrained in the very ardour of his heart and the greatness of his soul. It was a spectacle that made her forget the actual questions at issue. This was no stage play; and yet she had caught herself looking at him with bated breath as at a great actor on a darkened stage in some simple and tremendous drama. He extorted from her a response to the forces that seemed to tear at his single-minded brain, at his guileless breast. He shook her with his own struggles, he possessed her with his emotions and imposed his personality as if its tragedy were the only thing worth considering in this matter. And yet what had she to do with all those obscure and barbarous things? Obviously nothing. Unluckily she had been taken into the confidence of that man's passionate perplexity, a confidence provoked apparently by nothing but the power of her personality. She was flattered, and even more, she was touched by it; she was aware of something that resembled gratitude and provoked a sort of emotional return as between equals who had secretly recognized each other's value. Yet at the same time she regretted not having been left in the dark; as much in the dark as Mr Travers himself or d'Alcacer, though as to the latter it was impossible to say how much precise, unaccountable, intuitive knowledge was buried under his unruffled manner.

D'Alcacer was the sort of man whom it would be much easier to suspect of anything in the world than ignorance – or stupidity. Naturally he couldn't know anything definite or even guess at the bare outline of the facts, but somehow he must have scented the situation in those few days of contact with Lingard. He was an acute and sympathetic observer in all his secret aloofness from the life of men which was so very different from Jörgenson's secret divorce from the passions of this earth. Mrs Travers would have liked to share with d'Alcacer the burden (for it was a burden) of Lingard's story. After all, she had not provoked those confidences, neither had that unexpected adventurer from the sea laid on her an obligation of secrecy. No, not even by implication. He had never said to her that she was the *only* person whom he wished to know that story.

No. What he had said was that she was the only person to whom he *could* tell the tale himself, as if no one else on earth had the power to draw it from him. That was the sense and nothing more. Yes, it would have been a relief to tell d'Alcacer. It would have been a relief to her feeling of being shut off from the world alone with Lingard as if within the four walls of a romantic palace and in an exotic atmosphere. Yes, that relief and also another: that of sharing the responsibility with somebody fit to understand. Yet she shrank from it, with unaccountable reserve, as if by talking of Lingard with d'Alcacer she was bound to give him an insight into herself. It was a vague uneasiness and yet so persistent that she felt it, too, when she had to approach and talk to Lingard under d'Alcacer's eyes. Not that Mr d'Alcacer would ever dream of staring or even casting glances. But was he averting his eyes on purpose? That would be even more offensive.

'I am stupid,' whispered Mrs Travers to herself, with a complete and reassuring conviction. Yet she waited motionless till the footsteps of the two men stopped outside the deckhouse, then separated and died away, before she went out on deck. She came out on deck some time after her husband. As if in intended contrast to the conflicts of men a great aspect of serenity lay upon all visible things. Mr Travers had gone inside the Cage in which he really looked like a captive and thoroughly out of place. D'Alcacer had gone in there, too, but he preserved – or was it an illusion? – an air of independence. It was not that he put it on. Like Mr Travers he sat in a wicker armchair in very much the same attitude as the other gentleman and also silent; but there was somewhere a subtle difference which did away with the notion of captivity. Moreover, d'Alcacer had that peculiar gift of never looking out of place in any surroundings. Mrs Travers, in order to save her European boots for active service, had been persuaded to use a pair of leather sandals also extracted from that seaman's chest in the deckhouse. An additional fastening had been put on them but she could not avoid making a delicate clatter as she walked on the deck. No part of her costume made her feel so exotic. It also forced her to alter her usual gait and move with quick, short steps very much like Immada. 'I am robbing the girl of her clothes,' she had thought to herself, 'besides other things.' She knew by this time that a girl of such high rank would never dream of wearing anything that had been worn by somebody else.

At the slight noise of Mrs Travers' sandals d'Alcacer looked over the back of his chair. But he turned his head away at once and Mrs Travers, leaning her elbow on the rail and resting her head on the palm of her hand, looked across the calm surface of the lagoon, idly.

She was turning her back on the Cage, the fore-part of the deck and the edge of the nearest forest. That great erection of enormous solid trunks, dark, rugged columns festooned with writhing creepers and steeped in gloom, was so close to the bank that by looking over the side of the ship she could see inverted in the glassy belt of water its massive and black reflection on the reflected sky that gave the impression of a clear blue abyss seen through a transparent film. And when she raised her eyes the same abysmal immobility seemed to reign over the whole sun-bathed enlargement of that lagoon which was one of the secret places of the earth. She felt strongly her isolation. She was so much the only being of her kind moving within this mystery that even to herself she looked like an apparition without rights and without defence and that must end by surrendering to those forces which seemed to her but the expression of the unconscious genius of the place. Hers was the most complete loneliness, charged with a catastrophic tension. It lay about her as though she had been set apart within a magic circle. It cut off – but it did not protect. The footsteps that she knew how to distinguish above all others on that deck were heard suddenly behind her. She did not turn her head.

Since that afternoon when the gentlemen, as Lingard called them, had been brought on board, Mrs Travers and Lingard had not exchanged one significant word.

When Lingard had decided to proceed by way of negotiation she had asked him on what he based his hope of success; and he had answered her: 'On my luck.' What he really depended on was his prestige; but even if he had been aware of such a word he would not have used it, since it would have sounded like a boast. And, besides, he did really believe in his luck. Nobody, either white or brown, had ever doubted his word and that, of course, gave him great assurance in entering upon the negotiation. But the ultimate issue of it would be always a matter of luck. He said so distinctly to Mrs Travers at the moment of taking leave of her, with Jörgenson already waiting for him in the boat that was to take them across the lagoon to Belarab's stockade.

Startled by his decision (for it had come suddenly clinched by the words 'I believe I can do it'), Mrs Travers had dropped her hand into his strong open palm on which an expert in palmistry could have distinguished other lines than the line of luck. Lingard's hand closed on hers with a gentle pressure. She looked at him, speechless. He waited for a moment, then in an unconsciously tender voice he said: 'Well, wish me luck then.'

She remained silent. And he still holding her hand looked surprised at her hesitation. It seemed to her that she could not let him go, and he didn't know what to say till it occurred to her to make use of the power she knew she had over him. She would try it again. 'I am coming with you,' she declared with decision. 'You don't suppose I could remain here in suspense for hours, perhaps.'

He dropped her hand suddenly as if it had burnt him – 'Oh, yes, of course,' he mumbled with an air of confusion. One of the men over there was her husband! And nothing less could be expected from such a woman. He had really nothing to say but she thought he hesitated – 'Do you think my presence would spoil everything? I assure you I am a lucky person, too, in a way ... As lucky as you, at least,' she had added in a murmur and with a smile which provoked his responsive mutter – 'Oh, yes, we are a lucky pair of people.' – 'I count myself lucky in having found a man like you to fight my – our battles,' she said, warmly. 'Suppose you had not existed? ... You must let me come with you!' For the second time before her expressed wish to stand by his side he bowed his head. After all, if things came to the worst,

237

she would be as safe between him and Jörgenson as left alone on board the *Emma* with a few Malay spearmen for all defence. For a moment Lingard thought of picking up the pistols he had taken out of his belt preparatory to joining Jörgenson in the boat, thinking it would be better to go to a big talk completely unarmed. They were lying on the rail but he didn't pick them up. Four shots didn't matter. They could not matter if the world of his creation were to go to pieces. He said nothing of that to Mrs Travers but busied himself in giving her the means to alter her personal appearance. It was then that the sea-chest in the deckhouse was opened for the first time before the interested Mrs Travers who had followed him inside. Lingard handed to her a Malay woman's light cotton coat with jewelled clasps to put over her European dress. It covered half of her yachting skirt. Mrs Travers obeyed him without comment. He pulled out a long and wide scarf of white silk embroidered heavily on the edges and ends, and begged her to put it over her head and arrange the ends so as to muffle her face, leaving little more than her eyes exposed to view. – 'We are going amongst a lot of Mohammedans,' he explained. – 'I see. You want me to look respectable,' she jested. – 'I assure you, Mrs Travers,' he protested, earnestly, 'that most of the people there and certainly all the great men have never seen a white woman in their lives. But perhaps you would like better one of those other scarves? There are three in there.' – 'No, I like this one well enough. They are all very gorgeous. I see that the Princess is to be sent back to her land with all possible splendour. What a thoughtful man you are, Captain Lingard. That child will be touched by your generosity ... Will I do like this?'

'Yes,' said Lingard, averting his eyes. Mrs Travers followed him into the boat where the Malays stared in silence while Jörgenson, stiff and angular, gave no sign of life, not even so much as a movement of the eyes. Lingard settled her in the stern sheets and sat down by her side. The ardent sunshine devoured all colours. The boat swam forward on the glare heading for the strip of coral beach dazzling like a crescent of metal raised to a white heat. They landed. Gravely, Jörgenson opened above Mrs

Travers' head a big white cotton parasol and she advanced between the two men, dazed, as if in a dream and having no other contact with the earth but through the soles of her feet. Everything was still, empty, incandescent, and fantastic. Then when the gate of the stockade was thrown open she perceived an expectant and still multitude of bronze figures draped in coloured stuffs. They crowded the patches of shade under the three lofty forest trees left within the enclosure between the sun-smitten empty spaces of hard-baked ground. The broad blades of the spears decorated with crimson tufts of horsehair had a cool gleam under the outspread boughs. To the left a group of buildings on piles with long verandahs and immense roofs towered high in the air above the heads of the crowd, and seemed to float in the glare, looking much less substantial than their heavy shadows. Lingard, pointing to one of the smallest, said in an undertone, 'I lived there for a fortnight when I first came to see Belarab'; and Mrs Travers felt more than ever as if walking in a dream when she perceived beyond the rails of its verandah and visible from head to foot two figures in an armour of chain mail with pointed steel helmets crested with white and black feathers and guarding the closed door. A high bench draped in turkey cloth stood in an open space of the great audience shed. Lingard led her up to it, Jörgenson on her other side closed the parasol calmly, and when she sat down between them the whole throng before her eyes sank to the ground with one accord disclosing in the distance of the courtyard a lonely figure leaning against the smooth trunk of a tree. A white cloth was fastened round his head by a yellow cord. Its pointed ends fell on his shoulders, framing a thin dark face with large eyes, a silk cloak striped black and white fell to his feet, and in the distance he looked aloof and mysterious in his erect and careless attitude suggesting assurance and power.

Lingard, bending slightly, whispered into Mrs Travers' ear that that man, apart and dominating the scene, was Daman, the supreme leader of the Illanuns, the one who had ordered the capture of those gentlemen in order perhaps to force his hand. The two barbarous, half-naked figures covered with ornaments and charms, squatting at his feet with their heads enfolded in crimson and gold handkerchiefs and with straight swords lying across their knees, were the Pangerans who carried out the order, and had brought the captives into the lagoon. But the two men in chain armour on watch outside the door of the small house were Belarab's two particular body-guards, who got themselves up in that way only on very great occasions. They were the outward and visible sign that the prisoners were in Belarab's keeping, and this was good, so far. The pity was that the Great Chief himself was not there. Then Lingard assumed a formal pose and Mrs Travers stared into the great courtyard and with rows and rows of faces ranged on the ground at her feet felt a little giddy for a moment.

Every movement had died in the crowd. Even the eyes were still under the variegated mass of coloured head-kerchiefs: while beyond the open gate a noble palm tree looked intensely black against the glitter of the lagoon and the pale incandescence of the sky. Mrs Travers gazing that way wondered at the absence of Hassim and Immada. But the girl might have been somewhere within one of the houses with the ladies of Belarab's stockade. Then suddenly Mrs Travers became aware that another bench had been brought out and was already occupied by five men dressed in gorgeous silks, and embroidered velvets, round-faced and grave. Their hands reposed on their knees; but one amongst them clad in a white robe and with a large nearly black turban on his head leaned forward a little with his chin in his hand. His cheeks were sunken and his eyes remained fixed on the ground as if to avoid looking at the infidel woman.

She became aware suddenly of a soft murmur, and glancing at Lingard she saw him in an attitude of impassive attention. The momentous negotiations had begun, and it went on like this in low undertones with long pauses and in the immobility of all the attendants squatting on the ground with the distant figure of Daman far off in the shade towering over all the assembly. But in him, too, Mrs Travers could not detect the slightest movement while the slightly modulated murmurs went on enveloping her in a feeling of peace.

The fact that she couldn't understand anything of what was said soothed her apprehensions. Sometimes a silence fell and Lingard bending toward her would whisper, 'It isn't so easy,' and the stillness would be so perfect that she would hear the flutter of a pigeon's wing somewhere high up in the great overshadowing trees. And suddenly one of the men before her without moving a limb would begin another speech rendered more mysterious still by the total absence of action or play of feature. Only the watchfulness of the eyes which showed that the speaker was not communing with himself made it clear that this was not a spoken meditation but a flow of argument directed to Lingard who now and then uttered a few words either with a grave or a smiling expression. They were always followed by murmurs which seemed mostly to her to convey assent; and then a reflective silence would reign again and the immobility of the crowd would appear more perfect than before.

When Lingard whispered to her that it was now his turn to make a speech Mrs Travers expected him to get up and assert himself by some commanding gesture. But he did not. He remained seated, only his voice had a vibrating quality though he obviously tried to restrain it, and it travelled masterfully far into the silence. He spoke for a long time while the sun climbing the unstained sky shifted the diminished shadows of the trees, pouring on the heads of men its heat through the thick and motionless foliage. Whenever murmurs arose he would stop and, glancing fearlessly at the assembly, wait till they subsided. Once or twice, they rose to a loud hum and Mrs Travers could hear on the other side of her Jörgenson muttering something in his moustache. Beyond the rows of heads, Daman under the tree had folded his arms on his breast. The edge of the white cloth concealed his forehead and at his feet the two Illanun chiefs, half naked and bedecked with charms and ornaments of bright feathers, of shells, with necklaces of teeth, claws, and shining beads, remained cross-legged with their swords across their knees like two bronze idols. Even the plumes of their head-dresses stirred not.

'Sudah! It is finished!' A movement passed along all the

241

heads, the seated bodies swayed to and fro. Lingard had ceased speaking. He remained seated for a moment looking his audience all over and when he stood up together with Mrs Travers and Jörgenson the whole assembly rose from the ground together and lost its ordered formation. Some of Belarab's retainers, young broad-faced fellows, wearing a sort of uniform of check-patterned *sarongs*, black silk jackets, and crimson skull-caps set at a rakish angle, swaggered through the broken groups and ranged themselves in two rows before the motionless Daman and his Illanun chiefs in martial array. The members of the council who had left their bench approached the white people with gentle smiles and deferential movements of the hands. Their bearing was faintly propitiatory, only the man in the big turban remained fanatically aloof, keeping his eyes fixed on the ground.

'I have done it,' murmured Lingard to Mrs Travers. – 'Was it very difficult?' she asked. – 'No,' he said, conscious in his heart that he had strained to the fullest extent the prestige of his good name and that habit of deference to his slightest wish established by the glamour of his wealth and the fear of his personality in this great talk which after all had done nothing except put off the decisive hour. He offered Mrs Travers his arm ready to lead her away, but at the last moment did not move.

With an authoritative gesture Daman had parted the ranks of Belarab's young followers with the red skull-caps and was seen advancing toward the whites striking into an astonished silence all the scattered groups in the courtyard. But the broken ranks had closed behind him. The Illanun chiefs, for all their truculent aspect, were much too prudent to attempt to move. They had not needed for that the faint warning murmur from Daman. He advanced alone. The plain hilt of a sword protruded from the open edges of his cloak. The parted edges disclosed also the butts of two flintlock pistols. The Koran in a velvet case hung on his breast by a red cord of silk. He was pious, magnificent, and war-like, with calm movements and a straight glance from under the hem of the simple piece of linen covering his head. He carried himself rigidly and his bearing had a sort of solemn modesty.

Lingard said hurriedly to Mrs Travers that the man had met white people before and that, should he attempt to shake hands with her, she ought to offer her own covered with the end of her scarf. – 'Why?' she asked. 'Propriety?' – 'Yes, it will be better,' said Lingard and the next moment Mrs Travers felt her enveloped hand pressed gently by slender dark fingers and felt extremely Oriental herself when, with her face muffled to the eyes, she encountered the lustrous black stare of the sea-robbers' leader. It was only for an instant, because Daman turned away at once to shake hands with Lingard. In the straight, ample folds of his robes he looked very slender facing the robust white man.

'Great is your power,' he said, in a pleasant voice. 'The white men are going to be delivered to you.'

'Yes, they pass into my keeping,' said Lingard, returning the other's bright smile but otherwise looking grim enough with the frown which had settled on his forehead at Daman's approach. He glanced over his shoulder at a group of spearmen escorting the two captives who had come down the steps from the hut. At the sight of Daman barring as it were Lingard's way they had stopped at some distance and had closed round the two white men. Daman also glanced dispassionately that way.

'They were my guests,' he murmured. 'Please God I shall come soon to ask you for them . . . as a friend,' he added after a slight pause.

'And please God you will not go away empty handed,' said Lingard, smoothing his brow. 'After all you and I were not meant to meet only to quarrel. Would you have preferred to see them pass into Tengga's keeping?'

'Tengga is fat and full of wiles,' said Daman, disdainfully, 'a mere shopkeeper smitten by a desire to be a chief. He is nothing. But you and I are men that have real power. Yet there is a truth that you and I can confess to each other. Men's hearts grow quickly discontented. Listen. The leaders of men are carried forward in the hands of their followers; and common men's minds are unsteady, their desires changeable, and their thoughts not to be trusted. You are a great chief they say. Do not forget that I am a chief, too, and a leader of armed men.'

'I have heard of you, too,' said Lingard in a composed voice.

Daman had cast his eyes down. Suddenly he opened them very wide with an effect that startled Mrs Travers. – 'Yes. But do you see?' Mrs Travers, her hand resting lightly on Lingard's arm, had the sensation of acting in a gorgeously got-up play on the brilliantly lighted stage of an exotic opera whose accompaniment was not music but the varied strains of the all-pervading silence. – 'Yes, I see,' Lingard replied with a surprisingly confidential intonation. 'But power, too, is in the hands of a great leader.'

Mrs Travers watched the faint movements of Daman's nostrils as though the man were suffering from some powerful emotion, while under her fingers Lingard's forearm in its white sleeve was as steady as a limb of marble. Without looking at him she seemed to feel that with one movement he could crush that nervous figure in which lived the breath of the great desert haunted by his nomad, camel-riding ancestors. – 'Power is in the hand of God,' he said, all animation dying out of his face, and paused to wait for Lingard's 'Very true,' then continued with a fine smile, 'but He apportions it according to His will for His own purposes, even to those that are not of the Faith.'

'Such being the will of God you should harbour no bitterness against them in your heart.'

The low exclamation, 'Against those !' and a slight, dismissing gesture of a meagre dark hand out of the folds of the cloak were almost understandable to Mrs Travers in the perfection of their melancholy contempt, and gave Lingard a further insight into the character of the ally secured to him by the diplomacy of Belarab. He was only half reassured by this assumption of superior detachment. He trusted to the man's self-interest more; for Daman no doubt looked to the reconquered kingdom for the reward of dignity and ease. His father and grandfather (the men of whom Jörgenson had written as having been hanged for an example twelve years before) had been friends of Sultans, advisers of Rulers, wealthy financiers of the great raiding expeditions of the past. It was hatred that had turned Daman into a self-made outcast, till Belarab's diplomacy had drawn him out from some obscure and uneasy retreat.

In a few words Lingard assured Daman of the complete safety of his followers as long as they themselves made no attempt to get possession of the stranded yacht. Lingard understood very well that the capture of Travers and d'Alcacer was the result of a sudden fear, a move directed by Daman to secure his own safety. The sight of the stranded yacht shook his confidence completely. It was as if the secrets of the place had been betrayed. After all, it was perhaps a great folly to trust any white man, no matter how much he seemed estranged from his own people. Daman felt he might have been the victim of a plot. Lingard's brig appeared to him a formidable engine of war. He did not know what to think and the motive for getting hold of the two white men was really the wish to secure hostages. Distrusting the fierce impulses of his followers he had hastened to put them into Belarab's keeping. But everything in the Settlement seemed to him suspicious: Belarab's absence, Jörgenson's refusal to make over at once the promised supply of arms and ammunition. And now that white man had by the power of his speech got them away from Belarab's people. So much influence filled Daman with wonder and awe. A recluse for many years in the most obscure corner of the Archipelago, he felt himself surrounded by intrigues. But the alliance was a great thing, too. He did not want to quarrel. He was quite willing for the time being to accept Lingard's assurance that no harm should befall his people encamped on the sandbanks. Attentive and slight, he seemed to let Lingard's deliberate words sink into him. The force of that unarmed big man seemed overwhelming. He bowed his head slowly.

'Allah is our refuge,' he murmured, accepting the inevitable.

He delighted Mrs Travers not as a living being but like a clever sketch in colours, a vivid rendering of an artist's vision of some soul, delicate and fierce. His bright half-smile was extraordinary, sharp like clear steel, painfully penetrating. Glancing right and left Mrs Travers saw the whole courtyard smitten by the desolating fury of sunshine and peopled with shadows, their forms and colours fading in the violence of the light. The very brown tones of roof and wall dazzled the eye. Then Daman stepped aside. He was no longer smiling and Mrs Travers advanced with her hand on Lingard's arm through a heat so potent that it seemed to have a taste, a feel, a smell of its own. She moved on as if floating in it with Lingard's support.

'Where are they?' she asked.

'They are following us all right,' he answered. Lingard was so certain that the prisoners would be delivered to him on the beach that he never glanced back till, after reaching the boat, he and Mrs Travers turned about.

The group of spearmen parted right and left, and Mr Travers and d'Alcacer walked forward alone looking unreal and odd like their own day-ghosts. Mr Travers gave no sign of being aware of his wife's presence. It was certainly a shock to him. But d'Alcacer advanced smiling, as if the beach were a drawing-room.

With a very few paddlers the heavy old European-built boat moved slowly over the water that seemed as pale and blazing as the sky above. Jörgenson had perched himself in the bow. The other four white people sat in the stern sheets, the ex-prisoners side by side in the middle. Lingard spoke suddenly.

'I want you both to understand that the trouble is not over yet. Nothing is finished. You are out on my bare word.'

While Lingard was speaking Mr Travers turned his face away but d'Alcacer listened courteously. Not another word was spoken for the rest of the way. The two gentlemen went up the ship's side first. Lingard remained to help Mrs Travers at the foot of the ladder. She pressed his hand strongly and looking down at his upturned face:

'This was a wonderful success,' she said.

For a time the character of his fascinated gaze did not change. It was as if she had said nothing. Then he whispered, admiringly: 'You understand everything.'

She moved her eyes away and had to disengage her hand to which he clung for a moment, giddy, like a man falling out of the world.

3

Mrs Travers, acutely aware of Lingard behind her, remained gazing over the lagoon. After a time he stepped forward and placed himself beside her close to the rail. She went on staring at the sheet of water turned to deep purple under the sunset sky.

'Why have you been avoiding me since we came back from the stockade?' she asked in a deadened voice.

'There is nothing to tell you till Rajah Hassim and his sister Immada return with some news,' Lingard answered in the same tone. 'Has my friend succeeded? Will Belarab listen to any arguments? Will he consent to come out of his shell? Is he on his way back? I wish I knew! ... Not a whisper comes from there! He may have started two days ago and he may be now near the outskirts of the Settlement. Or he may have gone into camp half way down, from some whim or other; or he may be already arrived for all I know. We should not have seen him. The road from the hills does not lead along the beach.'

He snatched nervously at the long glass and directed it at the dark stockade. The sun had sunk behind the forests leaving the contour of the tree-tops outlined by a thread of gold under a band of delicate green lying across the lower sky. Higher up a faint crimson glow faded into the darkened blue overhead. The shades of the evening deepened over the lagoon, clung to the sides of the *Emma* and to the forms of the further shore. Lingard laid the glass down.

'Mr d'Alcacer, too, seems to have been avoiding me,' said Mrs Travers. 'You are on very good terms with him, Captain Lingard.'

'He is a very pleasant man,' murmured Lingard, absently. 'But he says funny things sometimes. He inquired the other day if there were any playing cards on board, and when I asked him if he liked card-playing, just for something to say, he told me with that queer smile of his that he had read a story of some people

247

condemned to death who passed the time before execution playing card games with their guards.'

'And what did you say?'

'I told him that there were probably cards on board somewhere – Jörgenson would know. Then I asked him whether he looked on me as a gaoler. He was quite startled and sorry for what he said.'

'It wasn't very kind of you, Captain Lingard.'

'It slipped out awkwardly and we made it up with a laugh.'

Mrs Travers leaned her elbows on the rail and put her head into her hands. Every attitude of that woman surprised Lingard by its enchanting effect upon himself. He sighed, and the silence lasted for a long while.

'I wish I had understood every word that was said that morning.'

'That morning,' repeated Lingard. 'What morning do you mean?'

'I mean the morning when I walked out of Belarab's stockade on your arm, Captain Lingard, at the head of the procession. It seemed to me that I was walking on a splendid stage in a scene from an opera, in a gorgeous show fit to make an audience hold its breath. You can't possibly guess how unreal all this seemed, and how artificial I felt myself. An opera you know ...'

'I know. I was a gold digger at one time. Some of us used to come down to Melbourne with our pockets full of money. I daresay it was poor enough to what you must have seen, but once I went to a show like that. It was a story acted to music. All the people went singing through it right to the very end.'

'How it must have jarred on your sense of reality,' said Mrs Travers, still not looking at him. 'You don't remember the name of the opera?'

'No. I never troubled my head about it. We – our lot never did.'

'I won't ask you what the story was like. It must have appeared to you like the very defiance of all truth. Would real people go singing through their life anywhere except in a fairy tale?'

'These people didn't always sing for joy,' said Lingard, simply. 'I don't know much about fairy tales.'

'They are mostly about princesses,' murmured Mrs Travers.

Lingard didn't quite hear. He bent his ear for a moment but she wasn't looking at him and he didn't ask her to repeat her remark. 'Fairy tales are for children, I believe,' he said. 'But that story with music I am telling you of, Mrs Travers, was not a tale for children. I assure you that of the few shows I have seen that one was the most real to me. More real than anything in life.'

Mrs Travers, remembering the fatal inanity of most opera librettos, was touched by these words as if there had been something pathetic in this readiness of response: as if she had heard a starved man talking of the delight of a crust of dry bread. 'I suppose you forgot yourself in that story, whatever it was,' she remarked in a detached tone.

'Yes, it carried me away. But I suppose you know the feeling.'

'No. I never knew anything of the kind, not even when I was a chit of a girl.' Lingard seemed to accept this statement as an assertion of superiority. He inclined his head slightly. Moreover, she might have said what she liked. What pleased him most was her not looking at him; for it enabled him to contemplate with perfect freedom the curve of her cheek, her small ear half hidden by the clear mesh of fine hair, the fascination of her uncovered neck. And her whole person was an impossible, an amazing and solid marvel which somehow was not so much convincing to the eyes as to something within him that was apparently independent of his senses. Not even for a moment did he think of her as remote. Untouchable – possibly! But remote – no. Whether consciously or unconsciously he took her spiritually for granted. It was materially that she was a wonder of the sort that is at the same time familiar and sacred.

'No,' Mrs Travers began again, abruptly. 'I never forgot myself in a story. It was not in me. I have not even been able to forget myself on that morning on shore which was part of my own story.'

'You carried yourself first rate,' said Lingard, smiling at the

249

nape of her neck, her ear, the film of escaped hair, the modelling of the corner of her eye. He could see the flutter of the dark eyelashes; and the delicate flush on her cheek had rather the effect of scent than of colour.

'You approved of my behaviour.'

'Just right, I tell you. My word, weren't they all struck of a heap when they made out what you were.'

'I ought to feel flattered. I will confess to you that I felt only half disguised and was half angry and wholly uncomfortable. What helped me, I suppose, was that I wanted to please . . .'

'I don't mean to say that they were exactly pleased,' broke in Lingard, conscientiously. 'They were startled more.'

'I wanted to please you,' dropped Mrs Travers, negligently. A faint, hoarse, and impatient call of a bird was heard from the woods as if calling to the oncoming night. Lingard's face grew hot in the deepening dusk. The delicate lemon yellow and ethereal green tints had vanished from the sky and the red glow darkened menacingly. The sun had set behind the black pall of the forest, no longer edged with a line of gold.

'Yes, I was absurdly self-conscious,' continued Mrs Travers in a conversational tone. 'And it was the effect of these clothes that you made me put on over some of my European – I almost said disguise; because you know in the present more perfect costume I feel curiously at home; and yet I can't say that these things really fit me. The sleeves of this silk under-jacket are rather tight. My shoulders feel bound, too, and as to the *sarong* it is scandalously short. According to rule it should have been long enough to fall over my feet. But I like freedom of movement. I have had very little of what I liked in life.'

'I can hardly believe that,' said Lingard. 'If it wasn't for your saying so . . .'

'I wouldn't say so to everybody,' she said, turning her head for a moment to Lingard and turning it away again to the dusk which seemed to come floating over the black lagoon. Far away in its depth a couple of feeble lights twinkled; it was impossible to say whether on the shore or on the edge of the more distant forest. Overhead the stars were beginning to come out, but faint yet, as if too remote to be reflected in the lagoon. Only to the west a setting planet shone through the red fog of the sunset glow. 'It was supposed not to be good for me to have much freedom of action. So at least I was told. But I have a suspicion that it was only unpleasing to other people.'

'I should have thought,' began Lingard, then hesitated and stopped. It seemed to him inconceivable that everybody should not have loved to make that woman happy. And he was impressed by the bitterness of her tone. Mrs Travers did not seem curious to know what he wanted to say and after a time she added, 'I don't mean only when I was a child. I don't remember that very well. I daresay I was very objectionable as a child.'

Lingard tried to imagine her as a child. The idea was novel to him. Her perfection seemed to have come into the world complete, mature, and without any hesitation or weakness. He had nothing in his experience that could help him to imagine a child of that class. The children he knew played about the village street and ran on the beach. He had been one of them. He had seen other children, of course, since, but he had not been in touch with them except visually and they had not been English children. Her childhood, like his own, had been passed in England, and that very fact made it almost impossible for him to imagine it. He could not even tell whether it was in town or in the country, or whether as a child she had ever seen the sea. And how could a child of that kind be objectionable? But he remembered that a child disapproved of could be very unhappy, and he said :

'I am sorry.'

Mrs Travers laughed a little. Within the muslin cage forms had turned to blurred shadows. Amongst them the form of d'Alcacer arose and moved. The systematic or else the morbid dumbness of Mr Travers bored and exasperated him, though, as a matter of fact, that gentleman's speeches had never had the power either to entertain or to soothe his mind.

'It's very nice of you. You have a great capacity for sympathy, but after all I am not certain on which side your sympathies lie. With me, or those much-tried people,' said Mrs Travers.

'With the child,' said Lingard, disregarding the bantering tone. 'A child can have a very bad time of it all to itself.'

'What can you know of it?' she asked.

'I have my own feelings,' he answered in some surprise.

Mrs Travers, with her back to him, was covered with confusion. Neither could she depict to herself his childhood as if he, too, had come into the world in the fullness of his strength and his purpose. She discovered a certain naïveness in herself and laughed a little. He made no sound.

'Don't be angry,' she said. 'I wouldn't dream of laughing at your feelings. Indeed your feelings are the most serious thing that ever came in my way. I couldn't help laughing at myself – at a funny discovery I made.'

'In the days of your childhood?' she heard Lingard's deep voice asking after a pause.

'Oh, no. Ages afterward. No child could have made that discovery. Do you know the greatest difference there is between us? It is this: That I have been living since my childhood in front of a show and that I never have been taken in for a moment by its tinsel and its noise or by anything that went on on the stage. Do you understand what I mean, Captain Lingard?'

There was a moment of silence. 'What does it matter? We are not children now.' There was an infinite gentleness in Lingard's deep tones. 'But if you have been unhappy then don't tell me that it has not been made up to you since. Surely you have only to make a sign. A woman like you.'

'You think I could frighten the whole world on to its knees?'

'No, not frighten.' The suggestion of a laugh in the deadened voice passed off in a catch of the breath. Then he was heard beginning soberly: 'Your husband ...' He hesitated a little and she took the opportunity to say coldly:

'His name is Mr Travers.'

Lingard didn't know how to take it. He imagined himself to have been guilty of some sort of presumption. But how on earth was he to call the man? After all he was her husband. That idea was disagreeable to him because the man was also inimical in a particularly unreasonable and galling manner. At the same time he was aware that he didn't care a bit for his enmity and had an idea that he would not have cared for his friendship either. And suddenly he felt very much annoyed.

'Yes. That's the man I mean,' he said in a contemptuous tone. 'I don't particularly like the name and I am sure I don't want to talk about him more than I can help. If he hadn't been your husband I wouldn't have put up with his manners for an hour. Do you know what would have happened to him if he hadn't been your husband?'

'No,' said Mrs Travers. 'Do you, Captain Lingard?'

'Not exactly,' he admitted. 'Something he wouldn't have liked, you may be sure.'

'While of course he likes this very much,' she observed. Lingard gave an abrupt laugh.

'I don't think it's in my power to do anything that he would like,' he said in a serious tone. 'Forgive me my frankness, Mrs Travers, but he makes it very difficult sometimes for me to keep civil. Whatever I have had to put up with in life I have never had to put up with contempt.'

'I quite believe that,' said Mrs Travers. 'Don't your friends call you King Tom?'

'Nobody that I care for. I have no friends. Oh, yes, they call me that ...'

'You have no friends?'

'Not I,' he said with decision. 'A man like me has no chums.'

'It's quite possible,' murmured Mrs Travers to herself.

'No, not even Jörgenson. Old crazy Jörgenson. He calls me King Tom, too. You see what that's worth.'

'Yes, I see. Or rather I have heard. That poor man has no tone, and so much depends on that. Now suppose I were to call you King Tom now and then between ourselves,' Mrs Travers' voice proposed, distantly tentative in the night that invested her person with a colourless vagueness of form.

She waited in the stillness, her elbows on the rail and her face in her hands as if she had already forgotten what she had said. She heard at her elbow the deep murmur of:

'Let's hear you say it.'

She never moved the least bit. The sombre lagoon sparkled faintly with the reflection of the stars.

'Oh, yes, I will let you hear it,' she said into the starlit space in a voice of unaccented gentleness which changed subtly as she went on. 'I hope you will never regret that you came out of your friendless mystery to speak to me, King Tom. How many days ago it was! And here is another day gone. Tell me how many more of them there must be? Of these blinding days and nights without a sound.'

'Be patient,' he murmured. 'Don't ask me for the impossible.'

'How do you or I know what is possible?' she whispered with a strange scorn. 'You wouldn't dare guess. But I tell you that every day that passes is more impossible to me than the day before.'

The passion of that whisper went like a stab into his breast. 'What am I to tell you?' he murmured, as if with despair. 'Remember that every sunset makes it a day less. Do you think I want you here?'

A bitter little laugh floated out into the starlight. Mrs Travers heard Lingard move suddenly away from her side. She didn't change her pose by a hair's breadth. Presently she heard d'Alcacer coming out of the Cage. His cultivated voice asked half playfully:

'Have you had a satisfactory conversation? May I be told something of it?'

'Mr d'Alcacer, you are curious.'

'Well, in our position, I confess ... You are our only refuge, remember.'

'You want to know what we were talking about,' said Mrs Travers, altering slowly her position so as to confront d'Alcacer whose face was almost indistinguishable. 'Oh, well, then, we talked about opera, the realities and illusions of the stage, of dresses, of people's names, and things of that sort.'

'Nothing of importance,' he said, courteously. Mrs Travers moved forward and he stepped to one side. Inside the Cage two Malay hands were hanging round lanterns, the light of which fell on Mr Travers' bowed head as he sat in his chair.

When they were all assembled for the evening meal Jörgenson strolled up from nowhere in particular as his habit was, and speaking through the muslin announced that Captain Lingard begged to be excused from joining the company that evening. Then he strolled away. From that moment till they got up from the table and the camp bedsteads were brought in not twenty words passed between the members of the party within the net. The strangeness of their situation made all attempts to exchange ideas very arduous: and apart from that each had thoughts which it was distinctly useless to communicate to the others. Mr Travers had abandoned himself to his sense of injury. He did not so much brood as rage inwardly in a dull, dispirited way. The impossibility of asserting himself in any manner galled his very soul. D'Alcacer was extremely puzzled. Detached in a sense from the life of men perhaps as much even as Jörgenson himself, he took yet a reasonable interest in the course of events and had not lost all his sense of self-preservation. Without being able to appreciate the exact values of the situation he was not one of those men who are ever completely in the dark in any given set of circumstances. Without being humorous he was a good-humoured man. His habitual, gentle smile was a true expression. More of a European than of a Spaniard he had that truly aristo-cratic nature which is inclined to credit every honest man with something of its own nobility and in its judgement is altogether independent of class feeling. He believed Lingard to be an honest man and he never troubled his head to classify him, except in the sense that he found him an interesting character. He had a sort of esteem for the outward personality and the bearing of that seaman. He found in him also the distinction of being nothing of a type. He was a specimen to be judged only by its own worth. With his natural gift of insight d'Alcacer told himself that many overseas adventurers of history were probably less worthy because obviously they must have been less simple. He didn't, however, impart those thoughts formally to Mrs Travers. In fact he avoided discussing Lingard with Mrs Travers who, he thought, was quite intelligent enough to appreciate the exact shade of his attitude. If that shade was fine, Mrs Travers was fine, too; and there was no need to discuss the colours of this adventure. Moreover, she herself seemed to avoid all direct discussion of the Lingard element in their fate. D'Alcacer was fine enough to be aware that those two seemed to understand each other in a way that was not obvious even to themselves. Whenever he saw them together he was always much tempted to observe them. And he yielded to the temptation. The fact of one's life depending on the phases of an obscure action authorizes a certain latitude of behaviour. He had seen them together repeatedly, communing openly or apart, and there was in their way of joining each other, in their poses and their ways of separating, something special and characteristic and pertaining to themselves only, as if they had been made for each other.

What he couldn't understand was why Mrs Travers should have put off his natural curiosity as to her latest conference with the Man of Fate by an incredible statement as to the nature of the conversation. Talk about dresses, opera, people's names. He couldn't take this seriously. She might have invented, he thought, something more plausible; or simply have told him that this was not for him to know. She ought to have known that he would not have been offended. Couldn't she have seen already that he accepted the complexion of mystery in her relation to that man completely, unquestionably; as though it had been something preordained from the very beginning of things. But he was not annoyed with Mrs Travers. After all it might have been true. She would talk exactly as she liked, and even incredibly, if it so pleased her, and make the man hang on her lips. And likewise she was capable of making the man talk about anything by a power of inspiration for simple or perverse. Opera! Dresses! Yes – about Shakespeare and the musical glasses! For a mere whim or for the deepest purpose. Women worthy of the name were like that. They were very wonderful. They rose to the occasion and sometimes above the occasion when things were bound to occur that would be comic or tragic (as it happened) but generally charged with trouble even to innocent beholders. D'Alcacer thought these thoughts without bitterness and even without irony. With his half-secret social reputation as a man of one great passion in a world of mere intrigues he liked all women. He liked them in their sentiment and in their hardness, in the tragic character of their foolish or clever impulses, at which he looked with a sort of tender seriousness.

He didn't take a favourable view of the position but he considered Mrs Travers' statement about operas and dresses as a warning to keep off the subject. For this reason he remained silent through the meal.

When the bustle of clearing away the table was over he strolled toward Mrs Travers and remarked very quietly:

'I think that in keeping away from us this evening the Man of Fate was well inspired. We dined like a lot of Carthusian monks.'

'You allude to our silence?'

'It was most scrupulous. If we had taken an eternal vow we couldn't have kept it better.'

'Did you feel bored?'

'*Pas du tout,*' d'Alcacer assured her with whimsical gravity. 'I felt nothing. I sat in a state of blessed vacuity. I believe I was the happiest of us three. Unless you, too, Mrs Travers ...'

'It's absolutely no use your fishing for my thoughts, Mr d'Alcacer. If I were to let you see them you would be appalled.'

'Thoughts really are but a shape of feelings. Let me congratulate you on the impassive mask you can put on those horrors you say you nurse in your breast. It was impossible to tell anything by your face.'

'You will always say flattering things.'

'Madame, my flatteries come from the very bottom of my heart. I have given up long ago all desire to please. And I was not trying to get at your thoughts. Whatever else you may expect from me you may count on my absolute respect for your privacy. But I suppose with a mask such as you can make for yourself you really don't care. The Man of Fate, I noticed, is not nearly as good at it as you are.'

'What a pretentious name. Do you call him by it to his face, Mr d'Alcacer?'

'No, I haven't the cheek,' confessed d'Alcacer, equably. 'And, besides, it's too momentous for daily use. And he is so simple that he might mistake it for a joke and nothing could be further from my thoughts. Mrs Travers, I will confess to you that I don't feel jocular in the least. But what can he know about people of our sort? And when I reflect how little people of our sort can know of such a man I am quite content to address him as Captain Lingard. It's common and soothing and most respectable and satisfactory; for Captain is the most empty of all titles. What is a Captain? Anybody can be a Captain; and for Lingard it's a name like any other. Whereas what he deserves is something special, significant, and expressive, that would match his person, his simple and romantic person.'

He perceived that Mrs Travers was looking at him intently. They hastened to turn their eyes away from each other.

'He would like your appreciation,' Mrs Travers let drop negligently.

'I am afraid he would despise it.'

'Despise it! Why, that sort of thing is the very breath of his nostrils.'

'You seem to understand him, Mrs Travers. Women have a singular capacity for understanding. I mean subjects that interest them; because when their imagination is stimulated they are not afraid of letting it go. A man is more mistrustful of himself, but women are born much more reckless. They push on and on under the protection of secrecy and silence, and the greater the obscurity of what they wish to explore the greater their courage.'

'Do you mean seriously to tell me that you consider me a creature of darkness?'

'I spoke in general,' remonstrated d'Alcacer. 'Anything else would have been an impertinence. Yes, obscurity is women's best friend. Their daring loves it; but a sudden flash of light disconcerts them. Generally speaking, if they don't get exactly at the truth they always manage to come pretty near to it.'

Mrs Travers had listened with silent attention and she allowed the silence to continue for some time after d'Alcacer had ceased. When she spoke it was to say in an unconcerned tone that as to this subject she had had special opportunities. Her self-possessed interlocutor managed to repress a movement of real curiosity under an assumption of conventional interest. 'Indeed,' he exclaimed, politely. 'A special opportunity. How did you manage to create it?'

This was too much for Mrs Travers. 'I! Create it!' she exclaimed, indignantly, but under her breath. 'How on earth do you think I could have done it?'

Mr d'Alcacer, as if communing with himself, was heard to murmur unrepentantly that indeed women seldom knew how they had 'done it', to which Mrs Travers in a weary tone returned the remark that no two men were dense in the same way. To this Mr d'Alcacer assented without difficulty. 'Yes, our brand presents more varieties. This, from a certain point of view, is obviously to our advantage. We interest ... Not that I imagine myself interesting to you, Mrs Travers. But what about the Man of Fate?'

'Oh, yes,' breathed out Mrs Travers.

'I see! Immensely!' said d'Alcacer in a tone of mysterious understanding. 'Was his stupidity so colossal?'

'It was indistinguishable from great visions that were in no sense mean and made up for him a world of his own.'

'I guessed that much,' muttered d'Alcacer to himself. 'But that, you know, Mrs Travers, that isn't good news at all to me. World of dreams, eh? That's very bad, very dangerous. It's almost fatal, Mrs Travers.'

'Why all this dismay? Why do you object to a world of dreams?'

'Because I dislike the prospect of being made a sacrifice of by those Moors. I am not an optimist like our friend, there,' he continued in a low tone nodding toward the dismal figure of Mr Travers huddled up in the chair. 'I don't regard all this as a farce and I have discovered in myself a strong objection to having my throat cut by those gorgeous barbarians after a lot of fatuous talk. Don't ask me why, Mrs Travers. Put it down to an absurd weakness.'

Mrs Travers made a slight movement in her chair, raising her hands to her head, and in the dim light of the lanterns d'Alcacer

saw the mass of her clear gleaming hair fall down and spread itself over her shoulders. She seized half of it in her hands which
looked very white, and with her head inclined a little on one side
she began to make a plait.

'You are terrifying,' he said after watching the movement of
her fingers for a while.

'Yes ...' she accentuated; interrogatively.

'You have the awfulness of the pre-destined. You, too, are the
prey of dreams.'

'Not of the Moors, then,' she uttered, calmly, beginning the
other plait. D'Alcacer followed the operation to the end. Close
against her, her diaphanous shadow on the muslin reproduced
her slightest movements. D'Alcacer turned his eyes away.

'No! No barbarian shall touch you. Because if it comes to that
I believe *he* would be capable of killing you himself.'

A minute elapsed before he stole a glance in her direction. She
was leaning back again, her hands had fallen on her lap and her
head with a plait of hair on each side of her face, her head incredibly changed in character and suggesting something medi-
eval, ascetic, drooped dreamily on her breast.

D'Alcacer waited, holding his breath. She didn't move. In
the dim gleam of jewelled clasps, the faint sheen of gold embroideries and the shimmer of silks, she was like a figure in a
faded painting. Only her neck appeared dazzlingly white in the
smoky redness of the light. D'Alcacer's wonder approached a
feeling of awe. He was on the point of moving away quietly
when Mrs Travers, without stirring in the least, let him hear the
words:

'I have told him that every day seemed more difficult to live.
Don't you see how impossible this is?'

D'Alcacer glanced rapidly across the Cage where Mr Travers
seemed to be asleep all in a heap and presenting a ruffled appearance like a sick bird. Nothing was distinct of him but the
bald patch on the top of his head.

'Yes,' he murmured, 'it is most unfortunate ... I understand
your anxiety, Mrs Travers, but ...'

'I am frightened,' she said.

He reflected a moment. 'What answer did you get?' he asked, softly.

'The answer was: "Patience".'

D'Alcacer laughed a little. – 'You may well laugh,' murmured Mrs Travers in a tone of anguish. – 'That's why I did,' he whispered. 'Patience! Didn't he see the horror of it?' – 'I don't know. He walked away,' said Mrs Travers. She looked immovably at her hands clasped in her lap, and then with a burst of distress, 'Mr d'Alcacer, what is going to happen?' – 'Ah, you are asking yourself the question at last. *That* will happen which cannot be avoided; and perhaps you know best what it is.' – 'No. I am still asking myself what he will do.' – 'Ah, that is not for me to know,' declared d'Alcacer. 'I can't tell you what he will do, but I know what will happen to him.' – 'To him, you say! To him!' she cried. – 'He will break his heart,' said d'Alcacer, distinctly, bending a little over the chair with a slight gasp at his own audacity – and waited.

'*Croyez-vous?*' came at last from Mrs Travers in an accent so coldly languid that d'Alcacer felt a shudder run down his spine.

Was it possible that she was that kind of woman, he asked himself. Did she see nothing in the world outside herself? Was she above the commonest kind of compassion? He couldn't suspect Mrs Travers of stupidity; but she might have been heartless and, like some women of her class, quite unable to recognize any emotion in the world except her own. D'Alcacer was shocked and at the same time he was relieved because he confessed to himself that he had ventured very far. However, in her humanity she was not vulgar enough to be offended. She was not the slave of small meannesses. This thought pleased d'Alcacer who had schooled himself not to expect too much from people. But he didn't know what to do next. After what he had ventured to say and after the manner in which she had met his audacity the only thing to do was to change the conversation. Mrs Travers remained perfectly still. 'I will pretend that I think she is asleep,' he thought to himself, meditating a retreat on tip-toe.

He didn't know that Mrs Travers was simply trying to recover the full command of her faculties. His words had given her a terrible shock. After managing to utter this defensive *'croyez-vous'* which came out of her lips cold and faint as if in a last effort of dying strength, she felt herself turn rigid and speechless. She was thinking, stiff all over with emotion: 'D'Alcacer has seen it! How much more has he been able to see?' She didn't ask herself that question in fear or shame but with a reckless resignation. Out of that shock came a sensation of peace. A glowing warmth passed through all her limbs. If d'Alcacer had peered by that smoky light into her face he might have seen on her lips a fatalistic smile come and go. But d'Alcacer would not have dreamed of doing such a thing, and, besides, his attention just then was drawn in another direction. He had heard subdued exclamations, had noticed a stir on the decks of the *Emma*, and even some sort of noise outside the ship.

'These are strange sounds,' he said.

'Yes, I hear,' Mrs Travers murmured, uneasily.

Vague shapes glided outside the Cage, barefoot, almost noiseless, whispering Malay words secretly.

'It seems as though a boat had come alongside,' observed d'Alcacer, lending an attentive ear. 'I wonder what it means. In our position . . .'

'It may mean anything,' interrupted Mrs Travers.

'Jaffir is here,' said a voice in the darkness of the after end of the ship. Then there were some more words in which d'Alcacer's attentive ear caught the word 'surat'.

'A message of some sort has come,' he said. 'They will be calling Captain Lingard. I wonder what thoughts or what dreams this call will interrupt.' He spoke lightly, looking now at Mrs Travers who had altered her position in the chair; and by their tones and attitudes these two might have been on board the yacht sailing the sea in perfect safety. 'You, of course, are the one who will be told. Don't you feel a sort of excitement, Mrs Travers?'

'I have been lately exhorted to patience,' she said in the same easy tone. 'I can wait and I imagine I shall have to wait till the morning.'

'It can't be very late yet,' he said. 'Time with us has been standing still for ever so long. And yet this may be the hour of fate.'

'Is this the feeling you have at this particular moment?'

'I have had that feeling for a considerable number of moments already. At first it was exciting. Now I am only moderately anxious. I have employed my time in going over all my past life.'

'Can one really do that?'

'Yes. I can't say I have been bored to extinction. I am still alive, as you see; but I have done with that and I feel extremely idle. There is only one thing I would like to do. I want to find a few words that could convey to you my gratitude for all your friendliness in the past, at the time when you let me see so much of you in London. I felt always that you took me on my own terms and that so kindly that often I felt inclined to think better of myself. But I am afraid I am wearying you, Mrs Travers.'

'I assure you you have never done that – in the past. And as to the present moment I beg you not to go away. Stay by me please. We are not going to pretend that we are sleepy at this early hour.'

D'Alcacer brought a stool close to the long chair and sat down on it. 'Oh, yes, the possible hour of fate,' he said. 'I have a request to make, Mrs Travers. I don't ask you to betray anything. What would be the good? The issue when it comes will be plain enough. But I should like to get a warning, just something that would give me time to pull myself together, to compose myself as it were. I want you to promise me that if the balance tips against us you will give me a sign. You could, for instance, seize the opportunity when I am looking at you to put your left hand to your forehead like this. It is a gesture that I have never seen you make, and so . . .'

'Jörgenson!' Lingard's voice was heard forward where the light of a lantern appeared suddenly. Then, after a pause, Lingard was heard again: 'Here!'

Then the silent minutes began to go by. Mrs Travers reclining in her chair and d'Alcacer sitting on the stool waited motionless without a word. Presently through the subdued murmurs and agitation pervading the dark deck of the *Emma* Mrs Travers

heard a firm footstep, and, lantern in hand, Lingard appeared
outside the muslin cage.

'Will you come out and speak to me?' he said, loudly. 'Not
you. The lady,' he added in an authoritative tone as d'Alcacer
rose hastily from the stool. 'I want Mrs Travers.'

'Of course,' muttered d'Alcacer to himself and as he opened
the door of the Cage to let Mrs Travers slip through he whispered
to her, 'This *is* the hour of fate.'

She brushed past him swiftly without the slightest sign that
she had heard the words. On the after deck between the Cage
and the deckhouse Lingard waited, lantern in hand. Nobody else
was visible about; but d'Alcacer felt in the air the presence of
silent and excited beings hovering outside the circle of light.
Lingard raised the lantern as Mrs Travers approached and d'Alcacer heard him say:

'I have had news which you ought to know. Let us go into the
deckhouse.'

D'Alcacer saw their heads lighted up by the raised lantern surrounded by the depths of shadow with an effect of a marvellous
and symbolic vision. He heard Mrs Travers say 'I would rather
not hear your news,' in a tone that made that sensitive observer
purse his lips in wonder. He thought that she was over-wrought,
that the situation had grown too much for her nerves. But this
was not the tone of a frightened person. It flashed through his
mind that she had become self-conscious, and there he stopped
in his speculation. That friend of women remained discreet even
in his thoughts. He stepped backward further into the Cage and
without surprise saw Mrs Travers follow Lingard into the deckhouse.

4

LINGARD stood the lantern on the table. Its light was very poor.
He dropped on to the sea-chest heavily. He, too, was over-
wrought. His flannel shirt was open at the neck. He had a broad

belt round his waist and was without his jacket. Before him, Mrs Travers, straight and tall in the gay silks, cottons, and muslins of her outlandish dress, with the ends of the scarf thrown over her head, hanging down in front of her, looked dimly splendid and with a black glance out of her white face. He said:

'Do you, too, want to throw me over? I tell you you can't do that now.'

'I wasn't thinking of throwing you over, but I don't even know what you mean. There seem to be no end of things I can't do. Hadn't you better tell me of something that I could do? Have you any idea yourself what you want from me?'

'You can let me look at you. You can listen to me. You can speak to me.'

'Frankly, I have never shirked doing all those things, whenever you wanted me to. You have led me ...'

'I led you!' cried Lingard.

'Oh! It was my fault,' she said, without anger. 'I must have dreamed then that it was you who came to me in the dark with the tale of your impossible life. Could I have sent you away?'

'I wish you had. Why didn't you?'

'Do you want me to tell you that you were irresistible? How could I have sent you away? But you! What made you come back to me with your very heart on your lips?'

When Lingard spoke after a time it was in jerky sentences.

'I didn't stop to think. I had been hurt. I didn't think of you people as ladies and gentlemen. I thought of you as people whose lives I held in my hand. How was it possible to forget you in my trouble? It is your face that I brought back with me on board my brig. I don't know why. I didn't look at you more than at any-body else. It took me all my time to keep my temper down lest it should burn you all up. I didn't want to be rude to you people, but I found it wasn't very easy because threats were the only argument I had. Was I very offensive, Mrs Travers?'

She had listened tense and very attentive, almost stern. And it was without the slightest change of expression that she said:

'I think that you bore yourself appropriately to the state of life to which it has pleased God to call you.'

'What state?' muttered Lingard to himself. 'I am what I am. They call me Rajah Laut, King Tom, and such like. I think it amused you to hear it, but I can tell you it is no joke to have such names fastened on one, even in fun. And those very names have in them something which makes all this affair here no small matter to anybody.'

She stood before him with a set, severe face. – 'Did you call me out in this alarming manner only to quarrel with me?' – 'No, but why do you choose this time to tell me that my coming for help to you was nothing but impudence in your sight? Well, I beg your pardon for intruding on your dignity.' – 'You misunderstood me,' said Mrs Travers, without relaxing for a moment her contemplative severity. 'Such a flattering thing had never happened to me before and it will never happen to me again. But believe me, King Tom, you did me too much honour. Jörgenson is perfectly right in being angry with you for having taken a woman in tow.' – 'He didn't mean to be rude,' protested Lingard, earnestly. Mrs Travers didn't even smile at this intrusion of a point of manners into the atmosphere of anguish and suspense that seemed always to arise between her and this man who, sitting on the sea-chest, had raised his eyes to her with an air of extreme candour and seemed unable to take them off again. She continued to look at him sternly by a tremendous effort of will.

'How changed you are,' he murmured.

He was lost in the depths of the simplest wonder. She appeared to him vengeful and as if turned forever into stone before his bewildered remorse. Forever. Suddenly Mrs Travers looked round and sat down in the chair. Her strength failed her but she remained austere with her hands resting on the arms of her seat. Lingard sighed deeply and dropped his eyes. She did not dare relax her muscles for fear of breaking down altogether and betraying a reckless impulse which lurked at the bottom of her dismay, to seize the head of d'Alcacer's Man of Fate, press it to her breast once, fling it far away, and vanish herself, vanish out of life like a wraith. The Man of Fate sat silent and bowed, yet with a suggestion of strength in his dejection. 'If I don't speak,'

Mrs Travers said to herself, with great inward calmness, 'I shall burst into tears.' She said aloud, 'What could have happened? What have you dragged me in here for? Why don't you tell me your news?'

'I thought you didn't want to hear. I believe you really don't want to. What is all this to you? I believe that you don't care anything about what I feel, about what I do and how I end. I verily believe that you don't care how you end yourself. I believe you never cared for your own or anybody's feelings. I don't think it is because you are hard, I think it is because you don't know, and don't want to know, and are angry with life.'

He flourished an arm recklessly, and Mrs Travers noticed for the first time that he held a sheet of paper in his hand.

'Is that your news there?' she asked, significantly. 'It's difficult to imagine that in this wilderness writing can have any significance. And who on earth here could send you news on paper? Will you let me see it? Could I understand it? Is it in English? Come, King Tom, don't look at me in this awful way.'

She got up suddenly, not in indignation, but as if at the end of her endurance. The jewelled clasps, the gold embroideries, gleamed elusively amongst the folds of her draperies which emitted a mysterious rustle.

'I can't stand this,' she cried. 'I can't stand being looked at like this. No woman could stand it. No woman has ever been looked at like this. What can you see? Hatred I could understand. What is it you think me capable of?'

'You are very extraordinary,' murmured Lingard, who had regained his self-possession before that outburst.

'Very well, and you are extraordinary, too. That's understood – here we are both under that curse and having to face together whatever may turn up. But who on earth could have sent you this writing?'

'Who?' repeated Lingard. 'Why, that young fellow that blundered on my brig in the dark, bringing a boatload of trouble alongside on that quiet night in Carimata Straits. The darkest night I have ever known. An accursed night.'

Mrs Travers bit her lip, waited a little, then asked quietly:
'What difficulty has he got into now?'

'Difficulty!' cried Lingard. 'He is immensely pleased with
himself, the young fool. You know, when you sent him to talk
to me that evening you left the yacht, he came with a loaded
pistol in his pocket. And now he has gone and done it.'

'Done it?' repeated Mrs Travers, blankly. 'Done what?'

She snatched from Lingard's unresisting palm the sheet of
paper. While she was smoothing it Lingard moved round and
stood close at her elbow. She ran quickly over the first lines, then
her eyes steadied. At the end she drew a quick breath and looked
up at Lingard. Their faces had never been so close together before and Mrs Travers had a surprising second of a perfectly new
sensation. She looked away. – 'Do you understand what this
means?' he murmured. Mrs Travers let her hand fall by her
side. – 'Yes,' she said in a low tone. 'The compact is broken.'

Carter had begun his letter without any preliminaries:

You cleared out in the middle of the night and took the lady away
with you. You left me no proper orders. But as a sailorman I looked
upon myself as left in charge of two ships while within half a mile on
that sandbank there were more than a hundred piratical cut-throats
watching me as closely as so many tigers about to leap. Days went by
without a word of you or the lady. To leave the ships outside and go
inland to look for you was not to be thought of with all those pirates
within springing distance. Put yourself in my place. Can't you imagine my anxiety, my sleepless nights? Each night worse than the
night before. And still no word from you. I couldn't sit still and
worry my head off about things I couldn't understand. I am a
sailorman. My first duty was to the ships. I had to put an end to this
impossible situation and I hope you will agree that I have done it in
a seamanlike way. One misty morning I moved the brig nearer the
sandbank and directly the mist cleared I opened fire on the praus of
those savages which were anchored in the channel. We aimed wide at
first to give those vagabonds that were on board a chance to clear
out and join their friends camped on the sands. I didn't want to
kill people. Then we got the long gun to bear and in about an hour
we had the bottom knocked out of the two praus. The savages on
the bank howled and screamed at every shot. They are mighty angry

but I don't care for their anger now, for by sinking their praus I have made them as harmless as a flock of lambs. They needn't starve on their sandbank because they have two or three dugouts hauled up on the sand and they may ferry themselves and their women to the mainland whenever they like.

I fancy I have acted as a seaman and as a seaman I intend to go on acting. Now I have made the ships safe I shall set about without loss of time trying to get the yacht off the mud. When that's done I shall arm the boats and proceed inshore to look for you and the yacht's gentry, and shan't rest till I know whether any or all of you are above earth yet.

I hope these words will reach you. Just as we had done the business of those praus the man you sent off that night in Carimata to stop our chief officer came sailing in from the west with our first gig in tow and the boat's crew all well. Your *serang* tells me he is a most trust-worthy messenger and that his name is Jaffir. He seems only too anxious to try to get to you as soon as possible. I repeat, ships and men have been made safe and I don't mean to give you up dead or alive.

'You are quick in taking the point,' said Lingard in a dull voice, while Mrs Travers, with the sheet of paper gripped in her hand, looked into his face with anxious eyes. 'He has been smart and no mistake.'

'He didn't know,' murmured Mrs Travers.

'No, he didn't know. But could I take everybody into my confidence?' protested Lingard in the same low tone. 'And yet who else could I trust? It seemed to me that he must have understood without being told. But he is too young. He may well be proud according to his lights. He has done that job outside very smartly – damn his smartness! And here we are with all our lives depending on my word – which is broken now, Mrs Travers. It is broken.'

Mrs Travers nodded at him slightly.

'They would sooner have expected to see the sun and the moon fall out of the sky,' Lingard continued with repressed fire. Next moment it seemed to have gone out of him and Mrs Travers heard him mutter a disconnected phrase ... 'The world down about my ears.'

'What will you do?' she whispered.

'What will I do?' repeated Lingard, gently. 'Oh, yes – do. Mrs Travers, do you see that I am nothing now. Just nothing.'

He had lost himself in the contemplation of her face turned to him with an expression of awed curiosity. The shock of the world coming down about his ears in consequence of Carter's smartness was so terrific that it had dulled his sensibilities in the manner of a great pain or of a great catastrophe. What was there to look at but that woman's face, in a world which had lost its consistency, its shape and its promises in a moment.

Mrs Travers looked away. She understood that she had put to Lingard an impossible question. What was presenting itself to her as a problem was to that man a crisis of feeling. Obviously Carter's action had broken the compact entered into with Daman and she was intelligent enough to understand that it was the sort of thing that could not be explained away. It wasn't horror that she felt, but a sort of consternation, something like the discomfiture of people who have just missed their train. It was only more intense. The real dismay had yet to make its way into her comprehension. To Lingard it was a blow struck straight at his heart.

He was not angry with Carter. The fellow had acted like a seaman. Carter's concern was for the ships. In this fatality Carter was a mere incident. The real cause of the disaster was somewhere else, was other, and more remote. And at the same time Lingard could not defend himself from a feeling that it was in himself, too, somewhere in the unexplored depths of his nature, something fatal and unavoidable. He muttered to himself:

'No. I am not a lucky man.'

This was but a feeble expression of the discovery of the truth that suddenly had come home to him as if driven into his breast by a revealing power which had decided that this was to be the end of his fling. But he was not the man to give himself up to the examination of his own sensations. His natural impulse was to grapple with the circumstances and that was what he was trying to do; but he missed now that sense of mastery which is half the battle. Conflict of some sort was the very essence of life. But this was something he had never known before. This was a conflict within himself. He had to face unsuspected powers, foes that he could not go out to meet at the gate. They were within, as though he had been bertayed by somebody, by some secret enemy. He was ready to look round for that subtle traitor. A sort of blankness fell on his mind and he suddenly thought: 'Why! It's myself.'

Immediately afterward he had a clear, merciless recollection of Hassim and Immada. He saw them far off beyond the forests. Oh, yes, they existed – within his breast!

'That was a night!' he muttered, looking straight at Mrs Travers. He had been looking at her all the time. His glance had held her under a spell, but for a whole interminable minute he had not been aware of her at all. At the murmur of his words she made a slight movement and he saw her again. – 'What night?' she whispered, timidly, like an intruder. She was astonished to see him smile. – 'Not like this one,' he said. 'You made me notice how quiet and still it was. Yes. Listen how still it is.'

Both moved their heads slightly and seemed to lend an ear. There was not a murmur, sigh, rustle, splash, or footfall. No whispers, no tremors, not a sound of any kind. They might have been alone on board the *Emma*, abandoned even by the ghost of Captain Jörgenson departed to rejoin the Barque *Wild Rose* on the shore of the Cimmerian sea. – 'It's like the stillness of the end,' said Mrs Travers in a low, equable voice. – 'Yes, but that, too, is false,' said Lingard in the same tone. – 'I don't understand,' Mrs Travers began, hurriedly, after a short silence. 'But don't use that word. Don't use it, King Tom! It frightens me by its mere sound.'

Lingard made no sign. His thoughts were back with Hassim and Immada. The young chief and his sister had gone up country on a voluntary mission to persuade Belarab to return to his stockade and to take up again the direction of affairs. They carried urgent messages from Lingard, who for Belarab was the very embodiment of truth and force, that unquestioned force

which had permitted Belarab to indulge in all his melancholy
hesitations. But those two young people had also some personal
prestige. They were Lingard's heart's friends. They were like
his children. But beside that, their high birth, their warlike
story, their wanderings, adventures, and prospects had given
them a glamour of their own.

5

THE very day that Travers and d'Alcacer had come on board
the *Emma* Hassim and Immada had departed on their mission;
for Lingard, of course, could not think of leaving the white
people alone with Jörgenson. Jörgenson was all right, but his
ineradicable habit of muttering in his moustache about 'throwing a lighted match amongst the powder barrels' had inspired
Lingard with a certain amount of mistrust. And, moreover, he
did not want to go away from Mrs Travers.

It was the only correct inspiration on Carter's part to send
Jaffir with his report to Lingard. That stout-hearted fighter,
swimmer, and devoted follower of the princely misfortunes of
Hassim and Immada, had looked upon his mission to catch the
chief officer of the yacht (which he had received from Lingard in
Carimata) as a trifling job. It took him a little longer than he
expected, but he had got back to the brig just in time to be sent
on to Lingard with Carter's letter after a couple of hours' rest.
He had the story of all the happenings from Wasub before he
left and, though his face preserved its grave impassivity, in his
heart he did not like it at all.

Fearless and wily, Jaffir was the man for difficult missions
and a born messenger – as he expressed it himself – 'to bear
weighty words between great men'. With his unfailing memory
he was able to reproduce them exactly, whether soft or hard, in
council or in private; for he knew no fear. With him there was
no need for writing which might fall into the hands of the
enemy. If he died on the way the message would die with him.
He had also the gift of getting at the sense of any situation and

an observant eye. He was distinctly one of those men from whom trustworthy information can be obtained by the leaders of great enterprises. Lingard did put several questions to him, but in this instance, of course, Jaffir could have only very little to say. Of Carter, whom he called the 'young one', he said that he looked as white men look when they are pleased with themselves; then added without waiting for a definite question – 'The ships out there are now safe enough, O Rajah Laut!' There was no elation in his tone.

Lingard looked at him blankly. When the Greatest of White Men remarked that there was yet a price to be paid for that safety, Jaffir assented by a 'Yes, by Allah!' without losing for a moment his grim composure. When told that he would be required to go and find his master and the lady Immada who were somewhere in the back country, in Belarab's travelling camp, he declared himself ready to proceed at once. He had eaten his fill and had slept three hours on board the brig and he was not tired. When he was young he used to get tired sometimes; but for many years now he had known no such weakness. He did not require the boat with paddlers in which he had come up into the lagoon. He would go alone in a small canoe. This was no time, he remarked, for publicity and ostentation. His pent-up anxiety burst through his lips. 'It is in my mind, Tuan, that death has not been so near them since that night when you came sailing in a black cloud and took us all out of the stockade.'

Lingard said nothing, but there was in Jaffir a faith in that white man which was not easily shaken. 'How are you going to save them this time, O Rajah Laut?' he asked, simply.

'Belarab is my friend,' murmured Lingard.

In his anxiety Jaffir was very outspoken. 'A man of peace!' he exclaimed in a low tone. 'Who could be safe with a man like that?' he asked, contemptuously.

'There is no war,' said Lingard.

'There is suspicion, dread, and revenge, and the anger of armed men,' retorted Jaffir. 'You have taken the white prisoners out of their hands by the force of your words alone. Is that so, Tuan?'

'Yes,' said Lingard.

'And you have them on board here?' asked Jaffir, with a glance over his shoulder at the white and misty structure within which by the light of a small oil flame d'Alcacer and Mrs Travers were just then conversing.

'Yes, I have them here.'

'Then, Rajah Laut,' whispered Jaffir, 'you can make all safe by giving them back.'

'Can I do that?' were the words breathed out through Lingard's lips to the faithful follower of Hassim and Immada.

'Can you do anything else?' was the whispered retort of Jaffir, the messenger accustomed to speak frankly to the great of the earth. 'You are a white man and you can have only one word. And now I go.'

A small, rough dug-out belonging to the *Emma* had been brought round to the ladder. A shadowy calash hovering respectfully in the darkness of the deck had already cleared his throat twice in a warning manner.

'Yes, Jaffir, go,' said Lingard, 'and be my friend.'

'I am the friend of a great prince,' said the other, sturdily. 'But you, Rajah Laut, were even greater. And great you will remain while you are with us, people of this sea and of this land. But what becomes of the strength of your arms before your own white people? Where does it go to, I say? Well, then, we must trust in the strength of your heart.'

'I hope that will never fail,' said Lingard, and Jaffir emitted a grunt of satisfaction. 'But God alone sees into men's hearts.'

'Yes. Our refuge is with Allah,' assented Jaffir, who had acquired the habit of pious turns of speech in the frequentation of professedly religious men, of whom there were many in Belarab's stockade. As a matter of fact, he reposed all his trust in Lingard who had with him the prestige of a providential man sent at the hour of need by heaven itself. He waited awhile, then: 'What is the message I am to take?' he asked.

'Tell the whole tale to the Rajah Hassim,' said Lingard. 'And tell him to make his way here with the lady his sister secretly and with speed. The time of great trouble has come. Let us, at least, be together.'

'Right! Right!' Jaffir approved, heartily. 'To die alone under the weight of one's enemies is a dreadful fate.'

He stepped back out of the sheen of the lamp by which they had been talking and making his way down into the small canoe he took up a paddle and without a splash vanished on the dark lagoon.

It was then that Mrs Travers and d'Alcacer heard Lingard call aloud for Jörgenson. Instantly the familiar shadow stood at Lingard's elbow and listened in detached silence. Only at the end of the tale it marvelled audibly: 'Here's a mess for you if you like.' But really nothing in the world could astonish or startle old Jörgenson. He turned away muttering in his moustache. Lingard remained with his chin in his hand and Jaffir's last words took gradual possession of his mind. Then brusquely he picked up the lamp and went to seek Mrs Travers. He went to seek her because he actually needed her bodily presence, the sound of her voice, the dark, clear glance of her eyes. She could do nothing for him. On his way he became aware that Jörgenson had turned out the few Malays on board the *Emma* and was disposing them about the decks to watch the lagoon in all directions. On calling Mrs Travers out of the Cage, Lingard was, in the midst of his mental struggle, conscious of a certain satisfaction in taking her away from d'Alcacer. He couldn't spare any of her attention to any other man, not the least crumb of her time, not the least particle of her thought! He needed it all. To see it withdrawn from him for the merest instant was irritating – seemed a disaster.

D'Alcacer, left alone, wondered at the imperious tone of Lingard's call. To this observer of shades the fact seemed considerable. 'Sheer nerves,' he concluded, to himself. 'The man is overstrung. He must have had some sort of shock.' But what could it be – he wondered to himself. In the tense stagnation of those days of waiting the slightest tremor had an enormous importance. D'Alcacer did not seek his camp bedstead. He didn't even sit down. With the palms of his hands against the edge of the table he leaned back against it. In that negligent attitude he preserved an alert mind which for a moment wondered whether

Mrs Travers had not spoiled Lingard a little. Yet in the suddenness of the forced association, where, too, d'Alcacer was sure
there was some moral problem in the background, he recognized
the extreme difficulty of weighing accurately the imperious de-
mands against the necessary reservations, the exact proportions
of boldness and caution. And d'Alcacer admired upon the whole
Mrs Travers' cleverness.

There could be no doubt that she had the situation in her
hands. That, of course, did not mean safety. She had it in her
hands as one may hold some highly explosive and uncertain
compound. D'Alcacer thought of her with profound sympathy
and with a quite unselfish interest. Sometimes in a street we
cross the path of personalities compelling sympathy and wonder,
but for all that we don't follow them home. D'Alcacer refrained
from following Mrs Travers any farther. He had become suddenly aware that Mr Travers was sitting up on his camp bedstead. He must have done it very suddenly. Only a moment before he had appeared plunged in the deepest slumber, and the
stillness for a long time now had been perfectly unbroken.
D'Alcacer was startled enough for an exclamation and Mr
Travers turned his head slowly in his direction. D'Alcacer
approached the bedstead with a certain reluctance.

'Awake?' he said.

'A sudden chill,' said Mr Travers. 'But I don't feel cold now.
Strange! I had the impression of an icy blast.'

'Ah!' said d'Alcacer.

'Impossible, of course!' went on Mr Travers. 'This stagnating
air never moves. It clings odiously to one. What time is it?'

'Really, I don't know.'

'The glass of my watch was smashed on that night when we
were so treacherously assailed by the savages on the sandbank,'
grumbled Mr Travers.

'I must say I was never so surprised in my life,' confessed
d'Alcacer. 'We had stopped and I was lighting a cigar, you may
remember.'

'No,' said Mr Travers. 'I had just then pulled out my watch.
Of course it flew out of my hand but it hung by the chain.
Somebody trampled on it. The hands are broken off short. It

keeps on ticking but I can't tell the time. It's absurd. Most provoking.'

'Do you mean to say,' asked d'Alcacer, 'that you have been winding it up every evening?'

Mr Travers looked up from his bedstead and he also seemed surprised. 'Why! I suppose I have.' He kept silent for a while. 'It isn't so much blind habit as you may think. My habits are the outcome of strict method. I had to order my life methodically. You know very well, my dear d'Alcacer, that without strict method I would not have been able to get through my work and would have had no time at all for social duties, which, of course, are of very great importance. I may say that, materially, method has been the foundation of my success in public life. There were never any empty moments in my day. And now this! ...' He looked all round the Cage ... 'Where's my wife?' he asked.

'I was talking to her only a moment ago,' answered d'Alcacer. 'I don't know the time. My watch is on board the yacht; but it isn't late, you know.'

Mr Travers flung off with unwonted briskness the light cotton sheet which covered him. He buttoned hastily the tunic which he had unfastened before lying down, and just as d'Alcacer was expecting him to swing his feet to the deck impetuously, he lay down again on the pillow and remained perfectly still.

D'Alcacer waited awhile and then began to pace the Cage. After a couple of turns he stopped and said, gently:

'I am afraid, Travers, you are not very well.'

'I don't know what illness is,' answered the voice from the pillow, to the great relief of d'Alcacer who really had not expected an answer. 'Good health is a great asset in public life. Illness may make you miss a unique opportunity. I was never ill.'

All this came out deadened in tone, as if the speaker's face had been buried in the pillow. D'Alcacer resumed his pacing.

'I think I asked you where my wife was,' said the muffled voice.

With great presence of mind d'Alcacer kept on pacing the

Cage as if he had not heard. – 'You know, I think she is mad,' went on the muffled voice. 'Unless I am.'

Again d'Alcacer managed not to interrupt his regular pacing. 'Do you know what I think?' he said, abruptly. 'I think, Travers, that you don't want to talk about her. I think that you don't want to talk about anything. And to tell you the truth I don't want to, either.'

D'Alcacer caught a faint sigh from the pillow and at the same time saw a small, dim flame appear outside the Cage. And still he kept on his pacing. Mrs Travers and Lingard coming out of the deckhouse stopped just outside the door and Lingard stood the deck-lamp on its roof. They were too far from d'Alcacer to be heard, but he could make them out: Mrs Travers, as straight as an arrow, and the heavy bulk of the man who faced her with a lowered head. He saw it in profile against the light and as if deferential in its slight droop. They were looking straight at each other. Neither of them made the slightest gesture.

'There is that in me,' Lingard murmured, deeply, 'which would set my heart harder than a stone. I am King Tom, Rajah Laut, and fit to look any man hereabouts in the face. I have my name to take care of. Everything rests on that.'

'Mr d'Alcacer would express this by saying that everything rested on honour,' commented Mrs Travers with lips that did not tremble, though from time to time she could feel the accelerated beating of her heart.

'Call it what you like. It's something that a man needs to draw a free breath. And look! – as you see me standing before you here I care for it no longer.'

'But I do care for it,' retorted Mrs Travers. 'As you see me standing here – I do care. This is something that is your very own. You have a right to it. And I repeat I do care for it.'

'Care for something of my own,' murmured Lingard, very close to her face. 'Why should you care for my rights?'

'Because,' she said, holding her ground though their foreheads were nearly touching, 'because if I ever get back to my life I don't want to make it more absurd by real remorse.'

Her tone was soft and Lingard received the breath of those

words like a caress on his face. D'Alcacer, in the Cage, made still another effort to keep up his pacing. He didn't want to give Mr Travers the slightest excuse for sitting up again and looking round.

'That I should live to hear anybody say they cared anything for what was mine!' whispered Lingard. 'And that it should be you – you, who have taken all hardness out of me.'

'I don't want your heart to be made hard. I want it to be made firm.'

'You couldn't have said anything better than what you have said just now to make it steady,' flowed the murmur of Lingard's voice with something tender in its depth. 'Has anybody ever had a friend like this?' he exclaimed, raising his head as if taking the starry night to witness.

'And I ask myself is it possible that there should be another man on earth that I could trust as I trust you. I say to you: Yes! Go and save what you have a right to and don't forget to be merciful. I will not remind you of our perfect innocence. The earth must be small indeed that we should have blundered like this into your life. It's enough to make one believe in fatality. But I can't find it in me to behave like a fatalist, to sit down with folded hands. Had you been another kind of man I might have been too hopeless or too disdainful. Do you know what Mr d'Alcacer calls you?'

Inside the Cage d'Alcacer, casting curious glances in their direction, saw Lingard shake his head and thought with slight uneasiness: 'He is refusing her something.'

'Mr d'Alcacer's name for you is the "Man of Fate",' said Mrs Travers, a little breathlessly.

'A mouthful. Never mind, he is a gentleman. It's what you ...'

'I call you all but by your Christian name,' said Mrs Travers, hastily. 'Believe me, Mr d'Alcacer understands you.'

'He is all right,' interjected Lingard.

'And he is innocent. I remember what you have said – that the innocent must take their chance. Well, then, do what is right.'

'You think it would be right? You believe it? You feel it?'

'At the time, in this place, from a man like you – Yes, it is right.'

Lingard thought that woman wonderfully true to him and wonderfully fearless with herself. The necessity to take back the two captives to the stockade was so clear and unavoidable now, that he believed nothing on earth could have stopped him from doing so, but where was there another woman in the world who would have taken it like this? And he reflected that in truth and courage there is found wisdom. It seemed to him that till Mrs Travers came to stand by his side he had never known what truth and courage and wisdom were. With his eyes on her face and having been told that in her eyes he appeared worthy of being both commanded and entreated, he felt an instant of complete content, a moment of, as it were, perfect emotional repose.

During the silence Mrs Travers with a quick side-glance noticed d'Alcacer as one sees a man in a mist, his mere dark shape arrested close to the muslin screen. She had no doubt that he was looking in their direction and that he could see them much more plainly than she could see him. Mrs Travers thought suddenly how anxious he must be; and she remembered that he had begged her for some sign, for some warning, beforehand, at the moment of crisis. She had understood very well his hinted request for time to get prepared. If he was to get more than a few minutes, *this* was the moment to make him a sign – the sign he had suggested himself. Mrs Travers moved back the least bit so as to let the light fall in front of her and with a slow, distinct, movement she put her left hand to her forehead.

'Well, then,' she heard Lingard's forcible murmur, 'well, then, Mrs Travers, it must be done tonight.'

One may be true, fearless, and wise, and yet catch one's breath before the simple finality of action. Mrs Travers caught her breath : 'Tonight! Tonight!' she whispered. D'Alcacer's dark and misty silhouette became more blurred. He had seen her sign and had retreated deeper within the Cage.

'Yes, tonight,' affirmed Lingard. 'Now, at once, within the hour, this moment,' he murmured, fiercely, following Mrs

Travers in her recoiling movement. She felt her arm being seized swiftly. 'Don't you see that if it is to do any good, that if they are not to be delivered to mere slaughter, it must be done while all is dark ashore, before an armed mob in boats comes clamouring alongside? Yes. Before the night is an hour older, so that I may be hammering at Belarab's gate while all the Settlement is still asleep.'

Mrs Travers didn't dream of protesting. For the moment she was unable to speak. This man was very fierce and just as suddenly as it had been gripped (making her think incongruously in the midst of her agitation that there would be certainly a bruise there in the morning) she felt her arm released and a penitential tone come into Lingard's murmuring voice.

'And even now it's nearly too late! The road was plain but I saw you in it and my heart failed me. I was there like an empty man and I dared not face you. You must forgive me. No, I had no right to doubt you for a moment. I feel as if I ought to go on my knees and beg your pardon for forgetting what you are, for daring to forget.'

'Why, King Tom, what is it?'

'It seems as if I had sinned,' she heard him say. He seized her by the shoulders, turned her about, moved her forward a step or two. His hands were heavy, his force irresistible, though he himself imagined he was handling her gently. 'Look straight before you,' he growled into her ear. 'Do you see anything?' Mrs Travers, passive between the rigid arms, could see nothing but, far off, the massed, featureless shadows of the shore.

'No, I see nothing,' she said.

'You can't be looking the right way,' she heard him behind her. And now she felt her head between Lingard's hands. He moved it the least bit to the right. 'There! See it?'

'No. What am I to look for?'

'A gleam of light,' said Lingard, taking away his hands suddenly. 'A gleam that will grow into a blaze before our boat can get half way across the lagoon.'

Even as Lingard spoke Mrs Travers caught sight of a red spark far away. She had looked often enough at the Settlement, as on the face of a painting on a curtain, to have its configuration fixed in her mind, to know that it was on the beach at its end furthest from Belarab's stockade.

'The brushwood is catching,' murmured Lingard in her ear. 'If they had some dry grass the whole pile would be blazing by now.'

'And this means . . .'

'It means that the news has spread. And it is before Tengga's enclosure on his end of the beach. That's where all the brains of the Settlement are. It means talk and excitement and plenty of crafty words. Tengga's fire! I tell you, Mrs Travers, that before half an hour has passed Daman will be there to make friends with the fat Tengga, who is ready to say to him "I told you so".'

'I see,' murmured Mrs Travers. Lingard drew her gently to the rail.

'And now look over there at the other end of the beach where the shadows are heaviest. That is Belarab's fort, his houses, his treasure, his dependants. That's where the strength of the Settlement is. I kept it up. I made it last. But what is it now? It's like a weapon in the hand of a dead man. And yet it's all we have to look to, if indeed there is still time. I swear to you I wouldn't dare land them in daylight for fear they should be slaughtered on the beach.'

'There is no time to lose,' whispered Mrs Travers, and Lingard, too, spoke very low.

'No, not if I, too, am to keep what is my right. It's you who have said it.'

'Yes, I have said it,' she whispered, without lifting her head. Lingard made a brusque movement at her elbow and bent his head close to her shoulder.

'And I who mistrusted you! Like Arabs do to their great men, I ought to kiss the hem of your robe in repentance for having doubted the greatness of your heart.'

'Oh! my heart!' said Mrs Travers, lightly, still gazing at the fire, which had suddenly shot up to a tall blaze. 'I can assure you it has been of very little account in the world.' She paused for a moment to steady her voice, then said, firmly, 'Let's get this over.'

'To tell you the truth the boat has been ready for some time.'

'Well, then ...'

'Mrs Travers,' said Lingard with an effort, 'they are people of your own kind.' And suddenly he burst out: 'I cannot take them ashore bound hand and foot.'

'Mr d'Alcacer knows. You will find him ready. Ever since the beginning he has been prepared for whatever might happen.'

'He is a man,' said Lingard with conviction. 'But it's of the other that I am thinking.'

'Ah, the other,' she repeated. 'Then, what about my thoughts? Luckily we have Mr d'Alcacer. I shall speak to him first.'

She turned away from the rail and moved toward the Cage.

'Jörgenson,' the voice of Lingard resounded all along the deck, 'get a light on the gangway.' Then he followed Mrs Travers slowly.

6

D'ALCACER, after receiving his warning, stepped back and leaned against the edge of the table. He could not ignore in himself a certain emotion. And indeed, when he had asked Mrs Travers for a sign he expected to be moved – but he had not expected the sign to come so soon. He expected this night to pass like other nights, in broken slumbers, bodily discomfort, and the unrest of disconnected thinking. At the same time he was surprised at his own emotion. He had flattered himself on the possession of more philosophy. He thought that this famous sense of self-preservation was a queer thing, a purely animal thing. 'For, as a thinking man,' he reflected, 'I really ought not to care.' It was probably the unusual that affected him. Clearly. If he had been lying seriously ill in a room in a hotel and had overheard some ominous whispers he would not have cared in the least. Ah, but then he would have been ill – and in illness one

grows so indifferent. Illness is a great help to unemotional behaviour, which of course is the correct behaviour for a man of
the world. He almost regretted he was not very ill. But, then,
Mr Travers was obviously ill and it did not seem to help him
much. D'Alcacer glanced at the bedstead where Mr Travers preserved an immobility which struck d'Alcacer as obviously
affected. He mistrusted it. Generally he mistrusted Mr Travers.
One couldn't tell what he would do next. Not that he could do
much one way or another, but that somehow he threatened to
rob the situation of whatever dignity it may have had as a
stroke of fate, as a call on courage. Mr d'Alcacer, acutely observant and alert for the slightest hints, preferred to look upon himself as the victim not of a swindle but of a rough man naïvely
engaged in a contest with heaven's injustice. D'Alcacer did not
examine his heart, but some lines of a French poet came into
his mind, to the effect that in all times those who fought with
an unjust heaven had possessed the secret admiration and love of
men. He didn't go so far as love but he could not deny to himself that this feeling toward Lingard was secretly friendly and –
well, appreciative. Mr Travers sat up suddenly. What a horrible
nuisance, thought d'Alcacer, fixing his eyes on the tips of his
shoes with the hope that perhaps the other would lie down again.
Mr Travers spoke.

'Still up, d'Alcacer?'

'I assure you it isn't late. It's dark at six, we dined before
seven, that makes the night long and I am not a very good
sleeper; that is, I cannot go to sleep till late in the night.'

'I envy you,' said Mr Travers, speaking with a sort of
drowsy apathy. 'I am always dropping off and the awakenings
are horrible.'

D'Alcacer, raising his eyes, noticed that Mrs Travers and
Lingard had vanished from the light. They had gone to the rail
where d'Alcacer could not see them. Some pity mingled with
his vexation at Mr Travers' snatchy wakefulness. There was
something weird about the man, he reflected. 'Jörgenson,' he
began aloud.

'What's that?' snapped Mr Travers.

'It's the name of that lanky old store-keeper who is always about the decks.'

'I haven't seen him. I don't see anybody. I don't know anybody. I prefer not to notice.'

'I was only going to say that he gave me a pack of cards; would you like a game of piquet?'

'I don't think I could keep my eyes open,' said Mr Travers in an unexpectedly confidential tone. 'Isn't it funny, d'Alcacer. And then I wake up. It's too awful.'

D'Alcacer made no remark and Mr Travers seemed not to have expected any.

'When I said my wife was mad,' he began, suddenly, causing d'Alcacer to start, 'I didn't mean it literally, of course.' His tone sounded slightly dogmatic and he didn't seem to be aware of any interval during which he had appeared to sleep. D'Alcacer was convinced more than ever that he had been shamming, and resigned himself wearily to listen, folding his arms across his chest. 'What I meant, really,' continued Mr Travers, 'was that she is the victim of a craze. Society is subject to crazes, as you know very well. They are not reprehensible in themselves, but the worst of my wife is that her crazes are never like those of the people with whom she naturally associates. They generally run counter to them. This peculiarity has given me some anxiety, you understand, in the position we occupy. People will begin to say that she is eccentric. Do you see her anywhere, d'Alcacer?'

D'Alcacer was thankful to be able to say that he didn't see Mrs Travers. He didn't even hear any murmurs, though he had no doubt that everybody on board the *Emma* was wide awake by now. But Mr Travers inspired him with invincible mistrust and he thought it prudent to add:

'You forget that your wife has a room in the deckhouse.'

This was as far as he would go, for he knew very well that she was not in the deckhouse. Mr Travers, completely convinced by the statement, made no sound. But neither did he lie down again. D'Alcacer gave himself up to meditation. The night seemed extremely oppressive. At Lingard's shout for Jörgenson, that in the profound silence struck his ears ominously, he raised his eyes and saw Mrs Travers outside the door of the Cage. He started forward but she was already within. He saw she was moved. She seemed out of breath and as if unable to speak at first.

'Hadn't we better shut the door?' suggested d'Alcacer.

'Captain Lingard's coming in,' she whispered to him. 'He has made up his mind.'

'That's an excellent thing,' commented d'Alcacer, quietly. 'I conclude from this that we shall hear something.'

'You shall hear it all from me,' breathed out Mrs Travers.

'Ah !' exclaimed d'Alcacer very low.

By that time Lingard had entered, too, and the decks of the *Emma* were all astir with moving figures. Jörgenson's voice was also heard giving directions. For nearly a minute the four persons within the Cage remained motionless. A shadowy Malay in the gangway said suddenly : 'Sudah Tuan,' and Lingard murmured, 'Ready, Mrs Travers.'

She seized d'Alcacer's arm and led him to the side of the Cage furthest from the corner in which Mr Travers' bed was placed, while Lingard busied himself in pricking up the wick of the Cage lantern as if it had suddenly occurred to him that this, whatever happened, should not be a deed of darkness. Mr Travers did nothing but turn his head to look over his shoulder.

'One moment,' said d'Alcacer, in a low tone and smiling at Mrs Travers' agitation. 'Before you tell me anything let me ask you : "Have *you* made up your mind?" ' He saw with much surprise a widening of her eyes. Was it indignation? A pause as of suspicion fell between those two people. Then d'Alcacer said apologetically : 'Perhaps I ought not to have asked that question,' and Lingard caught Mrs Travers' words, 'Oh, I am not afraid to answer that question.'

Then their voices sank. Lingard hung the lamp up again and stood idle in the revived light; but almost immediately he heard d'Alcacer calling him discreetly.

'Captain Lingard !'

He moved toward them at once. At the same instant Mr

Travers' head pivoted away from the group to its frontal position.

D'Alcacer, very serious, spoke in a familiar undertone.

'Mrs Travers tells me that we must be delivered up to those Moors on shore.'

'Yes, there is nothing else for it,' said Lingard.

'I confess I am a bit startled,' said d'Alcacer; but except for a slightly hurried utterance nobody could have guessed at anything resembling emotion.

'I have a right to my good name,' said Lingard, also very calm, while Mrs Travers near him, with half-veiled eyes, listened impassive like a presiding genius.

'I wouldn't question that for a moment,' conceded d'Alcacer. 'A point of honour is not to be discussed. But there is such a thing as humanity, too. To be delivered up helplessly . . .'

'Perhaps!' interrupted Lingard. 'But you needn't feel hopeless. I am not at liberty to give up my life for your own. Mrs Travers knows why. That, too, is engaged.'

'Always on your honour?'

'I don't know. A promise is a promise.'

'Nobody can be held to the impossible,' remarked d'Alcacer.

'Impossible! What is impossible? I don't know it. I am not a man to talk of the impossible or dodge behind it. I did not bring you here.'

D'Alcacer lowered his head for a moment. 'I have finished,' he said, gravely. 'That much I had to say. I hope you don't think I have appeared unduly anxious.'

'It's the best policy, too.' Mrs Travers made herself heard suddenly. Nothing of her moved but her lips, she did not even raise her eyes. 'It's the only possible policy. You believe me, Mr d'Alcacer? . . .' He made an almost imperceptible movement of the head . . . 'Well, then, I put all my hopes in you, Mr d'Alcacer, to get this over as easily as possible and save us all from some odious scene. You think perhaps that it is I who ought to . . .'

'No, no! I don't think so,' interrupted d'Alcacer. 'It would be impossible.'

'I am afraid it would,' she admitted, nervously.

D'Alcacer made a gesture as if to beg her to say no more and at once crossed over to Mr Travers' side of the Cage. He did not want to give himself time to think about his task. Mr Travers was sitting up on the camp bedstead with a light cotton sheet over his legs. He stared at nothing, and on approaching him d'Alcacer disregarded the slight sinking of his own heart at this aspect which seemed to be that of extreme terror. 'This is awful,' he thought. The man kept as still as a hare in its form.

The impressed d'Alcacer had to make an effort to bring himself to tap him lightly on the shoulder.

'The moment has come, Travers, to show some fortitude,' he said with easy intimacy. Mr Travers looked up swiftly. 'I have just been talking to your wife. She had a communication from Captain Lingard for us both. It remains for us now to preserve as much as possible our dignity. I hope that if necessary we will both know how to die.'

In a moment of profound stillness, d'Alcacer had time to wonder whether his face was as stony in expression as the one upturned to him. But suddenly a smile appeared on it, which was certainly the last thing d'Alcacer expected to see. An indubitable smile. A slightly contemptuous smile.

'My wife has been stuffing your head with some more of her nonsense.' Mr Travers spoke in a voice which astonished d'Alcacer as much as the smile, a voice that was not irritable nor peevish, but had a distinct note of indulgence. 'My dear d'Alcacer, that craze has got such a hold of her that she would tell you any sort of tale. Social impostors, mediums, fortune-tellers, charlatans of all sorts do obtain a strange influence over women. You have seen that sort of thing yourself. I had a talk with her before dinner. The influence that bandit has got over her is incredible. I really believe the fellow is half crazy himself. They often are, you know. I gave up arguing with her. Now, what is it you have got to tell me? But I warn you that I am not going to take it seriously.'

He rejected briskly the cotton sheet, put his feet to the ground and buttoned his jacket. D'Alcacer, as he talked, became aware

288

by the slight noise behind him that Mrs Travers and Lingard were leaving the Cage, but he went on to the end and then waited anxiously for the answer.

'See! She has followed him out on deck,' were Mr Travers' first words. 'I hope you understand that it is a mere craze. You can't help seeing that. Look at her costume. She simply has lost her head. Luckily the world needn't know. But suppose that something similar had happened at home. It would have been extremely awkward. Oh! yes, I will come. I will go anywhere. I can't stand this hulk, those people, this infernal Cage. I believe I should fall ill if I were to remain here.'

The inward detached voice of Jörgenson made itself heard near the gangway saying: 'The boat has been waiting for this hour past, King Tom.'

'Let us make a virtue of necessity and go with a good grace,' said d'Alcacer, ready to take Mr Travers under the arm persuasively, for he did not know what to make of that gentleman. But Mr Travers seemed another man. 'I am afraid, d'Alcacer, that you, too, are not very strong-minded. I am going to take a blanket off this bedstead ...' He flung it hastily over his arm and followed d'Alcacer closely. 'What I suffer mostly from, strange to say, is cold.'

Mrs Travers and Lingard were waiting near the gangway. To everybody's extreme surprise Mr Travers addressed his wife first.

'You were always laughing at people's crazes,' was what he said, 'and now you have a craze of your own. But we won't discuss that.'

D'Alcacer passed on, raising his cap to Mrs Travers, and went down the ship's side into the boat. Jörgenson had vanished in his own manner like an exorcised ghost, and Lingard, stepping back, left husband and wife face to face.

'Did you think I was going to make a fuss?' asked Mr Travers in a very low voice. 'I assure you I would rather go than stay here. You didn't think that? You have lost all sense or reality, of probability. I was just thinking this evening that I would rather be anywhere than here looking on at you. At your folly ...'

Mrs Travers' loud, 'Martin!' made Lingard wince, caused d'Alcacer to lift his head down there in the boat, and even Jörgenson, forward somewhere out of sight, ceased mumbling in his moustache. The only person who seemed not to have heard that exclamation was Mr Travers himself, who continued smoothly:

'... at the aberration of your mind, you who seemed so superior to common credulities. You are not yourself, not at all, and some day you will admit to me that ... No, the best thing will be to forget it, as you will soon see yourself. We shall never mention that subject in the future. I am certain you will be only too glad to agree with me on that point.'

'How far ahead are you looking?' asked Mrs Travers, finding her voice and even the very tone in which she would have addressed him had they been about to part in the hall of their town house. She might have been asking him at what time he expected to be home, while a footman held the door open and the brougham waited in the street.

'Not very far. This can't last much longer.' Mr Travers made a movement as if to leave her exactly as though he were rather pressed to keep an appointment. 'By the by,' he said, checking himself, 'I suppose the fellow understands thoroughly that we are wealthy. He could hardly doubt that.'

'It's the last thought that would enter his head,' said Mrs Travers.

'Oh, yes, just so.' Mr Travers allowed a little impatience to pierce under his casual manner. 'But I don't mind telling you that I have had enough of this. I am prepared to make – ah! – to make concessions. A large pecuniary sacrifice. Only the whole position is so absurd! He might conceivably doubt my good faith. Wouldn't it be just as well if you, with your particular influence, would hint to him that with me he would have nothing to fear? I am a man of my word.'

'That is the first thing he would naturally think of any man,' said Mrs Travers.

'Will your eyes never be opened?' Mr Travers began, irritably, then gave it up. 'Well, so much the better then. I give you a free hand.'

'What made you change your attitude like this?' asked Mrs Travers, suspiciously.

'My regard for you,' he answered without hesitation.

'I intended to join you in your captivity. I was just trying to persuade him . . .'

'I forbid you absolutely,' whispered Mr Travers, forcibly. 'I am glad to get away. I don't want to see you again till your craze is over.'

She was confounded by his secret vehemence. But instantly succeeding his fierce whisper came a short, inane society laugh and a much louder, 'Not that I attach any importance . . .'

He sprang away, as it were, from his wife, and as he went over the gangway waved his hand to her amiably.

Lighted dimly by the lantern on the roof of the deckhouse Mrs Travers remained very still with lowered head and an aspect of profound meditation. It lasted but an instant before she moved off and brushing against Lingard passed on with downcast eyes to her deck cabin. Lingard heard the door shut. He waited awhile, made a movement toward the gangway but checked himself and followed Mrs Travers into her cabin.

It was pitch dark in there. He could see absolutely nothing and was oppressed by the profound stillness unstirred even by the sound of breathing.

'I am going on shore,' he began, breaking the black and death-like silence enclosing him and the invisible woman. 'I wanted to say good-bye.'

'You are going on shore,' repeated Mrs Travers. Her voice was emotionless, blank, unringing.

'Yes, for a few hours, or for life,' Lingard said in measured tones. 'I may have to die with them or to die maybe for others. For you, if I only knew how to manage it, I would want to live. I am telling you this because it is dark. If there had been a light in here I wouldn't have come in.'

'I wish you had not,' uttered the same unringing woman's voice. 'You are always coming to me with those lives and those deaths in your hand.'

'Yes, it's too much for you,' was Lingard's undertoned comment. 'You could be no other than true. And you are innocent!

Don't wish me life, but wish me luck, for you are innocent –
and you will have to take your chance.'

'All luck to you, King Tom,' he heard her say in the darkness
in which he seemed now to perceive the gleam of her hair. 'I
will take my chance. And try not to come near me again for I am
weary of you.'

'I can well believe it,' murmured Lingard, and stepped out of
the cabin, shutting the door after him gently. For half a minute,
perhaps, the stillness continued, and then suddenly the chair fell
over in the darkness. Next moment Mrs Travers' head appeared
in the light of the lamp left on the roof of the deckhouse. Her
bare arms grasped the door posts.

'Wait a moment,' she said, loudly, into the shadows of the
deck. She heard no footsteps, saw nothing moving except the
vanishing white shape of the late Captain H. C. Jörgenson, who
was indifferent to the life of men. 'Wait, King Tom!' she insisted, raising her voice; then, 'I didn't mean it. Don't believe
me!' she cried, recklessly.

For the second time that night a woman's voice startled the
hearts of men on board the *Emma*. All except the heart of old
Jörgenson. The Malays in the boat looked up from their
thwarts. D'Alcacer, sitting in the stern sheets beside Lingard,
felt a sinking feeling of his heart.

'What's this?' he exclaimed. 'I heard your name on deck. You
are wanted, I think.'

'Shove off,' ordered Lingard, inflexibly, without even looking
at d'Alcacer. Mr Travers was the only one who didn't seem to
be aware of anything. A long time after the boat left the *Emma*'s
side he leaned toward d'Alcacer.

'I have a most extraordinary feeling,' he said in a cautious
undertone. 'I seem to be in the air – I don't know. Are we on
the water, d'Alcacer? Are you quite sure? But of course, we are
on the water.'

'Yes,' said d'Alcacer, in the same tone. 'Crossing the Styx –
perhaps.' He heard Mr Travers utter an unmoved 'Very likely,'
which he did not expect. Lingard, his hand on the tiller, sat like
a man of stone.

'Then your point of view has changed,' whispered d'Alcacer.

'I told my wife to make an offer,' went on the earnest whisper of the other man. 'A sum of money. But to tell you the truth I don't believe very much in its success.'

D'Alcacer made no answer and only wondered whether he didn't like better Mr Travers' other, unreasonable mood. There was no denying the fact that Mr Travers was a troubling person. Now he suddenly gripped d'Alcacer's forearm and added under his breath: 'I doubt everything. I doubt whether the offer will ever be made.'

All this was not very impressive. There was something pitiful in it: whisper, grip, shudder, as of a child frightened in the dark. But the emotion was deep. Once more that evening, but this time aroused by the husband's distress, d'Alcacer's wonder approached the borders of awe.

PART SIX

THE CLAIM OF LIFE AND
THE TOLL OF DEATH

'HAVE you got King Tom's watch in there?' said a voice that seemed not to attach the slightest importance to the question. Jörgenson, outside the door of Mrs Travers' part of the deck-house, waited for the answer. He heard a low cry very much like a moan, the startled sound of pain that may be sometimes heard in sick rooms. But it moved him not at all. He would never have dreamt of opening the door unless told to do so, in which case he would have beheld, with complete indifference, Mrs Travers extended on the floor with her head resting on the edge of the camp bedstead (on which Lingard had never slept), as though she had subsided there from a kneeling posture which is the attitude of prayer, supplication, or defeat. The hours of the night had passed Mrs Travers by. After flinging herself on her knees, she didn't know why, since she could think of nothing to pray for, had nothing to invoke, and was too far gone for such a futile thing as despair, she had remained there till the sense of exhaustion had grown on her to the point in which she lost her belief in her power to rise. In a half-sitting attitude, her head resting against the edge of the couch and her arms flung above her head, she sank into an indifference, the mere resignation of a worn-out body and a worn-out mind which often is the only sort of rest that comes to people who are desperately ill and is welcome enough in a way. The voice of Jörgenson roused her out of that state. She sat up, aching in every limb and cold all over.

Jörgenson, behind the door, repeated with lifeless obstinacy: 'Do you see King Tom's watch in there?'

Mrs Travers got up from the floor. She tottered, snatching at the air, and found the back of the armchair under her hand.

'Who's there?'

She was also ready to ask: 'Where am I?' but she remembered and at once became the prey of that active dread which had been lying dormant for a few hours in her uneasy and prostrate body. 'What time is it?' she faltered out.

'Dawn,' pronounced the imperturbable voice at the door. It seemed to her that it was a word that could make any heart sink with apprehension. Dawn! She stood appalled. And the toneless voice outside the door insisted:

'You must have Tom's watch there!'

'I haven't seen it,' she cried as if tormented by a dream.

'Look in that desk thing. If you push open the shutter you will be able to see.'

Mrs Travers became aware of the profound darkness of the cabin. Jörgenson heard her staggering in there. After a moment a woman's voice, which struck even him as strange, said in faint tones:

'I have it. It's stopped.'

'It doesn't matter. I don't want to know the time. There should be a key about. See it anywhere?'

'Yes, it's fastened to the watch,' the dazed voice answered from within. Jörgenson waited before making his request. 'Will you pass it out to me? There's precious little time left now!'

The door flew open, which was certainly something Jörgenson had not expected. He had expected but a hand with the watch protruded through a narrow crack. But he didn't start back or give any other sign of surprise at seeing Mrs Travers fully dressed. Against the faint clearness in the frame of the open shutter she presented to him the dark silhouette of her shoulders surmounted by a sleek head, because her hair was still in the two plaits. To Jörgenson, Mrs Travers in her un-European dress had always been displeasing, almost monstrous. Her stature, her gestures, her general carriage struck his eye as absurdly incongruous with a Malay costume, too ample, too free, too bold – offensive. To Mrs Travers, Jörgenson, in the dusk of the passage, had the aspect of a dim white ghost, and he chilled her by his ghost's aloofness.

He picked up the watch from her outspread palm without a word of thanks, only mumbling in his moustache, 'H'm, yes, that's it. I haven't yet forgotten how to count seconds correctly, but it's better to have a watch.'

She had not the slightest notion what he meant. And she did not care. Her mind remained confused and the sense of bodily discomfort oppressed her. She whispered, shamefacedly, 'I believe I've slept.'

'I haven't,' mumbled Jörgenson, growing more and more distinct to her eyes. The brightness of the short dawn increased rapidly as if the sun were impatient to look upon the Settlement. 'No fear of that,' he added, boastfully.

It occurred to Mrs Travers that perhaps she had not slept either. Her state had been more like an imperfect, half-conscious, quivering death. She shuddered at the recollection.

'What an awful night,' she murmured, drearily.

There was nothing to hope for from Jörgenson. She expected him to vanish, indifferent, like a phantom of the dead carrying off the appropriately dead watch in his hand for some unearthly purpose. Jörgenson didn't move. His was an insensible, almost a senseless presence! Nothing could be extorted from it. But a wave of anguish as confused as all her other sensations swept Mrs Travers off her feet.

'Can't you tell me something?' she cried.

For half a minute perhaps Jörgenson made no sound; then: 'For years I have been telling anybody who cared to ask,' he mumbled in his moustache. 'Telling Tom, too. And Tom knew what he wanted to do. How's one to know what *you* are after?'

She had never expected to hear so many words from that rigid shadow. Its monotonous mumble was fascinating, its sudden loquacity was shocking. And in the profound stillness that reigned outside it was as if there had been no one left in the world with her but the phantom of that old adventurer. He was heard again: 'What I could tell you would be worse than poison.'

Mrs Travers was not familiar with Jörgenson's consecrated phrases. The mechanical voice, the words themselves, his air of abstraction appalled her. And he hadn't done yet; she caught some more of his unconcerned mumbling: 'There is nothing I

don't know,' and the absurdity of the statement was also appalling. Mrs Travers gasped and with a wild little laugh :
'Then you know why I called after King Tom last night.'

He glanced away along his shoulder through the door of the deckhouse at the growing brightness of the day. She did so, too. It was coming. It had come! Another day! And it seemed to Mrs Travers a worse calamity than any discovery she had made in her life, than anything she could have imagined to come to her. The very magnitude of horror steadied her, seemed to calm her agitation as some kinds of fatal drugs do before they kill. She laid a steady hand on Jörgenson's sleeve and spoke quietly, distinctly, urgently.

'You were on deck. What I want to know is whether I was heard?'

'Yes,' said Jörgenson, absently. 'I heard you.' Then, as if roused a little, he added less mechanically : 'The whole ship heard you.'

Mrs Travers asked herself whether perchance she had not simply screamed. It had never occurred to her before that perhaps she had. At the time it seemed to her she had no strength for more than a whisper. Had she been really so loud? And the deadly chill, the night that had gone by her had left her body, vanished from her limbs, passed out of her in a flush. Her face was turned away from the light, and that fact gave her courage to continue. Moreover, the man before her was so detached from the shames and prides and schemes of life that he seemed not to count at all, except that somehow or other he managed at times to catch the mere literal sense of the words addressed to him – and answer them. And answer them! Answer unfailingly, impersonally, without any feeling.

'You saw Tom – King Tom? Was he here? I mean just then, at the moment. There was a light at the gangway. Was he on deck?'

'No. In the boat.'

'Already? Could I have been heard in the boat down there? You say the whole ship heard me – and I don't care. But could he hear me?'

'Was it Tom you were after?' said Jörgenson in the tone of a negligent remark.

'Can't you answer me?' she cried, angrily.

'Tom was busy. No child's play. The boat shoved off,' said Jörgenson, as if he were merely thinking aloud.

'You won't tell me, then?' Mrs Travers apostrophized him, fearlessly. She was not afraid of Jörgenson. Just then she was afraid of nothing and nobody. And Jörgenson went on thinking aloud.

'I guess he will be kept busy from now on and so shall I.'

Mrs Travers seemed ready to take by the shoulders and shake that dead-voiced spectre till it begged for mercy. But suddenly her strong white arms fell down by her side, the arms of an exhausted woman.

'I shall never, never find out,' she whispered to herself.

She cast down her eyes in intolerable humiliation, in intolerable desire, as though she had veiled her face. Not a sound reached the loneliness of her thought. But when she raised her eyes again Jörgenson was no longer standing before her.

For an instant she saw him all black in the brilliant and narrow doorway, and the next moment he had vanished outside, as if devoured by the hot blaze of light. The sun had risen on the Shore of Refuge.

When Mrs Travers came out on deck herself it was as it were with a boldly unveiled face, with wide-open and dry, sleepless eyes. Their gaze, undismayed by the sunshine, sought the innermost heart of things each day offered to the passion of her dread and of her impatience. The lagoon, the beach, the colours and the shapes struck her more than ever as a luminous painting on an immense cloth hiding the movements of an inexplicable life. She shaded her eyes with her hand. There were figures on the beach, moving dark dots on the white semicircle bounded by the stockades, backed by roof ridges above the palm groves. Further back the mass of carved white coral on the roof of the mosque shone like a white day-star. Religion and politics – always politics! To the left, before Tengga's enclosure, the loom of fire had changed into a pillar of smoke. But there were some big trees over there and she couldn't tell whether the night council had prolonged its sitting. Some vague forms were still moving there and she could picture them to herself: Daman, the supreme chief of sea-robbers, with a vengeful heart and the eyes of a gazelle; Sentot, the sour fanatic with the big turban, that other saint with a scanty loin cloth and ashes in his hair, and Tengga whom she could imagine from hearsay, fat, good-tempered, crafty, but ready to spill blood on his ambitious way and already bold enough to flaunt a yellow state umbrella at the very gate of Belarab's stockade – so they said.

She saw, she imagined, she even admitted now the reality of those things no longer a mere pageant marshalled for her vision with barbarous splendour and savage emphasis. She questioned it no longer – but she did not feel it in her soul any more than one feels the depth of the sea under its peaceful glitter or the turmoil of its grey fury. Her eyes ranged afar, unbelieving and fearful – and then all at once she became aware of the empty Cage with its interior in disorder, the camp bedsteads not taken away, a pillow lying on the deck, the dying flame like a shred of dull yellow stuff inside the lamp left hanging over the table. The whole struck her as squalid and as if already decayed, a flimsy and idle phantasy. But Jörgenson, seated on the deck with his back to it, was not idle. His occupation, too, seemed fantastic and so truly childish that her heart sank at the man's utter absorption in it. Jörgenson had before him, stretched on the deck, several bits of rather thin and dirty-looking rope of different lengths from a couple of inches to about a foot. He had (an idiot might have amused himself in that way) set fire to the ends of them. They smouldered with amazing energy, emitting now and then a splutter, and in the calm air within the bulwarks sent up very slender, exactly parallel threads of smoke, each with a vanishing curl at the end; and the absorption with which Jörgenson gave himself up to that pastime was enough to shake all confidence in his sanity.

In one half-opened hand he was holding the watch. He was also provided with a scrap of paper and the stump of a pencil. Mrs Travers was confident that he did not either hear or see her.

'Captain Jörgenson, you no doubt think . . .'

He tried to wave her away with the stump of the pencil. He did not want to be interrupted in his strange occupation. He was playing very gravely indeed with those bits of string. 'I lighted them all together,' he murmured, keeping one eye on the dial of the watch. Just then the shortest piece of string went out, utterly consumed. Jörgenson made a hasty note and remained still while Mrs Travers looked at him with stony eyes thinking that nothing in the world was any use. The other threads of smoke went on vanishing in spirals before the attentive Jörgenson.

'What are you doing?' asked Mrs Travers, drearily.

'Timing match . . . precaution . . .'

He had never in Mrs Travers' experience been less spectral than then. He displayed a weakness of the flesh. He was impatient at her intrusion. He divided his attention between the threads of smoke and the face of the watch with such interest that the sudden reports of several guns breaking for the first time for days the stillness of the lagoon and the illusion of the painted scene failed to make him raise his head. He only jerked it sideways a little. Mrs Travers stared at the wisps of white vapour floating above Belarab's stockade. The series of sharp detonations ceased and their combined echoes came back over the lagoon like a long-drawn and rushing sigh.

'What's this?' cried Mrs Travers.

'Belarab's come home,' said Jörgenson.

The last thread of smoke disappeared and Jörgenson got up. He had lost all interest in the watch and thrust it carelessly into his pocket, together with the bit of paper and the stump of pencil. He had resumed his aloofness from the life of men, but approaching the bulwark he condescended to look toward Belarab's stockade.

'Yes, he is home,' he said very low.

'What's going to happen?' cried Mrs Travers. 'What's to be done?' Jörgenson kept up his appearance of communing with himself.

'I know what to do,' he mumbled.

'You are lucky,' said Mrs Travers, with intense bitterness.

It seemed to her that she was abandoned by all the world. The opposite shore of the lagoon had resumed its aspect of a painted scene that would never roll up to disclose the truth behind its

blinding and soulless splendour. It seemed to her that she had
said her last words to all of them: to d'Alcacer, to her husband, to
Lingard himself – and that they had all gone behind the curtain
forever out of her sight. Of all the white men Jörgenson alone
was left, that man who had done with life so completely that his
mere presence robbed it of all heat and mystery, leaving nothing
but its terrible, its revolting insignificance. And Mrs Travers was
ready for revolt. She cried with suppressed passion:

'Are you aware, Captain Jörgenson, that I am alive?'

He turned his eyes on her, and for a moment she was daunted
by their cold glassiness. But before they could drive her away,
something like the gleam of a spark gave them an instant's animation.

'I want to go and join them. I want to go ashore,' she said,
firmly. 'There!'

Her bare and extended arm pointed across the lagoon, and
Jörgenson's resurrected eyes glided along the white limb and
wandered off into space.

'No boat,' he muttered.

'There must be a canoe. I know there is a canoe. I want it.'

She stepped forward compelling, commanding, trying to con-
centrate in her glance all her will power, the sense of her own
right to dispose of herself and her claim to be served to the last
moment of her life. It was as if she had done nothing. Jörgenson
didn't flinch.

'Which of them are you after?' asked his blank, unringing
voice.

She continued to look at him; her face had stiffened into a
severe mask; she managed to say distinctly:

'I suppose you have been asking yourself that question for
some time, Captain Jörgenson?'

'No. I am asking you now.'

His face disclosed nothing to Mrs Travers' bold and weary
eyes. 'What could you do over there?' Jörgenson added, as merciless, as irrepressible and sincere as though he were the embodiment of that inner voice that speaks in all of us at times and, like
Jörgenson, is offensive and difficult to answer.

'Remember that I am not a shadow but a living woman still, Captain Jörgenson. I can live and I can die. Send me over to share their fate.'

'Sure you would like to?' asked the roused Jörgenson in a voice that had an unexpected living quality, a faint vibration which no man had known in it for years. 'There may be death in it,' he mumbled, relapsing into indifference.

'Who cares?' she said, recklessly. 'All I want is to ask Tom a question and hear his answer. That's what I would like. That's what I must have.'

2

ALONG the hot and gloomy forest path, neglected, overgrown and strangled in the fierce life of the jungle, there came a faint rustle of leaves. Jaffir, the servant of princes, the messenger of great men, walked, stooping, with a broad chopper in his hand. He was naked from the waist upward, his shoulders and arms were scratched and bleeding. A multitude of biting insects made a cloud about his head. He had lost his costly and ancient head-kerchief, and when in a slightly wider space he stopped in a listening attitude anybody would have taken him for a fugitive.

He waved his arms about, slapping his shoulders, the sides of his head, his heaving flanks; then, motionless, listened again for a while. A sound of firing, not so much made faint by distance as muffled by the masses of foliage, reached his ears, dropping shots which he could have counted if he had cared to. 'There is fighting in the forest already,' he thought. Then putting his head low in the tunnel of vegetation he dashed forward out of the horrible cloud of flies, which he actually managed for an instant to leave behind him. But it was not from the cruelty of insects that he was flying, for no man could hope to drop that escort, and Jaffir in his life of a faithful messenger had been accustomed, if such an extravagant phrase may be used, to be eaten alive. Bent

305

nearly double he glided and dodged between the trees, through the undergrowth, his brown body streaming with sweat, his firm limbs gleaming like limbs of imperishable bronze through the mass of green leaves that are forever born and forever dying. For all his desperate haste he was no longer a fugitive; he was simply a man in a tremendous hurry. His flight, which had begun with a bound and a rush and a general display of great presence of mind, was a simple issue from a critical situation. Issues from critical situations are generally simple if one is quick enough to think of them in time. He became aware very soon that the attempt to pursue him had been given up, but he had taken the forest path and had kept up his pace because he had left his Rajah and the lady Immada beset by enemies on the edge of the forest, as good as captives to a party of Tengga's men.

Belarab's hesitation had proved too much even for Hassim's hereditary patience in such matters. It is but becoming that weighty negotiations should be spread over many days, that the same requests and arguments should be repeated in the same words, at many successive interviews, and receive the same evasive answers. Matters of state demand the dignity of such a procedure as if time itself had to wait on the power and wisdom of rulers. Such are the proceedings of embassies and the dignified patience of envoys. But at this time of crisis Hassim's impatience obtained the upper hand; and though he never departed from the tradition of soft speech and restrained bearing while following with his sister in the train of the pious Belarab, he had his moments of anger, of anxiety, of despondency. His friendships, his future, his country's destinies were at stake, while Belarab's camp wandered deviously over the back country as if influenced by the vacillation of the ruler's thought, the very image of uncertain fate.

Often no more than the single word 'Good' was all the answer vouchsafed to Hassim's daily speeches. The lesser men, companions of the Chief, treated him with deference; but Hassim could feel the opposition from the women's side of the camp working against his cause in subservience to the mere caprice of the new wife, a girl quite gentle and kind to her dependants, but whose imagination had run away with her completely and had made her greedy for the loot of the yacht from mere simplicity and innocence. What could Hassim, that stranger, wandering and poor, offer for her acceptance? Nothing. The wealth of his far-off country was but an idle tale, the talk of an exile looking for help.

At night Hassim had to listen to the anguished doubts of Immada, the only companion of his life, child of the same mother, brave as a man, but in her fears a very woman. She whispered them to him far into the night while the camp of the great Belarab was hushed in sleep and the fires had sunk down to mere glowing embers. Hassim soothed her gravely. But he, too, was a native of Wajo where men are more daring and quicker of mind than other Malays. More energetic, too, and energy does not go without an inner fire. Hassim lost patience and one evening he declared to his sister Immada: 'Tomorrow we leave this ruler without a mind and go back to our white friend.'

Therefore next morning, letting the camp move on the direct road to the settlement, Hassim and Immada took a course of their own. It was a lonely path between the jungle and the clearings. They had two attendants with them, Hassim's own men, men of Wajo; and so the lady Immada, when she had a mind to, could be carried, after the manner of the great ladies of Wajo who need not put foot to the ground unless they like. The lady Immada, accustomed to the hardships that are the lot of exiles, preferred to walk, but from time to time she let herself be carried for a short distance out of regard for the feelings of her attendants. The party made good time during the early hours, and Hassim expected confidently to reach before evening the shore of the lagoon at a spot very near the stranded *Emma*. At noon they rested in the shade near a dark pool within the edge of the forest; and it was there that Jaffir met them, much to his and their surprise. It was the occasion of a long talk. Jaffir, squatting on his heels, discoursed in measured tones. He had entranced listeners. The story of Carter's exploit amongst the Shoals had not reached Belarab's camp. It was a great shock to Hassim, but the sort of half smile with which he had been listening to Jaffir never altered its character. It was the Princess Immada who cried out in distress and wrung her hands. A deep silence fell.

Indeed, before the fatal magnitude of the fact it seemed even to those Malays that there was nothing to say and Jaffir, lowering his head, respected his Prince's consternation. Then, before that feeling could pass away from that small group of people seated round a few smouldering sticks, the noisy approach of a large party of men made them all leap to their feet. Before they could make another movement they perceived themselves discovered. The men were armed as if bound on some warlike expedition. Amongst them Sentot, in his loin cloth and with unbound wild locks, capered and swung his arms about like the lunatic he was. The others' astonishment made them halt, but their attitude was obviously hostile. In the rear a portly figure flanked by two attendants carrying swords was approaching prudently. Rajah Hassim resumed quietly his seat on the trunk of a fallen tree, Immada rested her hand lightly on her brother's shoulder, and Jaffir, squatting down again, looked at the ground with all his faculties and every muscle of his body tensely on the alert.

'Tengga's fighters,' he murmured, scornfully.

In the group somebody shouted, and was answered by shouts from afar. There could be no thought of resistance. Hassim slipped the emerald ring from his finger stealthily and Jaffir got hold of it by an almost imperceptible movement. The Rajah did not even look at the trusty messenger.

'Fail not to give it to the white man,' he murmured.

'Thy servant hears, O Rajah. It's a charm of great power.'

The shadows were growing to the westward. Everybody was silent, and the shifting group of armed men seemed to have drifted closer. Immada, drawing the end of a scarf across her face, confronted the advance with only one eye exposed. On the flank of the armed men Sentot was performing a slow dance but he, too, seemed to have gone dumb.

'Now go,' breathed out Rajah Hassim, his gaze levelled into space immovably.

For a second or more Jaffir did not stir, then with a sudden leap from his squatting posture he flew through the air and struck the jungle in a great commotion of leaves, vanishing instantly like a swimmer diving from on high. A deep murmur of surprise arose in the armed party, a spear was thrown, a shot was fired, three or four men dashed into the forest, but they soon returned crestfallen with apologetic smiles; while Jaffir, striking an old path that seemed to lead in the right direction, ran on in solitude, raising a rustle of leaves, with a naked parang in his hand and a cloud of flies about his head. The sun declining to the westward threw shafts of light across his dark path. He ran at a springy half-trot, his eyes watchful, his broad chest heaving, and carrying the emerald ring on the forefinger of a clenched hand as though he were afraid it should slip off, fly off, be torn from him by an invisible force, or spirited away by some enchantment. Who could tell what might happen? There were evil forces at work in the world, powerful incantations, horrible apparitions. The messenger of princes and of great men, charged with the supreme appeal of his master, was afraid in the deepening shade of the forest. Evil presences might have been lurking in that gloom. Still the sun had not set yet. He could see its face through the leaves as he skirted the shore of the lagoon. But what if Allah's call should come to him suddenly and he die as he ran!

He drew a long breath on the shore of the lagoon within about a hundred yards from the stranded bows of the *Emma*. The tide was out and he walked to the end of a submerged log and sent out a hail for a boat. Jörgenson's voice answered. The sun had sunk behind the forest belt of the coast. All was still as far as the eye could reach over the black water. A slight breeze shivered a little.

*

At the same moment Carter, exhausted by thirty hours of uninterrupted toil at the head of whites and Malays in getting the yacht afloat, dropped into Mrs Travers' deck chair, on board the *Hermit*, said to the devoted Wasub: 'Let a good watch be kept tonight, old man,' glanced contentedly at the setting sun and fell asleep.

3

THERE was in the bows of the *Emma* an elevated grating over the heel of her bowsprit whence the eye could take in the whole range of her deck and see every movement of her crew. It was a spot safe from eavesdroppers, though, of course, exposed to view. The sun had just set on the supreme content of Carter when Jörgenson and Jaffir sat down side by side between the knight-heads of the *Emma* and, public but unapproachable, impressive and secret, began to converse in low tones.

Every Wajo fugitive who manned the hulk felt the approach of a decisive moment. Their minds were made up and their hearts beat steadily. They were all desperate men determined to fight and to die and troubling not about the manner of living or dying. This was not the case with Mrs Travers who, having shut herself up in the deckhouse, was profoundly troubled about those very things, though she, too, felt desperate enough to welcome almost any solution.

Of all the people on board she alone did not know anything of that conference. In her deep and aimless thinking she had only become aware of the absence of the slightest sound on board the *Emma*. Not a rustle, not a footfall. The public view of Jörgenson and Jaffir in deep consultation had the effect of taking all wish to move from every man.

Twilight enveloped the two figures forward while they talked, looking in the stillness of their pose like carved figures of European and Asiatic contrasted in intimate contact. The deepening dusk had nearly effaced them when at last they rose without warning, as it were, and thrilling the heart of the beholders by the sudden movement. But they did not separate at once. They lingered in their high place as if awaiting the fall of complete darkness, a fit ending to their mysterious communion. Jaffir had given Jörgenson the whole story of the ring, the symbol of a friendship matured and confirmed on the night of defeat, on the night of flight from a far-distant land sleeping unmoved under the wrath and fire of heaven.

310

'Yes, Tuan,' continued Jaffir, 'it was first sent out to the white man, on a night of mortal danger, a present to remember a friend by. I was the bearer of it then even as I am now. Then, as now, it was given to me and I was told to save myself and hand the ring over in confirmation of my message. I did so and that white man seemed to still the very storm to save my Rajah. He was not one to depart and forget him whom he had once called his friend. My message was but a message of good-bye, but the charm of the ring was strong enough to draw all the power of that white man to the help of my master. Now I have no words to say. Rajah Hassim asks for nothing. But what of that? By the mercy of Allah all things are the same, the compassion of the Most High, the power of the ring, the heart of the white man. Nothing is changed, only the friendship is a little older and love has grown because of the shared dangers and long companionship. Therefore, Tuan, I have no fear. But how am I to get the ring to the Rajah Laut? Just hand it to him. The last breath would be time enough if they were to spear me at his feet. But alas! the bush is full of Tengga's men, the beach is open and I could never even hope to reach the gate.'

Jörgenson, with his hands deep in the pockets of his tunic, listened, looking down. Jaffir showed as much consternation as his nature was capable of.

'Our refuge is with God,' he murmured. 'But what is to be done? Has your wisdom no stratagem, O Tuan?'

Jörgenson did not answer. It appeared as though he had no stratagem. But God is great and Jaffir waited on the other's immobility, anxious but patient, perplexed yet hopeful in his grim way, while the night flowing on from the dark forest near by hid their two figures from the sight of observing men. Before the silence of Jörgenson Jaffir began to talk practically. Now that Tengga had thrown off the mask Jaffir did not think that he could land on the beach without being attacked, captured, nay killed, since a man like he, though he could save himself by taking flight at the order of his master, could not be expected to surrender without a fight. He mentioned that in the exercise of his important functions he knew how to glide like a shadow, creep like a snake, and almost burrow his way underground. He was Jaffir who had never been foiled. No bog, morass, great river or jungle could stop him. He would have welcomed them. In many respects they were the friends of a crafty messenger. But that was an open beach, and there was no other way, and as things stood now every bush around, every tree trunk, every deep shadow of house or fence would conceal Tengga's men or such of Daman's infuriated partisans as had made already their way to the Settlement. How could he hope to traverse the distance between the water's edge and Belarab's gate which now would remain shut night and day? Not only himself but anybody from the *Emma* would be sure to be rushed upon and speared in twenty places.

He reflected for a moment in silence.

'Even you, Tuan, could not accomplish the feat.'

'True,' muttered Jörgenson.

When, after a period of meditation, he looked round, Jaffir was no longer by his side. He had descended from the high place and was probably squatting on his heels in some dark nook on the fore deck. Jörgenson knew Jaffir too well to suppose that he would go to sleep. He would sit there thinking himself into a state of fury, then get away from the *Emma* in some way or other, go ashore and perish fighting. He would, in fact, run amok; for it looked as if there could be no way out of the situation. Then, of course, Lingard would know nothing of Hassim and Immada's captivity for the ring would never reach him – the ring that could tell its own tale. No, Lingard would know nothing. He would know nothing about anybody outside Belarab's stockade till the end came, whatever the end might be, for all those people that lived the life of men. Whether to know or not to know would be good for Lingard Jörgenson could not tell. He admitted to himself that here there was something that he, Jörgenson, could not tell. All the possibilities were wrapped up in doubt, uncertain, like all things pertaining to the life of men. It was only when giving a short thought to himself that Jörgenson had no doubt. He, of course, would know what to do.

On the thin face of that old adventurer hidden in the night

not a feature moved, not a muscle twitched, as he descended in his turn and walked aft along the decks of the *Emma*. His faded eyes, which had seen so much, did not attempt to explore the night, they never gave a glance to the silent watchers against whom he brushed. Had a light been flashed on him suddenly he would have appeared like a man walking in his sleep: the somnambulist of an eternal dream. Mrs Travers heard his footsteps pass along the side of the deckhouse. She heard them – and let her head fall again on her bare arms thrown over the little desk before which she sat.

Jörgenson, standing by the taffrail, noted the faint reddish glow in the massive blackness of the further shore. Jörgenson noted things quickly, cursorily, perfunctorily, as phenomena unrelated to his own apparitional existence of a visiting ghost. They were but passages in the game of men who were still playing at life. He knew too well how much that game was worth to be concerned about its course. He had given up the habit of thinking for so long that the sudden resumption of it irked him exceedingly, especially as he had to think on toward a conclusion. In that world of eternal oblivion, of which he had tasted before Lingard made him step back into the life of men, all things were settled once for all. He was irritated by his own perplexity which was like a reminder of that mortality made up of questions and passions from which he had fancied he had freed himself forever. By a natural association his contemptuous annoyance embraced the existence of Mrs Travers, too, for how could he think of Tom Lingard, of what was good or bad for King Tom, without thinking also of that woman who had managed to put the ghost of a spark even into his own extinguished eyes? She was of no account; but Tom's integrity was. It was of Tom that he had to think, of what was good or bad for Tom in that absurd and deadly game of his life. Finally he reached the conclusion that to be given the ring would be good for Tom Lingard. Just to be given the ring and no more. The ring and no more.

'It will help him to make up his mind,' muttered Jörgenson in his moustache, as if compelled by an obscure conviction. It was only then that he stirred slightly and turned away from the loom of the fires on the distant shore. Mrs Travers heard his footsteps passing again along the side of the deckhouse – and this time never raised her head. That man was sleepless, mad, childish, and inflexible. He was impossible. He haunted the decks of that hulk aimlessly . . .

It was, however, in pursuance of a very distinct aim that Jörgenson had gone forward again to seek Jaffir.

The first remark he had to offer to Jaffir's consideration was that the only person in the world who had the remotest chance of reaching Belarab's gate on that night was that tall white woman the Rajah Laut had brought on board, the wife of one of the captive white chiefs. Surprise made Jaffir exclaim, but he wasn't prepared to deny that. It was possible that for many reasons, some quite simple and others very subtle, those sons of the Evil One belonging to Tengga and Daman would refrain from killing a white woman walking alone from the water's edge to Belarab's gate. Yes, it was just possible that she might walk unharmed.

'Especially if she carried a blazing torch,' muttered Jörgenson in his moustache. He told Jaffir that she was sitting now in the dark, mourning silently in the manner of white women. She had made a great outcry in the morning to be allowed to join the white men on shore. He, Jörgenson, had refused her the canoe. Ever since she had secluded herself in the deckhouse in great distress.

Jaffir listened to it all without particular sympathy. And when Jörgenson added, 'It is in my mind, O Jaffir, to let her have her will now,' he answered by a 'Yes, by Allah! let her go. What does it matter?' of the greatest unconcern, till Jörgenson added:

'Yes. And she may carry the ring to the Rajah Laut.'

Jörgenson saw Jaffir, the grim and impassive Jaffir, give a perceptible start. It seemed at first an impossible task to persuade Jaffir to part with the ring. The notion was too monstrous to enter his mind, to move his heart. But at last he surrendered in an awed whisper, 'God is great, Perhaps it is her destiny.'

Being a Wajo man he did not regard women as untrustworthy or unequal to a task requiring courage and judgement. Once he got over the personal feeling he handed the ring to Jörgenson with only one reservation, 'You know, Tuan, that she must on no account put it on her finger.'

'Let her hang it round her neck,' suggested Jörgenson, readily.

As Jörgenson moved toward the deckhouse it occurred to him that perhaps now that woman Tom Lingard had taken in tow might take it into her head to refuse to leave the *Emma*. This did not disturb him very much. All those people moved in the dark. He himself at that particular moment was moving in the dark. Beyond the simple wish to guide Lingard's thought in the direction of Hassim and Immada, to help him to make up his mind at last to a ruthless fidelity to his purpose Jörgenson had no other aim. The existence of those whites had no meaning on earth. They were the sort of people that pass without leaving footprints. That woman would have to act in ignorance. And if she refused to go then in ignorance she would have to stay on board. He would tell her nothing.

As a matter of fact, he discovered that Mrs Travers would simply have nothing to do with him. She would not listen to what he had to say. She desired him, a mere weary voice confined in the darkness of the deck cabin, to go away and trouble her no more. But the ghost of Jörgenson was not easily exorcised. He, too, was a mere voice in the outer darkness, inexorable, insisting that she should come out on deck and listen. At last he found the right words to say.

'It is something about Tom that I want to tell you. You wish him well, don't you?'

After this she could not refuse to come out on deck, and once there she listened patiently to that white ghost muttering and mumbling above her drooping head.

'It seems to me, Captain Jörgenson,' she said after he had ceased, 'that you are simply trifling with me. After your behaviour to me this morning, I can have nothing to say to you.'

'I have a canoe for you now,' mumbled Jörgenson.

'You have some new purpose in view now,' retorted Mrs

Travers with spirit. 'But you won't make it clear to me. What is it that you have in your mind?'

'Tom's interest.'

'Are you really his friend?'

'He brought me here. You know it. He has talked a lot to you.'

'He did. But I ask myself whether you are capable of being anybody's friend.'

'You ask yourself!' repeated Jörgenson, very quiet and morose. 'If I am not his friend I should like to know who is.'

Mrs Travers asked, quickly: 'What's all this about a ring? What ring?'

'Tom's property. He has had it for years.'

'And he gave it to you? Doesn't he care for it?'

'Don't know. It's just a thing.'

'But it has a meaning as between you and him. Is that so?'

'Yes. It has. He will know what it means.'

'What does it mean?'

'I am too much his friend not to hold my tongue.'

'What! To me!'

'And who are you?' was Jörgenson's unexpected remark. 'He has told you too much already.'

'Perhaps he has,' whispered Mrs Travers, as if to herself. 'And you want that ring to be taken to him?' she asked, in a louder tone.

'Yes. At once. For his good.'

'Are you certain it is for his good? Why can't you . . .'

She checked herself. That man was hopeless. He would never tell anything and there was no means of compelling him. He was invulnerable, unapproachable . . . He was dead.

'Just give it to him,' mumbled Jörgenson as though pursuing a mere fixed idea. 'Just slip it quietly into his hand. He will understand.'

'What is it? Advice, warning, signal for action?'

'It may be anything,' uttered Jörgenson, morosely, but as it were in a mollified tone. 'It's meant for his good.'

'Oh, if I only could trust that man!' mused Mrs Travers, half aloud.

Jörgenson's slight noise in the throat might have been taken for an expression of sympathy. But he remained silent.

'Really, this is most extraordinary!' cried Mrs Travers, suddenly aroused. 'Why did you come to me? Why should it be my task? Why should you want me specially to take it to him?'

'I will tell you why,' said Jörgenson's blank voice. 'It's because there is no one on board this hulk that can hope to get alive inside that stockade. This morning you told me yourself that you were ready to die – for Tom – or with Tom. Well, risk it then. You are the only one that has half a chance to get through – and Tom, maybe, is waiting.'

'The only one,' repeated Mrs Travers with an abrupt movement forward and an extended hand before which Jörgenson stepped back a pace. 'Risk it! Certainly! Where's that mysterious ring?'

'I have got it in my pocket,' said Jörgenson, readily; yet nearly half a minute elapsed before Mrs Travers felt the characteristic shape being pressed into her half-open palm. 'Don't let anybody see it,' Jörgenson admonished her in a murmur. 'Hide it somewhere about you. Why not hang it round your neck?'

Mrs Travers' hand remained firmly closed on the ring.

'Yes, that will do,' she murmured, hastily. 'I'll be back in a moment. Get everything ready.' With those words she disappeared inside the deckhouse and presently threads of light appeared in the interstices of the boards. Mrs Travers had lighted a candle in there. She was busy hanging that ring round her neck. She was going. Yes – taking the risk for Tom's sake.

'Nobody can resist that man,' Jörgenson muttered to himself with increasing moroseness. '*I* couldn't.'

4

Jörgenson, after seeing the canoe leave the ship's side, ceased to live intellectually. There was no need for more thinking, for any display of mental ingenuity. He had done with it all. All his notions were perfectly fixed and he could go over them in the same ghostly way in which he haunted the deck of the *Emma*. At the sight of the ring Lingard would return to Hassim and Immada, now captives, too, though Jörgenson certainly did not think them in any serious danger. What had happened really was that Tengga was now holding hostages, and those Jörgenson looked upon as Lingard's own people. They were his. He had gone in with them deep, very deep. They had a hold and a claim on King Tom just as many years ago people of that very race had had a hold and a claim on him, Jörgenson. Only Tom was a much bigger man. A very big man. Nevertheless, Jörgenson didn't see why he should escape his own fate – Jörgenson's fate – to be absorbed, captured, made their own either in failure or in success. It was an unavoidable fatality and Jörgenson felt certain that the ring would compel Lingard to face it without flinching. What he really wanted Lingard to do was to cease to take the slightest interest in those whites – who were the sort of people that left no footprints.

Perhaps, at first sight, sending that woman to Lingard was not the best way toward that end. Jörgenson, however, had a distinct impression in which his morning talk with Mrs Travers had only confirmed him, that those two had quarrelled for good. As, indeed, was unavoidable. What did Tom Lingard want with any woman? The only woman in Jörgenson's life had come in by way of exchange for a lot of cotton stuffs and several brass guns. This fact could not but affect Jörgenson's judgement since obviously in this case such a transaction was impossible. Therefore the case was not serious. It didn't exist. What did exist was Lingard's relation to the Wajo exiles, a great and warlike adventure such as no rover in those seas had ever attempted.

That Tengga was much more ready to negotiate than to fight, the old adventurer had not the slightest doubt. How Lingard would deal with him was not a concern of Jörgenson's. That would be easy enough. Nothing prevented Lingard from going to see Tengga and talking to him with authority. All that ambitious person really wanted was to have a share in Lingard's wealth, in Lingard's power, in Lingard's friendship. A year before Tengga had once insinuated to Jörgenson, 'In what way am I less worthy of being a friend than Belarab?'

It was a distinct overture, a disclosure of the man's innermost mind. Jörgenson, of course, had met it with a profound silence. His task was not diplomacy but the care of stores.

After the effort of connected mental processes in order to bring about Mrs Travers' departure he was anxious to dismiss the whole matter from his mind. The last thought he gave to it was severely practical. It occurred to him that it would be advisable to attract in some way or other Lingard's attention to the lagoon. In the language of the sea a single rocket is properly a signal of distress, but, in the circumstances, a group of three sent up simultaneously would convey a warning. He gave his orders and watched the rockets go up finely with a trail of red sparks, a bursting of white stars high up in the air, and three loud reports in quick succession. Then he resumed his pacing of the whole length of the hulk, confident that after this Tom would guess that something was up and set a close watch over the lagoon. No doubt these mysterious rockets would have a disturbing effect on Tengga and his friends and cause a great excitement in the Settlement; but for that Jörgenson did not care. The Settlement was already in such a turmoil that a little more excitement did not matter. What Jörgenson did not expect, however, was the sound of a musket-shot fired from the jungle facing the bows of the *Emma*. It caused him to stop dead short. He had heard distinctly the bullet strike the curve of the bow forward. 'Some hot-headed ass fired that,' he said to himself, contemptuously. It simply disclosed to him the fact that he was already besieged on the shore side and set at rest his doubts as to the length Tengga was prepared to go. Any length! Of course there was still time

for Tom to put everything right with six words, unless ...
Jörgenson smiled, grimly, in the dark and resumed his tireless
pacing.

What amused him was to observe the fire which had been
burning night and day before Tengga's residence suddenly
extinguished. He pictured to himself the wild rush with bamboo buckets to the lagoon shore, the confusion, the hurry and
jostling in a great hissing of water midst clouds of steam. The
image of the fat Tengga's consternation appealed to Jörgenson's
sense of humour for about five seconds. Then he took up the
binoculars from the roof of the deckhouse.

The bursting of the three white stars over the lagoon had
given him a momentary glimpse of the black speck of the canoe
taking over Mrs Travers. He couldn't find it again with the
glass, it was too dark; but the part of the shore for which it was
steered would be somewhere near the angle of Belarab's stockade
nearest to the beach. This Jörgenson could make out in the faint
rosy glare of fires burning inside. Jörgenson was certain that
Lingard was looking toward the *Emma* through the most convenient loophole he could find.

As obviously Mrs Travers could not have paddled herself
across, two men were taking her over; and for the steersman she
had Jaffir. Though he had assented to Jörgenson's plan, Jaffir
was anxious to accompany the ring as near as possible to its
destination. Nothing but dire necessity had induced him to part
with the talisman. Crouching in the stern and flourishing his
paddle from side to side he glared at the back of the canvas deck
chair which had been placed in the middle for Mrs Travers.
Wrapped up in the darkness she reclined in it with her eyes
closed, faintly aware of the ring hung low on her breast. As the
canoe was rather large it was moving very slowly. The two men
dipped their paddles without a splash; and surrendering herself
passively, in a temporary relaxation of all her limbs, to this
adventure Mrs Travers had no sense of motion at all. She, too,
like Jörgenson, was tired of thinking. She abandoned herself to
the silence of that night full of roused passions and deadly purposes. She abandoned herself to an illusory feeling; to the im-

pression that she was really resting. For the first time in many days she could taste the relief of being alone. The men with her were less than nothing. She could not speak to them; she could not understand them; the canoe might have been moving by enchantment – if it did move at all. Like a half-conscious sleeper she was on the verge of saying to herself, 'What a strange dream I am having.'

The low tones of Jaffir's voice stole into it quietly, telling the men to cease paddling, and the long canoe came to a rest slowly, no more than ten yards from the beach. The party had been provided with a torch which was to be lighted before the canoe touched the shore, thus giving a character of openness to this desperate expedition. 'And if it draws fire on us,' Jaffir had commented to Jörgenson, 'well, then, we shall see whose fate it is to die on this night.'

'Yes,' had muttered Jörgenson. 'We shall see.'

Jörgenson saw at last the small light of the torch against the blackness of the stockade. He strained his hearing for a possible volley of musketry fire but no sound came to him over the broad surface of the lagoon. Over there the man with the torch, the other paddler, and Jaffir himself impelling with a gentle motion of his paddle the canoe toward the shore, had the glistening eyeballs and the tense faces of silent excitement. The ruddy glare smote Mrs Travers' closed eyelids but she didn't open her eyes till she felt the canoe touch the strand. The two men leaped instantly out of it. Mrs Travers rose, abruptly. Nobody made a sound. She stumbled out of the canoe on to the beach and almost before she had recovered her balance the torch was thrust into her hand. The heat, the nearness of the blaze confused and blinded her till, instinctively, she raised the torch high above her head. For a moment she stood still, holding aloft the fierce flame from which a few sparks were falling slowly.

A naked bronze arm lighted from above pointed out the direction and Mrs Travers began to walk toward the featureless black mass of the stockade. When after a few steps she looked back over her shoulder, the lagoon, the beach, the canoe, the men she had just left had become already invisible. She was alone bearing up a blazing torch on an earth that was a dumb shadow shifting under her feet. At last she reached firmer ground and the dark length of the palisade untouched as yet by the light of the torch seemed to her immense, intimidating. She felt ready to drop from sheer emotion. But she moved on.

'A little more to the left,' shouted a strong voice.

It vibrated through all her fibres, rousing like the call of a trumpet, went far beyond her, filled all the space. Mrs Travers stood still for a moment, then casting far away from her the burning torch ran forward blindly with her hands extended toward the great sound of Lingard's voice, leaving behind her the light flaring and spluttering on the ground. She stumbled and was only saved from a fall by her hands coming in contact with the rough stakes. The stockade rose high above her head and she clung to it with widely open arms, pressing her whole body against the rugged surface of that enormous and unscaled palisade. She heard through it low voices inside, heavy thuds; and felt at every blow a slight vibration of the ground under her feet. She glanced fearfully over her shoulder and saw nothing in the darkness but the expiring glow of the torch she had thrown away and the sombre shimmer of the lagoon bordering the opaque darkness of the shore. Her strained eyeballs seemed to detect mysterious movements in the darkness and she gave way to irresistible terror, to a shrinking agony of apprehension. Was she to be transfixed by a broad blade, to the high, immovable wall of wood against which she was flattening herself desperately, as though she could hope to penetrate it by the mere force of her fear? She had no idea where she was, but as a matter of fact she was a little to the left of the principal gate and almost exactly under one of the loopholes of the stockade. Her excessive anguish passed into insensibility. She ceased to hear, to see, and even to feel the contact of the surface to which she clung. Lingard's voice somewhere from the sky above her head was directing her, distinct, very close, full of concern.

'You must stoop low. Lower yet.'

The stagnant blood of her body began to pulsate languidly. She stooped low – lower yet – so low that she had to sink on her knees, and then became aware of a faint smell of wood smoke mingled with the confused murmur of agitated voices. This came to her through an opening no higher than her head in her kneeling posture, and no wider than the breadth of two stakes. Lingard was saying in a tone of distress:

'I couldn't get any of them to unbar the gate.'

She was unable to make a sound. – 'Are you there?' Lingard asked, anxiously, so close to her now that she seemed to feel the very breath of his words on her face. It revived her completely; she understood what she had to do. She put her head and shoulders through the opening, was at once seized under the arms by an eager grip and felt herself pulled through with an irresistible force and with such haste that her scarf was dragged off her head, its fringes having caught in the rough timber. The same eager grip lifted her up, stood her on her feet without her having to make any exertion toward that end. She became aware that Lingard was trying to say something, but she heard only a confused stammering expressive of wonder and delight in which she caught the words 'You ... you ...' deliriously repeated. He didn't release his hold of her; his helpful and irresistible grip had changed into a close clasp, a crushing embrace, the violent taking possession by an embodied force that had broken loose and was not to be controlled any longer. As his great voice had done a moment before, his great strength, too, seemed able to fill all space in its enveloping and undeniable authority. Every time she tried instinctively to stiffen herself against its might, it reacted, affirming its fierce will, its uplifting power. Several times she lost the feeling of the ground and had a sensation of helplessness without fear, of triumph without exultation. The inevitable had come to pass. She had foreseen it – and all the time in that dark place and against the red glow of camp fires within the stockade the man in whose arms she struggled remained shadowy to her eyes – to her half-closed eyes. She thought suddenly, 'He will crush me to death without knowing it.'

323

He was like a blind force. She closed her eyes altogether. Her head fell back a little. Not instinctively but with wilful resignation and as it were from a sense of justice she abandoned herself to his arms. The effect was as though she had suddenly stabbed him to the heart. He let her go so suddenly and completely that she would have fallen down in a heap if she had not managed to catch hold of his forearm. He seemed prepared for it and for a moment all her weight hung on it without moving its rigidity by a hair's breadth. Behind her Mrs Travers heard the heavy thud of blows on wood, the confused murmurs and movements of men.

A voice said suddenly 'It's done' with such emphasis that though, of course, she didn't understand the words it helped her to regain possession of herself; and when Lingard asked her very little above a whisper: 'Why don't you say something?' she answered, readily, 'Let me get my breath first.'

Round them all sounds had ceased. The men had secured again the opening through which those arms had snatched her into a moment of self-forgetfulness which had left her out of breath but uncrushed. As if something imperative had been satisfied she had a moment of inward serenity, a period of peace without thought while, holding to that arm that trembled no more than an arm of iron, she felt stealthily over the ground for one of the sandals which she had lost. Oh, yes, there was no doubt of it, she had been carried off the earth, without shame, without regret. But she would not have let him know of that dropped sandal for anything in the world. That lost sandal was as symbolic as a dropped veil. But he did not know of it. He must never know. Where was that thing? She felt sure that they had not moved an inch from that spot. Presently her foot found it and still gripping Lingard's forearm she stooped to secure it properly. When she stood up, still holding his arm, they confronted each other, he rigid in an effort of self-command but feeling as if the surges of the heaviest sea that he could remember in his life were running through his heart; and the woman as if emptied of all feeling by her experience, without thought yet, but beginning to regain her sense of the situation and the memory of the immediate past.

'I have been watching at that loophole for an hour, ever since they came running to me with that story of the rockets,' said Lingard. 'I was shut up with Belarab then. I was looking out when the torch blazed and you stepped ashore. I thought I was dreaming. But what could I do? I felt I must rush to you but I dared not. That clump of palms is full of men. So are the houses you saw that time you came ashore with me. Full of men. Armed men. A trigger is soon pulled and when once shooting begins ... And you walking in the open with that light above your head! I didn't dare. You were safer alone. I had the strength to hold myself in and watch you come up from the shore. No! No man that ever lived had seen such a sight. What did you come for?'

'Didn't you expect somebody? I don't mean me, I mean a messenger?'

'No!' said Lingard, wondering at his own self-control. 'Why did he let you come?'

'You mean Captain Jörgenson? Oh, he refused at first. He said that he had your orders.'

'How on earth did you manage to get round him?' said Lingard in his softest tones.

'I did not try,' she began and checked herself. Lingard's question, though he really didn't seem to care much about an answer, had aroused afresh her suspicion of Jörgenson's change of front. 'I didn't have to say very much at the last,' she continued, gasping yet a little and feeling her personality, crushed to nothing in the hug of those arms, expand again to its full significance before the attentive immobility of that man. 'Captain Jörgenson has always looked upon me as a nuisance. Perhaps he had made up his mind to get rid of me even against your orders. Is he quite sane?'

She released her firm hold of that iron forearm which fell slowly by Lingard's side. She had regained fully the possession of her personality. There remained only a fading, slightly breathless impression of a short flight above that earth on which her feet were firmly planted now. 'And is that all?' she asked herself, not bitterly, but with a sort of tender contempt.

'He is so sane,' sounded Lingard's voice, gloomily, 'that if I had listened to him you would not have found me here.'

'What do you mean by here? In this stockade?'

'Anywhere,' he said.

'And what would have happened then?'

'God knows,' he answered. 'What would have happened if the world had not been made in seven days? I have known you for just about that time. It began by me coming to you at night – like a thief in the night. Where the devil did I hear that? And that man you are married to thinks I am no better than a thief.'

'It ought to be enough for you that I never made a mistake as to what you are, that I come to you in less than twenty-four hours after you left me contemptuously to my distress. Don't pretend you didn't hear me call after you. Oh, yes, you heard. The whole ship heard me for I had no shame.'

'Yes, you came,' said Lingard, violently. 'But have you really come? I can't believe my eyes! Are you really here?'

'This is a dark spot, luckily,' said Mrs Travers. 'But can you really have any doubt?' she added, significantly.

He made a sudden movement toward her, betraying so much passion that Mrs Travers thought, 'I shan't come out alive this time,' and yet he was there, motionless before her, as though he had never stirred. It was more as though the earth had made a sudden movement under his feet without being able to destroy his balance. But the earth under Mrs Travers' feet had made no movement and for a second she was overwhelmed by wonder not at this proof of her own self-possession but at the man's immense power over himself. If it had not been for her strange inward exhaustion she would perhaps have surrendered to that power. But it seemed to her that she had nothing in her worth surrendering, and it was in a perfectly even tone that she said, 'Give me your arm, Captain Lingard. We can't stay all night on this spot.'

As they moved on she thought, 'There is real greatness in that man.' He was great even in his behaviour. No apologies, no explanations, no abasement, no violence, and not even the slightest tremor of the frame holding that bold and perplexed soul. She knew that for certain because her fingers were resting lightly on Lingard's arm while she walked slowly by his side as though he were taking her down to dinner. And yet she couldn't suppose for a moment that, like herself, he was emptied of all emotion. She never before was so aware of him as a dangerous force. 'He is really ruthless,' she thought. They had just left the shadow of the inner defences about the gate when a slightly hoarse, apologetic voice was heard behind them repeating insistently, what even Mrs Travers' ear detected to be a sort of formula. The words were: 'There is this thing – there is this thing – there is this thing.' They turned round.

'Oh, my scarf,' said Mrs Travers.

A short, squat, broad-faced young fellow having for all costume a pair of white drawers was offering the scarf thrown over both his arms, as if they had been sticks, and holding it respectfully as far as possible from his person. Lingard took it from him and Mrs Travers claimed it at once. 'Don't forget the proprieties,' she said. 'This is also my face veil.'

She was arranging it about her head when Lingard said, 'There is no need. I am taking you to those gentlemen.' – 'I will use it all the same,' said Mrs Travers. 'This thing works both ways, as a matter of propriety or as a matter of precaution. Till I have an opportunity of looking into a mirror nothing will persuade me that there isn't some change in my face.' Lingard swung half round and gazed down at her. Veiled now she confronted him boldly. 'Tell me, Captain Lingard, how many eyes were looking at us a little while ago?'

'Do you care?' he asked.

'Not in the least,' she said. 'A million stars were looking on, too, and what did it matter? They were not of the world I know. And it's just the same with the eyes. They are not of the world I live in.'

Lingard thought: 'Nobody is.' Never before had she seemed to him more unapproachable, more different and more remote. The glow of a number of small fires lighted the ground only, and brought out the black bulk of men lying down in the thin drift of smoke. Only one of these fires, rather apart and burning

327

in front of the house which was the quarter of the prisoners, might have been called a blaze and even that was not a great one. It didn't penetrate the dark space between the piles and the depth of the verandah above where only a couple of heads and the glint of a spear-head could be seen dimly in the play of the light. But down on the ground outside, the black shape of a man seated on a bench had an intense relief. Another intensely black shadow threw a handful of brushwood on the fire and went away. The man on the bench got up. It was d'Alcacer. He let Lingard and Mrs Travers come quite close up to him. Extreme surprise seemed to have made him dumb.

'You didn't expect . . .' began Mrs Travers with some embarrassment before that mute attitude.

'I doubted my eyes,' struck in d'Alcacer, who seemed embarrassed, too. Next moment he recovered his tone and confessed simply: 'At the moment I wasn't thinking of you, Mrs Travers.' He passed his hand over his forehead. 'I hardly know what I was thinking of.'

In the light of the shooting-up flame Mrs Travers could see d'Alcacer's face. There was no smile on it. She could not remember ever seeing him so grave and, as it were, so distant. She abandoned Lingard's arm and moved closer to the fire.

'I fancy you were very far away, Mr d'Alcacer,' she said.

'This is the sort of freedom of which nothing can deprive us,' he observed, looking hard at the manner in which the scarf was drawn across Mrs Travers' face. 'It's possible I was far away,' he went on, 'but I can assure you that I don't know where I was. Less than an hour ago we had a great excitement here about some rockets, but I didn't share in it. There was no one I could ask a question of. The captain here was, I understood, engaged in a most momentous conversation with the king or the governor of this place.'

He addressed Lingard, directly. 'May I ask whether you have reached any conclusion as yet? That Moor is a very dilatory person, I believe.'

'Any direct attack he would, of course, resist,' said Lingard. 'And, so far, you are protected. But I must admit that he is rather angry with me. He's tired of the whole business. He loves peace above anything in the world. But I haven't finished with him yet.'

'As far as I understood from what you told me before,' said Mr d'Alcacer, with a quick side glance at Mrs Travers' uncovered and attentive eyes, 'as far as I can see he may get all the peace he wants at once by driving us two, I mean Mr Travers and myself, out of the gate on to the spears of those other enraged barbarians. And there are some of his counsellors who advise him to do that very thing no later than the break of day I understand.'

Lingard stood for a moment perfectly motionless.

'That's about it,' he said in an unemotional tone, and went away with a heavy step without giving another look at d'Alcacer and Mrs Travers, who after a moment faced each other.

'You have heard?' said d'Alcacer. 'Of course that doesn't affect your fate in any way, and as to him he is much too prestigious to be killed light-heartedly. When all this is over you will walk triumphantly on his arm out of this stockade; for there is nothing in all this to affect his greatness, his absolute value in the eyes of those people – and indeed in any other eyes.' D'Alcacer kept his glance averted from Mrs Travers and as soon as he had finished speaking busied himself in dragging the bench a little way further from the fire. When they sat down on it he kept his distance from Mrs Travers. She made no sign of unveiling herself and her eyes without a face seemed to him strangely unknown and disquieting.

'The situation in a nutshell,' she said. 'You have arranged it all beautifully, even to my triumphal exit. Well, and what then? No, you needn't answer, it has no interest. I assure you I came here not with any notion of marching out in triumph, as you call it. I came here, to speak in the most vulgar way, to save your skin – and mine.'

Her voice came muffled to d'Alcacer's ears with a changed character, even to the very intonation. Above the white and embroidered scarf her eyes in the firelight transfixed him, black and so steady that even the red sparks of the reflected glare did

not move in them. He concealed the strong impression she
made. He bowed his head a little.

'I believe you know perfectly well what you are doing.'

'No! I don't know,' she said, more quickly than he had ever
heard her speak before. 'First of all, I don't think he is as safe
as you imagine. Oh, yes, he has prestige enough, I don't question that. But you are apportioning life and death with too
much assurance ...'

'I know my portion,' murmured d'Alcacer, gently.

A moment of silence fell in which Mrs Travers' eyes ended by
intimidating d'Alcacer, who looked away. The flame of the fire
had sunk low. In the dark agglomeration of buildings, which
might have been called Belarab's palace, there was a certain
animation, a flitting of people, voices calling and answering, the
passing to and fro of lights that would illuminate suddenly a
heavy pile, the corner of a house, the eaves of a low-pitched
roof, while in the open parts of the stockade the armed men
slept by the expiring fires.

Mrs Travers said, suddenly, 'That Jörgenson is not friendly to
us.'

'Possibly.'

With clasped hands and leaning over his knees d'Alcacer had
assented in a very low tone. Mrs Travers, unobserved, pressed
her hands to her breast and felt the shape of the ring, thick,
heavy, set with a big stone. It was there, secret, hung against her
heart, and enigmatic. What did it mean? What could it mean?
What was the feeling it could arouse or the action it could pro-
voke? And she thought with compunction that she ought to
have given it to Lingard at once, without thinking, without
hesitating. 'There! This is what I came for. To give you this.'
Yes, but there had come an interval when she had been able to
think of nothing, and since then she had had the time to reflect
– unfortunately. To remember Jörgenson's hostile, contemptuous
glance enveloping her from head to foot at the break of a day
after a night of lonely anguish. And now while she sat there
veiled from his keen sight there was that other man, that
d'Alcacer, prophesying. O yes, triumphant. She knew already

what that was. Mrs Travers became afraid of the ring. She felt ready to pluck it from her neck and cast it away.

'I mistrust him,' she said. – 'You do!' exclaimed d'Alcacer, very low. – 'I mean that Jörgenson. He seems a merciless sort of creature.' – 'He is indifferent to everything,' said d'Alcacer. – 'It may be a mask.' – 'Have you some evidence, Mrs Travers?'

'No,' said Mrs Travers without hesitation. 'I have my instinct.'

D'Alcacer remained silent for a while as though he were pursuing another train of thought altogether, then in a gentle, almost playful tone: 'If I were a woman,' he said, turning to Mrs Travers, 'I would always trust my intuition.' – 'If you were a woman, Mr d'Alcacer, I would not be speaking to you in this way because then I would be suspect to you.'

The thought that before long perhaps he would be neither man nor woman but a lump of cold clay crossed d'Alcacer's mind, which was living, alert, and unsubdued by the danger. He had welcomed the arrival of Mrs Travers simply because he had been very lonely in that stockade, Mr Travers having fallen into a phase of sulks complicated with shivering fits. Of Lingard, d'Alcacer had seen almost nothing since they had landed, for the Man of Fate was extremely busy negotiating in the recesses of Belarab's main hut; and the thought that his life was being a matter of arduous bargaining was not agreeable to Mr d'Alcacer. The Chief's dependants and the armed men garrisoning the stockade paid very little attention to him apparently, and this gave him the feeling of his captivity being very perfect and hopeless. During the afternoon, while pacing to and fro in the bit of shade thrown by the glorified sort of hut inside which Mr Travers shivered and sulked misanthropically, he had been aware of the more distant verandahs becoming filled now and then by the muffled forms of women of Belarab's household taking a distinct and curious view of the white man. All this was irksome. He found his menaced life extremely difficult to get through. Yes, he welcomed the arrival of Mrs Travers who brought with her a tragic note into the empty gloom.

'Suspicion is not in my nature, Mrs Travers, I assure you, and I hope that you on your side will never suspect either my reserve or my frankness. I respect the mysterious nature of your conviction, but hasn't Jörgenson given you some occasion to . . .'

'He hates me,' said Mrs Travers, and frowned at d'Alcacer's incipient smile. 'It isn't a delusion on my part. The worst is that he hates me not for myself. I believe he is completely indifferent to my existence. Jörgenson hates me because as it were I represent you two who are in danger, because it is you two that are the trouble and I . . . Well !'

'Yes, yes, that's certain,' said d'Alcacer, hastily. 'But Jörgenson is wrong in making you the scapegoat. For if you were not here cool reason would step in and would make Lingard pause in his passion to make a king out of an exile. If we were murdered it would certainly make some stir in the world in time and he would fall under the suspicion of complicity with those wild and inhuman Moors. Who would regard the greatness of his day-dreams, his engaged honour, his chivalrous feelings? Nothing could save him from that suspicion. And being what he is, you understand me, Mrs Travers (but you know him much better than I do), it would morally kill him.'

'Heavens !' whispered Mrs Travers. 'This has never occurred to me.' Those words seemed to lose themselves in the folds of the scarf without reaching d'Alcacer, who continued in his gentle tone :

'However, as it is, he will be safe enough whatever happens. He will have your testimony to clear him.'

Mrs Travers stood up, suddenly, but still careful to keep her face covered, she threw the end of the scarf over her shoulder.

'I fear that Jörgenson,' she cried with suppressed passion. 'One can't understand what that man means to do, I think him so dangerous that if I were, for instance, entrusted with a message bearing on the situation, I would . . . suppress it.'

D'Alcacer was looking up from the seat, full of wonder. Mrs Travers appealed to him in a calm voice through the folds of the scarf :

'Tell me, Mr d'Alcacer, you who can look on it calmly, wouldn't I be right?'

'Why, has Jörgenson told you anything?'

'Directly – nothing, except a phrase or two which really I could not understand. They seemed to have a hidden sense and he appeared to attach some mysterious importance to them that he dared not explain to me.'

'That was a risk on his part,' exclaimed d'Alcacer. 'And he trusted you. Why you, I wonder!'

'Who can tell what notions he has in his head? Mr d'Alcacer, I believe his only object is to call Captain Lingard away from us. I understood it only a few minutes ago. It has dawned upon me. All he wants is to call him off.'

'Call him off,' repeated d'Alcacer, a little bewildered by the aroused fire of her conviction. 'I am sure I don't want him called off any more than you do; and, frankly, I don't believe Jörgenson has any such power. But upon the whole, and if you feel that Jörgenson has the power, I would – yes, if I were in your place I think I would suppress anything I could not understand.'

Mrs Travers listened to the very end. Her eyes – they appeared incredibly sombre to d'Alcacer – seemed to watch the fall of every deliberate word and after he had ceased they remained still for an appreciable time. Then she turned away with a gesture that seemed to say: 'So be it.'

D'Alcacer raised his voice suddenly after her. 'Stay! Don't forget that not only your husband's but my head, too, is being played at that game. My judgement is not ...'

She stopped for a moment and freed her lips. In the profound stillness of the courtyard her clear voice made the shadows at the nearest fires stir a little with low murmurs of surprise.

'Oh, yes, I remember whose heads I have to save,' she cried. 'But in all the world who is there to save that man from himself?'

D'ALCACER sat down on the bench again. 'I wonder what she knows,' he thought, 'and I wonder what I have done.' He wondered also how far he had been sincere and how far affected by a very natural aversion from being murdered obscurely by ferocious Moors with all the circumstances of barbarity. It was a very naked death to come upon one suddenly. It was robbed of all helpful illusions, such as the free will of a suicide, the heroism of a warrior, or the exaltation of a martyr. 'Hadn't I better make some sort of fight of it?' he debated with himself. He saw himself rushing at the naked spears without any enthusiasm. Or wouldn't it be better to go forth to meet his doom (somewhere outside the stockade on that horrible beach) with calm dignity. 'Pah! I shall be probably speared through the back in the beastliest possible fashion,' he thought with an inward shudder. It was certainly not a shudder of fear, for Mr d'Alcacer attached no high value to life. It was a shudder of disgust because Mr d'Alcacer was a civilized man and though he had no illusions about civilization he could not but admit the superiority of its methods. It offered to one a certain refinement of form, a comeliness of proceedings and definite safeguards against deadly surprises. 'How idle all this is,' he thought, finally. His next thought was that women were very resourceful. It was true, he on meditating with unwonted cynicism, that strictly speaking they had only one resource but, generally, it served – it served.

He was surprised by his supremely shameless bitterness at this juncture. It was so uncalled for. This situation was too complicated to be entrusted to a cynical or shameless hope. There was nothing to trust to. At this moment of his meditation he became aware of Lingard's approach. He raised his head eagerly. D'Alcacer was not indifferent to his fate and even to Mr Travers' fate. He would fain learn ... But one look at Lingard's face was enough. 'It's no use asking him anything,' he said to himself, 'for he cares for nothing just now.'

Lingard sat down heavily on the other end of the bench, and d'Alcacer, looking at his profile, confessed to himself that this was the most masculinely good-looking face he had ever seen in his life. It was an expressive face, too, but its present expression was also beyond d'Alcacer's past experience. At the same time its quietness set up a barrier against common curiosities and even common fears. No, it was no use asking him anything. Yet something should be said to break the spell, to call down again this man to the earth. But it was Lingard who spoke first.

'Where has Mrs Travers gone?'

'She has gone . . . where naturally she would be anxious to go first of all since she has managed to come to us,' answered d'Alcacer, wording his answer with the utmost regard for the delicacy of the situation.

The stillness of Lingard seemed to have grown even more impressive. He spoke again.

'I wonder what those two can have to say to each other.'

He might have been asking that of the whole darkened part of the globe, but it was d'Alcacer who answered in his courteous tones.

'Would it surprise you very much, Captain Lingard, if I were to tell you that those two people are quite fit to understand each other thoroughly? Yes? It surprises you! Well, I assure you that seven thousand miles from here nobody would wonder.'

'I think I understand,' said Lingard, 'but don't you know the man is light-headed? A man like that is as good as mad.'

'Yes, he has been slightly delirious since seven o'clock,' said d'Alcacer. 'But believe me, Captain Lingard,' he continued, earnestly, and obeying a perfectly disinterested impulse, 'that even in his delirium he is far more understandable to her and better able to understand her than . . . anybody within a hundred miles from here.'

'Ah!' said Lingard, without any emotion, 'so you don't wonder. You don't see any reason for wonder.'

'No, for, don't you see, I do know.'

'What do you know?'

'Men and women, Captain Lingard, which you . . .'

'I don't know any woman.'

'You have spoken the strictest truth there,' said d'Alcacer, and for the first time Lingard turned his head slowly and looked at his neighbour on the bench.

'Do you think she is as good as mad, too?' asked Lingard in a startled voice.

D'Alcacer let escape a low exclamation. No, certainly he did not think so. It was an original notion to suppose that lunatics had a sort of common logic which made them understandable to each other. D'Alcacer tried to make his voice as gentle as possible while he pursued: 'No, Captain Lingard, I believe the woman of whom we speak is and will always remain in the fullest possession of herself.'

Lingard, leaning back, clasped his hands round his knees. He seemed not to be listening and d'Alcacer, pulling a cigarette case out of his pocket, looked for a long time at the three cigarettes it contained. It was the last of the provision he had on him when captured. D'Alcacer had put himself on the strictest allowance. A cigarette was only to be lighted on special occasions; and now there were only three left and they had to be made to last till the end of life. They calmed, they soothed, they gave an attitude. And only three left! One had to be kept for the morning, to be lighted before going through the gate of doom – the gate of Belarab's stockade. A cigarette soothed, it gave an attitude. Was this the fitting occasion for one of the remaining two? D'Alcacer, a true Latin, was not afraid of a little introspection. In the pause he descended into the innermost depths of his be-ing, then glanced up at the night sky. Sportsman, traveller, he had often looked up at the stars before to see how time went. It was going very slowly. He took out a cigarette, snapped-to the case, bent down to the embers. Then he sat up and blew out a thin cloud of smoke. The man by his side looked with his bowed head and clasped knee like a masculine rendering of mournful meditation. Such attitudes are met with sometimes on the sculptures of ancient tombs. D'Alcacer began to speak:

'She is a representative woman and yet one of those of whom there are but very few at any time in the world. Not that they are very rare but that there is but little room on top. They are the iridescent gleams on a hard and dark surface. For the world is hard, Captain Lingard, it is hard, both in what it will remember and in what it will forget. It is for such women that people toil on the ground and underground and artists of all sorts invoke their inspiration.'

Lingard seemed not to have heard a word. His chin rested on his breast. D'Alcacer appraised the remaining length of his cigarette and went on in an equable tone through which pierced a certain sadness:

'No, there are not many of them. And yet they are all. They decorate our life for us. They are the gracious figures on the drab wall which lies on this side of our common grave. They lead a sort of ritual dance, that most of us have agreed to take seriously. It is a very binding agreement with which sincerity and good faith and honour have nothing to do. Very binding. Woe to him or her who breaks it. Directly they leave the pageant they get lost.'

Lingard turned his head sharply and discovered d'Alcacer looking at him with profound attention.

'They get lost in a maze,' continued d'Alcacer, quietly. 'They wander in it lamenting over themselves. I would shudder at that fate for anything I loved. Do you know, Captain Lingard, how people lost in a maze end?' he went on holding Lingard by a steadfast stare. 'No? ... I will tell you then. They end by hating their very selves, and they die in disillusion and despair.'

As if afraid of the force of his words d'Alcacer laid a soothing hand lightly on Lingard's shoulder. But Lingard continued to look into the embers at his feet and remained insensible to the friendly touch. Yet d'Alcacer could not imagine that he had not been heard. He folded his arms on his breast.

'I don't know why I have been telling you all this,' he said, apologetically. 'I hope I have not been intruding on your thoughts.'

'I can think of nothing,' Lingard declared, unexpectedly. 'I only know that your voice was friendly; and for the rest –'

'One must get through a night like this somehow,' said

337

d'Alcacer. 'The very stars seem to lag on their way. It's a common belief that a drowning man is irresistibly compelled to review his past experience. Just now I feel quite out of my depth, and whatever I have said has come from my experience. I am sure you will forgive me. All that it amounts to is this: that it is natural for us to cry for the moon but it would be very fatal to have our cries heard. For what could any one of us do with the moon if it were given to him? I am speaking now of us – common mortals.'

It was not immediately after d'Alcacer had ceased speaking but only after a moment that Lingard unclasped his fingers, got up, and walked away. D'Alcacer followed with a glance of quiet interest the big, shadowy form till it vanished in the direction of an enormous forest tree left in the middle of the stockade. The deepest shade of the night was spread over the ground of Belarab's fortified courtyard. The very embers of the fires had turned black, showing only here and there a mere spark; and the forms of the prone sleepers could hardly be distinguished from the hard ground on which they rested, with their arms lying beside them on the mats. Presently Mrs Travers appeared quite close to d'Alcacer, who rose instantly.

'Martin is asleep,' said Mrs Travers in a tone that seemed to have borrowed something of the mystery and quietness of the night.

'All the world's asleep,' observed d'Alcacer, so low that Mrs Travers barely caught the words. 'Except you and I, and one other who has left me to wander about in the night.'

'Was he with you? Where has he gone?'

'Where it's darkest I should think,' answered d'Alcacer, secretly. 'It's no use going to look for him; but if you keep perfectly still and hold your breath you may presently hear his footsteps.'

'What did he tell you?' breathed out Mrs Travers.

'I didn't ask him anything. I only know that something has happened which has robbed him of his power of thinking ... Hadn't I better go to the hut? Don Martin ought to have someone with him when he wakes up.' Mrs Travers remained perfectly still and even now and then held her breath with a vague fear of hearing those footsteps wandering in the dark. D'Alcacer had disappeared. Again Mrs Travers held her breath. No. Nothing. Not a sound. Only the night to her eyes seemed to have grown darker. Was that a footstep? 'Where could I hide myself?' she thought. But she didn't move.

*

After leaving d'Alcacer, Lingard threading his way between the fires found himself under the big tree, the same tree against which Daman had been leaning on the day of the great talk when the white prisoners had been surrendered to Lingard's keeping on definite conditions. Lingard passed through the deep obscurity made by the outspread boughs of the only witness left there of a past that for endless ages had seen no mankind on this shore defended by the Shallows, around this lagoon over-shadowed by the jungle. In the calm night the old giant, without shudders or murmurs in its enormous limbs, saw the restless man drift through the black shade into the starlight.

In that distant part of the courtyard there were only a few sentries who, themselves invisible, saw Lingard's white figure pace to and fro endlessly. They knew well who that was. It was the great white man. A very great man. A very rich man. A possessor of fire-arms, who could dispense valuable gifts and deal deadly blows, the friend of their Ruler, the enemy of his enemies, known to them for years and always mysterious. At their posts, flattened against the stakes near convenient loop-holes, they cast backward glances and exchanged faint whispers from time to time.

Lingard might have thought himself alone. He had lost touch with the world. What he had said to d'Alcacer was perfectly true. He had no thought. He was in the state of a man who, having cast his eyes through the open gates of Paradise, is rendered insensible by that moment's vision to all the forms and matters of the earth; and in the extremity of his emotion ceases even to look upon himself but as the subject of a sublime experience which exalts or unfits, sanctifies or damns – he didn't know

which. Every shadowy thought, every passing sensation was like
a base intrusion on that supreme memory. He couldn't bear it.

When he had tried to resume his conversation with Belarab
after Mrs Travers' arrival he had discovered himself unable to
go on. He had just enough self-control to break off the interview
in measured terms. He pointed out the lateness of the hour, a
most astonishing excuse to people to whom time is nothing and
whose life and activities are not ruled by the clock. Indeed
Lingard hardly knew what he was saying or doing when he
went out again leaving everybody dumb with astonishment at
the change in his aspect and in his behaviour. A suspicious
silence reigned for a long time in Belarab's great audience room
till the Chief dismissed everybody by two quiet words and a
slight gesture.

*

With her chin in her hand in the pose of a sybil trying to read
the future in the glow of dying embers, Mrs Travers, without
holding her breath, heard quite close to her the footsteps which
she had been listening for with mingled alarm, remorse, and
hope.

She didn't change her attitude. The deep red glow lighted her
up dimly, her face, the white hand hanging by her side, her feet
in their sandals. The disturbing footsteps stopped close to her.

'Where have you been all this time?' she asked, without
looking round.

'I don't know,' answered Lingard. He was speaking the exact
truth. He didn't know. Ever since he had released that woman
from his arms everything but the vaguest notions had departed
from him. Events, necessities, things – he had lost his grip on
them all. And he didn't care. They were futile and impotent;
he had no patience with them. The offended and astonished
Belarab, d'Alcacer with his kindly touch and friendly voice, the
sleeping men, the men awake, the Settlement full of unrestful
life and the restless Shallows of the coast, were removed from
him into an immensity of pitying contempt. Perhaps they
existed. Perhaps all this waited for him. Well, let all this wait;

let everything wait, till tomorrow or to the end of time, which could now come at any moment for all he cared – but certainly till tomorrow.

'I only know,' he went on with an emphasis that made Mrs Travers raise her head, 'that wherever I go I shall carry you with me – against my breast.'

Mrs Travers' fine ear caught the mingled tones of suppressed exultation and dawning fear, the ardour and the faltering of those words. She was feeling still the physical truth at the root of them so strongly that she couldn't help saying in a dreamy whisper:

'Did you mean to crush the life out of me?'

He answered in the same tone:

'I could not have done it. You are too strong. Was I rough? I didn't mean to be. I have been often told I didn't know my own strength. You did not seem able to get through that opening and so I caught hold of you. You came away in my hands quite easily. Suddenly I thought to myself, "now I will make sure." '

He paused as if his breath had failed him. Mrs Travers dared not make the slightest movement. Still in the pose of one in quest of hidden truth she murmured, 'Make sure?'

'Yes. And now I am sure. You are here – here! Before I couldn't tell.'

'Oh, you couldn't tell before,' she said.

'No.'

'So it was reality that you were seeking.'

He repeated as if speaking to himself: 'And now I am sure.'

Her sandalled foot, all rosy in the glow, felt the warmth of the embers. The tepid night had enveloped her body; and still under the impression of his strength she gave herself up to a momentary feeling of quietude that came about her heart as soft as the night air penetrated by the feeble clearness of the stars. 'This is a limpid soul,' she thought.

'You know I always believed in you,' he began again. 'You know I did. Well. I never believed in you so much as I do now,

341

as you sit there, just as you are, and with hardly enough light to make you out by.'

It occurred to her that she had never heard a voice she liked so well – except one. But that had been a great actor's voice; whereas this man was nothing in the world but his very own self. He persuaded, he moved, he disturbed, he soothed by his inherent truth. He had wanted to make sure and he had made sure apparently; and too weary to resist the waywardness of her thoughts Mrs Travers reflected with a sort of amusement that apparently he had not been disappointed. She thought, 'He believes in me. What amazing words. Of all the people that might have believed in me I had to find this one here. He believes in me more than in himself.' A gust of sudden remorse tore her out from her quietness, made her cry out to him:

'Captain Lingard, we forget how we have met, we forget what is going on. We mustn't. I won't say that you place your belief wrongly but I have to confess something to you. I must tell you how I came here tonight. Jörgenson . . .'

He interrupted her forcibly but without raising his voice.

'Jörgenson. Who's Jörgenson? You came to me because you couldn't help yourself.'

This took her breath away. 'But I must tell you. There is something in my coming which is not clear to me.'

'You can tell me nothing that I don't know already,' he said in a pleading tone. 'Say nothing. Sit still. Time enough tomorrow. Tomorrow! The night is drawing to an end and I care for nothing in the world but you. Let me be. Give me the rest that is in you.'

She had never heard such accents on his lips and she felt for him a great and tender pity. Why not humour this mood in which he wanted to preserve the moments that would never come to him again on this earth? She hesitated in silence. She saw him stir in the darkness as if he could not make up his mind to sit down on the bench. But suddenly he scattered the embers with his foot and sank on the ground against her feet, and she was not startled in the least to feel the weight of his head on her knee. Mrs Travers was not startled but she felt profoundly moved. Why should she torment him with all those questions of freedom and captivity, of violence and intrigue, of life and death? He was not in a state to be told anything and it seemed to her that she did not want to speak, that in the greatness of her compassion she simply could not speak. All she could do for him was to rest her hand lightly on his head and respond silently to the slight movement she felt, sigh or sob, but a movement which suddenly immobilized her in an anxious emotion.

*

About the same time on the other side of the lagoon Jörgenson, raising his eyes, noted the stars and said to himself that the night would not last long now. He wished for daylight. He hoped that Lingard had already done something. The blaze in Tengga's compound had been re-lighted. Tom's power was unbounded, practically unbounded. And he was invulnerable.

Jörgenson let his old eyes wander amongst the gleams and shadows of the great sheet of water between him and that hostile shore and fancied he could detect a floating shadow having the characteristic shape of a man in a small canoe.

'O! Ya! Man!' he hailed. 'What do you want?' Other eyes, too, had detected that shadow. Low murmurs arose on the deck of the *Emma*. 'If you don't speak at once I shall fire,' shouted Jörgenson, fiercely.

'No, white man,' returned the floating shape in a solemn drawl. 'I am the bearer of friendly words. A chief's words. I come from Tengga.'

'There was a bullet that came on board not a long time ago – also from Tengga,' said Jörgenson.

'That was an accident,' protested the voice from the lagoon. 'What else could it be? Is there war between you and Tengga? No, no, O white man! All Tengga desires is a long talk. He has sent me to ask you to come ashore.'

At these words Jörgenson's heart sank a little. This invitation meant that Lingard had made no move. Was Tom asleep or altogether mad?

343

'The talk would be of peace,' declared impressively the shadow which had drifted much closer to the hulk now.

'It isn't for me to talk with great chiefs,' Jörgenson returned, cautiously.

'But Tengga is a friend,' argued the nocturnal messenger. 'And by that fire there are other friends – your friends, the Rajah Hassim and the lady Immada, who send you their greetings and who expect their eyes to rest on you before sunrise.'

'That's a lie,' remarked Jörgenson, perfunctorily, and fell into thought, while the shadowy bearer of words preserved a scandalized silence, though, of course, he had not expected to be believed for a moment. But one could never tell what a white man would believe. He had wanted to produce the impression that Hassim and Immada were the honoured guests of Tengga. It occurred to him suddenly that perhaps Jörgenson didn't know anything of the capture. And he persisted.

'My words are all true, Tuan. The Rajah of Wajo and his sister are with my master. I left them sitting by the fire on Tengga's right hand. Will you come ashore to be welcomed amongst friends?'

Jörgenson had been reflecting profoundly. His object was to gain as much time as possible for Lingard's interference which indeed could not fail to be effective. But he had not the slightest wish to entrust himself to Tengga's friendliness. Not that he minded the risk; but he did not see the use of taking it.

'No!' he said, 'I can't go ashore. We white men have ways of our own and I am chief of this hulk. And my chief is the Rajah Laut, a white man like myself. All the words that matter are in him and if Tengga is such a great chief let him ask the Rajah Laut for a talk. Yes, that's the proper thing for Tengga to do if he is such a great chief as he says.'

'The Rajah Laut has made his choice. He dwells with Belarab, and with the white people who are huddled together like trapped deer in Belarab's stockade. Why shouldn't you meantime go over where everything is lighted up and open and talk in friendship with Tengga's friends, whose hearts have been made sick by many doubts; Rajah Hassim and the lady Immada

344

and Daman, the chief of the men of the sea, who do not know now whom they can trust unless it be you, Tuan, the keeper of much wealth.'

The diplomatist in the small dugout paused for a moment to give special weight to the final argument:

'Which you have no means to defend. We know how many armed men there are with you.'

'They are great fighters,' Jörgenson observed, unconcernedly spreading his elbows on the rail and looking over at the floating black patch of characteristic shape whence proceeded the voice of the wily envoy of Tengga. 'Each man of them is worth ten of such as you can find in the Settlement.'

'Yes, by Allah. Even worth twenty of these common people. Indeed, you have enough with you to make a great fight but not enough for victory.'

'God alone gives victory,' said suddenly the voice of Jaffir, who, very still at Jörgenson's elbow, had been listening to the conversation.

'Very true,' was the answer in an extremely conventional tone. 'Will you come ashore, O white man, and be the leader of chiefs?'

'I have been that before,' said Jörgenson, with great dignity, 'and now all I want is peace. But I won't come ashore amongst people whose minds are so much troubled, till Rajah Hassim and his sister return on board this ship and tell me the tale of their new friendship with Tengga.'

His heart was sinking with every minute, the very air was growing heavier with the sense of oncoming disaster, on that night that was neither war nor peace and whose only voice was the voice of Tengga's envoy, insinuating in tone though menacing in words.

'No, that cannot be,' said that voice. 'But, Tuan, verily Tengga himself is ready to come on board here to talk with you. He is very ready to come and indeed, Tuan, he means to come on board here before very long.'

'Yes, with fifty war-canoes filled with the ferocious rabble of the Shore of Refuge,' Jaffir was heard commenting, sarcastically, over the rail; and a sinister muttered 'It may be so,' ascended alongside from the black water.

Jörgenson kept silent as if waiting for a supreme inspiration and suddenly he spoke in his other-world voice: 'Tell Tengga from me that as long as he brings with him Rajah Hassim and the Rajah's sister, he and his chief men will be welcome on deck here, no matter how many boats come along with them. For that I do not care. You may go now.'

A profound silence succeeded. It was clear that the envoy was gone, keeping in the shadow of the shore. Jörgenson turned to Jaffir.

'Death amongst friends is but a festival,' he quoted, mumbling in his moustache.

'It is, by Allah,' assented Jaffir with sombre fervour.

6

THIRTY-SIX hours later Carter, alone with Lingard in the cabin of the brig, could almost feel during a pause in his talk the oppressive, the breathless peace of the Shallows awaiting another sunset.

'I never expected to see any of you alive,' Carter began in his easy tone, but with much less carelessness in his bearing as though his days of responsibility amongst the Shoals of the Shore of Refuge had matured his view of the external world and of his own place therein.

'Of course not,' muttered Lingard.

The listlessness of that man whom he had always seen acting under the stress of a secret passion seemed perfectly appalling to Carter's youthful and deliberate energy. Ever since he had found himself again face to face with Lingard he had tried to conceal the shocking impression with a delicacy which owed nothing to training but was as intuitive as a child's.

While justifying to Lingard his manner of dealing with the situation on the Shore of Refuge, he could not for the life of him help asking himself what was this new mystery. He was also young enough to long for a word of commendation.

'Come, Captain,' he argued; 'how would you have liked to come out and find nothing but two half-burnt wrecks stuck on the sands – perhaps?'

He waited for a moment, then in sheer compassion turned away his eyes from that fixed gaze, from that harassed face with sunk cheeks, from that figure of indomitable strength robbed of its fire. He said to himself: 'He doesn't hear me,' and raised his voice without altering its self-contained tone:

'I was below yesterday morning when we felt the shock, but the noise came to us only as a deep rumble. I made one jump for the companion but that precious Shaw was before me yelling "Earthquake! Earthquake!" and I am hanged if he didn't miss his footing and land down on his head at the bottom of the stairs. I had to stop to pick him up but I got on deck in time to see a mighty black cloud that seemed almost solid pop up from behind the forest like a balloon. It stayed there for quite a long time. Some of our calashes on deck swore to me that they had seen a red flash above the tree-tops. But that's hard to believe. I guessed at once that something had blown up on shore. My first thought was that I would never see you any more and I made up my mind at once to find out all the truth you have been keeping away from me. No, sir! Don't you make a mistake! I wasn't going to give you up, dead or alive.'

He looked hard at Lingard while saying these words and saw the first sign of animation pass over that ravaged face. He saw even its lips move slightly; but there was no sound, and Carter looked away again.

'Perhaps you would have done better by telling me everything; but you left me behind on my own to be your man here. I put my hand to the work I could see before me. I am a sailor. There were two ships to look after. And here they are both for you, fit to go or to stay, to fight or to run, as you choose.' He watched with bated breath the effort Lingard had to make to utter the two words of the desired commendation:

'Well done!'

'And I am your man still,' Carter added, impulsively, and hastened to look away from Lingard, who had tried to smile at him and had failed. Carter didn't know what to do next, remain in the cabin or leave that unsupported strong man to himself. With a shyness completely foreign to his character and which he could not understand himself, he suggested in an engaging murmur and with an embarrassed assumption of his right to give advice:

'Why not lie down for a bit, sir? I can attend to anything that may turn up. You seem done up, sir.'

He was facing Lingard, who stood on the other side of the table in a leaning forward attitude propped up on rigid arms and stared fixedly at him – perhaps? Carter felt on the verge of despair. This couldn't last. He was relieved to see Lingard shake his head slightly.

'No, Mr Carter. I think I will go on deck,' said the Captain of the famous brig *Lightning*, while his eyes roamed all over the cabin. Carter stood aside at once, but it was some little time before Lingard made a move.

The sun had sunk already, leaving that evening no trace of its glory on a sky clear as crystal and on the waters without a ripple. All colour seemed to have gone out of the world. The oncoming shadow rose as subtle as a perfume from the black coast lying athwart the eastern semicircle; and such was the silence within the horizon that one might have fancied oneself come to the end of time. Black and toylike in the clear depths and the final stillness of the evening the brig and the schooner lay anchored in the middle of the main channel with their heads swung the same way. Lingard, with his chin on his breast and his arms folded, moved slowly here and there about the poop. Close and mute like his shadow, Carter, at his elbow, followed his movements. He felt an anxious solicitude ...

It was a sentiment perfectly new to him. He had never before felt this sort of solicitude about himself or any other man. His personality was being developed by new experience, and as he was very simple he received the initiation with shyness and self-mistrust. He had noticed with innocent alarm that Lingard had not looked either at the sky or over the sea, neither at his own ship nor the schooner astern; not along the decks, not aloft, not anywhere. He had looked at nothing! And somehow Carter felt himself more lonely and without support than when he had been left alone by that man in charge of two ships entangled amongst the shallows and environed by some sinister mystery. Since that man had come back instead of welcome relief Carter felt his responsibility rest on his young shoulders with tenfold weight. His profound conviction was that Lingard should be roused.

'Captain Lingard,' he burst out in desperation; 'you can't say I have worried you very much since this morning when I received you at the side, but I must be told something. What is it going to be with us? Fight or run?'

Lingard stopped short and now there was no doubt in Carter's mind that the Captain was looking at him. There was no room for any doubt before that stern and inquiring gaze. 'Aha!' thought Carter. 'This has startled him'; and feeling that his shyness had departed he pursued his advantage. 'For the fact of the matter is, sir, that, whatever happens, unless I am to be your man you will have no officer. I had better tell you at once that I have bundled that respectable, crazy, fat Shaw out of the ship. He was upsetting all hands. Yesterday I told him to go and get his dunnage together because I was going to send him aboard the yacht. He couldn't have made more uproar about it if I had proposed to chuck him overboard. I warned him that if he didn't go quietly I would have him tied up like a sheep ready for slaughter. However, he went down the ladder on his own feet, shaking his fist at me and promising to have me hanged for a pirate some day. He can do no harm on board the yacht. And now, sir, it's for you to give orders and not for me – thank God!'

Lingard turned away, abruptly. Carter didn't budge. After a moment he heard himself called from the other side of the deck and obeyed with alacrity.

'What's that story of a man you picked up on the coast last evening?' asked Lingard in his gentlest tone. 'Didn't you tell me something about it when I came on board?'

'I tried to,' said Carter, frankly. 'But I soon gave it up. You didn't seem to pay any attention to what I was saying. I thought you wanted to be left alone for a bit. What can I know of your ways, yet, sir? Are you aware, Captain Lingard, that since this morning I have been down five times at the cabin door to look at you? There you sat ...'

He paused and Lingard said: 'You have been five times down in the cabin?'

'Yes. And the sixth time I made up my mind to make you take some notice of me. I can't be left without orders. There are two ships to look after, a lot of things to be done ...'

'There is nothing to be done,' Lingard interrupted with a mere murmur but in a tone which made Carter keep silent for a while.

'Even to know that much would have been something to go by,' he ventured at last. 'I couldn't let you sit there with the sun getting pretty low and a long night before us.'

'I feel stunned yet,' said Lingard, looking Carter straight in the face, as if to watch the effect of that confession.

'Were you very near that explosion?' asked the young man with sympathetic curiosity and seeking for some sign on Lingard's person. But there was nothing. Not a single hair of the Captain's head seemed to have been singed.

'Near,' muttered Lingard. 'It might have been my head.' He pressed it with both hands, then let them fall. 'What about that man?' he asked, brusquely. 'Where did he come from? ... I suppose he is dead now,' he added in an envious tone.

'No, sir. He must have as many lives as a cat,' answered Carter. 'I will tell you how it was. As I said before I wasn't going to give you up, dead or alive, so yesterday when the sun went down a little in the afternoon I had two of our boats manned and pulled in shore, taking soundings to find a passage if there was one. I meant to go back and look for you with the brig or without the brig – but that doesn't matter now. There were three or four floating logs in sight. One of the calashes in my boat made out something red on one of them. I thought it was worth while to go and see what it was. It was that man's *sarong*. It had got entangled amongst the branches and prevented him rolling into the water. I was never so glad, I assure you, as when we found out that he was still breathing. If we could only nurse him back to life, I thought, he could perhaps tell me a lot of things. The log on which he hung had come out of the mouth of the creek and he couldn't have been more than half a day on it by my calculation. I had him taken down the main hatchway and put into a hammock in the 'tween-decks. He only just breathed then, but some time during the night he came to himself and got out of the hammock to lie down on a mat. I suppose he was more comfortable that way. He recovered his speech only this morning and I went down at once and told you of it, but you took no notice. I told you also who he was but I don't know whether you heard me or not.'

'I don't remember,' said Lingard under his breath.

'They are wonderful, those Malays. This morning he was only half alive, if that much, and now I understand he has been talking to Wasub for an hour. Will you go down to see him, sir, or shall I send a couple of men to carry him on deck?'

Lingard looked bewildered for a moment.

'Who on earth is he?' he asked.

'Why, it's that fellow whom you sent out, that night I met you, to catch our first gig. What do they call him? Jaffir, I think. Hasn't he been with you ashore, sir? Didn't he find you with the letter I gave him for you? A most determined looking chap. I knew him again the moment we got him off the log.'

Lingard seized hold of the royal backstay within reach of his hand. Jaffir! Jaffir! Faithful above all others; the messenger of supreme moments; the reckless and devoted servant! Lingard felt a crushing sense of despair. 'No, I can't face this,' he whispered to himself, looking at the coast black as ink now before his eyes in the world's shadow that was slowly encompassing the grey clearness of the Shallow Waters. 'Send Wasub to me. I am going down into the cabin.'

He crossed over to the companion, then checking himself suddenly: 'Was there a boat from the yacht during the day?' he asked as if struck by a sudden thought. – 'No, sir,' answered Carter. 'We had no communication with the yacht today.' –

'Send Wasub to me,' repeated Lingard in a stern voice as he went down the stairs.

The old *serang* coming in noiselessly saw his Captain as he had seen him many times before, sitting under the gilt thunderbolts, apparently as strong in his body, in his wealth, and in his knowledge of secret words that have a power over men and elements, as ever. The old Malay squatted down within a couple of feet from Lingard, leaned his back against the satinwood panel of the bulkhead, then raising his old eyes with a watchful and benevolent expression to the white man's face, clasped his hands between his knees.

'Wasub, you have learned now everything. Is there no one left alive but Jaffir? Are they all dead?'

'May you live!' answered Wasub; and Lingard whispered an appalled 'All dead!' to which Wasub nodded slightly twice. His cracked voice had a lamenting intonation. 'It is all true! It is all true! You are left alone, Tuan; you are left alone!'

'It was their destiny,' said Lingard at last, with forced calmness. 'But has Jaffir told you of the manner of this calamity? How is it that he alone came out alive from it to be found by you?'

'He was told by his lord to depart and he obeyed,' began Wasub, fixing his eyes on the deck and speaking just loud enough to be heard by Lingard, who, bending forward in his seat, shrank inwardly from every word and yet would not have missed a single one of them for anything.

For the catastrophe had fallen on his head like a bolt from the blue in the early morning hours of the day before. At the first break of dawn he had been sent for to resume his talk with Belarab. He had felt suddenly Mrs Travers remove her hand from his head. Her voice speaking intimately into his ear: 'Get up. There are some people coming,' had recalled him to himself. He had got up from the ground. The light was dim, the air full of mist; and it was only gradually that he began to make out forms above his head and about his feet: trees, houses, men sleeping on the ground. He didn't recognize them. It was but a cruel change of dream. Who could tell what was real in this world? He looked about him, dazedly; he was still drunk with the deep draught of oblivion he had conquered for himself. Yes – but it was she who had let him snatch the cup. He looked down at the woman on the bench. She moved not. She had remained like that, still for hours, giving him a waking dream of rest without end, in an infinity of happiness without sound and movement, without thought, without joy; but with an infinite ease of content, like a world-embracing reverie breathing the air of sadness and scented with love. For hours she had not moved.

'You are the most generous of women,' he said. He bent over her. Her eyes were wide open. Her lips felt cold. It did not shock him. After he stood up he remained near her. Heat is a consuming thing, but she with her cold lips seemed to him indestructible – and, perhaps, immortal!

Again he stooped, but this time it was only to kiss the fringe of her head scarf. Then he turned away to meet the three men, who, coming round the corner of the hut containing the prisoners, were approaching him with measured steps. They desired his presence in the Council room. Belarab was awake.

They also expressed their satisfaction at finding the white man awake, because Belarab wanted to impart to him information of the greatest importance. It seemed to Lingard that he had been awake ever since he could remember. It was as to being alive that he felt not so sure. He had no doubt of his existence; but was this life – this profound indifference, this strange contempt for what his eyes could see, this distaste for words, this unbelief in the importance of things and men? He tried to regain possession of himself, his old self which had things to do, words to speak as well as to hear. But it was too difficult. He was seduced away by the tense feeling of existence far superior to the mere consciousness of life, and which in its immensity of contradictions, delight, dread, exultation and despair could not be faced and yet was not to be evaded. There was no peace in it. But who wanted peace? Surrender was better, the dreadful ease of slack limbs in the sweep of an enormous tide and in a divine emptiness of mind. If this was existence then he knew that he existed.

And he knew that the woman existed, too, in the sweep of the tide, without speech, without movement, without heat! Indestructible – and, perhaps, immortal!

7

WITH the sublime indifference of a man who has had a glimpse through the open doors of Paradise and is no longer careful of mere life, Lingard had followed Belarab's anxious messengers. The stockade was waking up in a subdued resonance of voices. Men were getting up from the ground, fires were being rekindled. Draped figures flitted in the mist amongst the buildings; and through the mat wall of a bamboo house Lingard heard the feeble wailing of a child. A day of mere life was beginning; but in the Chief's great Council room several wax candles and a couple of cheap European lamps kept the dawn at bay, while the morning mist which could not be kept out made a faint reddish halo round every flame.

Belarab was not only awake, but he even looked like a man who had not slept for a long time. The creator of the Shore of Refuge, the weary Ruler of the Settlement, with his scorn of the unrest and folly of men, was angry with his white friend who was always bringing his desires and his troubles to his very door. Belarab did not want any one to die but neither did he want any one in particular to live. What he was concerned about was to preserve the mystery and the power of his melancholy hesitations. These delicate things were menaced by Lingard's brusque movements, by that passionate white man who believed in more than one God and always seemed to doubt the power of Destiny. Belarab was profoundly annoyed. He was also genuinely concerned, for he liked Lingard. He liked him not only for his strength, which protected his clear-minded scepticism from those dangers that beset all rulers, but he liked him also for himself. That man of infinite hesitations, born from a sort of mystic contempt for Allah's creation, yet believed absolutely both in Lingard's power and in his boldness. Absolutely. And yet, in the marvellous consistency of his temperament, now that the moment had come, he dreaded to put both power and fortitude to the test.

Lingard could not know that some little time before the first break of dawn one of Belarab's spies in the Settlement had found his way inside the stockade at a spot remote from the lagoon, and that a very few moments after Lingard had left the Chief in consequence of Jörgenson's rockets, Belarab was listening to an amazing tale of Hassim and Immada's capture and of Tengga's determination, very much strengthened by that fact, to obtain possession of the *Emma*, either by force or by negotiation, or by some crafty subterfuge in which the Rajah and his sister could be made to play their part. In his mistrust of the universe, which seemed almost to extend to the will of God himself, Belarab was very much alarmed, for the material power of Daman's piratical crowd was at Tengga's command; and who could tell whether this Wajo Rajah would remain loyal in the circumstances? It was also very characteristic of him whom the original settlers of the Shore of Refuge called the Father of Safety, that he did not say anything of this to Lingard, for he was afraid of rousing Lingard's fierce energy which would even carry away himself and all his people and put the peace of so many years to the sudden hazard of a battle.

Therefore Belarab set himself to persuade Lingard on general considerations to deliver the white men, who really belonged to Daman, to that supreme Chief of the Illanuns and by this simple proceeding detach him completely from Tengga. Why should he, Belarab, go to war against half the Settlement on their account? It was not necessary, it was not reasonable. It would be even in a manner a sin to begin a strife in a community of True Believers. Whereas with an offer like that in his hand he could send an embassy to Tengga who would see there at once the downfall of his purposes and the end of his hopes. At once! That moment! ... Afterward the question of a ransom could be arranged with Daman in which he, Belarab, would mediate in the fullness of his recovered power, without a rival and in the sincerity of his heart. And then, if need be, he could put forth all his power against the chief of the sea-vagabonds who would, as a matter of fact, be negotiating under the shadow of the sword.

Belarab talked, low-voiced and dignified, with now and then a subtle intonation, a persuasive inflexion or a half-melancholy smile in the course of the argument. What encouraged him most was the changed aspect of his white friend. The fierce power of his personality seemed to have turned into a dream. Lingard listened, growing gradually inscrutable in his continued silence, but remaining gentle in a sort of rapt patience as if lapped in the wings of the Angel of Peace himself. Emboldened by that transformation, Belarab's counsellors seated on the mats murmured loudly their assent to the views of the Chief. Through the thickening white mist of tropical lands, the light of the tropical day filtered into the hall. One of the wise men got up from the floor and with prudent fingers began extinguishing the waxlights one by one. He hesitated to touch the lamps, the flames of which looked yellow and cold. A puff of the morning breeze entered the great room, faint and chill. Lingard, facing Belarab in a wooden armchair, with slack limbs and in the divine emptiness of a mind enchanted by a glimpse of Paradise, shuddered profoundly.

A strong voice shouted in the doorway without any ceremony and with a sort of jeering accent:

'Tengga's boats are out in the mist.'

Lingard half rose from his seat, Belarab himself could not repress a start. Lingard's attitude was a listening one, but after a moment of hesitation he ran out of the hall. The inside of the stockade was beginning to buzz like a disturbed hive.

Outside Belarab's house Lingard slowed his pace. The mist still hung. A great sustained murmur pervaded it and the blurred forms of men were all moving outward from the centre toward the palisades. Somewhere amongst the buildings a gong clanged. D'Alcacer's raised voice was heard:

'What is happening?'

Lingard was passing then close to the prisoners' house. There was a group of armed men below the verandah and above their heads he saw Mrs Travers by the side of d'Alcacer. The fire by which Lingard had spent the night was extinguished, its embers scattered, and the bench itself lay overturned. Mrs Travers must have run up on the verandah at the first alarm. She and d'Alcacer up there seemed to dominate the tumult which was now subsiding. Lingard noticed the scarf across Mrs Travers' face. D'Alcacer was bareheaded. He shouted again:

'What's the matter?'

'I am going to see,' shouted Lingard back.

He resisted the impulse to join those two, dominate the tumult, let it roll away from under his feet – the mere life of men, vain like a dream and interfering with the tremendous sense of his own existence. He resisted it, he could hardly have told why. Even the sense of self-preservation had abandoned him. There was a throng of people pressing close about him yet careful not to get in his way. Surprise, concern, doubt were depicted in all those faces; but there were some who observed that the great white man making his way to the lagoon side of the stockade wore a fixed smile. He asked at large:

'Can one see any distance over the water?'

One of Belarab's headmen who was nearest to him answered:

'The mist has thickened. If you see anything, Tuan, it will be but a shadow of things.'

The four sides of the stockade had been manned by that time. Lingard, ascending the banquette, looked out and saw the lagoon shrouded in white, without as much as a shadow on it, and so still that not even the sound of water lapping the shore reached his ears. He found himself in profound accord with this blind and soundless peace.

'Has anything at all been seen?' he asked incredulously.

Four men were produced at once who had seen a dark mass of boats moving in the light of the dawn. Others were sent for. He hardly listened to them. His thought escaped him and he stood motionless, looking out into the unstirring mist pervaded by the perfect silence. Presently Belarab joined him, escorted by three grave, swarthy men, himself dark-faced, stroking his short grey

357

beard with impenetrable composure. He said to Lingard, 'Your
white man doesn't fight,' to which Lingard answered, 'There is
nothing to fight against. What your people have seen, Belarab,
were indeed but shadows on the water.' Belarab murmured,
'You ought to have allowed me to make friends with Daman last
night.'

A faint uneasiness was stealing into Lingard's breast.

A moment later d'Alcacer came up, inconspicuously watched
over by two men with lances, and to his anxious inquiry
Lingard said: 'I don't think there is anything going on. Listen
how still everything is. The only way of bringing the matter to
a test would be to persuade Belarab to let his men march out and
make an attack on Tengga's stronghold this moment. Then we
would learn something. But I couldn't persuade Belarab to
march out into this fog. Indeed, an expedition like this might
end badly. I myself don't believe that all Tengga's people are on
the lagoon ... Where is Mrs Travers?'

The question made d'Alcacer start by its abruptness which
revealed the woman's possession of that man's mind. 'She is
with Don Martin, who is better but feels very weak. If we are to
be given up, he will have to be carried out to his fate. I can
depict to myself the scene. Don Martin carried shoulder high
surrounded by those barbarians with spears, and Mrs Travers
with myself walking on each side of the stretcher. Mrs Travers
has declared to me her intention to go out with us.'

'Oh, she has declared her intention,' murmured Lingard,
absent-mindedly.

D'Alcacer felt himself completely abandoned by that man.
And within two paces of him he noticed the group of Belarab
and his three swarthy attendants in their white robes, preserving
an air of serene detachment. For the first time since the stranding on the coast d'Alcacer's heart sank within him. 'But perhaps,' he went on, 'this Moor may not in the end insist on giving
us up to a cruel death, Captain Lingard.'

'He wanted to give you up in the middle of the night, a few
hours ago,' said Lingard, without even looking at d'Alcacer who
raised his hands a little and let them fall. Lingard sat down on

the breech of a heavy piece mounted on a naval carriage so as to command the lagoon. He folded his arms on his breast. L'Alcacer asked, gently:

'We have been reprieved then?'

'No,' said Lingard. 'It's I who was reprieved.'

A long silence followed. Along the whole line of the manned stockade the whisperings had ceased. The vibrations of the gong had died out, too. Only the watchers perched in the highest boughs of the big tree made a slight rustle amongst the leaves.

'What are you thinking of, Captain Lingard?' d'Alcacer asked in a low voice. Lingard did not change his position.

'I am trying to keep it off,' he said in the same tone.

'What? Trying to keep thought off?'

'Yes.'

'Is this the time for such experiments?' asked d'Alcacer.

'Why not? It's my reprieve. Don't grudge it to me, Mr d'Alcacer.'

'Upon my word I don't. But isn't it dangerous?'

'You will have to take your chance.'

D'Alcacer had a moment of internal struggle. He asked himself whether he should tell Lingard that Mrs Travers had come to the stockade with some sort of message from Jörgenson. He had it on the tip of his tongue to advise Lingard to go and see Mrs Travers and ask her point blank whether she had anything to tell him; but before he could make up his mind the voices of invisible men high up in the tree were heard reporting the thinning of the fog. This caused a stir to run along the four sides of the stockade.

Lingard felt the draught of air in his face, the motionless mist began to drive over the palisades and, suddenly, the lagoon came into view with a great blinding glitter of its wrinkled surface and the faint sound of its wash rising all along the shore. A multitude of hands went up to shade the eager eyes, and exclamations of wonder burst out from many men at the sight of a crowd of canoes of various sizes and kinds lying close together with the effect as of an enormous raft, a little way off the side of the *Emma*. The excited voices rose higher and higher. There was no doubt about Tengga's being on the lagoon. But what was Jörgenson about? The *Emma* lay as if abandoned by her keeper and her crew, while the mob of mixed boats seemed to be meditating an attack.

For all his determination to keep thought off to the very last possible moment, Lingard could not defend himself from a sense of wonder and fear. What was Jörgenson about? For a moment Lingard expected the side of the *Emma* to wreath itself in puffs of smoke, but an age seemed to elapse without the sound of a shot reaching his ears.

The boats were afraid to close. They were hanging off, irresolute; but why did Jörgenson not put an end to their hesitation by a volley or two of musketry if only over their heads? Through the anguish of his perplexity Lingard found himself returning to life, to mere life with its sense of pain and mortality, like a man awakened from a dream by a stab in the breast. What did this silence of the *Emma* mean? Could she have been already carried in the fog? But that was unthinkable. Some sounds of resistance must have been heard. No, the boats hung off because they knew with what desperate defence they would meet; and perhaps Jörgenson knew very well what he was doing by holding his fire to the very last moment and letting the craven hearts grow cold with the fear of a murderous discharge that would have to be faced. What was certain was that this was the time for Belarab to open the great gate and let his men go out, display his power, sweep through the further end of the Settlement, destroy Tengga's defences, do away once for all with the absurd rivalry of that intriguing amateur boatbuilder. Lingard turned eagerly toward Belarab but saw the Chief busy looking across the lagoon through a long glass resting on the shoulder of a stooping slave. He was motionless like a carving. Suddenly he let go the long glass which some ready hands caught as it fell and said to Lingard:

'No fight.'

'How do you know?' muttered Lingard, astounded.

'There are three empty sampans alongside the ladder,' said Belarab in a just audible voice. 'There is bad talk there.'

'Talk? I don't understand,' said Lingard slowly.

But Belarab had turned toward his three attendants in white robes, with shaven polls under skull-caps of plaited grass, with prayer beads hanging from their wrists, and an air of superior calm on their dark faces: companions of his desperate days, men of blood once and now imperturbable in their piety and wisdom of trusted counsellors.

'This white man is being betrayed,' he murmured to them with the greatest composure.

D'Alcacer, uncomprehending, watched the scene: the Man of Fate puzzled and fierce like a disturbed lion, the white-robed Moors, the multitude of half-naked barbarians, squatting by the guns, standing by the loopholes in the immobility of an arranged display. He saw Mrs Travers on the verandah of the prisoners' house, an anxious figure with a white scarf over her head. Mr Travers was no doubt too weak after his fit of fever to come outside. If it hadn't been for that, all the whites would have been in sight of each other at the very moment of the catastrophe which was to give them back to the claims of their life, at the cost of other lives sent violently out of the world. D'Alcacer heard Lingard asking loudly for the long glass and saw Belarab make a sign with his hand, when he felt the earth receive a violent blow from underneath. While he staggered to it the heavens split over his head with a crash in the lick of a red tongue of flame; and a sudden dreadful gloom fell all round the stunned d'Alcacer, who beheld with terror the morning sun, robbed of its rays, glow dull and brown through the sombre murk which had taken possession of the universe. The *Emma* had blown up; and when the rain of shattered timbers and mangled corpses falling into the lagoon had ceased, the cloud of smoke hanging motionless under the livid sun cast its shadow afar on the Shore of Refuge where all strife had come to an end.

A great wail of terror ascended from the Settlement and was succeeded by a profound silence. People could be seen bolting in unreasoning panic away from the houses and into the fields. On the lagoon the raft of boats had broken up. Some of them were sinking, others paddling away in all directions. What was left above water of the *Emma* had burst into a clear flame under the shadow of the cloud, the great smoky cloud that hung solid and unstirring above the tops of the forest, visible for miles up and down the coast and over the Shallows.

The first person to recover inside the stockade was Belarab himself. Mechanically he murmured the exclamation of wonder, 'God is great,' and looked at Lingard. But Lingard was not looking at him. The shock of the explosion had robbed him of speech and movement. He stared at the *Emma* blazing in a distant and insignificant flame under the sinister shadow of the cloud created by Jörgenson's mistrust and contempt for the life of men. Belarab turned away. His opinion had changed. He regarded Lingard no longer as a betrayed man but the effect was the same. He was no longer a man of any importance. What Belarab really wanted now was to see all the white people clear out of the lagoon as soon as possible. Presently he ordered the gate to be thrown open and his armed men poured out to take possession of the Settlement. Later Tengga's houses were set on fire and Belarab, mounting a fiery pony, issued forth to make a triumphal progress surrounded by a great crowd of headmen and guards.

That night the white people left the stockade in a cortège of torch bearers. Mr Travers had to be carried down to the beach, where two of Belarab's war-boats awaited their distinguished passengers. Mrs Travers passed through the gate on d'Alcacer's arm. Her face was half veiled. She moved through the throng of spectators displayed in the torchlight looking straight before her. Belarab, standing in front of a group of headmen, pretended not to see the white people as they went by. With Lingard he shook hands, murmuring the usual formulas of friendship; and when he heard the great white man say, 'You shall never see me again,' he felt immensely relieved. Belarab did not want to see that white man again, but as he responded to the pressure of Lingard's hand he had a grave smile.

'God alone knows the future,' he said.

Lingard walked to the beach by himself, feeling a stranger to all men and abandoned by the All-Knowing God. By that time the first boat with Mr and Mrs Travers had already got away out of the blood-red light thrown by the torches upon the water. D'Alcacer and Lingard followed in the second. Presently the dark shade of the creek, walled in by the impenetrable forest, closed round them and the splash of the paddles echoed in the still, damp air.

'How do you think this awful accident happened?' asked d'Alcacer, who had been sitting silent by Lingard's side.

'What is an accident?' said Lingard with a great effort. 'Where did you hear of such a thing? Accident! Don't disturb me, Mr d'Alcacer. I have just come back to life and it has closed on me colder and darker than the grave itself. Let me get used ... I can't bear the sound of a human voice yet.'

8

AND now, stoical in the cold and darkness of his regained life, Lingard had to listen to the voice of Wasub telling him Jaffir's story. The old *serang*'s face expressed a profound dejection and there was infinite sadness in the flowing murmur of his words.

'Yes, by Allah! They were all there: that tyrannical Tengga, noisy like a fool; the Rajah Hassim, a ruler without a country; Daman, the wandering chief, and the three Pangerans of the sea-robbers. They came on board boldly, for Tuan Jörgenson had given them permission, and their talk was that you, Tuan, were a willing captive in Belarab's stockade. They said they had waited all night for a message of peace from you or from Belarab. But there was nothing, and with the first sign of day they put out on the lagoon to make friends with Tuan Jörgenson; for, they said, you, Tuan, were as if you had not been, possessing no more power than a dead man, the mere slave of these strange white people, and Belarab's prisoner. Thus Tengga talked. God had taken from him all wisdom and all fear. And then he must have thought he was safe while Rajah Hassim and the lady Immada were on board. I tell you they sat

363

there in the midst of your enemies, captive! The lady Immada, with her face covered, mourned to herself. The Rajah Hassim made a sign to Jaffir and Jaffir came to stand by his side and talked to his lord. The main hatch was open and many of the Illanuns crowded there to look down at the goods that were inside the ship. They had never seen so much loot in their lives. Jaffir and his lord could hear plainly Tuan Jörgenson and Tengga talking together. Tengga discoursed loudly and his words were the words of a doomed man, for he was asking Tuan Jörgenson to give up the arms and everything that was on board the *Emma* to himself and to Daman. And then he said, "We shall fight Belarab and make friends with these strange white people by behaving generously to them and letting them sail away unharmed to their own country. We don't want them here. You, Tuan Jörgenson, are the only white man I care for." They heard Tuan Jörgenson say to Tengga: "Now you have told me everything there is in your mind you had better go ashore with your friends and return tomorrow." And Tengga asked: "Why! would you fight me tomorrow rather than live many days in peace with me?" and he laughed and slapped his thigh. And Tuan Jörgenson answered:

' "No, I won't fight you. But even a spider will give the fly time to say its prayers."

'Tuan Jörgenson's voice sounded very strange and louder than ever anybody had heard it before. O Rajah Laut, Jaffir and the white man had been waiting, too, all night for some sign from you; a shot fired or a signal-fire, lighted to strengthen their hearts. There had been nothing. Rajah Hassim, whispering, ordered Jaffir to take the first opportunity to leap overboard and take to you his message of friendship and good-bye. Did the Rajah and Jaffir know what was coming? Who can tell? But what else could they see than calamity for all Wajo men, whatever Tuan Jörgenson had made up his mind to? Jaffir prepared to obey his lord, and yet with so many enemies' boats in the water he did not think he would ever reach the shore; and as to yourself he was not at all sure that you were still alive. But he said nothing of this to his Rajah. Nobody was looking their way.

Jaffir pressed his lord's hand to his breast and waited his opportunity. The fog began to blow away and presently everything was disclosed to the sight. Jörgenson was on his feet, he was holding a lighted cigar between his fingers. Tengga was sitting in front of him on one of the chairs the white people had used. His followers were pressing round him, with Daman and Sentot who was muttering incantations; and even the Pangerans had moved closer to the hatchway. Jaffir's opportunity had come but he lingered by the side of his Rajah. In the clear air the sun shone with great force. Tuan Jörgenson looked once more toward Belarab's stockade, O Rajah Laut! But there was nothing there, not even a flag displayed – that had not been there before. Jaffir looked that way, too, and as he turned his head he saw Tuan Jörgenson, in the midst of twenty spear-blades that could in an instant have been driven into his breast, put the cigar in his mouth and jump down the hatchway. At that moment Rajah Hassim gave Jaffir a push toward the side and Jaffir leaped overboard.

'He was still in the water when all the world was darkened round him as if the life of the sun had been blown out of it in a crash. A great wave came along and washed him on shore, while pieces of wood, iron, and the limbs of torn men were splashing round him in the water. He managed to crawl out of the mud. Something had hit him while he was swimming and he thought he would die. But life stirred in him. He had a message for you. For a long time he went on crawling under the big trees on his hands and knees, for there is no rest for a messenger till the message is delivered. At last he found himself on the left bank of the creek. And still he felt life stir in him. So he started to swim across, for if you were in this world you were on the other side. While he swam he felt his strength abandoning him. He managed to scramble on to a drifting log and lay on it like one who is dead, till we pulled him into one of our boats.'

Wasub ceased. It seemed to Lingard that it was impossible for mortal man to suffer more than he suffered in the succeeding moment of silence crowded by the mute images as of universal destruction. He felt himself gone to pieces as though the violent expression of Jörgenson's intolerable mistrust of the life of men had shattered his soul, leaving his body robbed of all power of resistance and of all fortitude, a prey forever to infinite remorse and endless regrets.

'Leave me, Wasub,' he said. 'They are all dead – but I would sleep.'

Wasub raised his dumb old eyes to the white man's face.

'Tuan, it is necessary that you should hear Jaffir,' he said, patiently.

'Is he going to die?' asked Lingard in a low, cautious tone as though he were afraid of the sound of his own voice.

'Who can tell?' Wasub's voice sounded more patient than ever. 'There is no wound on his body but, O Tuan, he does not wish to live.'

'Abandoned by his God,' muttered Lingard to himself.

Wasub waited a little before he went on, 'And, Tuan, he has a message for you.'

'Of course. Well, I don't want to hear it.'

'It is from those who will never speak to you again,' Wasub persevered, sadly. 'It is a great trust. A Rajah's own words. It is difficult for Jaffir to die. He keeps on muttering about a ring that was for you, and that he let pass out of his care. It was a great talisman !'

'Yes. But it did not work this time. And if I go and tell Jaffir why he will be able to tell his Rajah, O Wasub, since you say that he is going to die ... I wonder where they will meet,' he muttered to himself.

Once more Wasub raised his eyes to Lingard's face.

'Paradise is the lot of all True Believers,' he whispered, firm in his simple faith.

The man who had been undone by a glimpse of Paradise exchanged a profound look with the old Malay. Then he got up. On his passage to the main hatchway the commander of the brig met no one on the decks, as if all mankind had given him up except the old man who preceded him and that other man dying in the deepening twilight, who was awaiting his coming.

Below, in the light of the hatchway, he saw a young calash with a broad yellow face and his wiry hair sticking up in stiff wisps through the folds of his head-kerchief, holding an earthenware water-jar to the lips of Jaffir extended on his back on a pile of mats.

A languid roll of the already glazed eyeballs, a mere stir of black and white in the gathering dusk showed that the faithful messenger of princes was aware of the presence of the man who had been so long known to him and his people as the King of the Sea. Lingard knelt down close to Jaffir's head, which rolled a little from side to side and then became still, staring at a beam of the upper deck. Lingard bent his ear to the dark lips. 'Deliver your message,' he said in a gentle tone.

'The Rajah wished to hold your hand once more,' whispered Jaffir so faintly that Lingard had to guess the words rather than hear them. 'I was to tell you,' he went on – and stopped suddenly.

'What were you to tell me?'

'To forget everything,' said Jaffir with a loud effort as if beginning a long speech. After that he said nothing more till Lingard murmured, 'And the lady Immada?'

Jaffir collected all his strength. 'She hoped no more,' he uttered, distinctly. 'The order came to her while she mourned, veiled, apart. I didn't even see her face.'

Lingard swayed over the dying man so heavily that Wasub, standing near by, hastened to catch him by the shoulder. Jaffir seemed unaware of anything, and went on staring at the beam.

'Can you hear me, O Jaffir?' asked Lingard.

'I hear.'

'I never had the ring. Who could bring it to me?'

'We gave it to the white woman – may Jehannum be her lot!'

'No! It shall be my lot,' said Lingard with despairing force, while Wasub raised both his hands in dismay. 'For, listen, Jaffir, if she had given the ring to me it would have been to one that was dumb, deaf, and robbed of all courage.'

It was impossible to say whether Jaffir had heard. He made no

sound, there was no change in his awful stare, but his prone
body moved under the cotton sheet as if to get further away
from the white man. Lingard got up slowly and making a sign
to Wasub to remain where he was, went up on deck without
giving another glance to the dying man. Again it seemed to him
that he was pacing the quarter-deck of a deserted ship. The
mulatto steward, watching through the crack of the pantry door,
saw the Captain stagger into the cuddy and fling-to the door behind him with a crash. For more than an hour nobody approached that closed door till Carter coming down the companion stairs spoke without attempting to open it.

'Are you there, sir?' The answer 'You may come in,' com-
forted the young man by its strong resonance. He went in.

'Well?'

'Jaffir is dead. This moment. I thought you would want to
know.'

Lingard looked persistently at Carter, thinking that now Jaffir
was dead there was no one left on the empty earth to speak to
him a word of reproach; no one to know the greatness of his
intentions, the bond of fidelity between him and Hassim and
Immada, the depth of his affection for those people, the earnestness of his visions, and the unbounded trust that was his reward.
By the mad scorn of Jörgenson flaming up against the life of
men, all this was as if it had never been. It had become a secret
locked up in his own breast forever.

'Tell Wasub to open one of the long-cloth bales in the hold,
Mr Carter, and give the crew a cotton sheet to bury him
decently according to their faith. Let it be done tonight. They
must have the boats, too. I suppose they will want to take him
on the sandbank.'

'Yes, sir,' said Carter.

'Let them have what they want, spades, torches ... Wasub
will chant the right words. Paradise is the lot of all True Believers. Do you understand me, Mr Carter? Paradise! I wonder
what it will be for him! Unless he gets messages to carry
through the jungle, avoiding ambushes, swimming in storms
and knowing no rest, he won't like it.'

368

Carter listened with an unmoved face. It seemed to him that the Captain had forgotten his presence.

'And all the time he will be sleeping on that sandbank,' Lingard began again, sitting in his old place under the gilt thunderbolts suspended over his head with his elbows on the table and his hands to his temples. 'If they want a board to set up at the grave let them have a piece of an oak plank. It will stay there – till the next monsoon. Perhaps.'

Carter felt uncomfortable before that tense stare which just missed him and in that confined cabin seemed awful in its piercing and far-off expression. But as he had not been dismissed he did not like to go away.

'Everything will be done as you wish it, sir,' he said. 'I suppose the yacht will be leaving the first thing tomorrow morning, sir?'

'If she doesn't we must give her a solid shot or two to liven her up – eh, Mr Carter?'

Carter did not know whether to smile or to look horrified. In the end he did both, but as to saying anything he found it impossible. But Lingard did not expect an answer.

'I believe you are going to stay with me, Mr Carter?'

'I told you, sir, I am your man if you want me.'

'The trouble is, Mr Carter, that I am no longer the man to whom you spoke that night in Carimata.'

'Neither am I, sir, in a manner of speaking.'

Lingard, relaxing the tenseness of his stare, looked at the young man, thoughtfully.

'After all, it is the brig that will want you. She will never change. The finest craft afloat in these seas. She will carry me about as she did before, but . . .'

He unclasped his hands, made a sweeping gesture.

Carter gave all his naïve sympathy to that man who had certainly rescued the white people but seemed to have lost his own soul in the attempt. Carter had heard something from Wasub. He had made out enough of this story from the old *serang*'s pidgin English to know that the Captain's native friends, one of them a woman, had perished in a mysterious catastrophe. But the why of it, and how it came about, remained still quite in-comprehensible to him. Of course, a man like the Captain would feel terribly cut up . . .

'You will be soon yourself again, sir,' he said in the kindest possible tone.

With the same simplicity Lingard shook his head. He was thinking of the dead Jaffir with his last message delivered and untroubled now by all these matters of the earth. He had been ordered to tell him to forget everything. Lingard had an inward shudder. In the dismay of his heart he might have believed his brig to lie under the very wing of the Angel of Desolation – so oppressive, so final and hopeless seemed the silence in which he and Carter looked at each other, wistfully.

Lingard reached for a sheet of paper amongst several lying on the table, took up a pen, hesitated a moment, and then wrote :

'Meet me at day-break on the sandbank.'

He addressed the envelope to Mrs Travers, Yacht *Hermit*, and pushed it across the table.

'Send this on board the schooner at once, Mr Carter. Wait a moment. When our boats shove off for the sandbank have the forecastle gun fired. I want to know when that dead man has left the ship.'

He sat alone, leaning his head on his hand, listening, listen-ing endlessly, for the report of the gun. Would it never come? When it came at last muffled, distant, with a slight shock through the body of the brig, he remained still with his head leaning on his hand but with a distinct conviction, with an almost physical certitude, that under the cotton sheet shrouding the dead man something of himself, too, had left the ship.

9

IN a roomy cabin, furnished and fitted with austere comfort, Mr Travers reposed at ease in a low bed-place under a snowy white sheet and a light silk coverlet, his head sunk in a white pillow of extreme purity. A faint scent of lavender hung about the fresh linen. Though lying on his back like a person who is seriously ill Mr Travers was conscious of nothing worse than a great fatigue. Mr Travers' restfulness had something faintly triumphant in it. To find himself again on board his yacht had soothed his vanity and had revived his sense of his own importance. He contemplated it in a distant perspective, restored to its proper surroundings and unaffected by an adventure too extraordinary to trouble a superior mind or even to remain in one's memory for any length of time. He was not responsible. Like many men ambitious of directing the affairs of a nation, Mr Travers disliked the sense of responsibility. He would not have been above evading it in case of need, but with perverse loftiness he really, in his heart, scorned it. That was the reason why he was able to lie at rest and enjoy a sense of returning vigour. But he did not care much to talk as yet, and that was why the silence in the stateroom had lasted for hours. The bulkhead lamp had a green silk shade. It was unnecessary to admit for a moment the existence of impudence or ruffianism. A discreet knocking at the cabin door sounded deferential.

Mrs Travers got up to see what was wanted, and returned without uttering a single word to the folding armchair by the side of the bed-place, with an envelope in her hand which she tore open in the greenish light. Mr Travers remained incurious but his wife handed to him an unfolded sheet of paper which he condescended to hold up to his eyes. It contained only one line of writing. He let the paper fall on the coverlet and went on reposing as before. It was a sick man's repose. Mrs Travers in the armchair, with her hands on the arm-rests, had a great dignity of attitude.

'I intend to go,' she declared after a time.

'You intend to go,' repeated Mr Travers in a feeble, deliberate voice. 'Really, it doesn't matter what you decide to do. All this is of so little importance. It seems to me that there can be no possible object.'

'Perhaps not,' she admitted. 'But don't you think that the uttermost farthing should always be paid?'

Mr Travers' head rolled over on the pillow and gave a covertly scared look at that outspoken woman. But it rolled back again at once and the whole man remained passive, the very embodiment of helpless exhaustion. Mrs Travers noticed this, and had the unexpected impression that Mr Travers was not so ill as he looked. 'He's making the most of it. It's a matter of diplomacy,' she thought. She thought this without irony, bitterness, or disgust. Only her heart sank a little lower and she felt that she could not remain in the cabin with that man for the rest of the evening. For all life – yes! But not for that evening.

'It's simply monstrous,' murmured the man, who was either very diplomatic or very exhausted, in a languid manner. 'There is something abnormal in you.'

Mrs Travers got up swiftly.

'One comes across monstrous things. But I assure you that of all the monsters that wait on what you would call a normal existence the one I dread most is tediousness. A merciless monster without teeth or claws. Impotent. Horrible!'

She left the stateroom, vanishing out of it with noiseless resolution. No power on earth could have kept her in there for another minute. On deck she found a moonless night with a velvety tepid feeling in the air, and in the sky a mass of blurred starlight, like the tarnished tinsel of a worn-out, very old, very tedious firmament. The usual routine of the yacht had been already resumed, the awnings had been stretched aft, a solitary round lamp had been hung as usual under the main boom. Out of the deep gloom behind it d'Alcacer, a long, loose figure, lounged in the dim light across the deck. D'Alcacer had got promptly in touch with the store of cigarettes he owed to the Governor General's generosity. A large, pulsating spark glowed, illuminating redly the design of his lips under the fine dark moustache, the tip of his nose, his lean chin. D'Alcacer reproached himself for an unwonted light-heartedness which had somehow taken possession of him. He had not experienced that sort of feeling for years. Reprehensible as it was he did not want anything to disturb it. But as he could not run away openly from Mrs Travers he advanced to meet her.

'I do hope you have nothing to tell me,' he said with whimsical earnestness.

'I? No! Have you?'

He assured her he had not, and proffered a request. 'Don't let us tell each other anything, Mrs Travers. Don't let us think of anything. I believe it will be the best way to get over the evening.' There was real anxiety in his jesting tone.

'Very well,' Mrs Travers assented, seriously. 'But in that case we had better not remain together.' She asked, then, d'Alcacer to go below and sit with Mr Travers who didn't like to be left alone. 'Though he, too, doesn't seem to want to be told anything,' she added, parenthetically, and went on : 'But I must ask you something else, Mr d'Alcacer. I propose to sit down in this chair and go to sleep – if I can. Will you promise to call me about five o'clock? I prefer not to speak to any one on deck, and, moreover, I can trust you.'

He bowed in silence and went away slowly. Mrs Travers, turning her head, perceived a steady light at the brig's yard-arm, very bright among the tarnished stars. She walked aft and looked over the taffrail. It was exactly like that other night. She half expected to hear presently the low, rippling sound of an advancing boat. But the universe remained without a sound. When she at last dropped into the deck chair she was absolutely at the end of her power of thinking. 'I suppose that's how the condemned manage to get some sleep on the night before the execution,' she said to herself a moment before her eyelids closed as if under a leaden hand.

She woke up, with her face wet with tears, out of a vivid dream of Lingard in chain-mail armour and vaguely recalling a Crusader, but bare-headed and walking away from her in the depths of an impossible landscape. She hurried on to catch up with him but a throng of barbarians with enormous turbans came between them at the last moment and she lost sight of him forever in the flurry of a ghastly sandstorm. What frightened her most was that she had not been able to see his face. It was then that she began to cry over her hard fate. When she woke up the tears were still rolling down her cheeks and she perceived in the light of the deck-lamp d'Alcacer arrested a little way off.

'Did you have to speak to me?' she asked.

'No,' said d'Alcacer. 'You didn't give me time. When I came as far as this I fancied I heard you sobbing. It must have been a delusion.'

'Oh, no. My face is wet yet. It was a dream. I suppose it is five o'clock. Thank you for being so punctual. I have something to do before sunrise.'

D'Alcacer moved nearer. 'I know. You have decided to keep an appointment on the sandbank. Your husband didn't utter twenty words in all these hours but he managed to tell me that piece of news.'

'I shouldn't have thought,' she murmured, vaguely.

'He wanted me to understand that it had no importance,' stated d'Alcacer in a very serious tone.

'Yes. He knows what he is talking about,' said Mrs Travers in such a bitter tone as to disconcert d'Alcacer for a moment. 'I don't see a single soul about the decks,' Mrs Travers continued, almost directly.

'The very watchmen are asleep,' said d'Alcacer.

'There is nothing secret in this expedition, but I prefer not to call anyone. Perhaps you wouldn't mind pulling me off yourself in our small boat.'

It seemed to her that d'Alcacer showed some hesitation. She added: 'It has no importance, you know.'

He bowed his assent and preceded her down the side in silence. When she entered the boat he had the sculls ready and directly she sat down he shoved off. It was so dark yet that but for the brig's yard-arm light he could not have kept his direction. He pulled a very deliberate stroke, looking over his shoulder frequently. It was Mrs Travers who saw first the faint gleam of the uncovered sandspit on the black, quiet water.

'A little more to the left,' she said. 'No, the other way ...' D'Alcacer obeyed her directions but his stroke grew even slower than before. She spoke again. 'Don't you think that the uttermost farthing should always be paid, Mr d'Alcacer?'

D'Alcacer glanced over his shoulder, then: 'It would be the only honourable way. But it may be hard. Too hard for our common fearful hearts.'

'I am prepared for anything.'

He ceased pulling for a moment ... 'Anything that may be found on a sandbank,' Mrs Travers went on. 'On an arid, insignificant, and deserted sandbank.'

D'Alcacer gave two strokes and ceased again.

'There is room for a whole world of suffering on a sandbank, for all the bitterness and resentment a human soul may be made to feel.'

'Yes, I suppose you would know,' she whispered while he gave a stroke or two and again glanced over his shoulder. She murmured the words:

'Bitterness, resentment,' and a moment afterward became aware of the keel of the boat running up on the sand. But she didn't move, and d'Alcacer, too, remained seated on the thwart with the blades of his sculls raised as if ready to drop them and back the dinghy out into deep water at the first sign.

Mrs Travers made no sign, but she asked, abruptly: 'Mr d'Alcacer, do you think I shall ever come back?'

Her tone seemed to him to lack sincerity. But who could tell what this abruptness covered – sincere fear or mere vanity? He asked himself whether she was playing a part for his benefit, or only for herself.

'I don't think you quite understand the situation, Mrs Travers. I don't think you have a clear idea either of his simplicity or of his visionary's pride.'

She thought, contemptuously, that there were other things which d'Alcacer didn't know and surrendered to a sudden temptation to enlighten him a little.

'You forget his capacity for passion and that his simplicity doesn't know its own strength.'

There was no mistaking the sincerity of that murmur. 'She has felt it,' d'Alcacer said to himself with absolute certitude. He wondered when, where, how, on what occasion? Mrs Travers stood up in the stern sheets suddenly and d'Alcacer leaped on the sand to help her out of the boat.

'Hadn't I better hang about here to take you back again?' he suggested, as he let go her hand.

'You mustn't!' she exclaimed, anxiously. 'You must return to the yacht. There will be plenty of light in another hour. I will come to this spot and wave my handkerchief when I want to be taken off.'

At their feet the shallow water slept profoundly, the ghostly gleam of the sands baffled the eye by its lack of form. Far off, the growth of bushes in the centre raised a massive black bulk against the stars to the southward. Mrs Travers lingered for a moment near the boat as if afraid of the strange solitude of this lonely sandbank and of this lone sea that seemed to fill the whole encircling universe of remote stars and limitless shadows. 'There is nobody here,' she whispered to herself.

'He is somewhere about waiting for you, or I don't know the man,' affirmed d'Alcacer in an undertone. He gave a vigorous shove which sent the little boat into the water.

*

D'Alcacer was perfectly right. Lingard had come up on deck long before Mrs Travers woke up with her face wet with tears. The burial party had returned hours before and the crew of the brig was plunged in sleep, except for two watchmen, who at Lingard's appearance retreated noiselessly from the poop. Lingard, leaning on the rail, fell into a sombre reverie of his past. Reproachful spectres crowded the air, animated and vocal, not in the articulate language of mortals but assailing him with faint sobs, deep sighs, and fateful gestures. When he came to himself and turned about they vanished, all but one dark shape without sound or movement. Lingard looked at it with secret horror.

'Who's that?' he asked in a troubled voice.

The shadow moved closer: 'It's only me, sir,' said Carter, who had left orders to be called directly the Captain was seen on deck.

'Oh, yes, I might have known,' mumbled Lingard in some confusion. He requested Carter to have a boat manned and when after a time the young man told him that it was ready, he said 'All right!' and remained leaning on his elbow.

'I beg your pardon, sir,' said Carter after a longish silence, 'but are you going some distance?'

'No, I only want to be put ashore on the sandbank.'

Carter was relieved to hear this, but also surprised. 'There is nothing living there, sir,' he said.

'I wonder,' muttered Lingard.

'But I am certain,' Carter insisted. 'The last of the women and children belonging to those cut-throats were taken off by the sampans which brought you and the yacht-party out.'

He walked at Lingard's elbow to the gangway and listened to his orders.

'Directly there is enough light to see flags by, make a signal to the schooner to heave short on her cable and loose her sails. If there is any hanging back give them a blank gun, Mr Carter. I will have no shilly-shallying. If she doesn't go at the word, by heavens, I will drive her out. I am still master here – for another day.'

＊

The overwhelming sense of immensity, of disturbing emptiness, which affects those who walk on the sands in the midst of the sea, intimidated Mrs Travers. The world resembled a limitless flat shadow which was motionless and elusive. Then against the southern stars she saw a human form that isolated and lone appeared to her immense: the shape of a giant outlined amongst the constellations. As it approached her it shrank to common proportions, got clear of the stars, lost its awesomeness, and became menacing in its ominous and silent advance. Mrs Travers hastened to speak.

'You have asked for me. I am come. I trust you will have no reason to regret my obedience.'

He walked up quite close to her, bent down slightly to peer into her face. The first of the tropical dawn put its characteristic cold sheen into the sky above the Shore of Refuge.

Mrs Travers did not turn away her head.

'Are you looking for a change in me? No. You won't see it.

377

Now I know that I couldn't change even if I wanted to. I am made of clay that is too hard.'

'I am looking at you for the first time,' said Lingard. 'I never could see you before. There were too many things, too many thoughts, too many people. No, I never saw you before. But now the world is dead.'

He grasped her shoulders, approaching his face close to hers. She never flinched.

'Yes, the world is dead,' she said. 'Look your fill then. It won't be for long.'

He let her go as suddenly as though she had struck him. The cold white light of the tropical dawn had crept past the zenith now and the expanse of the shallow waters looked cold, too, without stir or ripple within the enormous rim of the horizon where, to the west, a shadow lingered still.

'Take my arm,' he said.

She did so at once, and turning their backs on the two ships they began to walk along the sands, but they had not made many steps when Mrs Travers perceived an oblong mound with a board planted upright at one end. Mrs Travers knew that part of the sands. It was here she used to walk with her husband and d'Alcacer every evening after dinner, while the yacht lay stranded and her boats were away in search of assistance – which they had found – which they had found! This was something that she had never seen there before. Lingard had suddenly stopped and looked at it moodily. She pressed his arm to rouse him and asked 'What is this?'

'This is a grave,' said Lingard in a low voice, and still gazing at the heap of sand. 'I had him taken out of the ship last night. Strange,' he went on in a musing tone, 'how much a grave big enough for one man only can hold. His message was to forget everything.'

'Never, never,' murmured Mrs Travers. 'I wish I had been on board the *Emma* . . . You had a madman there,' she cried out, suddenly. They moved on again, Lingard looking at Mrs Travers who was leaning on his arm.

'I wonder which of us two was mad,' he said.

'I wonder you can bear to look at me,' she murmured. Then Lingard spoke again.

'I had to see you once more.'

'That abominable Jörgenson,' she whispered to herself.

'No, no, he gave me my chance – before he gave me up.'

Mrs Travers disengaged her arm and Lingard stopped, too, facing her in a long silence.

'I could not refuse to meet you,' said Mrs Travers at last. 'I could not refuse you anything. You have all the right on your side and I don't care what you do or say. But I wonder at my own courage when I think of the confession I have to make.' She advanced, laid her hand on Lingard's shoulder and spoke earnestly. 'I shuddered at the thought of meeting you again. And now you must listen to my confession.'

'Don't say a word,' said Lingard in an untroubled voice and never taking his eyes from her face. 'I know already.'

'You can't,' she cried. Her hand slipped off his shoulder. 'Then why don't you throw me into the sea?' she asked, passionately. 'Am I to live on hating myself?'

'You mustn't!' he said with an accent of fear. 'Haven't you understood long ago that if you had given me that ring it would have been just the same?'

'Am I to believe this? No, no! You are too generous to a mere sham. You are the most magnanimous of men but you are throwing it away on me. Do you think it is remorse that I feel? No. If it is anything it is despair. But you must have known that – and yet you wanted to look at me again.'

'I told you I never had a chance before,' said Lingard in an unmoved voice. 'It was only after I heard they gave you the ring that I felt the hold you have got on me. How could I tell before? What has hate or love to do with you and me? Hate. Love. What can touch you? For me you stand above death itself; for I see now that as long as I live you will never die.'

They confronted each other at the southern edge of the sands as if afloat on the open sea. The central ridge heaped up by the winds masked from them the very mastheads of the two ships and the growing brightness of the light only augmented the

sense of their invincible solitude in the awful serenity of the
world. Mrs Travers suddenly put her arm across her eyes and
averted her face.

Then he added:

'That's all.'

Mrs Travers let fall her arm and began to retrace her steps,
unsupported and alone. Lingard followed her on the edge of
the sand uncovered by the ebbing tide. A belt of orange light
appeared in the cold sky above the black forest of the Shore of
Refuge and faded quickly to gold that melted soon into a
blinding and colourless glare. It was not till after she had passed
Jaffir's grave that Mrs Travers stole a backward glance and
discovered that she was alone. Lingard had left her to herself.
She saw him sitting near the mount of sand, his back bowed, his
hands clasping his knees, as if he had obeyed the invincible call
of his great visions haunting the grave of the faithful messenger.
Shading her eyes with her hand Mrs Travers watched the
immobility of that man of infinite illusions. He never moved, he
never raised his head. It was all over. He was done with her.
She waited a little longer and then went slowly on her way.

Shaw, now acting second mate of the yacht, came off with
another hand in a little boat to take Mrs Travers on board. He
stared at her like an offended owl. How the lady could suddenly
appear at sunrise waving her handkerchief from the sandbank
he could not understand. For, even if she had managed to row
herself off secretly in the dark, she could not have sent the
empty boat back to the yacht. It was to Shaw a sort of improper
miracle.

D'Alcacer hurried to the top of the side ladder and as they
met on deck Mrs Travers astonished him by saying in a
strangely provoking tone:

'You were right. I have come back.' Then with a little laugh
which impressed d'Alcacer painfully she added with a nod
downward, 'and Martin, too, was perfectly right. It was
absolutely unimportant.'

She walked on straight to the taffrail and d'Alcacer followed
her aft alarmed at her white face, at her brusque movements, at

the nervous way in which she was fumbling at her throat. He waited discreetly till she turned round and thrust out toward him her open palm on which he saw a thick gold ring set with a large green stone.

'Look at this, Mr d'Alcacer. This is the thing which I asked you whether I should give up or conceal – the symbol of the last hour – the call of the supreme minute. And he said it would have made no difference! He is the most magnanimous of men and the uttermost farthing has been paid. He has done with me. The most magnanimous . . . but there is a grave on the sands by which I left him sitting with no glance to spare for me. His last glance on earth! I am left with this thing. Absolutely unimportant. A dead talisman.' With a nervous jerk she flung the ring overboard, then with a hurried entreaty to d'Alcacer, 'Stay here a moment. Don't let anybody come near us,' she burst into tears and turned her back on him.

*

Lingard returned on board his brig and in the early afternoon the *Lightning* got under way, running past the schooner to give her a lead through the maze of Shoals. Lingard was on deck but never looked once at the following vessel. Directly both ships were in clear water he went below saying to Carter: 'You know what to do.'

'Yes, sir,' said Carter.

Shortly after his Captain had disappeared from the deck Carter laid the main topsail to the mast. The *Lightning* lost her way while the schooner with all her light kites abroad passed close under her stern holding on her course. Mrs Travers stood aft very rigid, gripping the rail with both hands. The brim of her white hat was blown upward on one side and her yachting skirt stirred in the breeze. By her side d'Alcacer waved his hand courteously. Carter raised his cap to them.

During the afternoon he paced the poop with measured steps, with a pair of binoculars in his hand. At last he laid the glasses down, glanced at the compass-card and walked to the cabin sky-light which was open.

381

'Just lost her, sir,' he said. All was still down there. He raised his voice a little.

'You told me to let you know directly I lost sight of the yacht.'

The sound of a stifled groan reached the attentive Carter and a weary voice said, 'All right, I am coming.'

When Lingard stepped out on the poop of the *Lightning* the open water had turned purple already in the evening light, while to the east the Shallows made a steely glitter all along the sombre line of the shore. Lingard, with folded arms, looked over the sea. Carter approached him and spoke quietly.

'The tide has turned and the night is coming on. Hadn't we better get away from these Shoals, sir?'

Lingard did not stir.

'Yes, the night is coming on. You may fill the main topsail, Mr Carter,' he said and he relapsed into silence with his eyes fixed in the southern board where the shadows were creeping stealthily toward the setting sun. Presently Carter stood at his elbow again.

'The brig is beginning to forge ahead, sir,' he said in a warning tone.

Lingard came out of his absorption with a deep tremor of his powerful frame like the shudder of an uprooted tree.

'How was the yacht heading when you lost sight of her?' he asked.

'South as near as possible,' answered Carter. 'Will you give me a course to steer for the night, sir?'

Lingard's lips trembled before he spoke but his voice was calm.

'Steer north,' he said.

READ MORE IN PENGUIN

In every corner of the world, on every subject under the sun, Penguin represents quality and variety – the very best in publishing today.

For complete information about books available from Penguin – including Puffins, Penguin Classics and Arkana – and how to order them, write to us at the appropriate address below. Please note that for copyright reasons the selection of books varies from country to country.

In the United Kingdom: Please write to *Dept. EP, Penguin Books Ltd, Bath Road, Harmondsworth, West Drayton, Middlesex UB7 ODA*

In the United States: Please write to *Consumer Sales, Penguin Putnam Inc., P.O. Box 999, Dept. 17109, Bergenfield, New Jersey 07621-0120.* VISA and MasterCard holders call 1-800-253-6476 to order Penguin titles

In Canada: Please write to *Penguin Books Canada Ltd, 10 Alcorn Avenue, Suite 300, Toronto, Ontario M4V 3B2*

In Australia: Please write to *Penguin Books Australia Ltd, P.O. Box 257, Ringwood, Victoria 3134*

In New Zealand: Please write to *Penguin Books (NZ) Ltd, Private Bag 102902, North Shore Mail Centre, Auckland 10*

In India: Please write to *Penguin Books India Pvt Ltd, 210 Chiranjiv Tower, 43 Nehru Place, New Delhi 110 019*

In the Netherlands: Please write to *Penguin Books Netherlands bv, Postbus 3507, NL-1001 AH Amsterdam*

In Germany: Please write to *Penguin Books Deutschland GmbH, Metzlerstrasse 26, 60594 Frankfurt am Main*

In Spain: Please write to *Penguin Books S. A., Bravo Murillo 19, 1° B, 28015 Madrid*

In Italy: Please write to *Penguin Italia s.r.l., Via Benedetto Croce 2, 20094 Corsico, Milano*

In France: Please write to *Penguin France, Le Carré Wilson, 62 rue Benjamin Baillaud, 31500 Toulouse*

In Japan: Please write to *Penguin Books Japan Ltd, Kaneko Building, 2-3-25 Koraku, Bunkyo-Ku, Tokyo 112*

In South Africa: Please write to *Penguin Books South Africa (Pty) Ltd, Private Bag X14, Parkview, 2122 Johannesburg*